Surviving Custer

Surviving Custer

* * *

J. R. Gregg

iUniverse LLC
Bloomington

SURVIVING CUSTER

iUniverse books may be ordered through booksellers or by contacting:

iUniverse LLC
1663 Liberty Drive
Bloomington, IN 47403
www.iuniverse.com
1-800-Authors (1-800-288-4677)

ISBN: 978-1-4759-8688-4 (sc)
ISBN: 978-1-4759-8689-1 (hc)
ISBN: 978-1-4759-8690-7 (ebk)

Library of Congress Control Number: 2013907054

Printed in the United States of America.

iUniverse rev. date: 6/20/2013

For Suzann

*A woman of compassion, integrity, intelligence,
and more courage than seems possible.*

Acknowledgements

This story could not have been told without the wisdom and friendship of Joe Eagle Elk, Chub Black Bear, and their families. I am grateful to Kitty Deernose, retired curator of the Little Bighorn Battlefield archives, for helping me gain access to the whole battlefield, and to Jim Court for taking me up to the Crow's Nest and down Reno Creek. Thanks also to the NPS Rangers at the Bear Paw Battlefield for showing me the ground where Chief Joseph surrendered. Thanks to Joanne and Jim for help with the early drafts. Finally, thanks to John Lyke's for his years of encouragement and total support, which made it possible to tell the story.

Chapter 1: The Scout

April 30, 1876

Dan Murphy and Sam Streeter of Company A, Seventh Cavalry, were a half mile ahead of their squad that was scouting for two deserters from Fort Abraham Lincoln. Dan didn't know the deserters that well—Hogan and Snively from C Troop. Best guess was they were heading for the Black Hills, gold fever being what it was.

Reaching the crest of a long rise, they saw ten Sioux down below. The Indians were heading northwest at a slow walk, moving like they still owned this part of the country. Hell, they'd given it up back in '68.

Dan was quite aware that stumbling across renegades would complicate the scout. Worse yet, it messed up a peaceful afternoon when a gentle wind bore the new grass smell of spring and the sun warmed a man's bones after a hard winter stretched out by March blizzards. There was no choice now but to determine what the Indians were doing this far north.

Wiping the alkali dust off his face, Dan handed the field glasses to the eagle-eyed rookie from Massachusetts.

"I make out four braves," Dan said. "That right?"

"Three braves and one old man," Sam replied. "Four squaws dragging a travois, two boys."

"And one extra pony with a travois?"

"Yes," Sam said. He turned toward Dan. "We're going to stop them, right?"

"Damn it! You spooked 'em."

Below, the lead brave pulled up and pointed at them, warned when the glasses swung the sun's reflection past him. The others drew abreast and sat their horses facing the two cavalrymen, the uneasy quiet broken by the metallic clicks of cartridges being levered into the Indians' Winchesters. Meanwhile the two Indian boys galloped their ponies up the little hill on the far side of them.

"Go tell Jim and get Charley up here quick!" Dan said.

"We're going to stop them, aren't we?"

"Just get Charley quick."

Studying the renegades, Dan squinted, the old lines deepening above his half-bent nose as he watched the two boys disappear over the ridge. The sun disappeared behind a cloud.

"There's dust over that rise," Charley Smrka said when he came up.

Dan said, "Two boys went over there when they saw us."

"More people too."

"You think so?"

"Five travois. That's two, maybe three lodges."

The two boys reappeared with four mounted braves. One carried a lance with strips of red cloth and eagle feathers tied to it. The other three had Springfields—two carbines and a rifle.

Three minutes later Sergeant Jim Lawton reached the crest with the rest of the squad. Corporal Bull Judd and Jubal Tinker had been with Company A since '72. The other three were rookies who had enlisted six months before: Jake Picard was from Chicago, Ernst Albrecht from Germany, and Elvin Crane from Troy, New York.

At Jim's command the squad formed a line along the crest, nine cavalrymen on coal-black horses, carbines loaded and in hand. The Indians stared back, unmoved by the show of force.

"What're they doing this far north?" Jim asked Charley.

"Don't know," Charley replied.

Sam said, "We've got them outgunned, Sergeant!"

Jim ignored him, watching as the women, the old man, and the boys started northwest again. The seven braves remained still, staring up at the troopers. The one in the middle looked to be forty and well over six feet. He was a strong-looking man with his head cocked back, not so much to look up the hill but to challenge anyone put off by the angry scar running from his left eye to his chin, narrowly missing the proud nose but cutting straight across the lips. He rode a chestnut of fifteen hands—no pony, that.

"They ain't in no hurry," Jim said. "Charley, see what you can find out."

Charley handed his carbine to Dan before starting down the slope. He dismounted a few yards from the leader and began talking in a mix of halting Lakota and English. The Indian replied with a rapid-fire string of words until Charley cut him off with a gesture and said something. Whatever it was, it brought a lopsided smile to the man's face, and he slowed down considerably. The two conversed for a few minutes, and then Charley swung himself up into the saddle and returned up the hill. When he reached the top and turned, the Indian leader raised his rifle over his head and launched into a lengthy harangue. Finally finished, he turned slowly and the seven braves started northwest again. It looked like all of them were chuckling.

"They're Hunkpapa Sioux," Charley said.

"What'd he say?" Jim asked.

"Said there's buffalo three days west of here. After the hunt they'll go back to Standing Rock. "

"You believe him?"

"The buffalo part, not the rest. They'll prob'ly go on to Powder River an' find Sitting Bull."

"Okay. He say anythin' about the boys we're lookin' for?" Jim asked.

"Said they ain't seen 'em, but them two carbines say otherwise," Charley said.

"Yeah. What was he spoutin' at the end?"

"The speech? Somethin' about they're real strong an' we ain't."

"Sure and he was taunting us," Dan said. He removed his hat and ran a hand over his balding pate.

Two more boys came over the rise and remained there, staring at the cavalrymen. They couldn't have been older than twelve. Jim stared back, and then he glanced over at the line of troopers—straight enough for parade. When he turned back, the boys were angling down the slope to fall in behind the braves. Within minutes the party gained enough distance so you couldn't tell one rider from another. Meanwhile, the dust cloud behind the hill moved, paralleling the Indians' course.

The smell of spring returned as the clouds moved on and the sun began warming Dan again, as if nothing had gone on down below. He wondered how many warriors were behind that hill.

Charley admired how the Hunkpapas used the rolling country to half-hide the size of their party, and he was damn sure the two deserters were dead. The carbines clinched that. The only thing in doubt was how many more braves were on the other side of the hill, but the answer wasn't important. Their orders were to find the deserters and get back to Fort Lincoln.

Jim said, "Best thing is to follow them Indians' trail back. Prob'ly we'll find them poor boys south, southeast of here."

With that the squad started down the slope in a column of twos behind Jim. Dan and Sam were first, followed by Bull Judd and Elvin Crane, Jubal Tinker and Ernst Albrecht, and then Charley and Jake Picard.

Jake figured he was lucky to have Charley showing him the ropes. He was an old hand who was in the cavalry during The War, and he knew the ways of the Sioux, which was rare in the company.

"Them carbines, they got 'em off the deserters—you think?" Jake asked.

"Yeah," Charley said.

"How come you so sure?"

Charley pointed to a knoll three miles ahead. Four black specks were circling high above it.

Sam had been watching the birds for five minutes when the sergeant motioned him forward and ordered him to follow at a trot. They dismounted on top of the next rise. Jim handed over the glasses and told him to scan the area under the vultures.

Sam took a quick look, stiffened, and lowered them instantly to wipe the lenses clean. He took his time focusing carefully. A scattering of shapeless scraps and two whitish objects littered the ground. *Maybe a couple of Yorkshire hogs stretched out sleeping,* he thought, *but that didn't make sense out here.* He wiped his eyes.

"What do you see?" Sergeant Lawton's question had a bite.

Heart pounding, Sam refocused, hoping they were pigs but knowing they were cavalrymen.

"Two men. White. Stripped." His mind leaped back two years, picturing the bodies they'd found after the Williamsburg flood. Digging debris out of mud-filled cellars, they found corpses underneath it all. Most of them were people he'd known: Old Man Perkins, crushed beneath a floor beam; Sarah Pelky and her two little girls, pulled half-naked from the sucking mud; twelve-year-old John Dickinson, his flaxen curls in a mud-stuck tangle; Althea Jenner, her dead eyes open like she was still staring at that wall of water, knowing she was done for.

"Thought so," Jim said. "No sign of life?"

"No."

"Check all around, far as you can see. Anything?"

"Nothing except for a kind of wide trail. Probably from the Sioux we ran into."

"What you think happened?" Jake asked Sam when the squad pulled up a hundred yards from the dead men.

Unable to tear his eyes away from the corpses, Sam couldn't answer. He swallowed, trying to concentrate on his horse. Blaster was tossing his head, snorting, dancing lightly until training overrode instinctual skittishness triggered by the smell of death, a smell not yet sensed by humans yet obvious to the horse. Oddly, Sam's mind had kept on insisting they *were* hogs that had wandered off from a careless emigrant, but at a hundred yards, he surrendered.

They were men—men with sun-browned necks and wrists and skin the color of fine, white ash. They looked pallid, lifeless, stained with blood baked red-brown, like life-size rag dolls cast aside by a feeble-minded giant or God himself, a leg bent under the wrong way, a neck strangely twisted too far to the side, the skull caved in. Sam went blind. Without conscious decision, the lids shut everything out, only to spring open again as Blaster settled between Dan and Jake, shuddering the way horses do as he took his solemn place in the shallow arc of mounted men studying the remains of fools who guessed wrong.

"Sure, and there they are," Dan said.

"Yeah, it's them," Jim said. His men sat motionless, their mounts not entirely easy.

Blaster half-heartedly tossed his head once more, and then like the others he let it fall to browse on wisps of grass, while testing Sam's intentions through the tension on the reins.

Jim nodded to Charley, who dismounted and began to survey the stuff scattered on the ground. He covered the area carefully to get a sense of how the men were attacked and killed. Horses and all they held were gone, as were blouses, trousers, and boots, along with saddlebags, blankets, and canteens. The men's begrimed shirts and drawers were tossed aside. A picket pin was half-hidden under a discarded feedbag next to one of the corpses. One spent cartridge lay near the other. Parallel sets of pony tracks bisected the powdery earth. Hogan's body (the shorter of the two), lay directly in their path.

Snively's corpse lay on its back. A shallow groove in the dirt showed where the head dragged when a scavenger pulled the man's boots. The skull showed blood-streaked white where the scalp was ripped off. The right leg crossed the left at the ankle, ludicrously suggesting a carefree attitude. An arm stretched haphazardly toward the slope rising twenty paces away. A thick streak of dried blood extended downward from a puncture wound in the upper chest. The dirt under the right thigh was thoroughly stained with blood. There were two jagged lance wounds, either one fatal—one to the heart, the other split the leg's big artery. Snively was not an unhandsome man, but now the chiseled features sagged into flatness under a four-day stubble. An expression of surprise remained in the set of his mouth, thin lips slightly ajar. Unseeing eyes stared into nothingness, the blue in them already flat. The man's genitals rested half-deflated in the hairy crotch, already melding into the whole. Of no more use as carnal appendage, the limp penis lay unmolested.

Hogan's body was on its side, grotesquely skewed. One arm was twisted around along the torso's side, hand wrong way out. Broken just above the elbow, the long bone's shattered end poked through skin torn jagged. The other arm lay outstretched, a sweat-stained bandanna still clutched in its hand. Bone-white occipital shards and flinders peppered the lucent gray of brain behind and below the skull's clotted crown. The left thighbone was shattered, the leg then bent under the torso at an improbable angle.

Two short arrows slanted upward from each cadaver, feather guides trimmed precisely, their markings identical. Jim pictured two ten-year-old boys sending the arrows home after the bodies had been stripped—a deed for boasting next time they saw their cousins.

The vultures circled lazily overhead, waiting for the squad to move on and leave the feast below. Off to the south, a lone, spotted eagle soared two hundred feet further up, intent on some other prey.

Jubal eased himself forward in the saddle to smooth out an irksome fold in his trousers while waiting for orders. He wasn't one to get worked up over dead men, especially these two. Only fools would pull foot and head off through Sioux country, especially when Sitting Bull had his folks all lathered up. Beside him Ernst tilted his head back, eyes following the eagle riding the currents above. *A picture of contentment,* Jubal thought. No matter what, Jubal felt the oversized German with a boy's face always seemed to find something in life to enjoy.

"What you starin' at?" Jubal asked him.

"The eagle."

"I knowed thet much. What're you seein'?"

"He soars."

"Uh huh," Jubal sighed. "So what about him?"

"The country he sees entire up high. From here to the Indians we come to before." He paused, his eyes following the raptor's soaring flight. "Up there to soar I wish that. It is good. You wish that also?"

"Not without wings an' a whole lot of 'sperience."

"What experience?"

"'Sperience usin' them wings."

Chapter 2: Burying the Deserters

★ ★ ★

Jim Lawton watched Jake Picard swivel in the saddle, probably wondering if there were more Sioux around. Jake then started to dismount, as if to join Charley, but he stopped, probably recalling being dressed down early in the morning for getting down to pick up a coin he'd spied on the ground. Jim smiled, remembering how he had shouted, "Picard, don't you never dismount 'fore I tell you!"

One thing was for sure, death didn't bother Jake. He'd seen plenty of it in Chicago from sickness, stabbings, gunfire, winter cold, and plain bad luck. He said that after the Chicago fire in '71 its stench persisted for days, so death was part of life for him. Jake shifted in the saddle again but not from nervousness—his ass was sore.

"Jubal, you git up that hill there an' spy it out four ways," Jim ordered. "Here, take the glasses. Dan, see if there's any personals we oughtta take back." Jim turned to Bull Judd, the stocky, flat-faced corporal. "Bull, take Crane and find a ditch or somethin', maybe over where the hill drops off sudden, bottom of the slope. Work some clods an' dirt loose to cover them boys three feet deep or more. Albrecht, you take the horses. Link 'em up an' take 'em up the hill. Set the picket line downwind of that flat spot. Don't want 'em gittin' skitterish, so take 'em around this here field. You understand?"

"*Ja,* Sergeant," Albrecht said.

"Picard, you and Streeter drag the corpses over to Bull. Use yer gum blankets. Soon's you git done, police the whole area. I don't want no sign of cav'lry left—not a cartridge, not a shod hoof print. Can't have no Injuns findin' the graves, hear?"

Neither man moved.

"Git a move on, fer Chrissake!" Jim shouted.

The two men nodded. Jake dismounted and started to untie his gum blanket from the saddle. Sam sat, still frozen, until Albrecht came over and took Blaster by the bridle. He then dismounted but remained still, without purpose.

Dan stood next to Hogan's corpse.

Jim called over, "Ain't stiffened up, is he?"

The Irishman pushed hard at the dead weight with his boot, finally flopping it onto its back. The head rolled, then settled. Sightless eyes stared at a distant universe. A red scar traversed the left cheekbone.

"Not much yet. This one is Hogan. Got that slash back in January," Dan said.

"Uh huh. Well, let's git 'er done, then," Jim said. He sat absently for a few seconds, his mind pushing aside the image of a mule his pa put down when he was a tyke. It was the first time he'd looked into eyes that couldn't see.

Sam stood like a statue in the town square, immobile, frozen. He wouldn't admit it, but death frightened, angered, and numbed him. His eyes darted from one grotesque corpse to the other and back again, taking in every tiny detail, as if memorizing them, but the images wouldn't stick. Something far back in his mind kept his eyes moving past them.

Blaster sidestepped a tumbleweed bouncing lightly past. Sam sensed Dan and Sergeant Lawton talking beside him. On his left Jake cursed quietly. Everything might as well have been happening a mile away. His stomach heaved, yet he failed to heed the sensation. Time was at rest, its passing not registering. To the west the sky was deep blue, crossed by a far-flung band of clouds. From behind its lower edge a pale orange sun was about to make a late-afternoon appearance, its power magnified by some combination of factors unknown.

"Streeter, git movin' fer Chrissake!" It was Jim.

"Huh?" Sam asked, coming out of his reverie, trying to remember the sergeant's instructions.

"Your poncho, Sam," Ernst whispered, fretting over his friend's pain.

Ordinarily quick, Sam fumbled with the ties on his saddle before he could free the cloth. His face chalky, he turned toward Dan.

"Wake up, lad, and get moving," the man said quietly, coming through cold and firm. "Now!"

The command broke through his daze, prompting a familiar parade of thoughts through his mind as he began walking, eyes down. He was Jonah Streeter's son, damn it. Private Jonah Streeter, Company C, Fifteenth Regiment Massachusetts Infantry, killed in battle at Sharpsburg, Maryland, on September 17, 1862, at the battle they called Antietam. And he was Sam Streeter, Company A, Seventh Regiment, United States Cavalry, the best Indian-fighting regiment in the nation.

He struggled then willed his eyes up to stare at Dan's belt. The sight of copper cartridges side by side strengthened him. Daniel Murphy, veteran trooper of the Seventh, both of them soldiering in Dakota Territory, doing what had to be done. He moved forward, straightening up, one hand automatically making sure his holster flap was secure and the other clutching the gum blanket.

As Dan snatched a brass button from the dirt next to Snively's stringy remains, Sam's eyes passed quickly from the lifeless face to the chest wound to the blood-soaked dirt under the leg. He couldn't help but stare at the shriveling penis, peculiarly tan in contrast to the skim milk of the belly—one of those fleeting images that threatened to remain etched in visual memory for a lifetime. Shamed, he looked away, then up at Dan.

"He's gone, lad. See?" Dan kicked the corpse lightly. A semisoft, dead weight, it easily absorbed the blow. "Nobody there, not even a ghost. Same with the other one," Dan said.

Sam didn't respond.

"Look at him!" Dan shouted unexpectedly. The rookie recoiled, staggering back before catching himself. "You wanted to soldier, didn't you? Then look at him! Do it! That's right. Now lay the poncho next to him. No! Gum side up! Don't want him leaking into the cloth, do you?"

Sam steeled himself to do what he had to do. He looked at the grayish, blood-streaked chest, fixing his eyes on it while spreading the poncho. Dan tossed Snively's gray-grimed drawers over the crotch. He nodded at Jake, who came around, bent down, and rolled the lean corpse over and onto the poncho. In the process, the right arm flopped onto the bare ground. Jake stepped away, then dug his hands into the dirt and rubbed them together.

"Good," Dan said. "Now get Hogan on a poncho and drag them both over to Bull. After that, police the area. Clean as a whistle, lads." Starting toward Jim, he looked back and said, "Sam, put Snively's arm on the blanket."

Sam couldn't do it. He could not actually touch the dead hand lying there, palm up. "Your boot," Jake said, reading Sam's mind.

"What?"

"Push it with your boot."

Before he grasped what Jake was saying, Sam's foot responded, nudging the lifeless forearm closer to the torso. From there a slight kick propelled the limb smack against the corpse's hip. Half-smiling with stupid satisfaction, Sam followed Jake over to the other corpse. Charley sat his horse, waiting for Jim to return from his own look around. Absently massaging the back of his neck, he watched the eagle, wondering how many Sioux had left the agencies for Powder River country. Rumors said Sitting Bull had five hundred warriors and a lot more were coming. He didn't think it was an exaggeration this time. The enlisted Indian scouts at the post talked about five, maybe six hundred lodges by June. Everyone wanted to be there for the last great buffalo hunt. The scouts said, "Next year and forever, no buffalo. Just the *Wasicu's* cows, a meat gristly with stupidity and empty of spirit."

He almost smiled as he recalled sharing his whiskey with old trappers and the White scouts hired by the regiment. He learned from their stories, signs to look for, and some Lakota. Recently he learned more Lakota from Humaza, a scout from Spotted Tail's agency. However, it was not enough to call it a second language, like the Czech he spoke when they came to Pennsylvania coal country from Silesia. His mother had died the winter he was seven, and he had started picking coal when he was eight. Some time in there the old words slipped away. After that, there was nothing but the mines, the taunts, and the beatings by his father and brothers. The whole stinking mess from his past broke through again, like a river boiling up in a flood.

"Fuck it!" he muttered, pulling himself into the here and now. He looked over at Jake and Sam then away. He hated burial details ever since '68, when he was escorting Sheridan back to Washita to find the remains of Major Elliot and sixteen men caught in an ambush. It left him sick inside. It wasn't only the butchery though. He never understood why the sons of bitches didn't look for them after they took the village.

That was when he started studying up on Indians—and on officers. Nobody except Dan knew what he'd learned about Lakota ways of war and honor. The ways of officers was a whole different thing. He had learned some of that in The War and a lot more in the Seventh.

Jim walked over and hunkered down, looking for his report. On his way to join them, Dan hollered at Jake and Sam over his shoulder.

"Throw Hogan's drawers and shirt on top of his corpse. And, Sam, make sure you shut his eyes."

Jim turned to Charley and said, "How'd them boys git caught?"

"Walkin' their horses," Charley began, breaking off from watching the eagle. "Three mounted warriors spotted 'em comin'—prob'ly from up there—then hid in the coulee. When the troopers got to here, two braves rode straight in, with one trailing. Snively was quick. Got off a shot and was workin' on another when he caught a lance. Hogan's horse bolted an' yanked him to the side. Got brained by one rider, knocked him under the other's pony. That busted him up real bad. Braves caught the horses, took the scalps an' what stuff they wanted, and then waited while the women took everything else. Younger boys left their arrows in 'em," he said, his words still a monotone.

"Braggin' rights," Dan said.

"Yeah. Good enough to tell about all winter," Charley said.

"Why'd they use a lance an' clubs?" Jim wondered. "You think they were tryin' to be quiet in case more of us were coming?"

Charley let the idea hang in the still air, staring off at Sam. Jake was busy with the job, while Sam stood to the side, studying something on the ground.

"Whadaya think?" Jim asked.

"No," Charley said. "They wasn't scared of that. A lance gets big coup—brainin' does too, 'specially if the guy's armed." He looked up and located the eagle again. It was lower now. "Saves cartridges too."

"You're right," Dan said. "Well, they've got cartridges to spare now, and two good carbines and Colts to boot."

"An' two US sorrels," Charley said. "Another thing, they didn't linger. The pony herd never stopped movin'."

"Losin' two horses, that'll piss The Gen'ral off," Jim said.

"Yes, but he's a forgiving man," Dan joked. "And being Company C mounts, they go on brother Tom's account, remember."

"Uh huh," Jim said, standing up. "Well, me an' Charley gotta git some wood an' set up a bivouac. Dan, you git to houndin' Streeter. He's over there dreamin' again."

★ ★ ★

Dan's remark about soldiering got Sam going, although deep down dead people made him uneasy. He picked up Hogan's filthy shirt by one sleeve and tossed it. He aimed for the head, but it landed on the gum blanket. The drawers were a little farther off, all bloody, the crotch stained shit-brown. Refusing to think, he kicked them onto the broken corpse.

"Jake!" he called. "Give me a hand here, will you?"

"For what?"

"Help me roll him onto the poncho. I can't do it by myself."

"Shit, I did."

Jake was right. Determined, Sam tried to push the spongy corpse over, but it hardly moved—too much dead weight. It might as well have been held to the ground by suction, like a logging sled in mud. Only this was dry, so the suction had to be unearthly, a distinctly devilish force. He wrenched his mind out of the ghoulish reverie and dropped down, hands on the ground behind him and knees up. Placing one heel on Hogan's shoulder and the other on the bulging hip, he pushed, then pushed harder. The boots sunk into the mushiness, but the body itself remained planted. Angry, he scooted his ass up and tried again and again, shoving and grunting until he got the loathsome blob rocking. Up it went onto its side where it teetered a second before toppling over onto the cloth with a muffled thump and then an abrupt sigh. Rising from the dirt, he whacked the dust out of his trousers. Only then did Sam notice Dan and Jake staring at him in wonder. He grinned self-consciously and remembered he had to close Hogan's eyes. But now the damn corpse was facedown. Red-faced, he grabbed a corner of the poncho and heaved, then yanked. The head flopped to the side.

"Thanks for small favors, God," he mumbled, still red-faced angry.

Although Sam had read that dead men's eyes stared sightlessly, there was something more in these eyes. Curious, a calm came over him as he knelt on one knee and looked into them. Nothing in there, but there had to be something! A trace of wisdom, maybe, the dead man knowing something he didn't. Was he crazy for looking for something in a dead man's eyes? A shudder surged through Sam like a wave rushing into a narrowing crevice then sliding back to the sea. He reached down and closed one of the dead eyes, then the other, his forefinger lingering a fraction of a second, as if puzzling over a sensation reminiscent of something in the past, now forgotten, yet altogether new at the same time.

Standing up he looked toward Jake but stared inward, puzzling over the new-old sensation of Hogan's eyelids on the pad of his forefinger, like the skin of a dressed-out rabbit or raccoon but softer. It gave but it was firm. Absurdly, he remembered a clay deposit by a brook in Cummington where he'd hide after the older boys took their pleasure on him. He was nine. The clay was slippery yet solid, soft yet firm, moldable when damp, crumbly when dry. On first touch it was cool, yet a reassuring warmth came from beneath its surface. At nine years old it wasn't entirely absurd to believe there was life within the clay. And now these eyes had life—didn't they? Inside of them? This was ludicrous!

"You okay?" Jake asked.

"Uh huh," Sam lied offhandedly. It wasn't the first time his mind had wandered into a world of inanities. Might not his senses abandon him for good someday? The question frightened him.

Sam's eyes met Jake's. Each one grabbed a corner of the poncho. They tugged and jerked until they got the dead weight moving and dragged it over to where Bull and Elvin Crane were loosening clods of dirt. Elvin was Bull's toady and none too bright.

Chapter 3: A Dakota Night

CATCHING HIS BREATH, SAM looked up the hill. Jubal was hunkered just below the crest. The horses were grazing, strung along a picket line halfway up. Ernst stood nearby, gazing at the western sky. The air was still, the late-afternoon sun warming the day one last time.

Bull's bark cut through, saying, "Streeter, what in Sam Hill ye lookin' at? Git the other corpse over here!" He hollered up the hill, telling Albrecht to go down to help, then turned to Elvin, who was kicking dirt onto the body.

"Hold on, nincompoop. Git him off the poncho first then lay him out," Bull said. He reached down, ripping a bandanna from Hogan's stiffening fingers, a garnet ring tucked in its folds. "Devils must of missed this," he mumbled, pocketing it. "Fix him flat on his back and lay this here cloth over his face. Git busy, Albrecht! Law's sakes, you see how they busted him up killin' him? Bloody heathens'll do that, ye know. Made him crawl while they laughed, then the women stove in his head. Them arrows are the brats' doins. That's how they learn their fiendish ways."

A half hour later Ernst came around to Thor's nigh side and was suddenly confronted by a western sky like he'd never seen before. The sun was poised above the horizon, framed by cumulus billows shouldered aside by its commanding power. The sky was dynamic, clouds gaining depth and color without pause, from white to pink and faint orange, from silver-gray to violet, from pink to red. Solid sheets of pure orange and meandering trails of deep purples, pinks, and true reds melded into an evolving, never-ending flow of color strong enough to affect all but the coldest of hearts.

The light was too bright to be eerie, yet it almost cast both ground and figure in two dimensions. The sun itself, now sinking, became an unbrilliant red disk, flattened like a circular stained-glass window through which majestic light flowed from a source other than itself. To the north a wavering, orange-tinted band grew darker until no orange remained but only pure red, deepening into what Ursula called "blood red." Ernst sighed, recalling the ten days they spent together, when she changed him forever.

"Albrecht! Stop your dreamin' an' get on with it!" It was Jim, *der Feldwebel.*

⋆ ⋆ ⋆

It was nearly dark when Jake and Sam finished cooking their bacon and hard bread mush. Jubal and Ernst were stretched out nearby, Jubal talking softly and Ernst gazing upward, half-listening. Beyond them, Bull was carping again about the "devilish savages," embellishing tales of desecrations, while Elvin sat slack-jawed, taking it all in. On the other side Jim, Charley, and Dan hunched close to the small fire, smoking their dudeens, the short-stemmed clay pipes favored by cavalrymen. Their tin cups of coffee were set next to the red coals. None of the three spoke.

"You don't bury no corpses before, huh?" Jake asked Sam.

"Some. Flood in '74 took a few," Sam answered, breaking the hardtack into the hot grease.

"Right, you told 'bout that. Me an' my brother René, we buried the old lady."

"Your own mother?" Sam asked, looking up. "I mean, put her in the coffin and everything?"

"Sure. I was twelve. We got old Duffy to cart the box to the graveyard. Paid him two bits. Father Donovan, he told us get out. René give him couple of dollars so he tell us to dig a hole in the corner. Even said church words over the grave."

"Church words?" Sam asked.

"You know—them priests, they talk Latin like they got secrets with God."

"Okay. How'd your mother die?"

Jake shrugged and said, "Don't know."

They fell silent, concentrating on washing down the greasy mash with the fast-cooling coffee. A few paces away, Jubal got up and spit into the fire, then settled himself beside Jim. Ernst stayed near his tent, snoring softly.

"So how'd them boys git done in?" Jubal asked Jim, offering his tobacco around.

"Charley put it together. He'll tell it."

"Naw," Charley mumbled. "I'm getting this chaw goin'."

Jim told what Charley had said, including how the two men went down. He was telling how the women stripped the bodies when Bull walked over and hunkered down.

"So they niver did fort up?" Jubal asked.

"No, they walked right into it—horses bolted, they was cooked. Snively got off one shot, maybe two."

"That band we come across? They the ones?" Bull asked.

"Uh huh," Jim answered.

"Blasted heathens," Bull said. "We should of rubbed 'em out."

"Judas, Bull!" Jubal exclaimed. "We couldn't do that."

"Mebbe, but every last one of 'em deserves to die. Way they broke poor Hogan up, makin' him crawl," Bull said.

"Where'd you get that idea?" Dan snapped.

"Ye seen his legs. Why'd they do that?"

"That isn't what happened," Dan said. "They *rode* him down."

"Charley figgered it like thet," Jubal said. "An' Charley here ain't oftly wrong."

"Uh huh," Bull muttered. He looked up at the others. "I ain't gonna dispute Charley, but it could of happened like I said. Heathens love torturin' a man, ye know."

Jim said, "It's about dark, Bull, so git up on top. Streeter, you relieve him after you eat. Dan, you check the horses."

"How come you pissed off?" Jake asked Sam, who was looking disgusted.

"Just the way they talk, like they don't give a damn about savages butchering troopers."

"Them two boys, they took the long odds an' lost. That simple."

"Still, they were White men—massacred," Sam said. "And except for Bull, none of them care about getting even." Furious, he swallowed the last of his bacon mush and headed off to take a leak.

Watching his partner go, Jake shook his head. Sam was a strange one. He said the cavalry was the best place to be, that he couldn't wait until they tore into Sitting Bull. But for what? Indians never did anything to him. And what was so scary about a dead man?

Jake shifted his attention back to Charley, who was telling about coup and how sometimes Sioux warriors staked themselves out with no-retreat ropes. There was no mention of torture, but that didn't matter. Jake's old fear was there, just like back in December, when he asked Jubal about it.

"You say them Injuns torture a man," he'd said to Jubal. "You know guys that seen it?"

"Nobody gits away to tell it."

"So how come everybody thinks it?"

"'Cause it's a fact," Jubal said. "You skepticizin' me?"

"Christ no, but how come guys know for sure?"

"'Cause they do, that's why. Damn it, yer jist like them other Bowery Boys, don't b'lieve nothin'." He'd turned abruptly, as if to pull away from a spider web he'd walked into.

Just the possibility of torture spooked Jake, like the old nightmare did—the one with the iron-jawed bear trap. Shaking the thought out of his head, he started to clean up the two cups and meat cans, wondering what René was up to tonight, back in Chicago. It was later back there, so he'd be home with his wife and two kids, unless Tom Driscoll had him working late. And Marguerite? She'd be sound asleep, probably dreaming of her wedding day. That was her plan, to catch a swell rich enough to take away the worries, but a good man too. Whoever he was, he'd better treat her right. Nobody did her wrong and got away with it, because she'd always be Jake's woman, that simple. Sweet, sweet Marguerite was petite, soft in the right places, warm enough for both of them on a cold night, but tough as an alley cat when she needed to be. Marguerite was her real name, and she made sure everyone called her that—not Margaret, not Rita. "Never Rita," she said, eyes flashing. "It's Marguerite, always Marguerite!" Jake smiled, remembering how she pretended to resist the first time he called her "Reet." It fit with her quickness and her sharp temper. The nickname was theirs and theirs alone.

When Sam returned, he was still pissed off and only half-listened as Jake started up about his mother again.

"Drowned or froze in the river. Maybe she jump. Talk like that when she drank. Big sin, but Jesus Christ, what them priests know? Don't got no kids to feed. Let's eat them peaches," he said, digging in his saddlebag for the tin he'd bought.

Each man speared a slice in turn with his knife, then savored not only the fruit swimming in syrup but the quietness of the night itself. The western sky was cloudless, a blackness lit by the brilliance of the stellar infinity. Sam lost himself in the wonder of it for a minute or two.

"Should be clear tomorrow," he said.

"You sure look out for that weather. These peaches, they're real good," Jake said.

As if of one mind, they fell into the slowest of rhythms eating the canned fruit. Jake worked his blade smoothly, like an artist applying the last strokes carefully but with a playfulness well deserved after the strain of creativity. He lifted the skewered slices over his upturned face, letting each one slide off the blade into his yawning mouth. Sam was just as deliberate, though far less fanciful. Toward the end of the tin, he held a piece up and watched, fascinated to see gravity pull the slice down the blade's unmoving edge.

Jake resumed his story. "René bought a stone marker three years back."

The slice hung on the blade while a queasiness started in Sam's gut, caused by the orange flesh separating at the knife's edge.

"Old graveyard crowded up then. One guy say they got another grave on top of her, but ..."

Cut through, the fleshy pulp fell into Sam's lap. The two pieces lay in a fold of his trousers, half-hidden from the knife that automatically dove to reclaim what it had lost. He jerked his hand back, an image of a bloody gash in his groin flashing into consciousness. Shifting his grip, he reached for the fruit, finger and thumb extended.

"René said he don't care 'bout that. Her soul was gone."

Sam held the dripping pieces before his eyes, relieved they hadn't fallen in the dirt. Unnoticed, the queasiness grew while his eyes focused on finger and thumb. As he brought the flesh to his mouth, his stomach recoiled, but it was too late. The syrupy fruit was inside, his tongue and lips squeezing and slurping his fingers as well.

"Don't need to go there. Worms already eaten on it."

Sam's hand might as well have had a mind of its own, pushing the finger back that far in his mouth. Judas! He'd nearly triggered himself into puking. As it was, the finger was sour enough to make him gag, sour like the Dakota dirt. *The skin of the dead,* he thought wildly. His eyes bulged as he yanked the peach from his mouth and threw it down, spitting after it in disgust, struggling to keep from retching. Striving for control, a vivid picture of his fingertip on Hogan's dead eyelid flashed in his mind as waves of shuddering engulfed him.

"Hey, you okay?" Jake asked.

"I'm all right," Sam replied, still trying to control his gullet. "Too much sweet, I guess."

"You don't want the juice, huh?"

Sam shook his head—the thought of swallowing sickened him. Reaching for his canteen, he shook it, measuring how much water it held. Jake savored the last slice of fruit then tipped the tin back and drained the juice. He smiled, wiping his mouth.

"What the hell happen, Sam? You got real jerky, jammin' that fist down the throat."

"Nothing happened except that last peach slice was bad," Sam said, glowering.

"Must be, you heave like that."

"I wasn't heaving!" Sam shot back defensively. "Even if I was, what do you care?"

"Huh?"

"Let's face it, Jake. You don't give a damn about anything other than your own hide. That time in January when Grant and Heywood came back with toes near frozen, I didn't see you at the hospital visiting with them. And today, you hardly looked at those two boys. Could have been us for God's sake!"

"Not me. I don't run, not out here."

"Still, it didn't bother you a Goddamn bit!" With that Sam got up, about to stomp off but only to hear the sergeant remind him to relieve Bull. He was still muttering to himself when he got to the top of the hill.

"What's botherin' you, Sam?" Bull asked.

"We should have gone after those murdering Indians," Sam said.

"Think we could of caught 'em?"

"Sure, but we could have hung back and tracked them. After they went into camp, we could have pitched straight into them."

"Uh huh, an' wiped 'em out," Bull said.

"Maybe," Sam said. "At least hurt them really bad, which is why I joined the cavalry."

"But Captain Moylan didn't say nothin' about pitchin' into no Injuns."

"Still, General Sheridan's orders said they should stay on the reservation. I thought we were supposed to enforce that."

"Uh huh. Only Sergeant Lawton's gonna follow the captain's orders, which was to find Snively an' Hogan."

"Yes, but I enlisted to fight Indians, not bury deserters," Sam said.

"You'll be doin' plenty of that when we go after Sittin' Bull."

"Maybe."

Bull said, "You will fer sure, Sam, 'cause you got the makings of a good cav'lryman."

"What makes you think that?"

"Two things. Fer one, you got a good heart. Can see that the way you treat my li'l Maggie," Bull said, referring to the mongrel he kept in the barracks.

"Can't help but like Maggie," Sam said. "She's a good little dog. What's the other thing?"

"You hate Injuns," Bull said.

"Not exactly. I get real mad when they murder folks, but I don't hate them."

"Maybe not now, but you will when you fight 'em," Bull said. Starting to leave, he turned for a moment then said, "Anyway, yer a fine trooper, and yer gittin' better."

"Thanks," Sam said, surprised that the compliment left him uneasy. How come? And why was he picturing himself shooting Bull in the head? Judas Priest!

Chapter 4: The General

May 12, 1876

After refusing to sign the Sioux Treaty of 1868, Sitting Bull continued to roam the Montana Territory with over three thousand Sioux and Cheyenne followers. The government acted to put an end to his recalcitrance in December 1875, designating all Indians outside their reservations as hostile and ordering them to go to a reservation by the end of January. Knowing that Sitting Bull had no intention of complying, General Sheridan ordered General Crook's command in Wyoming to mount a campaign against the Indians' winter camps. It failed, leaving Sitting Bull and his people undisturbed, their numbers swelling in the spring when hundreds of reservation Indians went out to hunt buffalo.

Sheridan planned a second expedition for the spring. Under the overall direction of General Alfred Terry, it was to be a three-pronged attack aimed at the renegade villages in Powder River country. General Gibbon left Fort Ellis in April with 477 men, one Napoleon, and two Gatling guns. His command proceeded down the Yellowstone River. It would block any attempt by the renegades to move north and be ready to attack from the north and west. At Fort Fetterman in Wyoming, General Crook put together a column of fifteen companies of cavalry and five of infantry—over a thousand men—to go at Sitting Bull from the south. The Dakota column would attack Sitting Bull from the east. It would march west out of Fort Lincoln under General Alfred H. Terry, commander of the army's Department of Dakota. It included the twelve companies of General Custer's Seventh Cavalry, three infantry companies, forty enlisted Indian scouts, two civilian scouts, a battery of Gatling guns, a supply train of 150 wagons, and a beef herd.

On May 12 the regiment was camped a few miles south of Fort Lincoln, preparing for the expedition. That afternoon Dan, Charley, Sam, and Jake had ridden over to John Bringes's smithy to check out their horses' shoes. Bringes was the Company A farrier. It was a good hour before stable call when they finished, so Charley decided to go see his friend Humaza over at the scouts' camp. The other three tagged along. Humaza was a Brulé Sioux from Spotted Tail's Agency. ("Sioux" was first used by French Canadian frontiersmen who borrowed it from the Ojibwe language. The people of the Sioux Nation called themselves Lakota, which was also the name of their language. "Brulé" was the French term for the Sicaŋju band of the Lakota people.)

It was one of those blue-sky spring afternoons in Dakota Territory, with a chill in the westerly breeze and no warmth in the sun. The four troopers came over a rise forty yards from the scouts' camp and reined up quickly. There was General Custer in all his glory on one of his fine thoroughbreds, yapping at the scouts. Beaming down between the scattering of clouds, the sun's rays had singled him out for special radiance, which was no surprise, him having that way about him—the first one in a crowd your eyes would light on. One hardly noticed Lieutenant Varnum beside him, nor the two interpreters and the forty-odd scouts, the whole lot of them a faceless cluster of listeners. As usual, Custer was carrying on like God's true delegate, sitting ramrod straight in his doeskin jacket, running his mouth, and signing at the same time, ignoring his interpreter's struggle to keep up. Perhaps he thought the scouts ought to know enough English, seeing how they were drawing pay from the United States Army.

Charley said he was going to wait there and see Humaza, so

maybe the others should head back to the company. Sam would have none of it.

"Judas Priest," he said to Dan. "This is my chance to see General Custer. Up close, I mean."

Jake said, "Shit! We don't want him seeing us." Unlike Sam, Jake knew well the first rule of soldiering: never attract an officer's attention.

"You and Dan go on back if you want," Sam said. "I'm staying right here."

Charley gave Dan a look that said he'd better not leave Sam there. Dan had no problem with that. Trying to get the rookie to budge would cause a huge squawk anyway. Charley dismounted, intending to look like he had reason to hold up there until Custer left. Dan and Jake followed suit, but Sam remained in the saddle, staring slack-jawed at The General like he was the second coming.

Several minutes later it looked like The General was running out of wind. He turned to Lieutenant Varnum but suddenly changed his mind and started in on the poor condition of the scouts' ponies and how it was going to be a long and grueling march. He said the scouts should have taken better care of them, as if Indians needed instructions on the care of horses. Custer always maintained that he understood the Indian mind better than most White men.

Finally finished, Custer sat there a minute or two talking with Bloody Knife, his favorite scout, before starting back to headquarters. With that Charley handed his reins to Jake, took out his hoof pick, and lifted Augie's nigh fore hoof. Sam was still gawking at The General while Blaster sniffed the chewed-up ground, hoping to find a snatch of grass worth the effort.

As Custer drew close Sam's right arm twitched like it wanted to salute, but The General stared straight ahead and passed at the walk. Suddenly he yanked his horse around and came back to look down at Charley, who quickly dropped Augie's hoof and raised his hand as he straightened up.

"Smrka, isn't it? A Troop?" The General asked, waving off the salute. "Your mount okay?"

"Yes, sir. Picked up a stone," Charley said.

"Good, good. I was telling the lieutenant the animals better be in top shape. But you know that, being with the Seventh since when, sixty-seven?"

"Sixty-six. Fort Riley, sir."

"That's right. Murphy came a little later," he said, turning to Dan. "So, Sergeant Murphy, lost your stripes again?"

"Yes, sir," Dan said.

"Oh, yes, and not the first time, right? Tell me something, Private Murphy. You're out here with two greenhorns—showing them the ropes, I presume. How is it that this one here knows enough to rest his horse while the other uses his for a rocking chair?" Custer said, turning toward Sam, whose mouth was still agape. "Private, dismount!"

Sam scrambled down, catching his boot in the stirrup for a second that scared Blaster into a sideways dance and sprawled Sam to the ground. Red-faced, Sam looked up, trying to manage a salute while picking himself out of the dirt. Then the horse jerked his head, yanking his left arm up, forcing him into a sidewise stagger. The color drained from Sam's face as he regained his footing, bravely keeping his right hand against his campaign hat, the brim of which had flopped down to cover part of his face.

Custer let him stand there, deliberately refusing to return the salute. His voice rose a half octave in biting sarcasm.

"Tell me, Private, doesn't your mount deserve a rest?"

"Sir, I thought—"

Custer guffawed, finally returning Sam's salute with an off-handed wave and said, "Don't *think*, Private, just control your horse. And when you get back to camp, report to the first sergeant for latrine duty. And, Murphy, you make sure this melon-head learns how to treat his mount or he'll be walking to Powder River country."

With that Custer spurred his thoroughbred and raced off, leaving the four men breathing his dust. The picture of gloom,

Sam stood with reins in hand, squinting through the dust at the man who'd humiliated him for his own pleasure.

"Judas Priest, Dan. I sure messed that up," he said.

"True enough."

"So what do I do now?"

"Police the latrine," Dan offered.

"I mean about General Custer," Sam said. "How do I get him to see me differently?"

"See you differently? Lad, he doesn't know you exist," Dan said, wondering whether to laugh or throw up. "He had his fun, and now he's onto something else. So forget it, but tell Jim instead of The First."

"But General Custer told me—"

"Christ Almighty! Tell your duty sergeant first!" Dan nearly hollered. Exasperated, he looked over at Jake.

Jake shrugged and said, "Sam, he don't get things quick."

While they waited for Humaza, Sam said he didn't understand why Indians would scout for the army.

"How come, Charley? I mean, they're the enemy."

"Not the Rees," Charley said, meaning the Arikara.

"I meant the Sioux, like your friend," Sam asked. "What reason would they have?"

"Don't know."

"Think they're spies?"

"No."

"Why did your Indian friend join up?" he asked. Sam never kept his questions from getting under a man's skin.

"I don't know," Charley said as Humaza approached on foot.

"*Hau, kola,*" he said to Charley.

"*Hau,*" Charley replied, handing him a pouch of tobacco before turning to us. "This here's Jake Picard, that's Sam Streeter, and you know Dan."

The Indian glanced at Jake and Sam, nodding his head. He gave Dan his usual little smile and stuck out his hand.

"John Daniel Murphy, *wicasa wasté.*"

"*Pilamaya,*" Dan said, thanking him for the compliment. "You signed up again?"

"No. Go back to agency," Humaza said, glancing at the scouts' children playing nearby. He turned toward the wagons drawn up in rows. Beyond them were the seven hundred mules and a host of draft horses. He laughed softly. "Long march. Mules trouble all day, cry all night. Soldiers don't sleep. Pissed off."

Humaza and Charley hunkered down, talking by themselves, mostly in Lakota. Over the years Charley had picked up a lot of it. He could sign as well as anyone too, but he never let on about it. Some fool lieutenant would put him to work, costing a family man like Fred Gerard his job. Gerard was the interpreter.

"Might be some buffalo out there," he said to Humaza, smiling.

"Buffalo smell mule shit, move upwind." Both men chuckled.

"Custer, he talk about buffalo?" Charley asked.

"No. He say scouts take many ponies after soldiers kill *Tatanka Iyotake.*"

Across the campground the regimental band finished a tune it was practicing then broke into "Garryowen." Charley and Humaza smiled at each other.

"Hurry-up song," Humaza said.

"Uh huh. Hurry up, don't go nowhere," Charley said. They both smiled, like it was their private joke. "How're your people doin'?"

"Bad winter," Humaza said softly. "Cold. No food." He dropped to one knee. Staring into the afternoon sun gone pale, his chest heaved in a half spasm and then relaxed. "People need meat. Go to Powder River for buffalo. Hunkpapa, Mineconjous, Oglala, Sicaŋju. *Ota* lodges. *Ota* warriors. More than Custer say."

Charley hesitated before responding then said, "Maybe they'll scatter when we get close to 'em."

"*Hiya!* No! Custer say *Tatanka Iyotake* run away. Big lie! Custer know *Tatanka Iyotake* fight!"

"What makes you think he knows?"

"Custer's eyes! He talk to Rees, not look at Lakota scouts. Rees not see inside Custer's eyes," he said. He went on softly, mixing English with Lakota, glancing at the Arikara boys tending the ponies.

The bugle sounded Stable Call. Charley waited until the last note drifted away before straightening up. Then he spit out his used-up chaw, walked with small steps over to Augie, and mounted.

"Custer wrong," Humaza said. "Not like Washita. *Tatanka Iyotake, Ta' Shunke Witko* not sleep when *Wasicus* come."

"Yer prob'ly right. When do you leave?" Charley asked.

"Two days."

"I'll see you before that," Charley said, reining Augie around.

Riding beside Charley, Jake asked, "What was them Indian words: *Tatanka* something? And *Wasicus,* what's that one?"

"*Tatanka Iyotake* is Sitting Bull, and *Wasicus,* that means Whites. *Ta' Shunke Witko,* that's Crazy Horse. *Ota* means many. Oh yeah, *wicasa wasté* means good man," Charley added, glancing at Dan with a smile.

"Okay," Jake said. "An' what was that about Washita?"

"At the Washita we caught 'em asleep."

"You wipe 'em out?"

"No, but it was a big victory," Sam said. "Killed a hundred warriors."

"More like fifteen or twenty," Charley said. "And a helluva lot of women and kids. We lost twenty-one killed, thirteen wounded."

"Is Humaza going home again?" Dan asked.

"Yeah," Charley answered. "Then he'll prob'ly head for the Powder. A lot of his people are."

"And he thinks Sitting Bull will stand?"

"Yeah. He's got—" Charley started.

"If they stand, we'll wipe them out," Sam said, full of unfounded confidence.

"More than eight hundred warriors," Charley said, ignoring him.

"So what? The Seventh can handle them."

Charley shrugged. Giving Dan a look, he reined up to let Sam and Jake move ahead.

"What is it?" Dan asked.

"Humaza said Custer talks like he's worried the Sioux will scatter, but he thinks Custer's lyin'. The truth is he thinks they'll stand."

"Really?"

"Yeah," Charley said. "What's more is he thinks The General's worried."

"That's not like Custer."

"No, it's not. But Humaza seen it in his eyes."

Chapter 5: Partners and Uncles

★ ★ ★

DURING THE WAR CHARLEY had served under Custer in the Michigan Brigade. His regiment, the Sixth Michigan Cavalry, was sent to the Wyoming Territory after Appomattox. He first encountered Indians there in a fight with the Arapaho, along the upper reaches of the Tongue River. When the regiment was mustered out in '66, he enlisted in the Seventh when it formed up at Fort Riley. Dan joined the outfit five months later and partnered up with Charley.

Dan came from Boston. He was working in a print shop in '61 when his eighteen-year-old brother Franny joined the Twentieth Massachusetts Infantry. He enlisted the next day to watch out for him, maintaining that Franny was half-drunk when some flimflammer talked him and some other Irish innocents into filling out the Harvard boys' regiment. A year later he went down in a heap not two yards from him on that damnable September morning, although in the din and smoke Dan wasn't sure of it till he found his empty-eyed corpse that evening. Darling Franny! Just twenty, he was. And of such promise. The terrible loss left an aching hole in Dan's gut that never healed.

His mother died before war's end, and when Dan returned home, he found his sister married to a policeman and his sweetheart in a convent. His boss had moved the shop to Vermont, so he took what work he could find. Awash in self-blame over Franny and struggling, he decided eight months later to return to the army with its fixed routines and steadfast ways. He chose the cavalry to save his feet.

At first Dan hardly knew a curb bit from a spur, but Charley was there to show him the basics of horse husbandry. Close-mouthed, his bunkie never wasted words on matters cavalry or anything else, especially his past. But he was a good listener, a talent Dan appreciated. Over the months their respect for each other grew. They maintained good habits and shared their chores evenly. As old soldiers, they did the best they could about bad situations and moved on. Dan did give others some slack, but Charley didn't. When pestered by an ignoramus, he'd drive him away with a withering glower that would fry your drawers.

The fight at the Washita cemented their partnership. From then on they trusted each other as experienced, competent soldiers who knew how to fight while instinctively keeping one eye out for his partner's neck. A month later they were welcoming 1869 into their lives, and Dan had a hunch that Charley might open up.

"I've been wondering," he began, "during The War you must have seen enough corpses to have grown past any queasiness. So what threw you when we found Major Eliot's men?"

Charley froze up before Dan finished, glaring at him like he should get the hell out of there and leave the bottle behind. Dan quickly told him to forget it; it was none of his business. To his surprise, Charley's eyes softened. After a long moment, Charley glanced at his cup, but instead of drinking, he dug into a pocket for his tobacco. A full two minutes passed while he bit off a chaw and worked it around in his mouth until he had it like he wanted it. Then Charley began a recitation that rolled out scene after scene, bringing on a sorrow in Dan that mounted as the words maintained the drummer boy's brain-numbing beat, the one that pushed men forward into an earthly hell that only madmen could contrive.

"Maybe too long to tell, maybe not. We come from Bohemia. I was five. Father, two brothers an' me. *Matka,* she died on the boat. Went to Schuylkill County, Pennsylvania. Hard coal. No English. At school I learned to figure, speak English, read some."

The whisper of a smile appeared as he mimicked a child reading out loud. "'The dog ran. Can the boy catch the dog?' Not this boy—I didn't." The smile faded and was gone.

"When I was eight, no more school. Only the coal. Slate pickin' first, then into the mine. Mule boy. Slaved next to my father when I was thirteen. Mean son of a bitch, him. Get drunk an' beat me. Miklos an' Vasek, they was six an' eight years older. Beat on me for fun, them bastards." Charley stopped for a minute, worked the chaw around, and spit.

"Didn't you get pissed off?" Dan asked.

"Yeah, but that was how it worked since before we come over. I was fifteen when I raised my fists. They laid me right out—couldn't see straight for two days. Hid out but the old man grabbed me up an' dragged me back to work. Miklos an' Vasek, they kept on the same, beatin' on me. The old man he'd come home drunk, an' I'd wake up with him beatin' on me." He spit again and picked up his cup.

"How'd you get out of it?" Dan asked.

Charley went rigid, the cup partway to his mouth, his eyes glaring with rage, and said, "Sometimes you don't know nothin'." He spit to the side, drained his cup in two swallows, and walked out of the room.

Dan was shaken, sitting there picturing Charley braining him with the bottle, but then Charley returned and sat down, furious but under control.

"Shit!" he said, pouring himself another half cup. He stared into the distance, going back a long ways again. "Gonna finish it," he said, taking a sip. "After they knocked me cockeyed, there weren't no point fightin' back, so I'd cover up, but I got more hate in me every Goddamn time. A year later, one night I was awake when the old man, he come toward my corner, belt in hand. I shot out of bed, straight for the door. He hollered an' come after me. Miklos tripped me an' I went down. We had this club by the door—hickory. I grabbed hold of it, an' when the old man swung that belt down, I whacked him on the knee an' he staggered. I got up quick an' swung; hit him hard by the ear. Dropped him like a stone. Miklos come at me, an' I laid him out too. Vasek he went for the door fast. I clubbed his back, an' he went down on his face, cussin'. I went to smash his skull in but somethin' stopped me. Told him don't move and checked the old man. He was dead for sure, an' Miklos, he looked close to it. The hate stayed ice cold in my head. I could feel it, Goddamn it. But it left my hands 'cause they were shakin'. I was done."

Charley paused for a minute and took a large swallow. Dan followed suit, and then he started to ask something, but Charley put up his hand to stop him. He sat there, looking back in time some more. He started in again.

"That night I turned my back on all of it an' headed west. Hungry a lot. Took what work there was. A kindly preacher in Akron, he let me sleep in the barn. Got me work. Helped me talk better. In Michigan a blacksmith, he took me on. Learned horses from the hoof on up. Stayed there until The War come and I joined the Sixth Michigan Cavalry. Good duty.

"Corpses in The War didn't bother me none. Not like you. You're still dreamin' it over an' over. Guess I didn't give a Goddamn 'cause life hasn't been worth hanging on to," he said, taking another swallow. "A lot of them boys in The War was mangled too."

"Like those at the Washita," Dan said.

"No, that was different. Mortars an' shell fire mangled them. At the Washita braves did the manglin' with knives an' clubs. Lookin' at those corpses, I seen me smashin' the old man's head in, which I didn't do but maybe I should have," Charley said. He threw down the rest of his drink and looked off a ways. "Remembering's like scratching a boil. You ain't careful, you'll tear it open.

"I wondered how come the Cheyenne chopped up those men," he said. "I started listenin' to them old trappers that come through the post when they told about Indians. And I got to know some of the Indian scouts, learnin' their ways, how they got a diff'rent slant on things—like how they fought their wars, countin' coup, the spirit world, an' that kind of thing. Found out it wasn't hate that made 'em chop up those men. They were just fixin' 'em for the afterlife."

★ ★ ★

After the company picked up a bunch of recruits in the fall, it wasn't two weeks before Sam latched onto Dan like a cocklebur to wool socks. He'd lost his dad at Antietam when he was eight, so there was some sense in him seeing Dan as a kind of uncle. Dan put up with his wide-eyed admiration for Custer because it gave him a chance to show the lad some tricks of the trade that might help him hang on to his hair. And maybe, in a very small way, it would make up for losing Franny.

Sam had gone only a year and a half past grammar school, but he read everything in sight, which suited Dan fine. They both talked the king's English (or tried to), except Sam said "ayuh," with a long "a." A lot of people from the hill towns west of Boston talked that way. It bothered Dan for some reason. But the most vexing thing was that the lad believed every speck of jingoistic hogwash that came his way, especially the fish stories Custer wrote about himself being the greatest Indian fighter of all time. Dan was right—Sam had read Custer's every word in *Galaxy Magazine* and considered the whole of it God's honest truth.

As for Jake, it was almost natural that he looked up to Charley because, except for him being only five feet two and wiry, they were very much alike. Each one took life as it came and made the best of it—no dreams about tomorrow, no time wasted on yesterday, no illusions about today. Underneath the hardness, he was a good and fair-minded man, the same as Charley. Both came from risky worlds and mostly kept the past to themselves. And they were sharp-eyed, never missing a thing. They could read a man's intentions in a blink yet took their own sweet time in sizing people up. They even walked the same: short steps and almost pigeon-toed.

Chapter 6: The Three Rookies

WHILE SAM SAW CAVALRY life as a calling, Jake had enlisted under duress. His given name was Jacques. From Chicago, he was thin-faced with coal-black hair and dark, flashing eyes. From the city streets, he had no use for horses, less for the army, and detested the frontier. He was tough as nails, street-smart, and could speak English, French, and a little Ojibwe. He had made his living working in saloons as an all-around helper, afaro banker, and poker player.

Sam stood five feet ten with the broad shoulders and muscled arms that came from milking cows and plowing fields. His mouse-brown hair lay flat, his nose was bent some, and his cheeks showed apple-red when embarrassed or wrought up. He had plenty of brains and knew a little about a lot of things, some from life and some from reading every book and newspaper he came across.

He knew horses as well as John Bringes. For example, at first Jake had one hell of a time with Scar, the horse he drew. That was not surprising. He'd never had any use for horses, and Scar was plain ornery by nature. Sam jumped right in to help Jake out. No one could figure out how he did it, but in a day's time Jake and Scar were working together just fine. Sam's Blaster was a rambunctious animal of sixteen hands. A half-broken son of a bitch, he'd given old Tom Flanagan nothing but trouble. He would toss his head and prance away every time Tom picked up a bridle. But after two days Sam had the rip-snorter as docile as a priest's new altar boy. When Dan suggested he change his name to Sweetie Pie, Sam shook his head, saying that there was nothing sweet about him—he'd just had to learn who was boss.

Bunkies often bickered, but Sam and Jake would straight out quarrel. Sam was put off by the chip on Jake's shoulder, and Jake was baffled by Sam looking at Custer like he was Our Lord Jesus Christ. And yet they respected each other; you could feel it.

Ernst was oversized—big boned and six foot two—but he looked soft. Perhaps it was his youth, being no more than nineteen with a baby face, flaxen hair, and a ready smile. His cheeks were always rosy, not coming and going with his emotions like Sam's. The fact was, he rarely got angry and never seemed to be embarrassed. He was a rare one—truly comfortable with himself. Ordinarily as gentle as a spring breeze, you wouldn't think he was powerful, but don't mess with his friends.

He had enlisted after being falsely accused of theft in Cincinnati. The judge added a couple of years to his nineteen and gave him the choice of prison or the army, five years either way. (More than a few troopers came in by that route.) Funny how things work out—his father had sent him to America to avoid conscription in Germany.

The three of them started out together at Jefferson Barracks, the recruit depot in St. Louis. One night six men jumped Jake after a card game, going after his winnings. Sam piled in to help. They were overmatched even though Jake was a wildcat and Sam wouldn't stay down. Then Ernst Albrecht waded into the middle of it. He started pulling the thugs off and tossing them out of reach. With that, they all slunk off into the dark.

* * *

That evening after the run-in with The General, Dan and Charley were sitting on cracker boxes jawing with Sam, Jake, Ernst, and Jubal Tinker. Jubal was a genuine country boy out of the Missouri Ozarks. He joined the squad in '72, enlisting at Elizabethtown, Kentucky. Sprawled out, he was eyeing Ernst, his bunkmate.

"What you seein' out thar?" he asked Ernst.

"Everything!" Ernst said. "The people, all moving. Beautiful."

"Ain't nothin' beautiful 'bout five hunerd boys needin' a bath."

Bull then walked up with Elvin Crane. A rookie, Elvin hung near Bull like an organ grinder's monkey.

Jake brought up the subject of money. "Custer, he's back now. You think maybe we get paid?" It had been more than two months since they'd seen the paymaster.

Dan laughed and said, "You'd like it, all that money changing hands."

"I got to make a livin'," Jake said.

"Uh huh," Elvin said, glancing at Bull. "And I hear yer sharp at it."

"You mean somethin' by that?" Jake said.

Bull snarled. "Don't git yer hackles up, Picard. He don't mean nothin' at all."

"He better not," Jake answered, his eyes jumping between Bull and Elvin.

"It doesn't matter," Sam said quickly. "They're not going to pay us, not with all we've got to do. Men would be off spending it on booze, cards, and whores."

"For the whores we are too far," Ernst said.

"Nah," Jubal said. "Whar they's dollars, they's whores."

"Sam's right. If we get paid, we wouldn't be ready 'til July," Dan said.

"That be okay for me," Jake said.

Ernst laughed. "Jake, always you make the jokes."

Elvin kept glancing at Jake like he wanted to say something. Bull saw it and turned toward the company street, saying, "C'mon, Crane, we had enough jawin' fer one night." And the two men were gone.

"Anyway, we'll be working our tails off tomorrow," Sam said.

"Not for me," Ernst said. "I go with Sergeant Lawton to the range. He will teach me to shoot good."

"You think he can?" Sam asked.

"I will try, but the rifle I don't like."

"Carbine not rifle," Sam said.

"Name don't matter," Jake said. "You gotta learn to shoot, Ernst—to stay alive."

"*Ja*, but I am no good to shoot," Ernst said.

"You better get to be, so learn it!" Jake demanded.

★ ★ ★

Before falling asleep that night Ernst thought about Jake's insistence that he learn to shoot. It reminded him of Sergeant Steinbrecher's efforts to take him under his wing during the winter. When he was on shoveling detail, the old Prussian sergeant worked him harder and longer than the others, saying he expected more from a German boy. At one point Ernst was so exhausted he ended up in the hospital on the brink of pneumonia, prompting *der Feldwebel* (the sergeant) to bring him extra food and push the attendants into giving him better care. After Ernst recovered *der Feldwebel* often spoke passionately about the honor he'd had in serving in *der Zweites Garde-Dragoner-Regiment* of Prince Friedrich Carl Nicolaus's Second Army. He told glorious stories of routing the Austrians at Königgrätz in 1866 and the victories at Spicheren and Gravelotte in 1870, which Ernst listened to dutifully but without the old sergeant's enthusiasm.

★ ★ ★

The next evening Ernst told the others he'd had trouble just loading the carbine, never mind hitting a target.

"The sergeant said a cow would do better with nose bleeding," Ernst said.

Jim had given up after four wild shots and started questioning him. When Ernst reluctantly owned up to why he enlisted, Jim offered to put through a discharge for him. All he had to do was own up to being under twenty-one and the discharge would follow.

"You said okay?" Jake asked.

"*Nein.* I said I am twenty-one."

"How come?"

"For me the cavalry has good friends," Ernst said. He smiled.

"But them Injuns will kill you fer sure if you cain't even load yer piece," Jubal said.

"Who is dead and who lives is *das Verhängnis*. How you say … fate."

"Not in war," Sam said, like he knew something about it.

"*Ja*, in war also."

"Mebbe yer folks didn't know much about soldierin'," Jubal said.

"*Nein!* My father was in *der Landwehr* two years. My brother is *ein soldat* seven years, *ein Korporal*. He got the medal at Sedan in 1870. Also, my grandfather in Blücher's army, he was."

"At Waterloo?" Sam said, surprised and not a little pleased. "Blücher's Prussians saved Wellington that day. Boy, your grandfather must have been proud to be a Prussian."

"*Nein.* He was not Prussian. When I was nine he told it. The words I remember good. He said he was the Westphalian in Prussian cloth."

"But he beat Napoleon in a great victory," Sam insisted.

"No, he tells the words of history to be lies: 'Fuel to feed the ambitions of professors,'" Ernst said, pausing as if to gather his memories. He took a deep breath and then the torrent of it spilled out, restrained by neither years nor language. The way he used the word *Großvater* showed a respect for the man bordering on reverence. It was the clearest statement about the insanity of war Dan had ever heard.

"When my brother said *Großvater* was the hero, *Großvater* said, 'Hero? Ha! No heroes that day! At Ligny the French put us on the run all the way to Waterloo, their hussars close upon our tail. I walked and stood and quick-stepped and marched and double-timed until my feet were numb. I drank water fouled by men's blood and horse piss, slept in rain and mud, and marched again in filth, first this way then that until we heard the guns come close, the guns which stank of powder and shot and death, their thunder now *unbegreiflich* ... uh, not to be believed. We raced beyond the dead and bleeding to the very edge of the cloud of smoke with tiny sparks of flame inside and halted on command. A hero? No! I marched when told and turned when told. I was young. *Ich vass der Soldat gehorsam!* No more, no less. Even after a cannon ball smashed the head clear off *der Feldwebel* close beside me. And then it was *der Korporal's* turn to shout *'Feuren!'* and I fired, then again and again on command, exactly as they told me to do—to blindly kill men unseen until we charged, our blades seeking blood and flesh. Then we ran back to cleaner air to breathe and load and fire and load and fire at what? Smoke, for smoke was all there was to see. And when it stopped men writhed at our feet like fevered children groaning and pleading until they moaned their way into deaths we cheered silently because we loathed their screams.

"'All for Prussian glory. Prussia, a wilderness peopled by bloated bullies and beaten serfs. For the colonel on his splendid charger, eager to tell the world about his victory, how he drove Le Garde Imperial from the field. And tell it he did, although in the smoke he faced us up more east than south, and so we killed twenty Englanders whose own colonel endowed with that brilliance held by men of rank. He faced his men more west than south to murder twelve of us.

"'*Mein Gott,* boy, *die Kompanie* killed no French that day. But they say we fought a righteous war, a Holy War. That's what history says. Ha! War? *Was ist der Krieg? Das Schlachtaus, ah—*'"

"Slaughterhouse," Charley said.

"*Ja.* Let me think it in English," Ernst said, eyes half-shut. "*Ja,* 'a slaughterhouse with generals for butchers and men for meat to sate the greed and ambitions of kings and lords, the noble men of Prussia, and of England and France as well.'"

"You remember good," Jake said.

"*Ja,* he told it good, *mein Großvater.*"

"So why'd yer brother join the army?" Jubal asked.

"From when he is small, Johann *ein Krieger* he is," Ernst said.

"So soldierin's in his nature, but it ain't in yers."

"*Ja*," Ernst said, smiling.

Although he felt uneasy, Sam wouldn't give up. "But Ernst," he said, "can't you see that Napoleon had to be stopped? That Waterloo was a wonderful victory, maybe as glorious as Gettysburg?"

"Glorious? How many went down?" Charley asked Dan.

"Both sides? Some eight thousand killed. Twenty-eight thousand wounded."

Charley glowered at Sam and said, "No glory in that."

"But still—" Sam started.

"Jesus, Sam! They was there!" Jake said.

"Okay, okay," Sam said, standing up. He needed to escape the wisdom of Ernst's *Großvater.*

★ ★ ★

Sam stretched out when he returned to the group, staring at the heavens above.

"You know, the sky out here is extra special," he said. "It's like we're under a giant black bowl with pinpricks of light scattered all over the inside of it. You'd never see a sky like it back home."

"How come?" Jake asked.

"In Massachusetts the sky's more flat at night," Sam said.

"Massachusetts, the land of steady habits," Jubal said. "Ain't thet what they call it, Dan?"

"There are some who call it that," Dan replied.

"Call it what you want, it's a good part of the country," Sam said. "Someday I'd like to go back, but they don't need horse soldiers there. Besides, I like it out here."

"C'est la chose la plus insensée que j'aie jamais entendue!" Jake snarled, calling Sam crazy. "Dakota winters freeze your ass and summer's hot as hell. And them Indians, they're out to kill you."

"No," Sam argued. "They're after settlers, and I like being here to protect them."

"*Sacramère!*" Jake swore. "That was their choice not ours."

"Well, it's what we're paid to do," Sam said.

"That's enough!" Jubal exclaimed. "We're headin' out first thing tomorrow, ya know."

— Chapter 7: Off to Powder River Country —

* * *

May 17, 1876

Dan was in a sour state of mind when the regiment assembled, ready to move out. Having pulled guard detail the night before, the chill of the night was wedged deep in his bones as he stood at attention, Teddy's bridle in hand. He eyed The General on his prancing thoroughbred, squawking out this order and that, clearly uneasy under the eye of the dour-faced General Terry. Custer wouldn't put up with being a subordinate for long.

As they got underway he scanned the column ahead and the country to the sides. A heavy mist blanketed the river, held down by the cold morning air. A dozen antelope stood like bronze statues against the hillside, staring at the column of blue. The regiment marched onto Fort Lincoln's parade ground at seven o'clock, led by Varnum and his Indian scouts. Immediately, the Arikara women began their wailing, but it was the kids from Suds Row who grabbed the troopers' attention. They marched alongside the horses, exaggerating their steps the way young boys do, toodling away on little horns, beating on pans for drums, and waving sticks tied with scraps of cloth for flags. The racket made the horses skittish. Worried troopers tried to shoo the little kids away and then strained to gain a military bearing as the column turned toward the generals and their staffs lined up by the flagpole in front of officers' row. Even the most jaded trooper showed his best when passing in review. It came with being a cavalryman.

After the last company passed, General Terry and Custer assumed the lead. The band struck up "The Girl I Left Behind," and the column filed out of the parade ground by fours and started up the bluff. When it paused at the summit, Dan looked back down at the post. The barracks he called home looked much too small, the stables behind even smaller. The sutler's store was tiny, the steamboat at the landing a child's toy. Only the breadth of the Missouri River appeared undiminished by distance. Eyeing each man in turn, First Sergeant Heyn came down the line to take his position in the rear of A Troop. A bugle sounded up ahead and they began to move again, column of twos.

Dan and Charley rode behind Bull and Elvin. Charley maintained that Bull was built to be a miner; he was a short-armed, bow-legged, no-necked barrel of a man standing five foot five. Wide-jawed with a thick mustache below a nose flattened in brawls fueled by too much bragging mixed with alcohol, his pale blue eyes were deep-set below a broad forehead and thinning hair. All told, his squarish head was like that of a bulldog, which explained the nickname.

Bull had a way of making you uneasy. No matter what the expression on his face—pious, commanding, or reflecting a tiny streak of fear—you couldn't trust it. Pure rancor lay just beneath. When it came to people of color, he was entirely straightforward. Not only were they of inferior quality to him, they were the devil's own agents. Whenever he started in about that, Jake walked away, Charley gazed at the clouds, and Jubal's eyes rolled up as if to inspect his scalp from the inside.

He had a deep-rooted mean streak that showed through his pious insistence that Our Lord Jesus Christ saved him from a life of sin and debauchery. A half-reformed drunk, the Creature grabbed hold of him maybe twice a year. (The Creature was a term for whiskey, or the longing for it.) Dan drank with him just once. In his cups he bragged about riding with Chivington's Third Colorado Volunteers, a ragged hundred-day outfit. Its sole job was to kill Indians, which they sure as hell did at Sand Creek in '64. Bull sat there boasting how they rode in and "shot the living shit out of them heathens with hardly a loss to ourselves, shooting down old men, slaughtering ponies, splattering papoose brains, and taking a special kind of scalps offa them whorish fucking squaws." The filth of his rant was so depraved Dan was forced to leave—staying there meant strangling the son of a bitch.

The next day after his rant Bull tried his damndest to get Dan to tell him what he'd said, but Dan simply said, "Nothing," turned his back on him, and never mentioned Sand Creek again, except to tell Charley. Of course, neither one of them forgot the story nor the hideous pride Bull took in telling it.

Elvin Crane was a dimwitted recruit who arrived the summer before and wasted no time kissing Bull's arse. They ended up bunkmates, and rightly so—a wretch and his toady.

Ruminating about those two numbskulls added to the doldrums lodged in Dan's brain, but Jubal and Ernst's conversation behind him soon provided relief. Of course, any conversation involving Jubal Tinker brought on a smile, no matter the subject.

"It is good to see you chirky today," Ernst said.

"What d'you mean?" Jubal asked.

"Chirky is happy, you said."

"Uh huh."

"Yesterday you are not happy. You are, ah, nervous."

"Wa'n't nervous, jist a mite skitterish. The waitin' chafed on me," Jubal said. "Been two years since we went off like this."

"Then you go where?"

"Black Hills. 'Leven comp'nies then but no infantry. This here, it's the most bodacious expedition since the war. Nuff to make a man proud."

Jubal had grown up mudsill poor in Hickory County, Missouri, on a farm of just seventeen hardscrabble acres. The grind of poverty had worn his father down to where he leaped at the chance in '61 to "do something right." Proclaiming his devotion to the Confederacy, he joined Quantrill's Irregulars. Two years later he returned home to hide out after their barbaric raid on Lawrence, Kansas, and the fight at Baxter Springs. He rejoined the outfit later and stayed with it until Quantrill was killed in '65. Jubal's father then returned home and told his wife he was off to California and would send for her and the kids once he made his fortune. He was shot dead in a St. Joseph saloon two weeks later by a man whose wife and son perished in the Lawrence raid. His embittered widow made sure Jubal and the other kids knew the disgrace their father brought them by throwing in with Quantrill, a man she invariably called "that devilish polecat."

Jubal left home after his mother died in '71, making his way to St. Louis, where he found work on the steamers and eventually ended up on the Ohio River. He soon took to drinking. He was dogged by self-doubt, worrying he would come to no good like his father. It was not surprising, therefore, that in '72 he found himself on the bum in Louisville, Kentucky, drifting from town to town. In a sober moment he saw clearly where he was heading, the fright of it propelling him into the next full-fledged bender without delay. A day and a half later he found himself in the woodlands amongst a crowd of runagates led by sheeted Klansmen putting two young men to the torch for the capital crime of being the wrong color.

"The evil of it froze me up solid," Jubal said. "I fell to pukin' my guts out right thar, wond'rin' if I'd washed my supper down with horse piss 'stead of the beer I paid fer. It all lef' me of a mind thet I wa'n't no diff'rent from the old man throwing in with Satan when he emptied his pistol into them poor folks in Kansas."

The next afternoon found Jubal in Elizabethtown, where Seventh Cavalry was keeping watch on the Klan and seizing whatever illegal stills it could find. Seeing that the cavalrymen had bearing, he enlisted on the spot, aiming to scrub himself clean of the filth and misery of his past. The effect was immediate. He took pride in everything: his uniform, his Spencer carbine, and his horse Prince, a wily veteran of both field and parade ground. And Private Tinker stood tall for the first time in his twenty-one years.

★ ★ ★

That afternoon the column made camp by the Heart River. The paymaster appeared and set up shop. Card games started up shortly thereafter. A plentiful supply of whiskey surfaced as the evening wore on. Elvin came up with a pint of his own, the first swallows of which convinced him he was the equal of any player in sight. Later, with but four bits left, his muddled brain concluded he'd been rooked. One could see the matter festering inside his skull with the way he glanced at Jake; he was itching to tangle with him but too crocked to try. When the game broke up, Jake and Eddie O'Neil made a beeline over to H Troop to get into a no-limit game, where the serious players tried to parlay their winnings into enough to brag about.

Dan had just settled down with Charley and Jim for a last smoke when Bull stopped by. After lighting his clay pipe, he started carping about how some men didn't stand a chance against the "sharpies" in a card game.

"Didn't you leave a winner?" Dan asked.

"Sure, but I can spot a rigged hand. Some of the others can't."

"What do you mean a rigged hand?"

"You saw it. The way that half-pint was handlin' them cards," Bull said.

"What half-pint?"

"Picard. Him and O'Neil is city boys, both of 'em sharpies."

Jim said, "Best be careful, brandin' men like that."

"I ain't sayin' they was misdealin', but they got a way of winnin' when they want, is all. O'Neil, he's an old hand," Bull said while getting his pipe going again. He snuck a look at Charley gazing up at the stars, seemingly uninterested. "I played with a lotta guys over the years, but that Picard, he's different. You can't never trust him."

"Why's that?" Charley asked in his quiet way, his eyes still on the heavens.

"He's mostly Redskin with them eyes and the real black hair. You ever meet an Injun you can trust?"

"I have," Jim answered. "An' a lot of Whites I can't."

"Well not me. Way I see it, they're worse than yer average nigger," Bull said.

Charley got up and started for the latrine. Jim went with him.

Dan said, "Bull, do you think Our Lord Jesus Christ wants you hating Indians?"

"I don't hate 'em," he said. "But they're the devil's people. Them an' niggers."

With that Dan got up and followed Charley. Bull came right along.

"Don't get me wrong, Dan. I ain't lookin' to give Picard no grief. Not myself, but there's some that wouldn't mind seein' him hurt, you know."

"You think so?"

"Uh huh. There's a couple in C Troop still sore from last payday—what was it, four months ago? And some in A Troop too."

"Who?" Dan asked.

"I ain't sure, but remember he give Elvin a bad time about that tack last winter?"

"As I recall, Elvin switched bridles on him."

"Not how I heard it," Bull said. "Anyway, Elvin's still mad about it. And he's sure Picard gypped him today. He's got a short fuse, you know."

In the morning a tin of peaches was missing from Jake's saddlebag. Figuring it was Elvin, he talked with Charley about it. He said "*le beluet*" (the nincompoop) had been gunning for him from the beginning, probably because he was part Ojibwe. Jake figured he'd deal with it hard if Elvin brought his play into the open.

Chapter 8: At the Little Missouri

May 30, 1876

For the next ten days the column made its way through terrible weather: freezing cold and then wild hailstorms followed by days of sweltering heat with clouds of mosquitoes and swarms of grasshoppers. They were chilled to the bone, then sweltering day after day, the bugler telling the men when to saddle up, halt, drink, feed the horses, eat their beans, and sleep. After a day or two, one's mind was as numb as his keister, both ends dulled by the rhythmic sameness of it. At the end of the twelfth day, they set up camp by the Little Missouri River. Somehow General Terry had divined that Sitting Bull was along that stretch. However, there were no signs of him, so Terry sent Custer on a scout in force upstream the next day. That was May 30, a welcome day in camp for the men.

Borrowing a pole from John Bringes, Sam headed toward a little grove of cottonwoods downstream. There he found Captain Benteen, who not only welcomed him as a fellow angler but offered him some of his bait. They chatted for a few minutes, and then Sam decided to try his luck around the next bend. Thankful for the shade of a cottonwood in these badlands, he ruminated on how hard it was to get by in the Dakota Territory with its grass mostly brown and the half-sized trees. It seldom rained, and when it did, it came down in buckets and the constant wind cut into you like a scythe mowing timothy. Sure, he was lucky to be sitting beside what they called a river out here, pole in hand, but he was a New Englander at heart. He missed the woods and rivers and the hills. And he sure did miss the green of it.

Sam was born on July 24, 1854, in Northampton, Massachusetts, and raised in Chesterfield, a hill town fourteen miles northwest of there. Four years later his mother died in childbirth. His Aunt Ida Bradford took the baby, leaving Sam with his father, Jonah, who wasn't given to hard work. The farm barely sustained the two of them, but Jonah was a splendid father. He read all kinds of books to Sam about history, adventure, seafaring, and the Indians—books that brought an unimaginable world into his life.

When fire consumed the farmhouse in 1860, they moved to the Bradford farm in the valley. Jonah enlisted a year later. After his death in '62 the Bradfords sold both farms and moved to Ohio. They took his little sister with them but left Sam behind as a ward of the county. He couldn't understand why.

Over the next two years he was placed on five different farms where "state boys" worked to earn their keep. Luckily he ended up in Easthampton with a kindly older couple named Curtis. Mrs. Curtis belonged to the Social Library Association and made sure Sam had plenty to read. When Sam was eleven, Mr. Curtis loaned him enough to buy an older Yorkshire sow. He named her Katrinka. She not only became a kind of pet, she gave the family more than enough pork and bacon, and Sam had a little business selling the pigs. He kept a couple of gilts from her four litters before it was time to slaughter her. Of course he balked when Mr. Curtis insisted that Sam do the killing, but he was surprised how he didn't feel much of anything after swinging the hammer. Katrinka dropped like a stone, Mr. Curtis stuck her, they strung her up by the hocks, bled and gutted her, scalded and scraped the carcass, and then it was all about the butchering.

The best thing the old man did for Sam was to show him how to care for his fine team of Percherons. In time he learned to work them and, in the process, came to understand how they saw the world.

Mr. Curtis died unexpectedly when Sam was fifteen. Before moving to her daughter's home in Fiskdale, Mrs. Curtis found Sam a home in Williamsburg with her cousin who owned a livery. Starting as a stable boy, by eighteen Sam had steady work driving a team for a local sawmill. The disastrous flood of 1874 provided more than enough extra work to give him the stake he needed to travel.

The following March Sam journeyed to Sharpsburg, Maryland, where he hired a buggy to look around the battleground where his father was killed. He couldn't walk the entire path of the Fifteenth Massachusetts Infantry west from Antietam Creek that fateful morning, but he saw the open fields, imagining the three brigades marching in double lines, the men pressing forward resolutely through shell bursts and musket fire. He did get to walk through the West Woods to the attack's dreadful end. An hour later he stood over his father's grave in the unkempt cemetery by Boonsboro Pike. He sobbed uncontrollably while his mind insisted that it wasn't true, that his dad was not there, no matter what the marker said.

* * *

Dan was jawing with Charley and Jake when Sam returned from the river carrying a fine mess of trout, all cleaned and ready for the pan. It was enough to make a man's mouth water. He began telling how he found the surprisingly congenial Captain Benteen sitting by the stream with a beautifully crafted rod.

Jubal and Ernst arrived just as Sam was telling Charley that when he left the fish were still biting. A minute later Bull and Elvin walked up. Elvin was giggling.

"Share your laugh with us, boys," Dan said.

Elvin started to say something about a frog but Bull cut him off. "It wa'n't nothin'," he said, trying not to grin.

"Bullshit!" Sam said. "I saw you sliding a straw up a frog's ass and blow him up. Pissed me off, Bull."

"Wa'n't yer business," Bull snarled.

"So what happened with Benteen?" Dan asked Sam, trying to nudge him back to peaceful ground.

"He surprised me, talking like we were just two anglers."

"Boys in H Troop say he jaws with 'em a lot," Charley said.

"And I hear he plays baseball with his boys, like it's a real sport," Elvin said, glancing at Bull. "Horse crap! Wrasslin's the real sport."

"Chicago got a baseball team," Jake said

"Yeah, and maybe your team dances 'round the Maypole too," Elvin taunted.

"Shut your damn mouth!" Sam said, worried that Jake would blow up.

"Oh yeah, an' who's—"

"*Whoa!*" Jubal said. "You boys git The First lookin' this way, we'll all be dipped in shit."

Charley smiled. The others chuckled. Muttering, Elvin fell to scraping out the bowl of his pipe.

Dan said, "Bill Heyn isn't that bad."

"Yeah, he ain't 'tall like M Troop's first, ole John Ryan," Jubal said.

"What about him?" Sam asked.

"I didn't git all the perticulars, but I heard a man cut on a piece of harness, which calls fer comp'ny punishment. Ryan, he ignored thet an' strung him up by the thumbs right thar."

"Lost his stripes for it," Charley said.

"No, he didn't," Elvin sneered. "He's still M Troop's first."

"You're right, lad," Dan said. "But The General gave his stripes back to him."

"Why Custer do that?" Jake asked.

"Why Custer do that?" Elvin mimicked. "Hell, gen'rals do what they want. Ain't that right, Bull?"

"Yup, that's right."

"Hear that, runty!" Elvin said, sneering at Jake. "Yer brain's littler than I thought."

Jake stood up slowly, his dark eyes locked onto Elvin, his right hand emerging from his pocket and holding a clasp knife, his left reaching to open it. Elvin stiffened, ashen-faced. He quickly closed his own knife and pocketed it. Everyone sat stock-still.

"No need of that!" Dan said quietly. "The problem isn't—"

"Stay out of it," Jake said. "What you choose, Elvee? Take that back or bleed!"

"I was just arguin' with—"

"Choose, Goddamn it!"

"But—"

"Now!" Jake insisted, shifting the open knife from hand to hand, never taking his eyes from the dolt, starting toward him. Sam's face turned red. Charley half-smiled.

"That's enough, Picard," Bull declared, starting to rise. "He didn't mean—"

"Fuck off!" Jake hissed, eyes still locked on Elvin. "Choose now, Elvee."

"I was jest foolin'."

Jake shrugged and started toward him. "First I slice off that ear."

"No!" Elvin said. His right hand shot upward as if to protect his face. "I take it back."

"What you take back?"

"That yer brain's too little."

"What else?" Jake asked.

"Huh?"

"That runty stuff," Jake snarled, taking another step. "*Cré maudit!* Runty's 'bout pigs!"

"Okay, okay!" Elvin said. "I take that back too—the runty stuff."

With that Jake moved over to a chopping block and sat down, but he didn't hurry about it. The open knife remained in his hand. Settled, he went back to glaring at Elvin.

Dan tried to quiet things down, asking Charley if he still wanted to fish. He did.

"Good," Dan said, turning to Crane. "Now, Elvin, it did my heart good to hear you utter sweet phrases of reconciliation soon enough to be considered contemporaneous. For without such utterances your disputation with Private Picard might have proceeded to the letting of blood. I believe it would have been yours that we'd find staining this very ground. As Jubal pointed out, such excitement would surely capture the first sergeant's interest, thus endangering every one of us."

On occasion Dan thoroughly enjoyed using some of the fancier words in the dictionary that he pondered on cold winter nights. Elvin stood spellbound by his grandiloquence. Jake couldn't keep a smile from breaking through.

"But to keep the peace, laddie, I suggest you borrow young Streeter's pole and catch us an extraordinary mess of trout. Private Smrka is one of the Seventh Cavalry's finest anglers, and he'll gladly accompany you to the river's edge." Dan handed Sam's rod to the sulking young trooper. "Does that arrangement meet with your approval, Private Crane?"

Wordless, Elvin nodded his acquiescence and picked up the pole. Charley remained tight against his side as he stumbled from the circle. Jake watched them go. Only then did he return his knife to his pocket.

"Geehosaphat!" Jubal exclaimed. "One day thet Elvin's goin' to come clear offa the hinges."

"Ayuh," Sam said. "He's an idiot."

"Oh, he's a dimwit, fer sure," Jubal said. "Trouble be, he's tetched, to boot. One day all that stupid's gonna pour outta the crack in his head and he'll git hurt."

Dan wondered how close Jake would come to committing mayhem. For one thing, there were rumors of violence in his past life, and he did make a point of keeping both of his knives razor-sharp. Watching him hone them was a mesmerizing experience.

Jake returned to the matter of The General. "That Custer, he be cruel sometime, I think."

Bull disagreed. "Yer wrong. If he comes down hard, it's just to keep men in line."

"What you think, Dan?" Jake asked.

"Faith be, who knows what's inside a general's head?" Dan asked. "I wasn't surprised he gave back Ryan's stripes. Maybe he owed the sergeant a favor—or maybe he liked Ryan coming down hard like that, it being in his own nature. But Custer's attitudes matter not a whit. Out here each company works best following its own way, and Ryan's way works well for M Troop. That might be why he got his stripes back."

"I didn't think of it like that," Sam said.

"No difference to us," Jake said.

"That's right," Dan agreed. "What makes a difference is how we soldier."

"No two ways about it." Jim's steady voice surprised the others. Unnoticed, he'd walked up behind them. "Forget about Custer. Just do what you're told, do it good, watch out for the man next to you, and take care of yerself."

⋆ ⋆ ⋆

Later Jim approached Charley and Dan, worried that the trouble between Jake and Elvin could become deadly.

"You mean like them two M Troop boys in '74?" Charley asked. "What were their names?"

"Rollins and Turner," Dan said.

"Yeah, in the Black Hills," Jim said. "They'd been feudin' for two years, I heard. Finally Rollins shot him dead. We don't need nothin' like that, but the way Elvin's actin', Jake might get all hot an' kill the dumb sumbitch."

"Jake don't get hot," Charley said. "He gets cold."

"What do you mean?"

"He don't get all lathered up. He'll kill to save his skin or someone else's, but he'll do it with purpose, not 'cause he's pissed off."

Chapter 9: On to the Powder River

★ ★ ★

MAY 31, 1876–JUNE 7, 1876

May 31 was a Wednesday. Sam and Jake had pulled sentry duty the night before, and in the morning they were jawing with Charley and Dan while waiting for the march to commence. Jubal and Ernst joined them, carrying serious news. Just past midnight Jubal woke up to find Elvin crawling stealthily up to Sam and Jake's tent. He woke Ernst, who went and stood behind the skulker. Nearing the tent, Elvin drew his Colt, pulled the tent fly open carefully, thumbed the hammer back, and thrust the barrel into the opening. Finding no one inside, he cursed and turned, still on his knees, and bumped against Ernst's shins.

Jubal said, "Ernst tole him to 'uncock yer pistol,' which he did. He was fixin' to leave so I called his name, case he hadn't seen me squattin' there holdin' my carbine. I said what I seen didn't make no sense. Man wavin' a pistol under a body's nose is lookin' to git hisself hurt. Tole him if you two had been to home you'd of killed him, sure as cow's shit cow shit. Said if 'twas my tent I'd of shot him my own self, and I'm tender as a virgin's quim."

"Judas H. Priest!" Sam said, red-faced with fury.

"With you why does Elvin want the trouble?" Ernst asked Jake, but Jubal answered.

"Spleen's in his nature, thet's all."

"Spleen means spite," Sam said to Ernst.

"Uh huh," Jake said. "But there's more to it."

"Like what?" Sam asked.

Jake shrugged and said, "Bull's pushin' him."

His face reddening, Sam said, "Maybe, but it's still the idiot's doing, Goddamn it! Next time I'll take him apart!"

"He come for me not you," Jake said.

"Makes no difference!"

Jake stared at him with that steely cold look in his eyes, cold enough to send a chill through a man on a hot summer day.

"Okay, but he's mine, *une plorine*, a scared chicken," Jake said. "Sometime I kill him, but for now I cut him a little. Then he listen when I tell him stay away."

"That'll work," Charley said. "'Cept cutting him brings trouble."

"What you mean?"

"Cut him and he tells Bull. Bull goes to Jim, and Jim's gotta do something."

"How come?" Jake asked.

"That's how it works," Charley said. "If Jim don't come down on you, The First's gonna come down on him."

"How's The First gonna know?"

"Bull will tell him," Charley said.

"*Marde!*" Jake cursed. "So what am I s'posed to do?"

"Let me and Dan work it out."

"How?" Jake asked.

Charley glanced at Dan and shrugged.

"We'll talk to Bull," Dan said. "Use what play we have."

"Play?"

"What we got to change his mind," Charley said. "We've been savin' it up."

"Okay," Jake muttered, "but I'll cut him anyway, maybe."

"You can't do that," Sam said.

"What they gonna do? Ain't no jail out here."

"I tell you what," Dan said. "If Charley and I haven't fixed it by nightfall, you do what you please. Okay?"

"Okay," Jake said. And that was that.

★ ★ ★

The day's march was a hard one, crossing the Little Missouri, working up and out of the badlands, and then heading west toward Sentinel Butte. Close to sunset, Charley and Dan took Bull aside. Dan told him that, seeing how Elvin was not well-equipped in the brains department, maybe he could get him to stop making trouble for the squad. After all, everyone knew that Jim was concerned and Bull ought to back Jim up, him being the corporal.

Then Charley said, "So keep the numbskull away from Jake."

Of course it was no surprise when Bull resisted, saying that whatever Elvin did, Jake had it coming for humiliating him in front of everybody. Charley said that murder wasn't exactly the appropriate payback for public ridicule, and Bull acted surprised, like he didn't know anything about the night before. Dan started to press the matter, but Charley pushed him aside.

"Let's cut the horseshit," he said, glowering. "You got Elvin lookin' to you, and none of us want trouble. So you get that half-brain to back off."

"And what if I don't?" Bull said.

In half a second Charley had his face right close to Bull's, saying, "'Cause if you don't, we'll spread the word about how you was at Sand Creek shootin' kids an' taking them special kind of scalps offa them whorish fucking squaws—I think that's what you called 'em."

"Whadda *you* know 'bout Sand Creek?" Bull asked, his face turning red.

"Just what you told Dan."

"Goddamn it, I didn't tell Dan nothin'. He said that."

"I lied," Dan said with a smile.

"Well, you got it all wrong," Bull said. "Them heathens fought us something fierce."

"Even them whorish fucking squaws and their babies?" Charley roared, grabbing Bull by the shirt. "Like I said, let's cut the horseshit and go talk to Elvin."

Bull spluttered some but he had no choice in the matter, and the three of them cornered his half-cracked toady. Elvin's face turned ashen when Charley lit into him, looking so scared Dan thought he'd shit his drawers. When Bull got his say, Elvin said, "Okay, okay," before Bull got halfway through telling him to stay away from Jake.

★ ★ ★

After Dan and Charley left, Bull went off by himself and sat, honing his knife while Sand Creek played through his mind once again. At twenty he'd given up life as a drunken rock miner and signed on with the Third Colorado Volunteers, a hundred-day outfit raised to put the Arapaho and Cheyenne in their rightful place. The Reverend Colonel Chivington called for the extermination of all Indians, including the brats. ("Nits make lice," he'd preached.) Three months later they rode east and south to destroy Black Kettle's Cheyenne village on Sand Creek.

Bull tested the knife's edge with his thumb while the familiar images of that cold November morning ran through his head: The gang of uniformed riders, their yells forewarning the din to come; a whirling jumble of smoke and dust and dark-skinned savages running; troopers on horses careening every which way; the sounds of carbines barking, bullets whizzing and twanging, horses snorting, women screaming, and babies wailing; an old chief staggering backward, his chest cut through by troopers' lead. Then there was the weird yowling of another's death song in the middle of the tumult, and a Cheyenne girl coming toward them, waving a white cloth, three rounds sending her soul through the gates of Hades in an eyeblink, a human doll of rags left lifeless on a thin patch of snow. Bull's bunkie Schmidt tumbled, knocked from the saddle by a soldier's errant round. He saw an old squaw's backside as he rode her down, his carbine's bark sprawling her into the dirt, and felt Indian braids in his hand as he sliced and tore the bloody scalp from her devilish skull. Glancing up he saw a young warrior pointing an arrow straight at him. Flinching, his arm flew up as if to protect himself from the chilling stab of fear. Crack! Bull froze. A grizzled trooper's second round creased the boy's nose and tore into an already unseeing eye. Then came the biting taunt.

"You wanna warrior's scalp?" the veteran asked. "Take the boy's. He's pract'ly grown."

Shamed to the core, Bull left the boy untouched and went back to the killing, but the steam went out of him as he realized his drawers had filled with diarrheic shit.

When the troop returned to Denver, there were speeches and cheering crowds wanting to hear stories of the victory and see their booty, including the bloody scalps they'd sliced from men's skulls and women's privates. But their heroic tales sent the bleeding hearts to the pulpits and newspapers, crying it was no more than a "slaughter of innocents," as if the Cheyenne were people.

No matter what was said about it, Sand Creek became the defining moment of his life, confirming him as a living part of God's intention for Whites to rule over Indians, a bloodthirsty race more abominable than even the blackest of Ethiopians.

After the War, Bull found steady work in Denver as a full-time carpenter's helper and part-time drunk. Four years later a true Jezebel lured him into her satanic world of hedonists devoted to opiate delirium and perverse carnality. Caught in her web, he swung helplessly between the intoxicating joys of sadism and orgasmic bursts of excruciating galvanic pain, which somehow, deprived of rationality, he couldn't help but crave. In time she wrung from him all self-respect and then cast him on the dung heap.

Unable to erase the filthy images from his besotted mind, Bull staggered out of town, wandering east from one binge to the next until he reached the banks of the Mississippi near St. Louis. There an itinerant evangelist found him in a stinking alley behind a butcher shop and brought him to the path of Christian righteousness, where he swore off cussing, lust, and booze.

Struggling to maintain his Christian commitments, Bull concluded that redemption lay in stamping out the heathen. He enlisted at Jefferson Barracks in 1870 and was sent to the Seventh, a God-given assignment seeing as how Custer's regiment wiped out Black Kettle's Cheyenne at Washita. The next few years were frustrating, what with the regiment chasing moonshiners and the Klan in the south. In the Dakota Territory the closest they'd come to killing heathens was in '73, but this year they'd find a village, a big one, and they wouldn't leave the business unfinished. Now a true soldier of the Lord, Bull had finally redeemed himself for his sins. He made it a point to never talk about Sand Creek, but in private he believed that most troopers agreed with what he knew for a fact: a live Indian was no better than a nigger ten days dead.

⋆ ⋆ ⋆

That night a steady rain turned to snow by daybreak. Before long there were three or four inches on the ground, enough to ball up on the animals' hooves so the troop couldn't move. One wouldn't think it would get to a foot deep on the first day of June, but it did and it kept on going through that night. Misery prevailed for days. The horses couldn't graze, and the wood was so wet that the piddling fires couldn't warm a mouse. The Rees saw the storm as promising disaster, a prediction most of the men laughed off. Charley wasn't that sure. The Sioux scouts told him it was the just the latest trick the Spirits were playing on the *Wasicus,* and they'd bring a heat wave next. Sure enough, on June 4 General Terry was felled by sunstroke and finished that day's march in the ambulance. Still they pushed on through 117 miles of rugged country, and on June 7, they reached the Powder River, some twenty miles above the Yellowstone.

At dusk Dan stood on the river's bank with Jim, Charley, and Sam. Two hundred feet across, it was less than three feet at its deepest.

Jim said, "Damn, that was a long day, no two ways about it."

"I heard we made thirty-two miles," Sam said.

"All of that," Charley growled.

"Well, Sam, was the march as romantic as you thought it'd be?" Dan asked, smiling.

"If there was romance in it, it was lost in all the work."

"Work?"

"Ayuh. Seems like all we did was bridge gullies and manhandle wagons out of holes. You think we need all those wagons? The Indians don't," Sam said.

"This country's their house," Charley said.

"What do you mean?"

"They live inside it not against it."

"I still don't get it."

"They accept what it's got. We got necessaries we gotta bring along—and then take what else we want out of it."

"Guess you're right," Sam said, looking puzzled. "But we're here to make the land into something worthwhile. That's our rightful mission and the Seventh Cavalry's up to it, by God."

"You sound inspired," Dan said, suddenly longing to be alone. He caught Jim's eye and motioned toward the camp.

"C'mon, Charley," Jim said. "We gotta get back. You too, Streeter."

"You coming?" Sam asked Dan.

"I am not."

Dan turned and sat on a log half-buried in the fine-grained black sand, thinking if Sam hung on to his notions about the glory in war, he'd never learn what he needed to know. But the relentless truth-seeker in his mind shouted it was about Franny. Of course it was, but Sweet Jesus, Franny was gone and Sam was here now—and much too starry-eyed. Christ Almighty, just being in the regiment swelled the lad up, fancying the glory of fighting savages who massacred righteous settlers on the picturesque Western plains, the whole of it straight off the printed page. Amazing how a boy with such a good brain could fail to see how his asinine notions could get him killed.

Chapter 10: Hiatus at Powder River

★ ★ ★

June 7, 1876–June 15, 1876

On June 8 Companies A and I escorted General Terry down to the Yellowstone, where he boarded the *Far West* and steamed some fifteen miles up to Colonel Gibbon's camp. On the return the following afternoon, it suddenly turned cold and started to rain buckets. It was nearly ten o'clock that night before they got to the bivouac. Once more Montana weather had gone from one extreme to the other, with nothing in between.

Gibbon reported finding signs that Sitting Bull had been somewhere up Rosebud Creek. Wanting better intelligence, Terry ordered Major Reno to take six companies and reconnoiter up the Powder then down the Tongue River to the Yellowstone. The rest of the expedition marched down to the Yellowstone, where two traders on the *Far West* were selling canned goods, tobacco, and whiskey at a dollar a pint. Business was brisk. Charley picked up a pint to cover the next few days and an extra to hold for later in the month. Dan bought a couple, thinking he might get thoroughly soaked before they moved on.

The men spent the next four days mending tack, stowing their sabers away, and making sure their firearms were in good repair. No trooper's tailbone touched the saddle, a welcome rest for man and beast alike. John Bringes enlisted Sam's help going over the troop's horses, looking for problems the men ignored. Each company's first sergeant began picking men to leave at the depot, men unlikely to be of use in a fight. Sergeant Heyn named Ernst, but Jim and Gus Steinbrecher asked for a chance to prove his value. That afternoon they took Ernst down by the river to work him as a "four." When the cavalry dismounts in a fight, every fourth man takes four mounts to the rear. They felt Ernst could do this.

After Ernst mounted up, Jim and Gus brought out three horses. In no time at all he hooked up their link straps and was in the saddle again. Then Jim and Gus tried it while Sam, Jake, and Charley did their best to spook the horses, banging pans, yelling, screeching, and waving blankets. They ran through it five times. Not only did Ernst control the animals, he kept them calm. There was a certainty to it.

Two hours later Jim found Ernst sketching near the riverbank.

"I'll give you two dollars if you draw me," Jim said. "Send it home to my folks so they'll know I'm still real handsome."

"Okay, Sergeant, but I tell other men *das Porträt* I cannot draw."

"Why? You could make good money at it."

"*Ja*, but what I see I draw. You are okay I think with what I draw. But the truth in the face some men don't want. If I draw them they will be angry, so I don't draw anyone."

"I guess you're right," Jim said. "Okay, to save you trouble with 'em, we'll wait till we're back at the post. Then I'll send it home before they know you did it."

"Good. Thank you, Sergeant."

"But tell me, where'd you learn to draw so good?"

"I draw since I was young. Three, four years."

"Did you have a teacher?"

"*Ja,* a good one, and I learn more in Dusseldorf," Ernst said, smiling.

"That smile of yours, I bet you had a woman teacher in Dusseldorf?"

"*Ja,* Ursula," Ernst said, blushing. "*Sie war eine gute,* uh, *eine gute Lehrerin*. A good teacher. "

★ ★ ★

The second evening Charley found a little grove of cottonwoods up the Powder where he and Dan could do their drinking undisturbed. Each man brought a cup. Dan kept track of pace and amount, and Charley sipped gently. Sitting on the trunk of a fallen tree, Charley handed his cup over. Dan poured each an ounce and a half and recorked the pint. Charley carefully spilled a few drops on the ground, acknowledging "Something Greater than Himself," a Lakota ritual he'd picked up some time ago. It made a kind of sense to him. In turn, Dan raised his cup and silently offered his usual prayer for those who fell with the Twentieth Massachusetts, then threw the whiskey down, coughing with appreciation.

"Sure it's not 'Oh Be Joyful,' yet neither is it turpentine, for which I'm surely grateful," Dan said, reaching for the bottle.

Charley nodded, sipping just a bit, gaining a certain pleasure in sliding the booze over his tongue for the taste of it. This time he drained only half, then took out his pipe.

"Where's Jim?" Dan asked.

"With The First."

"Taking care of business, is he?"

"Yeah."

"Sure he knows what he's doing?"

"As good as you were, or better."

"Can't argue with that," Dan said, finishing the cup and uncorking the bottle. "He likes it, you know. Remember Bull's sanctimonious bullshit on that scout? I'd have blown my top, but Jim, he found a way to put the son of a bitch to good use."

"Yeah, you would've blown your top."

Dan thought about Jim, who enlisted in '69 straight off the family farm in Illinois. The youngest of five boys, he saw no future in staying there and left when he was twenty. After banging around from job to job, he enlisted on his twenty-first birthday and reenlisted five years later. He was a good judge of character, and as a sergeant he dealt easily with both the willing and the unwilling, putting each of his men to good use, as he did with cantankerous Bull and gentle Ernst. Firm but fair, Jim put up with neither bullshit nor nonsense. He would give a man a second chance but not a third. And he made good company, often throwing down a few with Charley and Dan. He was exactly the man a sensible soldier would choose as his sergeant.

"Sam Streeter's a pain in the arse," Dan said, breaking the silence.

"Maybe, but—"

"No maybes about it!" Dan sputtered. "He's worse than a carbuncle." He glanced at Charley's cup—still a half ounce in it. Dan drained his and reached for the pint again. "All he wants to know is the glories of ancient history. Worse yet, he believes every word Custer wrote. Remember that Black Hills hogwash?"

"Yeah, gold nuggets so big the horses pract'ly tripped over 'em," Charley said, chuckling. Then he finished his cup.

"Another?" Dan asked.

"Just a swallow."

Dan split the last of it one and three. Swirling his around, he started to raise it but checked himself, staring into the cup, thinking back to that first day with Sam. He knew he'd try to help him when first he saw the ancient ache of loss in his eye. Too bad the lad filled his fatherless void with dreams of glory that enslaved the brain so one couldn't grasp the hard-fast rule of soldiering. Death feasts on the careless.

"He's bent on dying for Custer 'cause he's hungry for glory," Dan said quietly while tossing down a bit too much. A drop of it caught in his windpipe, and it was a minute before he could continue.

"Goddamn it, Charley, how am I going to get Sam to keep his hair?"

"You can't, not till you get the bullshit out of his head," he said.

"You got a point there, my friend," Dan said, looking in his cup. There was only a wee bit left. For no good reason his gaze lifted to the rise on the other side of the Powder. Now blood red, the sun hung over the crest, readying itself for the final plunge. A majestic sight, no doubt, but could Dan enjoy it? No. His mind raced back and clung again to Antietam. No man who wasn't there could grasp the smallest piece of it, never mind get his mind around a slaughter so insanely monstrous. And there was dear Franny, who learned from Dan the ways of life after their Dad went down that warm spring night, trying to stop a runaway team of fancy Morgans. He could have done the job but for the young swell who'd whipped them up for the sport of it, so drunk he reveled in their wild-eyed bid to escape the lash. Suddenly fatherless at twelve, Franny looked for solace within the priest's enticing words until Dan cut through the web of them, forcing him to see what was fact and what was fancy, what was sin and what was not. Blessed with a brilliant mind, Franny had caught the eye of lawyer John O'Donnell for whom he did the chores and began to read for the law. But it was all for naught because that fateful August night in '61, he swallowed whole the lies of the huckster hired by bluebloods to fill the ranks of the Twentieth Massachusetts with Irish lads because, whatever the murderous cruelties of war, it was a sure-fire moneymaker. War was no place for a boy with possibilities, so Dan believed he should have been there to stop him, but no, he was in his cups at McGinty's and woke to find that his darling brother had signed up to fight for the noble sons of Harvard. So Dan joined too, thinking he could keep him off the butcher's bill. They got their first taste of war at Ball's Bluff in '61. Afterward, Franny raged on about the Confederates picking off Union boys caught helpless in the water, vowing to get even with the sons of bitches no matter what.

At Antietam Creek in '62 three brigades marched rank after rank into the West Woods, Franny ten men to Dan's left so no one ball or load of grape could take them both from mother and sister. That cautionary step mattered not, because Franny went down when a blast of canister hit the line from the front and a storm of musketry cut into them as well. With its left flank turned, the regiment fled north, leaving a jumble of sights etched in Dan's brain: John O'Leary knocked back and down, a Springfield leaning against a tree as if placed there by a sensible man, a severed arm, ramrod still clutched in its fist, leaves fluttering down from shattered limbs. He buried his brother that night near where he fell beneath a miraculously untouched maple. He marked the spot and thought of cursing a God who took boys' precious lives, but Dan stopped himself on the slim chance of eternal life because his blasphemy could mar His plan for Franny's rest, so instead he prayed as he'd been taught by nuns and priests long before he'd left their church but not his faith, not entirely. *God rest his soul,* Dan thought, knowing the awful truth—he should have been there that besotted night in '61 to save him from the smooth-tongued huckster.

In the months ahead, Dan shoved the guilt of it aside. No, he *buried* it for fear the distraction of it would cause his own death and leave his mom and sis alone. The irony was that neither disease nor shell nor ball touched him, but by war's end his dear mom had passed and young Kathleen had married well.

Fumbling with his pipe gone cold, Dan's mind turned back to Ball's Bluff, where by dusk he'd seen too many of the dead and mangled up close. Worse yet, he heard them—the haunting cries and moans drifting through the dark.

"No more," he said aloud, shutting down the ghostly flow.

He raised the cup and drank, leaving just enough to make the last of it, and followed Charley's eyes up to Polaris. How many had found their way looking to that constant star?

Charley broke the silence. "He's got pictures in his mind, ones of flag-wavin' glory."

"What?"

"Sam. He's got pictures like them in *Harper's,*" Charley said. "You gotta change 'em. Get him to picture it like it was."

"How?" Dan asked.

"Hell, you got a way with words. Tell him what happened, Goddamn it, but make him *feel* it."

Chapter 11: Onto the Tongue

★ ★ ★

DAN AWOKE NEXT MORNING in the grip of a grinding hangover, knowing once again the cost of satisfying the Big Thirst. He was leaning on a wagon when he spied Sam sauntering toward him, a stupid smile on his face and a hundred silly-ass questions in his skull. *Sweet Jesus,* Dan prayed, *make him just nod and go past.* No such luck.

"How are you?" Sam asked.

"Been better." Dan looked away, trying to discourage further conversation.

"You hear anything about the Sioux? Where they are?"

"Christ Almighty, I don't know everything."

"Charley could have heard something from the Rees."

"Charley talks with the Sioux not the Rees," Dan shot back, disgusted. His head was about to split.

"Right. Why did General Terry send Reno out? Colonel Gibbon's men saw the Sioux up Rosebud Creek two weeks ago. I asked Sergeant Lawton about it, but he just got angry."

He stood there with his face hanging out, waiting for an answer. Like a fool Dan thought he'd go away if he gave him one.

"Maybe Terry's worried they doubled back down the Tongue," Dan said. The cloud hanging over his brain was fast burgeoning into an ominous, pounding thunderhead behind his reddening complexion.

Oblivious, Sam started blabbering how Terry didn't understand Custer and his bringing pride to the regiment, and on and on.

Dan just stared at him, unhearing, looking for a hint of sensibility within those starry eyes. He finally cut him off, his words coming at measured pace, holding his exasperation in check as best he could.

"You are a blessed fool, Sam. What you're calling pride is naught but fancy by fools not knowing the difference between shadow soup and buffalo chips. Pride in one's regiment is based on accomplishment and not on a bushel of lies. And please say nothing more to Jim Lawton. He has more regard for porcupine piss than for speculations such as yours." Giving up, Dan shuddered with disgust, his stomach ready to heave.

* * *

Leaving behind all the wagons and some 150 men, the column set off on June 15 for the Tongue River, forty miles up the Yellowstone, where they were supposed to meet Major Reno's six companies. The mules were fitted with pack saddles. Each troop assigned several men to the pack train. At the Tongue they laid out company streets on an old Indian campground where driftwood pony shelters made for plenty of firewood. An Indian burial ground was there, the dead wrapped and placed in trees or on scaffolds. Custer personally set the tone by ordering Isaiah Dorman, translator for the Sioux scouts, to throw the remains of a respected warrior into the river. Then officers began robbing the dead, and the men gleefully followed, grabbing up clothing, beaded moccasins, and ceremonial articles. Not a few showed off their ill-found prizes as if they were trophies of victorious battle.

Dan stood between Jim and Bull, watching the ludicrous scene.

"Damn them numbskulls, robbin' graves like that," Jim said.

"Them ain't no graves," Bull said. "Injuns are just too lazy to dig a proper hole."

"Fer Chrissake, Bull. It's their way! You see one of the squad with them trinkets, lemme know."

"Uh huh," Bull mumbled, starting to leave. "I gotta find Crane. He's gittin' us some firewood."

As Bull moved off, Jim said, "Damn it, don't he know nothin?"

"Bull? Blinded by hate, he is," Dan said. "Especially when it comes to people of color."

"Don't know 'bout that, but I can't trust the sumbitch no more."

* * *

Bull found Elvin with another trooper.

"This here's Jack Cobb, from M Troop, Bull," Elvin said. "We pulled this old Injun down, and we got a couple little bags offa him."

"Just keep quiet about it, both of you. Jim says it's grave robbin'."

"But they ain't graves, fer Chrissakes!"

"He don't care. An' don't be usin' the Lord's name like that."

"Huh? Oh, I forgot."

"I'll see you later," Cobb said, starting toward M Troop's street.

"I'll come over later," Elvin said, pulling a small buckskin pouch from his pocket. It contained a tiny round stone and four silvery leaves of sage. "It's the first souvenir I got out of fightin' Injuns."

"Blazes! You ain't been in no fight!" Bull said.

"I know. Wonder what it is. Maybe the Ree scouts know."

"Blazes! Why ask them heathens? They just talk gibberish. You listen to me," Bull said, images from a cold morning twelve years before flashing in his mind. "We didn't come all this way just to play make-believe games. We come to kill Injuns."

"I know that."

"No, you don't, not really." Recalling that morning at Sand Creek, Bull was suddenly excited. He paused to catch his breath. "We gotta show 'em they can't go on depredatin' innocent White settlers."

"You're right, Bull," Elvin said.

"It's true. God meant this country to be the White man's, so we're like on a crusade. They'll find out when we surprise 'em when they're asleep," he said. "Now look here, scalps are the real souvenirs, 'cept ye wanna shake the lice out. Cheyenne all got lice, ye know."

"Cheyenne? I thought we're after the Sioux."

"We are," Bull said, trying to recover. "But Sittin' Bull's always got Cheyenne with him. Anyways, ye get yerself some real scalps to show yer grandkids."

"Did you ever get one?"

"Uh huh, but that's a story fer another time."

"Okay," Elvin said, glancing toward the company street. "I just hope we find Sittin' Bull quick so's we can whip his ass good an' get back to the post."

"Don't count on it," Bull said. "If they scatter, we'll be huntin' Injuns all summer. Anyways, you keep that pouch outta sight."

★ ★ ★

Later that day Jake was honing Sam's knife, the rhythmic strokes almost mesmerizing. "You know horses," he said to Sam, "but not the steel. Next time I find the good knife for you. Then I learn you to make the edge."

Jubal Tinker came back from the picket line. Lately his horse had been showing signs of lameness.

"How's that horse today?" Jake asked, looking up without missing a stroke with the stone.

"Ah, thet slew-footed boneshaker was pervaricatin' again. It's *me* thet's lame. Lame in the head."

"Huh?"

"Ole Prince was jist makin' like a gimp. He's a smart ole horse, or mebbe I'm the stupid-most trooper. Either way, he fries my onions fer sure."

"You hear anything 'bout that Reno?" Jake asked, handing the knife to Sam. After six days, everyone wondered when the Major and the rest of the regiment would show up.

"No. But I heard some G Troop boys come onto a trooper's skull."

"They did?" Sam asked.

"Yes siree Bob," Jubal said. "This one boy says they pried it up under a ole campfire. Gin'ral Custer was there, he said."

"Maybe it was an Indian," Sam said.

"Injuns put the dead in a tree," Jake said. Looking agitated, he stood up suddenly. "Couldn't it be a trapper?"

"No, they was scraps of uniform. Calv'ry," Jubal said, poking at the dirt with a stick.

"What did The General say?" Sam asked.

"Nothin', which was strange, seein' how he usually gits feverish 'bout them kind of things. However, thet G Troop boy speculated the Injuns burned him fer fun."

Nobody said anything for thirty seconds or so. Finally, Sam broke the uncomfortable silence.

"Well, this year we're going to get rid of them, so there'll be no more of that."

Jake started to leave and said, "Gonna see that guy who's got a game tonight." Obviously he didn't want to hear more.

A bit later Charley and Dan were passing the time when Jake walked up, wanting to talk with Charley. Dan started to leave, but Jake told him to stay.

"It's about Indian stuff, and you and Charley, I trust you guys, so it ain't nothing you can't hear."

"What's botherin' you?" Charley asked.

"What Jubal said 'bout that trooper's skull. D'you think they burnt that guy?"

Charley and Dan knew about Jake's fear of being captured and tortured and how he lost sleep over it.

"I don't know for sure, Jake, but I doubt it," Charley said. "He could have gone down in some fight years ago and them that buried him built that fire to hide his grave."

"I didn't think of that," Jake said, obviously still shaky. "I don't mind fighting Indians, but this here makes me want to go straight back to Chicago."

"You like Chicago," Dan said.

"Yeah. It's good there."

"So what are you doin' out here?"

"Not my choice."

"What do you mean?"

He didn't reply at first, but then he said, "What the hell, you don't run your mouth so I tell it."

Jake started in slowly at first, but pretty soon he was spilling about his brother René and how they stayed alive as kids and made their way as they got older.

"René, he got five years more'n me. We was up by the big lake, *Supérieur.* My mother, she was Ojibwe. Good people. The old man, he was French an' some other kind of Indian. Gone trappin' a lot. Come home and he drink hard. Me an' René, we fish a lot, trap rabbits, squirrels. Sometimes good, some hard, but René an' me, we was together. I had five years when Francine my sister she was born." He dug in his pocket for the makings and set about rolling one of his *zigounes.* "We go to Chicago when I had nine years. My mother and us."

"How come?" Charley asked.

"Leave the old man. Mean son of a bitch even sober," he said, lighting his smoke. "Me an' René, we learn English quick. I hawk papers. René work the hotels. After two years, he got in under a boss. Me, *un voleur à la tire.*"

"What's that?"

"Pickpocket. I was real good, but I got caught one time. They lock me up for three months. Bad. Got out an' tried *le cambriolage,* burglarin', but no fence give a kid the price. René, then he was right hand for Tom Driscoll, the big boss. I stay with him sometimes, practice the cards, work in the clubs, do what they want. Then I start dealin' the cards in the clubs. I had maybe sixteen years. Did other things but mostly the cards five years. The last year I run a saloon for a guy when he wasn't there. Lot of trouble in that business—fights, guys cheatin', stealin'. I was fixin' trouble all the time.

"Fat Dennis O'Reilly, real stupid, he got crazy drunk an' tried to shoot me when I threw him out. I kill him quick with the knife. That's the only way—quick.

"His brother, he's one big boss, so I got bad trouble. Got another place, hid out. My woman Marguerite, she stayed with me most of the time. Took a few days while René and his boss Tom Driscoll work it out with O'Reilly. He said it ain't my fault 'cause Fat Dennis always lookin' to get killed the way he was, but he's a boss so he gotta make me pay. Everybody know I hate the army, so that's how come. I gotta join the calv'ry to show he made me crawl—in horse shit is what he say. The deal keeps everybody happy, except old Jocko."

"Jocko?" Charley asked.

"That's my name there."

"You got yourself a damn good brother," Charley said.

"For sure," Dan said. "And that Marguerite? She must be special."

"Uh huh. Most women make trouble. Not Marguerite," he said, a smile breaking out. "She's warm on a cold night."

"You gonna see her again?" Charley asked.

"Don't know. I think she marry some swell, got a good life. She got the goods to snag one. She deserve that, an' she don't need no cav'lryman."

"How come you hated the cav'lry?"

"*Jésus-christ*, Charley, calv'ry's the worst thing. Long time back them troopers come to Chicago. Push guys aroun', hurt one little kid in the head. Me an' six other guys, we catch two of them *bâtards* an' beat 'em bad, break some arms. Shoulda killed 'em. An' horses, I don't need them, and I sure don't need no horseshit. Tell you that." Jake hesitated, then pressed on. "On top of that, O'Reilly wanted me stuck out here. He laughs, says I gotta save that last bullet for me, or the Indians they gonna cut my balls off and burn me up slow. Big laugh for him, you see that?"

"Yeah, but that ain't true, not with the Sioux."

"You said that before an' I try believin' it. *Sacramère,* I try like hell!" Jake said, smiling ruefully. Then he went back to what set him off. "Goddamn, what *you* think happen to that guy, that skull they dug up?"

"Don't know. If it was Indians, maybe they took his head into camp on a lance," Charley said.

"But that uniform."

"I don't know."

"Uh huh. Them Sioux don't capture nobody?"

"They only take the women, kids, an' horses. Men they kill," Charley said, grinning.

Jake smiled despite himself and said, "Okay, you tell it straight, but how come I still worry at that?"

"'Cause you ain't fought 'em. After that, it'll look diff'rent."

⋆ ⋆ ⋆

Jake woke up just past midnight feeling all closed in, like he couldn't get enough air. There was an insistent throb behind his left eye. Gradually the tension eased off as he filled his lungs with the cool air and gazed at the infinity above, eyes and mind searching for *l'étoile polaire,* like René had taught him when he was five by Lake Huron. René said, "Follow *l'étoile polaire* to the top of the world."

He drifted off, wondering if they'd catch the Sioux. According to Tinker, twelve companies were enough men to surround a village. They'd surprise them.

Ten minutes later Jake wrenched himself out from under the blanket, damp with sweat, clutching his sheath knife, still caught in the tunnel. *Marde!* They'd gotten too close. He had cut one of the Indians as he scrambled up to consciousness. *Le bâtard's* blood was still warm on his hands. Shaking his head to clear it, he leaned back on one elbow, trying to focus. Elvin Crane was standing not six feet away, looking bewildered. *Le gnochon!*

"Dégosse, viande à chien!"

"Easy, I just went out to piss," Elvin said, grinning. "You was yelpin' in yer sleep. That there's French, ain't it?"

Jake heaved himself up and said, "Get outta here. Go on!"

Elvin backed off, saying, "Okay, but I know French when I hear it. Makes you a breed for sure." Turning, he scurried into the dark.

Sacramère! Le bâtard would take that "breed for sure" shit back to Bull, bringing more trouble. Sitting on the blanket, Jake took out the big knife and ran his thumb along the blade. The best steel, honed perfectly. It could cut a man's balls off in his sleep and he wouldn't know it till morning. He slid it back in its sheath, making sure it was loose enough to draw. He stood and shook out the blanket, thinking ahead. If they fought the Indians, Jake would have to keep an eye out for Elvin and Bull. They'd try to pick him off in the thick of it.

Chapter 12: At Tongue River

★ ★ ★

June 16, 1876–June 18, 1876

There was no word from Reno on Saturday, June 17, making everybody restless. The NCOs kept everyone busy with made work—anything to keep time moving. Determined to change the mood, that evening Dan began a funny story about the previous summer in the Black Hills. Jubal Tinker took up where he left off, spinning a yarn about his old bunkie, Bobby Thorsen, falling into the Yellowstone in '73. Within minutes everyone's mood lightened up. Jake chuckled as Tinker answered questions about the skirmish that summer. The way he told it, Jubal was an authority on it, and why not? He was there.

"The Sioux you fought?" Ernst asked.

"Uh huh, Sitting Bull's Hunkpapas, Crazy Horse an' his Oglalas," Jubal said. "They was well armed too. Henrys an' Winchester repeaters, some breechloaders, old muskets."

"So what happened?" Jake asked.

"We was part of the biggest expedition I ever seen, near two thousand of us: cav'lry, infantry, scouts, teamsters, you name it. Surveyin' 'long the Yellowstone fer the railroad thet was comin'. Thet mornin', Gin'ral Custer, he took two comp'nies on a scout to lay out the best way fer the wagons to foller. 'Bout noon we come to this grove of trees close by the river that looked to be a likely spot fer thet night's camp. We picketed the horses in the grass and settled ourselves in the shade. 'Twa'n't long before the boys on watch hollered 'Injuns.' Thar was 'bout six of 'em chargin' in to stampede the horses, but they pulled up when some twenty boys let loose a volley while the rest of us saddled up all set to go after the son of a bitches.

"At first they pulled up like they was gonna stand, but then they'd go a little farther an' stop, an' then go an' stop agin'. Gin'ral Custer, he figgered they was baitin' us into a trap, so he had Captain Moylan take command whilst he took twenty of us an' follered 'em to whar some woods was ahead, close by the river. Thet's whar the Gin'ral goes ahead with jest his orderly an' baits *them*. Next thing we know hunerds of savages come pourin' outta the trees racin' their ponies straight at us, so we dismount an' make a skirmish line whilst Gin'ral Custer hightails it back. They come on somethin' fierce, hollering the way they do. A couple quick volleys staggered 'em considerable, an' they turned tail when we let fire agin. From there it was a all-out skedaddle."

"They could have charged right through you, couldn't they?" Sam asked. "Didn't have the heart fer it, I'd guess."

"And they prob'ly seen Moylan comin'," Charley said. "Indians ain't gonna waste men's lives, no more'n us."

The bottle was coming around, so Jubal took a swallow and looked around the circle. "I meant to tell you all how it was some kind of hot. Ain't thet right, Dan?"

"Sure and it was that," Dan said. "Well over a hundred."

"It was all of thet," Jubal said, catching a second quick swallow. "Anyways, thet wa'n't the end of it, not by a long shot. With the captain thar was ninety of us agin, so we worked our way two miles back to the woods whar we begun. Got the horses situated in the timber, one holder handlin' eight of 'em now. Thet was when Custer had us set up a skirmish line an' push out from the trees 'bout two hunerd yards where the ground give us some cover. A good two, three hunerd warriors in our front. Some of 'em tried slitherin' up close in the grass, which was fairly tall, whilst some others got their ponies lathered up an' come at us from one point or t'other, but we let fire an' they didn't git close. They tried settin' the grass afire, but it only smoked. We wa'n't goin' nowhar."

"So how'd you get away?" Jake asked.

"How'd we git away?" Jubal stretched one leg out, nudging a good-sized ember back into the fire. "Ah'll tell you how. We done it with discipline and superior gin'rulship, yes siree Bob. Our backs was to the river, an' they begun bunchin' up on our left front, hollerin' their jibberish, agitatin' to git the nerve to come straight at us. Was it skeery? Cain't say, but nary a boy wet his drawers, not by a drop. We jist set there waitin', Sharps cocked an' ready.

"Then when they's gittin' set fer their most bodacious attack, ole Custer, he gits us movin'. We mount up real fast, which befuddles 'em clear into next Tuesday. Then quick-like he orders a charge an' we go straight at 'em hell fer leather. Put 'em into the goldarndest scatteration you ever seen. Ain't that right, Dan?"

"It is that."

"One other thing," Charley said. "Both sides saw the dust cloud tellin' us the rest of the column was gettin' close."

"Uh huh, but we had 'em on the run. Chased 'em I don't know how fer till they couldn't but go home."

"And that's what's meant by generalmanship," Dan said, half in jest.

"'Xactly right, Dan," Jubal said. "The Gin'ral calculated it extryceptional. An' he'll do jist as good this time."

"Won't be no fight this time," Bull said. "They'll scatter."

"Do you think they will?" Sam asked Charley.

"Nope," Charley said, gazing steadily at the eager young trooper.

"Think we'll find them?"

Charley shrugged and Jubal answered instead. "You kin bet a month's pay on it. The gin'ral, he won't rest till we pitch into 'em."

"How come you say that?" Jake asked.

"I jist know it, Jake."

"Jubal's correct," Dan said, drawing vigorously on his pipe until the bowl glowed. "Attacking is in Custer's nature. On top of that, last month Grant cost him his pride, which is more important than life itself to him. He has to whip Sitting Bull to get it back, so if need be, we'll be chasing Indians till hell freezes over."

"But what if the Sioux are too many?" Ernst asked.

"There's never too many for Custer," Dan answered. "He truly believes he can't be beat. Besides, he's got no choice this time, like I said."

"Sitting Bull first sees us, he will move his people away?"

"Nope," Jubal said. "His braves won't see nothin' but scalps an' grain-fed horses fer the takin'."

"What you think?" Jake asked Charley.

"We'll find 'em an' they'll stand."

"I'm sure glad The General's leading us," Sam said. "Like Jubal said, he's a great man."

Jubal gave him a hard look, his eyes narrowing. "I only said he done his gin'rallin' good. As a man, he's out of true."

"Whadaya mean?" Jake asked.

"What I mean is there's more'n a few that don't trust him. Fact is, he'll piss on a man an' laugh square in front of his friends."

"You mean he's a prick," Jake said.

"Uh huh, but thet ain't the whole of it. He's strange in a way. Look here. We all like somethin'. Like you, Ernst, you liked the snow when it started, which don't make a lick of sense—not in Dakota Territory it don't. An' Charley, you like jawin' with yer Injun friends; Bull likes readin' his Bible; an' Dan, you're partial to philosophizing."

"And Jubal likes the hog farm on payday," Dan said.

"I sure do. But the gin'ral, he don't like nothin', not really. An' he sure don't like nobody 'cept his own damn self an' mebbe Miz Custer. That there's out of true."

"He likes his dogs, doesn't he?" Sam asked.

"Not really. What he likes is them doin' what he wants: lap his face, chase antelope, tear straight into a grizzly. He'll git a dog to run till he's used hisself up." There was a spark in Jubal's eye. "Now here's the thing. I fear thar's times he'll push men like they're his dogs. That's out of true fer sure."

Sam said, "But in battle, usually some men are killed following orders."

"Yup, some go down. But thar's a diff'rence 'tween goin' down fer the outfit an' goin' down fer him."

"But—"

"No buts about it. The time comes, you best fight fer yer outfit—not fer thet stuff you been readin' in books, an' not niver fer no gin'ral."

Later Dan said to Charley, "I can't deny that Jubal is persuasive, stringing words together in his inimitable, ingenuous fashion, but it's difficult to comprehend how he does it. The juxtaposition of his intelligence and his prosaic style appears paradoxical, you know?"

"Yeah."

"You're not going to tell me to shut up with the big words?"

"No. Your blatherin' gives me time to think."

"Sure, and about what are you thinking?"

"How Jubal's missing Bobby," Charley said.

"Yes, I never knew two bunkies so close," Dan said.

"Yeah. D'you remember how Jubal talked about Custer when he first joined up?"

"Yes. 'Gin'ral Custer's the most splendiferous ossifer in the world.'"

"The whole *wide* world," Charley said. "But the son of a bitch changed Jubal's mind that day in the Black Hills."

"He did that," Dan said. The moment was fixed in his memory like a stereopticon from Brady's camera.

The company was camped near the stream winding through Floral Valley. The afternoon air was filled with a perfume scent, which along with the magnificence of the hills and the valley seemed to overwhelm one's sense of proportion. The men were strung out along the stream, filling canteens and hooting at the fifteen or so who'd stripped down and plunged into the icy water, soaking off three weeks of dust and grime and alkali, whooping it up while splashing one another.

Jubal kneeled at water's edge, idly fashioning a garland of flowers. Bobby Thorsen was working his way to the shore in his wet Union suit, treading gingerly on the stream's bed of stones, scared of stepping in a hole. Couldn't swim a lick, he'd said. With his blue eyes, blond locks falling over his forehead, lithesome way he moved, and innocent smile, he was the picture of youthful vulnerability. There! After a last unsteady lurch a broad grin creased his face as he stood in front of Jubal. Pantomiming an imagined royal presentation, Jubal rose up and ceremoniously set the garland atop his bunkie's head.

"There you are, yer high an' mightiness," he joked. "A crown fer yer royal noggin."

Nobody noticed the Custer brothers who'd ridden up behind the crowd of men.

"Lookee here, Tom!" The General cracked to his brother, nudging his thoroughbred up behind Tinker. "Is this a trooper in love, do you think?" He laughed in that high-pitched way of his. "Private, who's that you've fallen in love with, some willowy Swede farm gal you've outfitted in shirt and drawers?"

Jubal's head snapped around, saw it was Custer, and turned crimson from embarrassment and tightly bound rage. The General leered at him for a moment, then assumed the air of a stern father.

"A word of advice, Private: save your lusting for the bawdy house!" With that the son of a bitch tossed his golden locks, twitched his spurs, and galloped off with his brother, cackling with laughter as they rode downstream to tell the story of "love in the ranks" to his circle of sycophants.

"Wha'd he say, Jubal?" Bobby asked. "Wha'd he say?"

"You jist shut yer mouth, Thorsen," Jubal spit back before turning, still red-faced, and started toward the camp.

The rest of the men turned away. A few smiled but most shook their heads. Charley stood off to the side, glaring with unspoken wrath at the Custer brothers as they disappeared around the river's bend.

Dan lay beneath his blanket, listening to Charley's familiar snores. What was the man's secret, finding peace in the night, every night? *Damn that Sam,* he thought, sending his mind skit-scatting like a water bug. His thoughts came tumbling out: Crossing the river at Fredericksburg, Brady's photographs, Spotsylvania, and coming home to find his sweetheart Mary Harrigan had become Sister Mary Catherine, the bride of Christ Himself. Sam Streeter hornswoggled by what he'd read, darling Dad telling how they'd throw out the Brits, as if passion, guts, and a few rusty pistols could dislodge those bloody bastards. Pride in the Twentieth Massachusetts, led by the Harvard boys, their fortunes made from Irish sweat.

And then she was there again, the woman at Washita. He'd been ordered to check for people hiding in the lodges. As he left the third one a young woman burst from the brush, a mounted trooper close behind. Desperate to escape, she ran, clutching her infant child, but the horse bore down, all fifteen hands and thousand pounds of him, snorting steam in the freezing cold, his eyes bulging as he strained against the pain of his rider's spurs digging into his hide, forcing him to ride her down. She glanced back and threw up an arm as the mount reared and leaped ahead, frantic the way a horse gets when forced upon a living human. His off shoulder smashed her into a tree, the baby tumbling under the animal's hooves as he danced to the side but couldn't avoid the child altogether. "Christ!" he'd called out as one hind shoe struck the tiny skull. Dragging a leg, the woman scuttled over and picked up her darling babe one last time, anxiously searching for signs of life, and then pulled the tiny robe up over the broken skull, as if to deny death's grip by hiding the wound. Not through, the trooper yanked his mount around. It was then that Dan saw him plain as day. The devil's own he was, squinty eyes set tight together, flashing madly as he raised his Colt and blew two holes in her chest. "Rot in hell, you filthy whore!" he cursed and raced off toward the river. Dan ran over and kneeled beside her, but she was quickly gone, stroking her baby's face until the last. He shut tight her eyelids, then arose, carbine at the ready. His knee was stained with red that changed to brown in time but never left the blue wool kersey nor his shaken soul.

And then a less troubling memory: running into one-armed Tommy Byrne in a St. Louis saloon, now a lawyer, saying God was a cruel son of a bitch and war a game He played for His own amusement. Sweet Jesus, Dan hadn't thought about Tommy in years.

Dan dreamed not of creeks and rills and emerald hills, but of miles and miles of buffalo grass burned to gray beneath the summer's sun.

Chapter 13: Jake Draws Blood

JUNE 19, 1876

Monday, June 19, crawled by slowly as everyone waited in vain for Reno to appear. That evening Jake helped break the tension, producing two pints of the Creature that he'd bought at the Powder, plus a third he'd taken off a G Troop man desperate to stay in the previous night's game. The whiskey not only lifted the men's spirits, it was just raw enough to give them something to complain about. Bull started in about rubbing out heathens, but nobody was interested, not this night. By the time the second pint was halfway around, Jubal was telling stories, each one wilder than the one before. Even Bull was chuckling.

Down on one knee, Jake was rolling another of his *zigounes.* When he looked up there was Elvin Crane staring at him across the fire; Elvin looked away right quick. Squatting, he was swaying just a bit—eight to five he'd make trouble.

Jubal was talking about his favorite whorehouse in Bismarck: "You boys know the one, but iffen you don't, you oughtter. Costs more'n yer ord'nary hog farm, but I guarantee you'll come away grinnin' like a tomcat at sunup. Well, thar was this ev'nin' me an' Bobby stopped in thar. Bein' as 'twas payday, they was but three girls to pick from, an' Bobby, he wa'n't shy in no whorehouse. 'Fore I knew it, he picked the best of the three an' was gone, leavin' me with a scarce-hipped ole witch an' one extry tiny one. Seein' as how she hadn't seen forty, I give her the nod an' headed fer the stairs."

With that Jubal pulled out his pipe, fumbled with it, taking his time filling and lighting it. Dan had to smile. Jubal would build up to a story's crucial point, then pull out that damn pipe and make you wait.

Jake caught Elvin staring again. This time the dolt held his gaze a few seconds before breaking off. The odds went up to twelve against five.

Jubal was still at it: "Down the hall you could hear somebody plowin' up a deep furrow, 'cept it wa'n't Bobby, him bein' a real slow goer. Always got his money's worth, you see. Now I was extry randy, sure to impress any whore willin' to work at it—me bein' such a young hot blood—an' this itty bitty whore, she wa'n't more'n four foot three, I swar, all ready to git 'er goin'. She's leg-spread sittin' on the bed, while I'm strugglin' with my drawers 'round my feet, desp'rate not to fall over 'cause I'm half-drunk, when the door flies open an' this crazy-eyed fat sergeant comes caterwaulin' in like some fat ole Hampshire boar. Sixth Infantry, he was." Jubal paused to take the pint coming around. "Lemme git a swaller whilst it's right here."

Jubal never let himself get truly drunk. He threw down just a half swallow before passing the bottle to Dan, and then he took his time wiping his mouth with that purple bandana of his. It looked like he was about to start in again but no, first he hocked up a lunger and spit it into the fire.

"Like I was sayin', this fat sergeant, he come caterwaulin'—"

"Hey, Picard!" It was Elvin. "How come you don't smoke a pipe like the rest us?" He was sitting on the ground now, one leg bent, the other straight out.

Jake gave him a cold stare through the smoke, then shrugged, barely moving his shoulders.

"That mean you don't know or somethin'?"

Jake barely nodded and turned slightly to the right as if to leave, but his eyes never left Elvin as he slipped his thumb under the rawhide loop that held the knife in its sheath, sliding it free.

"I'll tell you how come," Elvin went on, sneering. "Can't handle a man's smoke, so you took up makin' them twirly cigarettes. Prob'ly some whore of yers in Chicago learned you how."

His eyes still locked on him, Jake took a long drag on the cigarette, then pinched off the glowing end of it and slipped it into his pocket.

"Shut up," he said.

"Like I was sayin'," Jubal said, trying to divert Elvin. "This here fat sergeant—"

"I ain't done with Picard!" Elvin said, turning back to Jake. "The way you roll 'em up just so, I'm surprised yer army name ain't Nancy Boy 'stead of Jake. Hear that, boys? This here's Frenchy Picard, with the twiddly-diddly Nancy-boy fingers."

"Shut your mouth," Jake uttered, his hand moving to the knife.

"Who's gonna make me, Nancy Boy? Takes a bigger man—"

Jake's hand was a blur as the knife whistled across the fire and pierced Elvin's boot. He didn't see it until it was stuck there, quivering. Worse yet, its point was a good inch into his scrawny calf. The pain of it hit seconds later.

"Look at me, maggot," Jake said. "I tell you stop that talk but you didn't." He walked around the fire to retrieve the blade, glaring his disdain as he bent down, his face not a foot from Elvin's. "*Look* at me, maggot! You drunk?" Trembling now, Elvin barely managed to nod. "Talk some more, you get *le couteau* in the belly!"

Jake yanked the knife out and wiped its blade on Elvin's blouse before starting back around the fire. Elvin made as if to scurry away, but at the sound Jake wheeled around.

"Son of a bitch, don't you move!" he said, emphasizing each word. "I keep my eye on you while Jubal talk."

Elvin sat frozen, afraid to move. It wasn't until Tinker was back into the story that he slowly pulled off his boot, looking scared—probably thought he'd find a quart of blood in there.

Just then Jim came up into the firelight. Jubal glanced up as if to defer to him, but Jim told him to finish the story.

"So like I was sayin'," Jubal began, "this here fat sergeant come caterwaulin' through the door behind me, knockin' me onto my knees, my chin landin' on the edge of the bed. It dazed me fer a second, but I recovered an' Holy Geehosaphat! Thar I was, starin' straight into thet gal's quim not four inches from my nose. An' lemme tell you, such a sight will git you gulpin' whether it's yer first or yer hunerdth cross-eyed peek at the mother lode. Fact is, it's a sight you don't niver fergit, or git over, lemme tell you."

Jubal didn't get the laughter his stories usually produced, what with the tension still hanging there.

Jim said, "First off, we're movin' out tomorrow an' hooking up with Reno eleven miles upriver. And second, Picard an' Crane, you two stop this fuedin' or I'll trade one of you out. I'd hafta take another man's piss ant, but gettin' rid of you would be worth the trouble. You got that?"

"Any word on the Sioux?" Sam asked.

"Uh huh. A bunch of 'em went up Rosebud Creek, heading for the Little Bighorn. That's gotta be where Sitting Bull's at. Got plenty of grass for their ponies there."

* * *

It was after midnight when Jake woke up. He hadn't dreamed of the no-way-out tunnel, maybe because he'd cut Elvin. Drawing blood would set things right in a man's head. He had been dreaming of Marguerite. Dan said she "must be special." Hell, she was more than special. And now he had a hard-on. Gently teasing himself, he remembered her soul-soothing warmth that last time he was with her. How he had rested deep within her, motionless, totally aware of the good flowing between them. She surrounded him, he was inside her, and back the other way, savoring all as long as they could until the rising primal urgency set them thrusting and plunging deeper and harder until they burst into *la petite mort* on the mirror side of consciousness where they lay, drained of fluid and sweat and strength, until he saw that shy smile on her face as she watched him return to now. He had slept in peace until their time was gone, then awoke and there she was, the shadows on the quilt rounding over her willowy form, her hair a tangle from the wildness.

"Time, Marguerite," he murmured, gazing soft-eyed at the woman within the heap of covers. There was no response. His pinched face hardened.

"Marguerite! *Appareille!* What you think? Time you go!"

"To hell with you!" the girl spit back, her head rising above the covers. "I ain't one of your Goddamn whores, toss me out like that."

"Don't got no whores," he said icily. "You know that."

"Yes, I know, Jocko," she said. "But what's the hurry?"

"Today it's over," he answered distractedly, his mind scanning the various possibilities while his eyes took her in. Thin-faced and barely five feet tall, strong and supple, her perfectly proportioned form held the promise of a woman's fullness. Reflections of eighteen years bereft of comfort and trust showed only in her eyes. Even there, it took a practiced eye to discern the shadows of hard times.

"How you know that?" she asked, shrugging the rust-brown shift over her shoulders, sitting down and reaching for her boots.

"René said by today he'll have it worked out or not. I don't want you here." If it was bad, there could be blood. Worse than that, some of O'Reilly's guys might grab her.

"So how come you sent for me before? Huh?" she said, continuing with her boots.

"I got hungry." He smiled at her.

"And that cheese I brought, that was good for you?" she smiled back. No one played *la coquette* better.

"Oui, et le pain. Et le vin, aussi. But now you go, *ma petite bougrine."*

"Okay," she mumbled, then looked up. "It was good, Jocko?"

"Maybe," he teased.

"The best you ever had!" she flared. "Go on, tell me you had better!"

"Okay, I've had better," he laughed. "*Cré!* How come I don't lie no good to you?" He laughed again.

"'Cause it's good for you, making love with me, right? Go ahead, Jocko. The truth for once."

"Okay, just this one time." He paused, saddened by his need to hide both want and fear beneath studied indifference. "Yes, it is good with you, Reet. It is the best," he added in uncharacteristic openness.

"Thank you," she whispered, head down.

"Now you go," he told her, trying to resume the hardness he'd let slip aside.

"I will." She was pulling on her thick sweater but had started it front to back. Struggling, hidden within the twisted garment, raw passion spilled into words muffled by the folds of yarn. "Damn it, Jocko, I am happy you have peace with me. The only peace you get, yes?"

"No. Sometimes with the cards too."

"Stop the jokes. So now, no more peace? That isn't right, Jocko."

"*Comme on fait son lit se couche,*" he mumbled.

"You and your damn French!" she exploded. "Why you always say that stupid talk?"

"How come you don't?" he shouted back. "You're French!"

"'Cause I ain't no whore for no squaw man, that's why. 'Cause one day I catch me an educated guy with a fancy house and ev'rything else. That okay? Then no man kicks my ribs 'cause they think I come from the North. I'm from Chicago, Illinois! But you, you like all that French stuff. How come?"

"Don't know. Life too short for that dream 'bout 'some day,'" he said, tiring. "It don't never change."

The argument had lost its steam. He smiled playfully at her. "French is the language of love, *ma petite minoune.*"

"The sweetest pussy you'll ever have, *mon ami.*" She grinned, almost giggling. "I purr an' your heart, it jumps, huh?"

"Oui! C'est la meilleure minoune!" He laughed, then turned serious. "You one good woman." Good, tough, and honest—and needing the same kind of warm as he did.

"Yes. And I'm beautiful too," she teased.

"Beautiful for sure, *ma petite mère.* But now you go."

"I'm goin'." She strained to keep the tears back. The words burst through. "There got to be a way out of this, Jocko. Maybe René—"

He stopped her flatly, his voice icy, and said, "This here's my mess, not René's. Hey! Don't forget this," he said, softening. He held out her other sweater.

Balling it up, she started for the door then turned, her eyes glistening.

"Jocko? *C'est extra, étonnant!* You be careful." She whirled, reaching for the door.

"Uh huh," he answered. "And Reet? I don't forget you. And uh—"

"And what?" she demanded without turning around.

"You, uh, you stay warm, okay?"

Chapter 14: Up Rosebud Creek

★ ★ ★

June 20, 1876–June 24, 1876

The next morning was Tuesday, June 20. The column hooked up with Major Reno and continued up the Yellowstone to within two miles of Rosebud Creek. Colonel Gibbon's column of 450 men had come downriver from Fort Ellis and were camped across the river. Custer went aboard the *Far West* to confer with Gibbon and General Terry. They believed that Sitting Bull was on the Little Bighorn with about eight hundred warriors. Terry planned to strike them from two directions: Gibbon's column would march up the Bighorn and come up the Little Bighorn on June 26; Seventh Cavalry would set out on June 22, march seventy-odd miles up Rosebud Creek, and then head west over the hills and attack from above the village at sunrise on June 26.

Thursday, June 22, 1876

After five hard weeks of marching, the cavalrymen certainly were ready—weathered, lean, well trained, and eager to get on with the job. However, the regiment was markedly below its usual strength with just 566 men and thirty-one officers. With fifty scouts and civilians, the total came to 647. Each trooper carried one hundred rounds for his carbine, twenty-four for his Colt, and twelve pounds of oats for his horse. The pack train carried fifteen days of hard bread and coffee and twelve days of bacon, plus fifty extra rounds for each carbine. Knowing that in three and a half days they would be in position to attack, men began to think ahead. One could see it in the way they sat straighter in the saddle as they fell into line at noon, almost as if they were drilling on the parade ground. Conversations were terse—no laughter, no well-worn jokes. Passing in review before General Terry, the enlisted scouts sang their death songs and the buglers blew a cobbled up version of "Garryowen."

The sky was overcast, a misty, miserable day for sure. Swinging into line, a column of fours, a north wind blew up Dan's back, chilling him to the bone. They were riding two miles upriver to Rosebud Creek, and then would follow it south. Before long the sun broke through the gray overcast and the afternoon turned hot. Troopers began to shuck their blouses, turning the column from blue to gray. As if on cue, a million deer flies descended to torment both man and animal. Bitten to distraction, Sam talked about the summer of '61 when swarms of deer flies attacked him when he brought in the cows. It was just after his father had enlisted.

Dan paid no attention to Sam. His mind always pulled back into itself before a fight, automatically taking a mental inventory of his accouterments, the condition of his horse, the weather, the terrain, and those kinds of things. Then memories of the past would pop up: good times and bad; folks he missed and those he'd never see again, like Jerry O'Brien, who went down at Gettysburg, and stomach-churning faces like that son-of-a-bitch Father Duffy, whose lecherous hypocrisy still boiled his blood.

Despite the heat and the flies, it was a short and easy day's march. They camped at mile ten. Under the blanket that night he looked ahead. Three more days on the march and then they would attack at dawn on June 26.

Friday, June 23, 1876

It was still pitch black when Dan woke up, courtesy of a mule braying. No woman in labor ever sounded so distressed. After a "hardy" breakfast of coffee and a single cracker, the column was on the move at five, fording the creek five times in the first three miles. Finally they picked up the Indians' trail on the east bank and stuck with it. At mile nineteen they came across an old Indian campground, and then pressed on to mile twenty-five, where they rested at another campground. When the pack train caught up, they crossed to the creek's west side and continued to mile thirty-four and an even larger campsite. They had known of the campsites from Reno's reconnaissance, but Dan hadn't guessed they'd be so large. This one had earth-worn circles for at least four hundred lodges. There were bits and pieces of this and that left behind, and innumerable grooves from hundreds of travois poles.

Moving out, word came down the column that smoke signals had been spotted a few miles ahead. That caused a bit of excitement, but it turned out to be a mistake, so they went back to cussing the heat and swatting the infernal flies. They pushed on until four thirty before making camp, having travelled thirty-three miles since breakfast.

After stables they loafed around resting their weary butts. Jake asked how far they still had to go. The way he said it, you could sense his worry creeping up on him again.

"About forty miles," Charley said.

"So we camp two more nights before the fight, huh?"

"Yes," Dan responded. "We pitch into them the next morning."

"Just like at Washita," Sam said, always eager to share known history with the rest of the men. "Only not freezing cold."

"I could've used a piece of thet winter today," Jubal threw in. "Hot as a cricket in the oven, it was. 'Bout to feel sorry fer myself 'fore I remembered them boys on the pack train. 'Magine cussin' up them mules in this heat."

They'd left the pack train behind hours before, but it struggled into camp close to sundown. Jubal was right: the troopers with the mules were played out and pissed off.

Saturday, June 24, 1876

Saturday was extra long; a day to be endured, Jubal said later. A Troop was jammed up against the company ahead, so they started the day moving in fits and starts. Then three miles out, the scouts came trotting back, excited from an old village site ahead. When the column got to it, there was reason to be worked up. It was another big camp with nearly four hundred lodges and a White man's scalp hanging on a sun dance pole. George Herendeen, a civilian guide from Gibbon's column, surmised it was that of Private Stoker from Second Cavalry, killed by Sioux raiders a month before on the Yellowstone. The sight of it evoked oaths of vengeance from some, including Bull and Elvin.

Charley went over to hear what the scouts thought about it.

"Humaza's cousin Sina Luta says the Sioux had a sun dance here," he said when he came back. "Made sure we paid attention to it too."

"What do you mean?" Jim asked.

"Left a lot of signs for us," Charley said. "Stuff like painted stones, pictures in the dirt."

"Tellin' us what?"

"Tellin' us they know we're comin'. Say there'll be a big fight."

"I s'pose them signs say they'll take our scalps too," Bull offered sarcastically.

"That's right."

As they went farther, the signs of Indians traveling became more and more recent. At intervals tracks led off to the side, and the main trail on the valley's dusty floor broadened as they went along. The column maintained a relatively slow pace, covering only sixteen miles before halting at one o'clock, while scouts rode ahead to determine the meaning of the diverging tracks. Were the Sioux gathering or scattering? The scouts believed the former; they were certain that plenty of Indians had been coming out from the agencies recently.

Custer was in no hurry. Two hours more and they'd camp by

the creek. The next morning, they'd turn west and climb over the divide between Rosebud Creek and the Little Bighorn. They'd camp in a place where they couldn't be spotted and rest up until midnight. That would give the scouts plenty of time to reconnoiter, and Custer would have all the information he'd need. They'd start down the valley about one in the morning on June 26 and attack at dawn.

Mounting up again at five o'clock, Dan rode beside Sam. Charley and Jake were ahead of them, Jubal and Ernst behind. The column kept to a hard and steady pace. The riders looked like an enormous band of Missouri outlaws, their faces covered with bandanas to keep out the dust from the dried-up creek. It was hotter than the devil's kitchen, the heat coming at them from the burning sun and reflecting off the ground. In some stretches buffalo gnats waited by the millions to swarm all over anything exposed: eyes, ears, noses, and especially a horse's bunghole and filly-whacker. But no matter what, the first sergeant wasn't about to let a man use up his horse in spurts and stops. Dan was grateful that old Teddy kept the pace, because he did not fancy joining those already afoot, leading their played-out mounts.

Sam was a bother, worrying relentlessly about the long delay at the last halt. Dan finally told him Custer wanted to get a better read on Sitting Bull's strength. That didn't satisfy him in the least. After fielding several more of his "what ifs," Dan told Sam in no uncertain terms to quit pestering him. He couldn't get too irritated, however. He'd yet to meet the tenderfoot who wasn't fidgety before his first fight.

The march paralleled the ridge line of the Little Wolf Mountains off to the right for another twelve miles before it dipped, then rose in the distance to bend across the path. At about seven thirty, the column descended into another narrowing for a quarter mile, but as they came up from the draw, a fresh breeze cleared the dust and ahead was a sight perhaps more fantastic than believable.

"Mein Gott!" Ernst gasped, obviously awestruck, slowly turning his head to take in the whole panorama. On the right sat

a nearly perpendicular cliff beyond which the sun rested above the brownish-gray hills. Up ahead and to the left the forward companies were setting up camp close to a shallow creek. In between cliff and stream an unending spread of wild rose bushes held one's eye, a boundless profusion of color dotted just frequently enough with clumps of bushes to accent the carpet of pink and red. Above, streaks and smears of reds and orange and purple colored the cloud-streamed Montana sky, each shade deepening near the southwestern horizon, a vision at once peaceful yet exciting.

They camped at seven forty-five. after twenty-eight miles for the day. The sun disappeared behind the hills, and little fires flickered up and down the company street. A call came down to put them out as darkness enveloped the camp. Dan ended up sitting next to Jim in pitch blackness, barely able to make out his own hand. A man nearby coughed. Farther away, the officers began singing quietly. Before long they broke it up when The General called for an officers' meeting.

About ten o'clock First Sergeant Heyn walked up and said they'd be moving out at eleven. They didn't actually start moving until well after midnight. Heading west, they wound their way through some swampy ground and then into ravines and up a dry creek bed into the hills. Dan and Charley felt their way along in the blackness, guiding their horses as best they could by the sounds of others. The air was thick with dust. There hadn't been enough evening dew to keep it down. Alkali burned men's windpipes. Officers hooted and hollered down the trail with apparent disregard for stealth, trying to keep track of their companies. Some men wandered astray. Every sound was magnified in the darkness, the clattering of shod hoofs on the stony trail, the snorting of horses fighting the dust in their noses, the jangle of accouterments. Men whispered and hissed at each other. Not a few animals walked headlong into trees or the hind end of the horse ahead, while groggy riders meandered off until prompted to return by the dust-free air and a tinge of anxiety stemming from sensing they were absolutely alone. And there was always the bellyaching of men half-asleep, moving ever closer to an enemy waiting. It was the blind leading the blind for almost three long hours of frustration and uncertainty but unwavering resolve, moving inexorably toward an enemy of equal determination.

— Chapter 15: Moving Down Ash Creek —

★ ★ ★

June 25, 1876

The column halted somewhat more than halfway to the divide. The sky was a shade lighter but few men noticed. Some of them immediately slipped to the ground and dozed, reins in hand. The sun came up a little after four o'clock. Small fires for coffee lined the path. The little brook beside the trail was heavily alkaline, so they had to use water from their canteens.

"What's the word from the captain?" Dan asked when Jim returned from a sergeants' meeting with Heyn and Moylan.

"Scouts spied out the village," he said. "We was gonna hole up today, but they think we could of been spotted. Ain't surprising with this morning's fires."

"And the noise," Dan said. "Enough to wake the dead."

There had been a stir near headquarters. Custer, several Ree scouts, and the interpreter Gerard had mounted up. Jim said they were off to join Varnum up at the Crow's Nest, a lookout on the crest of the divide.

"Captain says to git ready to move out," he added. "The General's still worried they'll scatter."

"Nah, they're waiting for us," Charley said.

"Probably," Jim said. "But Custer thinks different."

"And he's wrong," Charley insisted.

"But he wants this fight," Dan said. "If there's any chance they'll run, we'll attack today."

"It'll be midafternoon before we get there," Charley said. "They'll be waitin' for us."

"No two ways about it," Jim said.

★ ★ ★

Orders came down. Men stirred, tightened cinches, slung their carbines, and leaned against horses, waiting to mount up. At eight forty-five they were on the march again. Even as high as they were, there still was no breeze. It was hot and getting hotter. There was not much sound except the ever-present squeak of leather on leather, the clatter of equipment, and the familiar sounds of hacking and hocking up lungers as they struggled against the caustic dust filling the air. A distant, gauzy kind of haze bleached out the rich blue sky and left the sun more a disk than a ball in the east where it hung, bent on broiling every living thing before the day was through.

Squinting, Sam unhooked the brim of his hat, choosing to put up with its floppiness to cut down the punishing glare. Charley was watching four buzzards circling to the west. He pointed to an eagle over the column ahead, a yellow-bellied marmot squirming in its talons. The magnificent raptor rode an invisible wave toward the rise where Custer went to spy out the village through the haze. Lodge pole pines rose on either side of the trail, providing patches of shade too brief to cut the heat.

A halt was called shortly after ten o'clock. Still in the saddle, Charley moved slowly toward the pines on the right and into a slight draw. The stillness was cold, deafening. A few minutes later he returned.

"A young Cheyenne in the trees over there," he said. "We stared at each other for a bit, then he moved off."

"He wearin' paint?" Jim asked.

"No."

"Okay, I'll tell The First."

Four men from E Troop were leading their horses past when one of them spotted Dan and walked over. It was Paddy O'Malley, an old comrade from the Twentieth Massachusetts. None too quick from the start, a grazed skull at Cold Harbor left him a bit off center with a twitch in the left eye.

"And a splendid good marnin' to you, Daniel."

"Sure, and a glorious morning it be, Paddy."

"Now, July the fifteenth, it be comin' up soon," O'Malley said, his eye twitching noticeably.

"Three weeks from yesterday," Dan replied. Each year the two of them celebrated the anniversary of the old regiment's mustering out. "Eleven years it is."

"Eleven. Now some there is as don't know how it was back then." Nervous, Paddy glanced back down the slope. "You and me, Daniel, we might of gone home in '64, but we signed over."

"Sure and stayed until the end, we did."

"You and me and ole Dennis, we outsmarted those Rebs that time, we did," Paddy went on. He twisted around, nervously scanning the trees.

"At Reams Station, you mean," Dan said. It was almost a ritual, repeated year after year. Although he played his part, Dan was concerned. It wasn't like Paddy to show nerves before a fight.

"Yes," O'Malley said, glancing at the trees again. "Now last night, Daniel, did you hear the faeries or no?"

"Not that I recall," Dan replied. That was it—the faeries. "And why is it you're askin', Paddy?"

"By my faith, Daniel, at that first halt we made I was played out. Dead asleep I was when the old terrors come an' stood me straight up. 'Twas then I heard the terrible keenin'. The ole banshee she was for sure. Up higher in the pines she was, Daniel."

"Sure and I heard it myself," Dan said, lying. "But that wa'n't the banshee, Paddy. 'Twas a painter screeching," It always angered him, the power of superstition to warp a man's brain, and he lied again, trying to calm his old compatriot. "Remember the night afore Spotsylvania? Thought I heard the old hag keenin' for sure, but the sentry said 'twas two cats going at it. Next day we charged into the jaws of hell, and not a ball come close to me precious self."

"Spotsylvania? Ah, the terrible loss we suffered there, but we pushed them out, we did. Won the day, Daniel."

"That we did, Paddy. And last night 'twas a painter for sure. Now go in peace, you old spalpeen. And you and me, we'll drink our share on the fifteenth." He chuckled, clapping his old friend on the shoulder.

Paddy smiled as best he could, but a glimmer of fear shone through his pale blue eyes.

⋆ ⋆ ⋆

It was just after eleven that morning when word came down that the column had been spotted. Because of this, it would follow the mostly dry Ash Creek down to the Little Bighorn and attack the village straight away. Nobody said much, but an unspoken urgency ran through the ranks as troopers prepared to move out. It showed in the horses, mince-stepping nervously while buckles and cinches were checked and rechecked. The men went over their accouterments one final time and made sure the Colts were loaded and cartridge belts full before the first sergeants came down each company's line.

At eleven forty-five they started out and got about a mile over the crest when General Custer called a halt and divided the outfit into battalions. Lieutenant Hare would take Company B and guard the pack train. Captain Benteen would lead D, H, and K Troops out to the left to make sure the hostiles weren't moving upstream toward the Bighorn Mountains. The General would lead C, E, F, I, and L Troops down the right side of Ash Creek. Major Reno would take A, G, and M Troops along the left bank. Custer's and Reno's battalions would alternate between the trot and the walk and attack the village from two sides.

Moving out, the ground sloped gradually down to what looked like flatland. Ash Creek meandered northwest for six miles before heading west into a darker smudge, the tree-lined Little Bighorn. A half mile to the left the blood bays of Benteen's H Troop were obliquing toward imposing bluffs, with D Troop's bays and the sorrels of K Troop in column behind. Sending Benteen out to block any Sioux moving south made it clear that The General wanted *all* of Sitting Bull's people.

Two hours later Custer's five companies on the other side of the creek were moving a shade faster than Reno's. Jake was looking over at C Troop, trying to spot his poker-playing friend Richard LaFleur. They loved to talk just enough French in a card game to piss off the others, giving themselves the edge they wanted.

The troop rode four abreast on a trail so wide that it looked like every Indian pony west of the Mississippi had come that way. There was so much dust on the horses one could hardly tell Company A's blacks from G Troop's sorrels. It was in Dan's eyes, ears, nose, and mouth, as well as down his windpipe. Another hour and Teddy's lungs would be full of the stuff.

"How yer mounts holdin' out?" Jim asked Sam and Jake, riding up alongside them.

"Blaster could use some water," Sam said, "but he's okay."

"Same for me an' Scar," Jake said.

"Oughtta be some up a ways," Jim said, staring hard at the two rookies' eyes. He rode on.

"Judas Priest!" Sam said. "It's too hot for fightin'!"

"Huh?"

"It's too damn hot to fight."

"Why you say that?" Jake asked.

"It just is, Goddamn it!" Sam said.

Sam looked pissed off, staring straight ahead, and then reddened, embarrassed.

"Sorry, Jake. It just struck me that way. Kind of stupid, I guess."

"Hell, no," Jake said, a smile on his face. "I tell Custer that last night. Killin' Injuns, that's a mornin' job. Cooler."

C Troop was riding parallel to the men again, across the creek.

There was LaFleur. Sensing he'd been spotted, he glanced over and threw up his hand in that kind of half salute men offer when there's nothing to say. Jake responded in kind.

Sam said, "There's going to be a fight; I can feel it—a big one."

"Maybe," Jake said. "But them Injuns don't kill us today."

"Why not?"

"Too Goddam hot for that!" Jake said, grinning again. "Serious though, Ernst goes down, you write that letter to his people."

"Yes."

"Same for me," he said, slipping it in.

"Okay," Sam agreed.

"In my footlocker, that tin box. Inside you get the address for René. You an' Ernst split the cash an' send the rest of that stuff to René. It's Renard not Picard."

"Okay."

"What you want, huh?" Jake asked.

"Nothing, I guess." Sam took a quick swallow from his canteen, then offered it to his bunkie. Jake shook his head, digging into the pocket of his blouse to inch out the pinched-off butt he'd been saving. Pulling the first drag deep into his lungs, he glanced at Dan and smiled.

"Things get tight; the smoke is good," he said.

* * *

The minutes ticked off, each man lost in his thoughts. Dan watched a meadowlark as it fluttered past, then banked around, gliding stiff-winged. Scattered clumps of spindly ash appeared out of the dust cloud alongside the dried-up creek. They were the size of young trees but probably full grown. Out here no tree came close to the size of those back east—not in this desert. Perched on a branch fifteen feet overhead, the meadowlark eyed each dust-covered horse and rider going by. In varying states of undress, the men looked like tramps, their faces set in ambivalent determination, marching toward an unknown prize promised by a man they neither disbelieved nor trusted entirely. The bird was joyfully free in contrast to the bridled horses and sullen-faced men. He broke into song, the notes tumbling down flute-like in a buoyant celebration of life, quite unlike the plaintive notes of the meadowlark stuck in memory from the day after Gettysburg. Here in the desert a meadowlark sang joyfully, while in the lush green of Pennsylvania his cousin's tune was but a two-note phrase, more lament than song.

Bull Judd stared at Ernst Albrecht from behind, noting how he sat transfixed by the meadowlark. Hundreds of lodges were just waiting to get pounced on and the Kraut was watching a stupid bird. Bull pictured how they'd slash into the heathens when a sharp-edged sliver of fear surprised him, piercing the inside of his stomach before slipping away. Albrecht's stupidity infuriated him. Why did The First drag him along anyway? The only thing he could do was hold the horses, and that wasn't for sure, not with bullets flying around his head. An even stronger shaft of fear silently raced up the inside of Bull's spine and into his throat, forcing a swallow. This time he urgently shoved it aside before insisting again that they should have left Albrecht behind with the crippled, the untrained, the too scared, and the just plain unwilling.

Bull was startled out of his reverie when his horse moved left to get around Ernst's. Jammed up because the lead troop was crossing the creek again, Company A had slowed to a stop.

— Chapter 16: To the Little Bighorn River —

★ ★ ★

June 25, 1876

Scar danced to the left, ears erect, testing Jake's resolve to stay in line. Horses were splashing up ahead, and thirst being a want far more compelling than hunger, Scar was intent on getting there without delay. Jake sawed him back into line just as the troop picked up the pace again.

"They want water, you think, maybe?" he asked, nodding at the animals.

"Yes. Keep a tight rein on," Sam said, all business.

"Okay, but Scar, he's not no trouble."

Minutes later Scar got a gulp or two as they crossed to Company C's side. It was almost two o'clock. According to Charley, it wasn't the best time of day for pitching into Indians.

Ernst half-listened to Jubal reciting a well-rehearsed litany of General Custer's many transgressions, from his treatment of deserters in '67 to putting off the last payday, all interspersed with examples of his prowess as a battlefield commander. He'd heard it several times before, but the C Troop rookie on his right gained a lesson in regimental history from listening. A red-winged blackbird suddenly flew up, its flash of red and yellow clear against the coal black sheen. Ernst leaned forward to pat the underside of Thor's neck. After the morning's inaction and uncertainty, the day had changed to one of direction and purpose. Going into battle was an impossible idea. Could it be happening? Up ahead Sergeant Steinbrecher had donned *das Käppi* he saved for drill and parades. "A soldier is obliged to dress the part," *der Feldwebel* had said, telling Ernst to wear *das Käppi* to show he was a civilized cavalryman, but Ernst misplaced the cap in the last-minute rush of leaving. *Der Feldwebel* would give him a tongue-lashing if he knew. The abbreviated song of the bird jerked him out of his worry and made him smile.

⋆ ⋆ ⋆

Dan felt the tension spreading along the column. It must have gotten to him, because he found himself whistling "Garryowen" under his breath. He put a halt to it, but it came back a minute or two later—damn tune wouldn't leave him be. Charley pointed to a little dust cloud atop some bluffs to the right, rising over the shallow valley. It had to be the scouts with Varnum, gaining a look down the Little Bighorn from up there. Dan unholstered his Colt and spun the cylinder, making sure it worked smoothly, and then replaced it, securing it with the strap. Charley ranged out to the right of C Troop. Knowing him, Dan figured he couldn't abide the wait and had to find out what was going on in front. He worked his way back as they approached an abandoned campground with a single tepee.

"It's an honored warrior's death lodge," Charley said. "Scouts on the bluff seen the village. Damn big, they say."

"No surprise, that. Where's Benteen?"

"Don't know, but he better catch up soon—the train too. We'll want the extra ammo on them mules."

Major Reno was near the lodge, watching The General talk animatedly with the Ree scouts. He said something to Reno and pointed forward. Immediately Reno's battalion moved ahead at a fast walk. Custer's battalion fell in behind. A bit later Dan made out a line of trees three or four miles ahead.

"Charley, is that the river?" he asked.

"Prob'ly," he said, reining Augie to the side to get a better look. "Yeah. It moves northwest under them bluffs. I guess the village is on its left bank."

★ ★ ★

Elvin Crane figured it was only an hour until the attack. The Indians would be skedaddling by now, the bastards. That's what Bull had said. He felt himself trembling. Was he afraid? No, probably just the excitement—not fear, Goddamn it. All he had to do was keep next to Bull and he'd be okay. "Get ready," he mumbled to himself, fingering the extra pistol rounds in the belt slung on his left side. If there was a fight, maybe he'd get a crack at that son-of-a-bitch Picard. Who would know in the thick of it? His stomach leaped, forcing a gulp. Had Bull seen it? Didn't look like it. Good. Just stay next to him.

★ ★ ★

The battalion went to the trot. *It was odd,* Dan thought, *riding straight into God-only-knows what,* and he was almost enjoying the ride. The fact was, Teddy had the smoothest trot in the cavalry, and they were practiced at it. Hands relaxed, Dan arched forward just enough to raise his keister. Glancing back he could make out The General's dust, his battalion heading for the bluffs above the river. He was probably going to find a ford and would go down on the village from the east. Of course with Custer the only thing predictable was that afterward he'd cozy up to one of his newspaper cronies and blow his horn harder than old Gabriel. Only Our Father knew where Benteen was, and the train. Lord, 130 men, maybe 160 with the scouts, charging a village of a thousand or more on the ready. He thought they could use every bit of Custer's luck today.

Dan watched the men ahead like he was still a sergeant, alert for a horse faltering or a trooper losing control. They crossed to the creek's left bank and splashed through a little brook coming in from the left, eyes smarting from the alkali. A holler came from ahead. At the gallop it was eight minutes to the river.

★ ★ ★

Jake's head snapped back, then his torso. One square-toed boot was out of its stirrup, his skimpy arse only brushing the cantle. He was hanging on though.

"Goddamn, Scar, you one quick son of a bitch!" Jake shouted, fighting to get fully back in the saddle, his foot finding the stirrup.

The column careened into and out of a gully, tossing him askew and scrambling again for his seat. Rump and boots finally in place, Jake went on cussing at Scar for being so damn eager to get where he hadn't been before, and probably would regret getting, "what with all them Sioux just waitin' for us both."

★ ★ ★

Sam looked to the left where the sun bore through the dust, blinding him for a second. In an instant he had a sharp, pulsating headache, the brightness intensifying the pain behind his left eye. It was ridiculous, going into his first battle with a pounding, one-sided headache.

★ ★ ★

Ernst found the ride a feverish blur, a smear of impressions against the reddish-brown background. What stood out was Thor's strength, the surges of incredible force as the animal's shoulder muscles bunched and flattened, stretching out and literally yanking them ahead. *Gott sei Dank* for Sergeant Steinbrecher, who spent extra time showing him how to handle horses' incredible power.

★ ★ ★

Jubal peered ahead, straining to see the timber through the dust.

Where in the hell was the village? Custer wouldn't have them at the gallop unless they were right close. Twisting around, he shouted, "Jim, whar's the village?" Jim shrugged, his face empty of expression.

★ ★ ★

Dan felt himself tense up, anticipating rifle fire from the brush and trees as they neared the river. It looked about twenty yards across, but there were no warriors—not a teepee in sight or a puff of smoke. Fifty yards to the river, Lieutenant Cooke, the regimental adjutant, appeared, hollering not to use the horses up. What was *he* doing here? Then he was gone, not to be seen again.

At the crossing, the horses plunged their noses deep into the stream, sucking up as much water as they could in splashing across. It was a good ford, only two feet deep with a firm bottom. On the other side they caught their wind. Troopers milled around for a bit, all the while keeping one eye on the bottomland ahead, searching for the village that should be there but wasn't, and then dismounted. Some of the men thought to fill their canteens; others forgot, concentrating on cinching up their girths and retying gear that had worked loose. There was not much talk, just half-voiced inquiries about one man spying something his bunkie hadn't, maybe an Indian or Custer, any scrap of information that made more sense than what they already knew, which was nothing. All the while the men kept an ear cocked for the order to move out. Knowing they were bound to charge down the bottomland, the next ten minutes flew by. If asked, most would say they were spoiling to get going, not extraordinary among men so charged up. Days later a man was heard to say he would have enjoyed the hiatus a lot more if he'd known what would follow. No one argued with him.

Captain Moylan was with Major Reno and his adjutant, Lieutenant Hodgson. Moylan was keeping an eye on The First so he could relay Reno's orders directly. The Major looked uncertain, but when someone hollered out they saw Custer up on the hills across the river, he started jabbering with the other officers as if he'd made a decision. However, another minute passed, then another.

What in tarnation is going on? Jubal wondered. They'd near spent the horses on a half-hour trot and a ten-minute canter without an Indian in sight, and now they were standing there doing nothing. It was not at all like General Custer by the Yellowstone, where he sat with his horse unruffled, waiting until just the right moment, and then barking out orders that were surefire and every little thing worked out just so. It was The General at his finest.

Jim used the wait to ready the squad for the charge. He told Dan to get Streeter's carbine sling corrected. Elvin's girth was loose, as usual. The dolt's cussed horse was a study in obduracy; he could set a record holding his breath, easily outlasting the blockhead's limited patience. Jim stood over both of them until the horse gave up, then looked over to where the captain stood, Bill Hardy the bugler at his side, ready to sound off. (Later on, Jim couldn't remember hearing any bugle calls, although they must have been sounded.) The company had pretty much sorted itself out by then. At least the long wait gave the animals a much-needed blow and a chance to settle the water in their bellies.

The bottomland was about a thousand yards wide, its edge on the left rising gently onto several successively higher benches. On the right the river ran northwest, its meandering banks lined with cottonwoods and willowy underbrush. Steep bluffs rose up on its far side. The bottomland extended some two miles before narrowing where a line of trees extended out from the river, stretching better than halfway across it. The village would be just beyond the line of trees. It *had* to be, because what looked to be riders were by the trees raising dust, probably warning the village.

Someone had spotted The General's column up on the bluffs a few minutes earlier. Moylan had told The First that Custer would support Reno by pitching into the village at the same time he did.

"Streeter!" Jim called out sharply. "Check yer carbine's sights. Jubal! Yer old horse git water? Picard! We go to the charge; stick yer ass on the saddle and get a grip with yer legs. That horse will leave you back in the dirt, you don't take hold. Crane! You do the same, you hear?"

Jim turned back to his mount, ran a hand down his neck, and then stepped away to look him in the eye. The horse minced back, then to the side.

"Easy, Storm, this ain't no race," he said. "You hold back some, hear?"

★ ★ ★

Dan took out his watch. Three minutes past three. Captain Moylan was in the saddle, Sergeant Heyn standing next to him—no breeze, no sound. The sun bore through the leaves onto his left thigh, warming a spot beneath the kersey fabric. He looked down the line, then turned and caught Charley's eye. They were ready.

"Mount!" The first sergeant's shout broke through the stillness.

Chapter 17: Charge!

THE COMPANY MOVED AHEAD quickly at the trot, column of fours. Two miles of dry bottomland lay ahead, the grass overgrazed. A chunk of dry horseshit flew up, hitting Dan in the face. Squinting, he grabbed his neckerchief and wiped furiously at his eyes, while Teddy fell behind a length and a half and the company advanced left front into a line of battle. After a bit he could see past the smart of it and spurred Teddy hard to regain his place, but they ended up between Ernst and Jubal. *Damn!* Charley was three places down the line. He went back to wiping the shit dust out of his eyes. The tears had just about done the job, but the stink of it stayed far up in his nose.

On Dan's left Ernst squinted, his eyes filled with grit and awash in tears, but he was posting smartly, feet sticking in the stirrups, looking like a champion rider with the reins in one hand while the other dabbed at his eyes with a purple bandana. Purple? Where did *that* come from? Dan wondered how the peace-loving boy would do when they closed on the Sioux.

G Troop came up on the right flank. M Troop and the Indian scouts were on the left. *How come?* Dan thought. He hadn't heard a bugle. No matter, it all made for a line of 130 riders sending up a rolling blanket of dust half the width of the bottom. Now the Indian scouts moved ahead, obliquing left, racing toward the bench to cut the main pony herd loose. The line of trees was a mile ahead. Hostiles were riding back and forth in front of it. An enormous dust cloud rose to the northwest, far beyond the tree line. *The pony herd?* Seven scouts veered off from Varnum's party and raced back behind the line, across the bottom, heading for a smaller cluster of ponies across the river—to the gallop!

It wasn't like this in the books Sam had read. He'd heard no bugle calls, just reacted to the men nearby, as in a silent dream. Still, when they swung into line of battle, a wave of exhilaration went through him. *Judas Priest! Charging the enemy!* The wind whistled past his ears, bending the shoddy brim of his hat flat against the crown. Blaster's neck stretched out like a clipper ship's bowsprit. *Running free?* He barely twitched one rein and Blaster instantly angled to the right, then straightened out again. *Good!* Lodge poles behind the trees. When they got inside the village, they would drive the Indians to cover, shooting whoever got in the way. "Punishing them" was how the officers put it. A quick look at Jake, doing really well for his first all-out charge. On impulse he reached for his Colt, but then decided to wait until they got close. He glanced toward the steep bluffs across the river. General Custer had to be up there by now, ready to charge the village from the east.

The Indians weren't about to scatter. The riders in front of the trees dashed out toward the line of troopers, shaking their fists and weapons, and then wheeled around, raced back, and out again. Their crazy hollers were drowned out by the hoofbeats of the troopers' horses. More warriors streamed out, riding back and forth, pulling back gradually, staying out of range. General Custer had turned that tactic around on them at the Yellowstone fight. Where was he now? Sam glanced at the bluffs. Not in sight, yet.

Riding twenty yards ahead of the line, Major Reno suddenly turned and halted the charge four or five hundred yards from where the timber looped out onto the bottom. *Dismount!* Men spilled from their saddles variously, some landing on the run or on all fours, some sprawled in the dust, a few facing to the rear. Four wild-eyed horses from M Troop galloped on without pause, their riders still in the saddle, sawing at the reins when they disappeared into the timber ahead. Dan silently urged—no, he willed—the four men to leap from their horses gone berserk. *No chance, gone for sure.* Then two reappeared, racing back. Jubal actually cheered. The other two were gone, poor bastards.

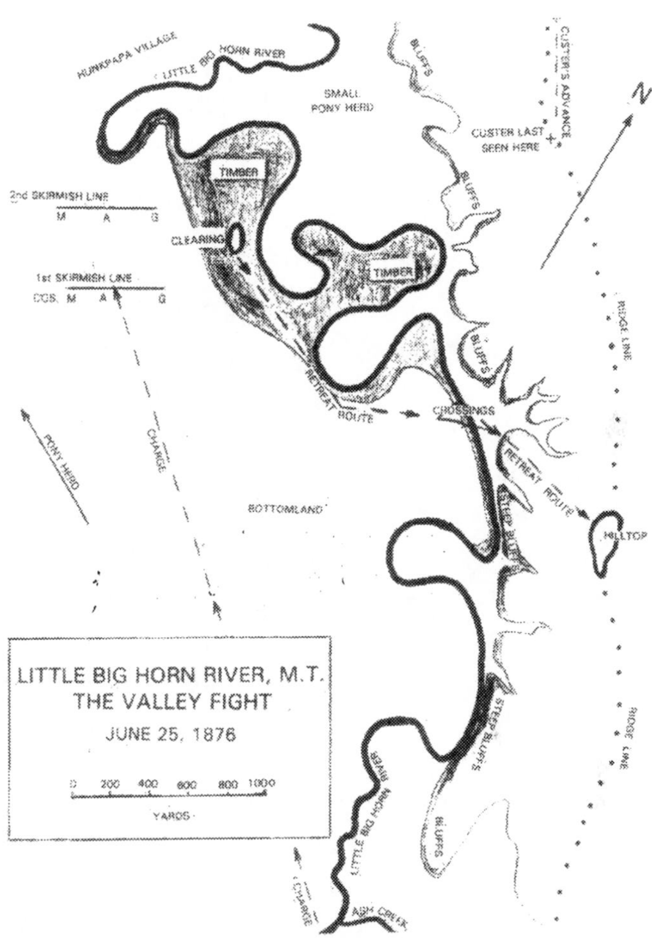

The skirmish line shaped up quickly, most troopers doing what they'd been trained to do. Remarkable, so many being under fire for the first time. No matter how they landed, every man came up with reins and loop straps in hand, ready to hand over to the horse holders. Ernst and Charley each took their four into the timber on the right flank. Troopers spaced themselves three to five yards apart, squinting over their carbines, trying their damnedest to pick out something to shoot at. The dust had thinned, but warriors were hard to find.

Jake looked calm, wiping the sweat from his eyes. Sam was on one knee, seating a cartridge in the Springfield's chamber. He'd dropped the first one, picked it up, and pocketed it. The second one went okay despite a shaking hand. He glanced over at Dan and shrugged, red-faced.

Major Reno ordered an advance. The men began moving forward, warily at first, watching for targets, some men firing at nothing. Bullets whizzed by their heads but the line never hesitated; after 150 yards it slowed and stopped. Grazed to the bone, the ground was pocked with prairie-dog holes. Company G's right flank was anchored at the timber on the east side. M Troop was hanging out on the left flank far short of the bench on the bottomland's western edge. The men went to ground, most of them kneeling, some on their bellies. Enough breeze so you had to breathe it. No sense shooting; the hostiles ahead were too far and hidden by the dust. Another bunch appeared beyond the left flank. The tops of lodges showed above the trees. The sun's rays bored through the haze, intent on broiling them. Jim dug out his watch: three-twenty.

Lying prone, Jubal waited patiently, searching for a warrior to shoot at. He concentrated on a spot in the timber three hundred yards away, where a shaft of sunlight came through. A minute later a brave appeared astride a chestnut pony, his face bisected with a line of yellow paint beneath his eyes, bold as all get-out in the sun's rays. A stillness came over Jubal, the sounds of the battlefield slipping away. Shifting his carbine, he reset its sight for the distance, and then settled his hips, melding with the dusty ground. Slowly, carefully he took aim, bringing the front sight up smoothly into the aperture. The young Indian carried a rifle, its brass shining in the sunlight. *A Winchester?* The hint of a smile appeared on Jubal's face when he squeezed the trigger, gently but persistently until the hammer let go. Click!

"Tarnation!" he cursed aloud.

Hastily, he half-cocked the carbine and thumbed the breechblock up, ejecting the faulty cartridge. Frustrated and with a sense of urgency rising from his gut, he still paused to examine the new cartridge before sliding it into the chamber and closing down the breechblock. Cocking the hammer, he resettled himself to take aim again.

"Goldurnit," he muttered while wiping the dust from his eye. He peered down the carbine's barrel once more, but the brave was gone like a mouse down a hole.

Jake looked over and saw that Sam's left ear was in the dirt. "Sam!" he hollered.

Sam just raised his arm to point at the bluffs rising on the other side of the timber. "Up there!" he yelled. "Looks like E Troop."

Jake turned and squinted, focusing on the sunny hillside. A thin line of dust rose from just below one of the peaks on the ridgeline, some three hundred feet above the river. A blur of gray horses was moving down into a coulee and out of sight. *Jésus-christ!* Custer was really going to charge the Sioux farther downstream.

Elvin Crane wondered how come Charley Smrka got to be a four, and Albrecht? He fired again, the puff of dust showing he'd fired short. Then another. Same thing. *Springfield's sights always got screwed up,* he thought. But it felt good just shooting at them heathens.

"Crane!" Bull hollered. "Save them cartridges fer when we charge."

"Okay," Elvin said, wondering what Bull was thinking. *Charge on foot? Stupid Reno's gonna get us all killed.*

"Goddamn it," he said, ignoring Bull and letting fly at an Indian riding back and forth two hundred yards away. Couldn't tell if it was short or long. Unconsciously he worked his shoulder as if to ease the soreness sure to come. The warrior slowed his horse considerably but continued erect in the saddle, his studied nonchalance showing his contempt for the cavalry. *The sonuvabitch of a no good bastard!* Thumbing the breechblock up, Elvin reloaded, then looked off to the west.

"Hey, Bull!" he called, squirming a couple feet closer to him.

"See them Redskins over on the left? I thought Varnum was out there with the scouts."

"Varnum's over here with the captain. Ain't seen his Rees."

"They must of pulled foot."

"Prob'ly," Bull said. "Ain't worth two cents."

★ ★ ★

Jim watched ten braves on foot come out of the line of trees. None wore paint. Maybe the village had been surprised after all. However, another twenty rode out of the trees, all wearing paint. They joined some braves running their ponies back and forth. Were they getting them going for a charge? Not likely, but maybe. A bunch more joined them. Too much movement to count, but definitely more than a hundred of them—maybe another fifty moving around M Troop's left flank. The intensity of cavalry fire grew steadily. It was amazing how rapidly a tenderfoot down the line could load and fire, not aiming a whit. Maybe he thought the *sound* of it would scare the Sioux out of coming at him.

An officer shouted a command from behind the line. Jim couldn't decipher it. Glancing back he saw Lieutenant Varnum working his way toward the timber. Suddenly two dozen Indian riders raced out of the dust toward the skirmish line. Fifteen more joined them from out of the timber, and then they all made a wide turn and trotted back. Dan was beside Jim. Kneeling, he drew a bead on an especially nervy brave riding a piebald pony with yellow slashes on its chest. He'd charged several times, then wheeled off to run parallel to the line, while hanging from the pony's off side before moving back to two hundred yards and resting. The man just sat there, staring at the troopers. Dan fired. The round fell barely short, sending up a puff of dust. The warrior threw his head back as if to laugh, his pride showing in how he sat the pony as it high-stepped off.

"Don't know how long we'll be here," Dan said, waiting for a better target. "They've already flanked us on the left. No one's been hit, have they?"

"None in A Troop I seen."

"This is not the place to be, only Reno doesn't see that yet. Maybe he'd wake up if an officer was hit."

"Maybe. I gotta check on Picard and Crane," Jim said, moving off.

⋆ ⋆ ⋆

Jake looked over at Jubal, who grinned and pointed at a cluster of young braves in a ditch about two hundred yards in front. Two or three would raise their heads at the same time, tempting the troopers to use up their ammunition. Taking his time, Jubal aimed and fired, then reloaded and aimed again, waiting for another head to pop up. Jake followed his example, but he flinched when pulling the trigger. *Jésus Christ!*

Jim grabbed Jake's shoulder, startling him, and said, "Easy, Jake. Just slide the cartridge in—uh huh—an' close the breechblock. Mash the thumb piece to be sure. Draw the hammer back. Okay, line 'er up good. You got it? Now think of that woman in Chicago. What's her name?"

"Huh?" Jake looked up. "Marguerite."

"Keep on aimin' an' think of Marguerite, all warm and close, an' yer squeezin' her soft an' nice. Just like yer squeezin' the trigger."

Blam!

"Sumbitch!" the sergeant exclaimed. "See that pony go down? You hit him! Behind the ditch. Sumbitch, you got him!"

"I shot at them guys in the ditch," Jake said.

"Just shows yer aimin' high. Let's see yer piece. Yeah, set 'er down to two hundred, that'll do it. Sumbitch, wait till ole Charley hears this."

Although unimpressed, Jake had to smile, thinking of Marguerite.

Reno was talking to Lieutenant Hodgson behind the skirmish

line. Gesturing excitedly, he pointed toward M Troop, then the village, and then toward the timber. Hodgson hurried toward G Troop. Lieutenant McIntosh met him halfway. Shortly after, McIntosh's men started making their way toward the timber. They were in good order at first, but seconds later three of them were jumping and flinching, as if they'd walked into a swarm of hornets, sending them scampering past the others. One dropped his carbine like it was a hot potato, practically throwing it down. Without missing a step the man behind him picked it up. Damn! They were catching fire from warriors in the timber upstream.

The First was coming down the line, stretching the company out to the right to fill the gap left by G Troop. The men complied raggedly, the natural tendency being to bunch up. Besides, they were busy shooting at the mounting number of warriors charging closer and closer before breaking off their runs. Fire from the timber upstream was getting heavier, more and more Indians gathering in there. Most of them were aiming high, but a scattering of rounds zipped through, too close for comfort.

"See that brave on the piebald?" Sam asked Dan. It was the proud warrior from before.

"Uh huh."

"He keeps comin' straight at us. 'Bout a hundred yards out he turns to our left. He hangs on the off side when he turns," Sam said, staring at the rider. "I'm gonna shoot the pony when he turns."

"Okay," Dan said. "I'll try and hit the brave."

The Indian started forward, drawing a couple of shots from down the line. He kept the pony going straight, pushing it into an all-out gallop.

"Fire quick when he turns," Dan said.

Leaning forward, the warrior was barely visible above the pony's flying mane as he raced toward the line, closing the distance rapidly and passing the spot where he turned before. Surprised, Dan raised up slightly to look over his rear sight just as the pony planted a foreleg to turn and Sam's carbine barked in the same instant. The little piebald stumbled, still turning, appeared to regain his footing, and then crumpled in a heap, his momentum carrying him forward as he fell, his lower jaw skidding through the dusty soil and the stunned rider still on his back. Dan aimed again but too quickly. He knew he missed when he pulled the trigger.

Sam reached for a new cartridge but fumbled it into the dirt as Jim fired. He missed too. The brave rolled off the dead pony, grabbed his lance, and stood, staggering as he regained his balance. With that he turned toward the skirmish line, raised his lance over his head, and hollered at them. He turned his back and started toward the trees as another rider galloped forward to rescue him. Four troopers fired, but the two Indians disappeared in the dust.

"Good shot, Sam," Dan said.

"I was lucky."

"No, that was a good shot," Jim said. "Okay, we gotta hang on a bit more. Then we're movin' out."

"Where to?" Sam asked.

"They'll work somethin' out." Jim nodded toward Reno and Hodgson.

I hope they do, Dan thought. "Jesus!" he yelled as a round scorched him. He worked his arm around to see if it still worked. The sleeve was cut and it burned like hell near the shoulder.

"You okay?" Sam asked.

"Yes."

"You sure?"

"Yes. Burnt the skin, that's all."

"Good. Judas, they could roll us up with a few more out there," Jim said, pointing out to the left.

"Maybe they won't," Dan said. "They don't often fight as an outfit, so—"

"Hope you're right," Sam said. "Anyway, General Custer should be hitting them about now. That will put them on the run, won't it?"

"Depends on how big the village is," Dan said.

"But he's got five companies."

"An' McClellan had six whole corps," Dan mumbled.

"What?" Sam asked.

"Nothing."

"We're on our own here," Jim said. He dug out his watch: three thirty-two. They'd been on the line just shy of a quarter hour.

The First came up, grabbed his shoulder, and pointed.

"Streeter!" Jim shouted. "Git to the timber an' cover us comin' in!"

Without answering, Sam started to rise. The buzz of a bullet whined past Dan's ear as loud as any he'd heard. Sam was down!

"Judas Priest!" Sam exclaimed, clamping his hat back on. There were a pair of holes in its crown, front and back. "That was awful close."

"Git goin'!" Jim shouted.

In a single motion Sam was up and running in a half-crouch while his mind remained stuck on the round that nearly put him down for good. He was going to die, no way around it. Today! He couldn't prevent it, not with hundreds of bullets coming at him, one of which was searching him out right now. *Goddamn it, how far to the timber? Fifty yards? God, let me get to those trees, please, God. Zzzzzz!* Forty yards. *Zzzzzz!* Twenty. Ten. *Whizzzz!* Damn! His boot found a hole, sending him flat out in the dirt like batter on a griddle, a sharp pain in his ankle. It pissed him off. He would not die—not today.

Scrambling up he made it to the shade and turned as he went down on one knee and fired. *Click!* Damn, he hadn't reloaded! "Slow down!" he said aloud, pulling two cartridges from his belt and palming them in his left hand before slipping a third into the carbine's breech. Six braves were clustered less than 150 yards from the line, working themselves up to charge. *As good a place to start as any.* As the shot went off he remembered his sights were set at two hundred. *Judas H. Priest!*

Chapter 18: In the Timber

THE TIMBER WAS ON the skirmish line's right flank. It ran alongside the river's left bank for some five hundred yards. Because of the stream's meandering, the timber ranged from five to well over a hundred yards wide, with the occasional box elder and black ash standing within thick groves of cottonwoods leafed out to shade the baking sun. The underbrush was thick, a tangle of willows, chokecherries, and thorny bullberry and rose bushes that would grab at you if you tried to plunge through them. Because the only paths through this tangle were deer and buffalo game trails, the bushes' upper branches whipped at a horse's face and threatened to unseat the rider. The woods were marked by occasional hollows, the remnants of ancient riverbeds dried up.

All three troops took positions in a dry meander that formed a wide arc three hundred yards upstream from the village. Good ground. They could hold the place the whole day if they didn't waste cartridges. Company A faced west and southwest along the cut bank, a man every three or four yards. Most of them had good cover, their boots well below the level of the flats they'd just left. Company G was on their right, nearest the village, while M Troop was situated on their left. Major Reno stood behind Company A in a small clearing, along with Hodgson, the orderlies, and Bloody Knife, Custer's favorite Ree scout. The horse holders remained together in the trees, most of them behind M Troop.

The cut bank made for some protection, and a tangle of bushes helped screen the men a little. Still, the willows and wild current bushes were sparse enough to allow a few clear lines of fire. Dan lay half on his side on the shallow slope just below the ground they had dashed across, cradling his carbine against his chest as he pulled out his bandana to wipe the sweat out of his eyes. More and more Indians were hollering their crazy, sing-song gibberish and getting close, creeping up on the troopers. Dan was parched. He had left his canteen slung on the saddle, in the best of hands with Charley.

Jake lay prone five yards to Dan's left, his head and arms above the top of the slope, drawing a bead on something or somebody. His shoulder jumped back when the Springfield fired.

"Goddam!" he swore, sliding back down the bank. Sensing Sam watching, he looked over. "I still got the flinch."

"You shot that pony," Sam said.

"Uh huh, but that wasn't what I shot at." Sam raised his eyebrows and, moving his eyes, silently urged Jake to look behind him. Elvin was hunkered there, immobile, glowering at the back of Jake's head.

"What're *you* doin'?" Jake barked.

"Whadda you care?" Elvin muttered.

"You sneak up like a snake, I gotta watch out. What you want?"

"Corporal Judd sent me over, that's what."

"Okay, but don't eye the back of my head. Get to shootin' Injuns."

"Why don't *you*, Picard?" Elvin shot back.

The tremor in Elvin's voice was easy to pick up. Fear as much as anything, but he was pissed off too. Like the rest of the men, he was stuck there, not knowing what Major Reno was going to decide next.

Jake turned his head as if to continue his conversation with Sam then quickly swiveled back at Elvin, taking him by surprise. The dolt had shifted his carbine so it was pointed at Jake.

"Don't point yer piece at me, you sonuvabitch!" Jake said, his eyes flitting to the Springfield, then locking up with Elvin's.

"Oh yeah." Elvin swung the carbine toward the brush.

"Good. Now go screw yourself, maggot!"

As if the curse had called for it, a drawn-out volley of shots came in, the lead buzzing and zinging through the air over their heads, some splatting into tree trunks and branches, others snapping off twigs and leaves. A cottonwood leaf fluttered to land on Jake's shoulder like a moth near the end of its time. Reflexively he brushed it off angrily.

"You sonuvabitches!" he hollered toward the flats, scrambling up the shallow bank to rest his carbine on its rim. An unpainted Hunkpapa boy of about fourteen sat on a pinto not seventy yards away, staring at him. Holding an ancient muzzleloader, he wore a puzzled expression on his face, as if he wondered why the chargers had come so far only to hole up short of the village. Jake lined up his sights—he couldn't miss. The carbine fired. When the smoke cleared the boy was still there. In fact, he sat on his pony for a moment before he barely touched him with his heels. The animal turned and headed for the village at a slow walk. Jake mumbled an oath in French, then shifted around on impulse, looking for Charley.

"Hey, Dan, what if our horses get hit?"

"Charley's okay," Dan told him.

Shielded by an old log and a clump of bushes on the cut bank's crest, Jim and Dan tried to get a handle on the situation. The fire had eased up considerably to their front. Out on the flats Indians were moving upstream and then circling back into the timber to their left, putting more pressure on M Troop. More warriors from the village were pitching into G Troop on their right. The number of those on the river's far bank was growing by the minute. In the brush Indians hollered back and forth, sending up an unending cacophony of bloodthirsty Lakota oaths. It was unnerving for the new men who still couldn't see them. When the Indians fired a single round, several troopers fired back, glad to have a faint idea of a hostile's location.

Dan slid down the bank and rested, the tension draining out of his neck muscles. Out of habit he ejected and reseated the cartridge in his carbine while collecting his thoughts. Jim scrambled down beside him.

"First thing, we gotta save ammo," Jim said. "No more firing wild."

"Right. You get that, Sam?" Dan said. "Then pass the word."

"What's Reno's thinking?" Jim asked. "We oughtta git movin'."

"Yes, and soon," Dan said. "And where's Custer?"

"I don't know. Oughtta be a couple miles downstream by now. Course, from there he cain't support us d'rectly. But wherever he pitches in, it might get these sumbitches off our backs."

Dan hoped Custer would get to it soon. If he did, then maybe Benteen's battalion would catch up, and maybe the pack train too, with their ammo reserves. Of course, ifs and maybes just made for bullshit. He wondered where Moylan's lieutenants were, DeRudio and Varnum. Was anyone moving men around to meet the fire from the east? Was there a plan? Reno had made mistakes, but it was poor communication that messed things up. When orders did come down, they were confusing. Men floundered without clear direction.

"Damn it!" Dan muttered, turning to Jim and asking what he thought.

Jim shrugged and said Reno had both thumbs up his ass, but they should keep their doubts from the rookies.

Just then Varnum rode behind the line, moving upstream. "Lieutenant!" Jim hollered to get his attention. "We s'posed to dig in here or we gonna move out?"

"Just stay there and hold 'em off," Varnum replied, riding on.

⋆ ⋆ ⋆

The firing picked up again. Sam let fly an answering shot, then cursed. He'd missed again. Hell, nobody could hit anything through the brush.

Men low on ammunition needed to get to their saddlebags to

replenish, so Varnum went to Company A's fours and called for them to follow him. However, horse holders from all three troops responded, bringing *every* animal to one spot in the willows behind them.

Confusion set in. The First ordered every second man to come off the line, find his horse, and get what ammunition he needed, then return to the line so the next man could get his. Not everyone heard him correctly, what with the Sioux firing in volleys and troopers firing back.

Making matters worse, someone hollered either "Charge!" or "They're gonna charge!" With that nobody was sure of who was supposed to be doing what. In the tumult of it, Elvin and some others immediately left the line, looking for their mounts in the trees and brush. Men began colliding on the poorly defined trails. Elvin was knocked sideways into a tree by another man's horse. Dan found him wandering along a path that turned toward the village. Seeing Dan, he turned pale and lurched into a run, fortunately in the right direction.

Jim was handling two squads, having stepped in for Sergeant Perkins, who'd taken a round in the shoulder. He stood behind Perkins's men, shouting nonstop, directing their fire, and telling them who was to go for ammunition and in what order. When little Kunz tried to dart by him out of turn, Jim tripped him, picked him up, and actually threw him back onto the line six feet away. Jim standing like a block of granite was exactly what the rookies needed—somebody to hang on to.

Disorder prevailed. No widespread panic, but discipline had broken down. Uncertainty about what men should do bred doubt as to whether their officers knew what *they* were doing. A few troopers lost all sense of direction. In addition, the Indians' skill with their horses was unsettling for those who'd never fought them before. Braves raced along the twisting trails, stopping in an instant, then dashing off in a different direction. No matter how many times they saw the trick, troopers stared in awe when a warrior fired at them from beneath his pony's neck.

A lot of men thought the hostiles had the better firearms. It was not surprising, since trying to rapidly load, fire, and reload a trap door Springfield without dropping cartridges into the dirt could be a hellish job with smoke and dust swirling in your face, bullets clipping leaves barely above your head and raising puffs of dust, especially when a screaming warrior bore down on you, riding a paint-streaked pony while getting off three rounds to your one with his Winchester. However, it appeared worse than it was. More than a few Indians had older, single-shot rifles, some of them muzzleloaders. Their supply of ammunition was limited too. Many of the younger ones used bows and arrows. Besides, with good ground and disciplined fire, a company could hold off Indians indefinitely using Springfield carbines. The Indians possibly knew that, and so they didn't mount mass charges.

* * *

Ernst held his four horses in a grove of willows twenty yards behind the line. A sudden volley of shots came from the left, followed by the sounds of men crashing through the underbrush. One burst out of the bushes, panting.

"Bring the horses up!" the man yelled as he hurried down the path. "We're pullin' out!"

Things were happening too fast. As Ernst started forward, Elvin dashed up and grabbed his mount. Bull's horse reared, spooking Thor into nearly yanking Ernst off his feet. Glaring at the animal, he spoke commandingly and started forward again as Jubal arrived and took Prince. Somewhere to the right a wounded horse screamed, the sound tearing at Ernst's gut. A man cursed and another responded, their cries adding to the tumult.

"Goddamn it, let go of thet horse! He's mine!"

"Okay, but he's a goner, see?"

"Christ! What am I gonna do?"

Bull hurried up the path toward his horse, his carbine in one hand, the other reaching up for the bridle despite having four steps to go. Ernst saw a strangeness in his eyes when Bull looked through him, unhooked the link strap, swung himself up into the saddle, and was gone. Ernst took a step back, then mounted Thor and started forward again. The path turned right and he saw Sergeant Steinbrecher on the ground ahead, still holding his reins as he lay there. The kepi gone, he was bleeding above his right ear.

"Sergeant!" Ernst shouted, leaping from Thor's back and going to Steinbrecher. *Der Feldwebel* looked up, mumbling incoherently as he regained his faculties.

"Albrecht, it is you! Give me a hand!" he commanded. Ernst helped him up, but the old Prussian couldn't stand without support.

Chapter 19: Reno's Clearing

★ ★ ★

MEN WERE MILLING AROUND without direction as Dan started back for Teddy. Why hadn't Reno ordered the men to fort up? It was good ground, and Indians wouldn't throw lives away against men dug in. He thought Benteen would be coming up before long. And then it dawned on him just as he and Jake reached Charley.

"Reno's thinking of making a run for it," he said.

Charley shook his head. "We get to runnin', they'll pick us off like buffaloes in the hunt."

Abruptly the fire slackened off, and there were no sounds of ponies in the brush. It bothered Dan. Going from a cock-sure charge to an aimless muddle in the timber looked weak, and Indians had a nose for weakness. Should have fired them up. Maybe they were holding back, wondering if the Major had lost his nerve. Dan pictured a host of braves stealing through the trees, hungry for coup, getting up close and ready to dash in alone, making the coup big enough to brag on all winter.

★ ★ ★

Jake tried to get at the ammunition in his saddlebags as they started out. It was difficult, the trail being so narrow. They mounted up when they got near Captain Moylan and waited for the company to assemble. Then they would move upstream to join Reno.

Suddenly someone hollered there was going to be a charge. With that a few troopers lost their heads, afraid of being left behind. Riders spurring their mounts forward ran into men on foot, knocking them aside. Men were cursing, shouting, and yelling as they searched desperately for horses being held only six feet away behind a clump of bushes. A few took mounts belonging to others; in the rising tumult, horse holders handed them over, leaving the rightful owners either afoot or forced to ride another man's horse.

Major Reno's clearing was small, jamming them up more than before. That gave some men a feeling of greater safety. The notion was ill-advised. Troopers should never get caught inside a crowd. Dan led the squad over to the west side, putting them apart from the crowded mix of men and horses. Out of the main thrust of things, they could move quickly if anything changed.

Jim joined them after Sergeant Perkins was fixed up. A few stragglers were cursing in the brush, trying to recover their horses. Major Reno was about twenty yards away with Bloody Knife and M Troop's Captain French beside him. Moylan sat his horse about ten paces from them. Neither Captain McIntosh nor Lieutenant Wallace were there from G Troop, nor were many of their men.

The Indians were working their way up close. Their occasional shots were a diversion and mostly unanswered. When a round flew narrowly overhead, the men ducked on reflex, causing some of the rookies to look chagrined, but the veterans saw nothing wrong with staying alive. Occasionally troopers heard the deeper bark of a Springfield from the brush downstream, where half of G Troop remained.

The First came over to the squad and asked if they'd seen Ernst. Nobody had seen him since he had led the horses into the timber a half hour ago. The First said Gus Steinbrecher was also missing, along with Gilbert, Bancroft, Taylor, and Corporal Roy.

Two men from M Troop rode over from the middle of the clearing. One was Jack Cobb, Elvin's friend from Tongue River. Big and awkward, he looked surprisingly nervous. Jake knew the other, Zach Purvis, a bewhiskered old card player from M Troop.

"How you makin' out?" Purvis asked.

"Okay," Jake replied.

"Too crowded fer me over thar. 'Sides, listenin' to the Major jabberin' first one way then t'other, it's more'n I can take. With The Gen'ral, we wouldn't be in this here fix."

Sam said, "You're right about that."

"Yup. How many's A Troop lost?" Purvis asked.

"Ain't seen nobody go down," Jake answered.

"You seen them four runaways goin' straight for the village? Ain't seen Smith an' Turley since. Meier caught a round, but he and ole Rutten, they made it back. Lost Sergeant O'Hara just 'fore we ran fer the trees," the old trooper said. "Klotzburger was hit turribly. Reckon he's a goner. Boy named Selkirk, he was hit an' hollered out, afeered he'd git left behind but he wa'n't."

"Is Elvin Crane here?" Cobb asked Dan.

"He was, but I don't see him now," Dan said. Looking around he spotted young Taylor on Steamboat, his ancient, short-winded mount. The horse looked ready to give up the ghost altogether, but that was usual for him.

Jim took out his watch: eight minutes before four. How long would they stay put? Reno, Bloody Knife, French, and Moylan were still huddled up, the Major gesturing toward the bluffs.

Crack! Bang ba-bam bang! Ba-bang bang! A storm of shots broke the quiet, ripping through the clearing. Bloody Knife's head snapped back in a red-tinged blur, brain matter flying, his body twisting and spilling to the ground. Reno's face was stippled with Bloody Knife's blood. In fact, every man and every horse close by was splattered. White smoke wafted upward from the brush beyond the clearing's edge. A horse reared, his rider throwing himself forward and bringing him down. Jake leaned into Scar's neck, steadying him. Furious, Jubal's face was flushed. Cobb's was a ghostly gray. Ten yards away a man clutched his stomach, calling out for his God before crumpling, moaning. Two others jumped down to help him. Trumpeter Hardy's horse danced sideways along with several others, less disturbed by the volley than by the wave of trepidation that swept through the clearing.

Major Reno steadied his mount while wiping a red bandana over his face and hollered, "Dismount!"

Captain French and Captain Moylan repeated the command but almost immediately Reno yelled, "Mount!" The two captains glanced at each other before hollering out the new order.

Men scrambled to regain their saddles, ordinarily a simple act, but the commotion around Major Reno spread like wildfire among the horses. Riders were caught in circle dances, one foot in the stirrup and one on the ground as their mounts twisted around like a child's whirligig toy, the tied-on accouterments clinking and clanking until in one heroic leap each man gained purchase, then clung desperately until he had his horse in hand. In the midst of it all, Major Reno ordered a charge. French and Moylan hollered it down, but before their companies could get in order, Reno was off, racing through the trees upstream, angling toward the open flats. He was followed by a ragged column, every man spurring his horse out of the timber and up the valley toward the ford they'd crossed an hour before.

Remarkably, Sam's and Jake's horses gave them no trouble, but Cobb had big problems. His seven-year-old Bay reared again and again, each time doing his best to yank the reins out of Cobb's hand. Adding to his frustration was a rightful fear of being left behind without a horse. Sam was unmoved by all the tumult. His horse still at rest, he stared at Cobb's predicament. Apparently he found the desperate look on Cobb's face amusing, because he was chuckling.

"Your horse likes it here," he kidded. "Wants to stay awhile."

Jim glanced over, glowering. "Streeter!" he hollered. "This ain't no joke! Go an' help the man, numbskull!"

Startled, Sam spurred Blaster over and took the plunging Bay's bridle with one hand and held firm, talking gently, which calmed the horse down instantly. Cobb sprang into the saddle before the horse could change his mind.

"Sorry," Sam said, mortified. "I guess I—"

But Cobb was gone before he could finish, angling to the right.

In fact, they were *all* gone, Jake, Jubal, Elvin, Bull, Charley, the whole bunch. Next thing he knew Bancroft, Switzer, Andrew Conner, and a couple of others raced by. Barely twitching his spurs, Blaster leaped ahead and he and Jim were off. Close behind, Dan tried to grasp why Reno had yelled "Charge!" He supposed one might say it was a charge, what with several Indians between them and the open flats. But in truth, it was a retreat. Later, some said it was a rout, while others called it a "sure 'nuff skedaddle."

★ ★ ★

Back in the brush, Ernst was helping Sergeant Steinbrecher gain the saddle when they heard the volley that killed Bloody Knife a hundred yards away. Turning toward the sound, they strained to make out what was happening. Behind them men from G Troop yelled excitedly and crashed their horses through the underbrush. Ernst felt the nonsensical impulse to tell them to be quiet, but then he heard the rumble of the battalion racing upstream. Five or six shots hissed and thunked into the brush and trees only feet away.

Startled, he swung himself up as Thor burst ahead, leaving his right foot searching for its stirrup. The path headed upstream, then veered obliquely right. Other troopers were pounding through the timber; every so often he'd catch a glimpse of one through the bushes. Steinbrecher raised his hand twenty yards from the edge of the woods and both men pulled up. Thor immediately lowered his head as far as Ernst would permit, snuffling in a patch of oat grass, but *der Feldwebel's* horse was in a frenzy, forcing the sergeant to keep a tight rein as the animal danced in place, his shoulders trembling, a compelling sight of enormous power barely contained. For an instant Ernst pictured that power captured on canvas. It shone in the animal's eyes, the way they bulged outward with the whites extra prominent, like those of men crazed by fear or rage. For two seconds he was the artist completely absorbed, the imminent danger absent from his mind.

Holding the frantic animal in check without apparent effort, *der Feldwebel* cocked his head, listening to determine the best course to take. Random shots continued through the branches overhead, and now other rounds came their way from downstream, their reports steadily closer. They finally captured Ernst's attention. He pulled Thor's head up and touched his side with a boot heel. The horse sidestepped to the far side of the path.

"Upstream we ride, out of the trees," *der Feldwebel* said, shouting to be heard. A bullet zinged over his head, forcing him low in the saddle. Another buzzed past, even closer. He forced a smile to reassure the rookie, but distorted by pressure, it appeared as the grimace of a man before the guillotine. "Follow me, and stay back two or three."

Zzzzzzz-thunk! A round smashed through his horse's ribs just in front of the sergeant's boot. *Thwack!* A second bullet crashed into the animal's head, buckling his front legs completely. Horse and rider plunged to the ground, pinning Steinbecher's leg beneath the horse's quivering body. Unable to extricate himself, *der Feldwebel* twisted around toward Ernst who was already out of his saddle, hurrying toward him and grabbing the animal's head with both hands, straining as if to force the horse to raise itself. Only then did Ernst realize the animal was dead.

Steinbecher pointed to his leg, urgently, muttering that it was pinned between the horse and a bare tree limb half-buried in silt left by spring floods. Digging with his hands, Ernst found the offending pole and bent to the job of extricating it. Suddenly a crazed, riderless cavalry mount came charging up the path. Ernst caught only a fleeting image of the big sorrel before it knocked him aside, bruising his knee against a tree and smashing the stock of his carbine. Crawling back, he grabbed the free end of the tree limb and muscled it back and forth until he could pull it out. Then he helped *der Feldwebel* get his leg out from beneath the dead horse.

"You are okay, Sergeant?" Ernst asked.

"My right leg is bad." He remained sitting on the ground.

"It is broken?"

Still agitated at being unhorsed, the sergeant merely shrugged, then shouted, "You don't catch that sorrel, no? *Dumkopf,* we must go now!" Shots rattled through the leaves nearby, accentuating his urgency.

Ernst hurried back to where Thor grazed peacefully, took the reins, and returned.

"You take my horse!" he urged, handing the reins over. "I will catch the sorrel." Half-expecting *der Feldwebel t*o refuse, he was relieved when Steinbrecher motioned for a hand up. He stood mostly on his left leg and took the reins. Ernst helped him mount. Then the sergeant threw him a salute, yanked Thor's head around, and raced off, chasing the sounds of the battalion pounding upstream, leaving more than a few men behind—the dead, the unhorsed, and some of the wounded as well. Ernst moved toward the sorrel, grazing in the brush twenty meters away, but when he reached out, the horse minced backward, tossed his head, and dashed away, following *der Feldwebel.*

Chapter 20: A Desperate Run

IT WAS A WILD-EYED, pell-mell run to God-only-knew where. No one took charge, for all Jim could tell. While half his mind was demanding that he stay low in the saddle and watch for hostiles, the other half pictured Reno spurring his horse so hard it leaped into a gallop. He'd heard neither bugle nor orders, although Captain Moylan shouted something he couldn't make out. He looked around again for the others, but it was hard to keep track of them in the tangle of trees, wild roses, willows, and dogwood.

"Easy, Storm," he muttered, slowing the horse. Bull was ahead, Crane close by him. Jubal passed by on old Prince. Dan and Sam were coming up from behind. *Where was Jake? What about Ernst?* Then he spotted Jake next to Crane's buddy from M Troop. *Goddamn it, where the hell was Ernst?* A streak of fear surprised him. He gulped, afraid he'd lost the young German. Charley came alongside.

"You seen Ernst?" Jim hollered.

"Not since we took the horses off the line," Charley answered.

Two rounds whizzed past, not really close. Scattered shots ahead out on the flats. Men were hollering on hidden paths not far behind, and others were very far behind. Storm careened around a bend and into a hollow where Dan and Sam were bunched up behind Bull. A riderless horse galloped into the draw, stumbled, recovered, and raced up out of it and was gone.

"Lead out, Bull!" Jim hollered, pointing to an opening. They reached the flats twenty seconds later, straight into the blinding sun as three troopers sped by at full gallop, one of them with his Colt in hand. *Easy to lose it like that.* When Jim's eyes adjusted to the light, there was Charley, ranging out from the timber's edge to scan the length of the column. He was probably trying to spot that sumbitch Reno. *Christ!* Forty-odd Sioux were riding parallel on the right, and twice that many coming up fast. You had to hand it to them: their ponies stretching out in a dead run, braves riding smoothly, no saddles, no effort.

Storm settled into a canter, pacing himself like a race horse, which was good except the stakes in this race were an awful lot higher. An idiotic phrase repeated itself inside his brain like a drumbeat in time with the steady three-beat gait: *"Don't you run, don't you run, don't you run."* Christ, running wasn't his choice. Like Charley said, an Indian's pony would go farther on less, and he'd outlast you without hardly trying. *Goddamn it, stop all the thinking! Don't you run, don't you run, don't you run.*

He saw an unhorsed civilian legging it toward the timber; it was Herendeen. The man knew the country well. Ahead, Stanislaus Roy slowed and fell back, his carbine missing, boot splattered with blood, horse slobbering dark red drivel. He caught Jim's eye and they exchanged off-hand salutes as he turned back toward the timber. More hostiles on the right, edging closer, crowding the strung-out column toward the river.

* * *

Dan caught up to Jack Cobb who was leaning forward in the saddle, holding on to the pommel as the column slowed. *Damn it, Major, don't change the pace out here. You'll get us slaughtered.* Then it picked up again, thanks be to God. Somehow Cobb had gotten into a bunch from M Troop on the timber's edge.

Over Dan's right shoulder three braves were thirty yards away and drawing closer. They had the speed and the angle, racing each other for the honor, and he was the prize. Twenty yards. A pinto was in the lead, thirteen hands, cream-white face, pinkish nose, black paint circling his left eye, streaks on his shoulder. Dan pulled his Colt and cocked it, then everything slowed down and went silent.

"Easy, Teddy, easy!" he yelled, glancing over. The lead warrior was only ten yards back now, a steel point on his lance, his face chalked white, black stripes over the eyes, one eagle feather, and no Winchester. *Good!* He took another look, and then another. Five yards off, the pony was bug-eyed, neck straight out, frothing, lathering, busting his heart for the rider, putting out more than he had. His dark eyes flashing, the warrior's high-pitched scream pierced the silence. He raised the lance and Dan fired, the bullet hitting off-center on his shoulder, his arm flinging up and back with him following it, twisting up and off the pinto's back. *There, you son of a bitch!* Riderless, the pony dashed ahead faster, still busting his heart for the warrior. Another look back. The two others were fading into the chickenshit-brown dust.

More hostiles appeared on the right, as close as forty yards off, hardly aiming as they pumped rounds into the column. Ahead, Reno must have veered left, the ragged column following like stampeding buffalo. Nothing the Sioux did better than chase down buffalo.

Dan slowed a bit and Jim came up alongside.

"You seen Ernst?" he asked. Dan shook his head. Jim rose in the stirrups and hollered ahead, the sound nearly lost in the tumultuous mix of thundering hoofbeats and the howling Indians. He hollered again: "Gawd damn it, Major! Why'd you put us on the run, you sumbitch?"

⋆ ⋆ ⋆

Bent on getting back to the trees, Elvin's horse began fighting the bit coming out of the timber. Elvin yanked him right. The horse swerved and stumbled, spilling him ass over teakettle, his carbine hitting the back of his head. He jumped up and stood, swaying, watching his mount moving toward the trees. He wondered what he was going to do, but he couldn't think it out. Dazed, his brain was off-center. Suddenly Jubal Tinker came charging past, tearing after the runaway horse. In seconds he brought him back and Elvin swung into the saddle. The whole thing took less than a half minute. Good thing, because a bunch of Indians were heading for them. Still woozy and trying not to panic, Elvin clung tight to the pommel. No sign the horse was shot. He probably stepped in a gopher hole.

★ ★ ★

Dan had slowed up to cover Jubal. As he picked up the pace, two horses collided up ahead, spilling one of the troopers. He was trying to get up when a warrior leaped off his pony, tomahawk in hand. *Whomp!* Stove in the skull with one blow. The brave went for the scalp as two others started toward Dan, who spurred Teddy into a straight-out gallop and flew past the brave's bloody work. The dead man was Jerry Malloy, a G Troop boy. Charley had traded tobacco with him back at Powder River. Whiskey cured, it was.

Teddy quickly made up the ground. Sam and Jake were in front of Jim, Jake so low in the saddle he was no more than a molehill stuck on Scar's back. Warriors started coming closer from the right, firing willy-nilly. Most were painted, and their horses as well. Jake had his Colt in his right hand. Every time an Indian rider broke off from the rest and started toward them, Jake raised the pistol, but he only fired once when one got inside of twenty paces. That one pulled up and kept his distance, at least for the moment. Then a warrior on a chestnut horse (not a pony) rode up on Sam's left, hollering something loud and wild enough to wake the dead. Sam looked back at him, pulled his Colt, and fired. Dan couldn't see if he had hit him, but the chestnut stumbled, fell back, and veered away.

Up ahead warriors began attacking ever more boldly. There was too much dust to figure their numbers, but they were letting fly a steady hail of lead with almost no return fire. At first the only ones coming close were coup-seekers making lone dashes toward the ragged column. Troopers that tried to drive off these single warriors soon emptied their Colts and their fire slackened. With that the warriors began coming closer in threes and fours, pushing the column steadily toward the left. All the while, Dan kept an eye on Teddy, watching for any sign he was hit or playing out.

Within the dust cloud ahead, Reno started obliquing toward the timber, and seconds later the column began to disappear into the trees. Dan figured that the Major had found a place where they could fort up and hold the bastards off until they got support from Custer. And Benteen should get there damn soon.

A minute later the column was in the trees. Dan was mistaken. Reno had kept going, tearing through the brush along an overgrown buffalo run, while behind him things had gone from bad to worse. The trees and brush split the column up, and the horses charged every which way, some under control, some not, their eyes bulging in desperation as they plunged through the ensnaring underbrush. Dan spotted an unseated man, whose left foot was caught in the stirrup, being dragged back toward the open flats by his crazed horse. Dan tried to help him, but Teddy got crowded into the bushes by Gus Steinbrecher charging ahead.

"Out of the way!" Gus shouted. "I go to my men in the front!"

Without thinking, Dan reined over to the side. Spent rounds buzzed over his head while he listened to the fight up ahead where Reno was. It was a loud, steady clamor of men fighting for their lives, yelling, cursing, the Indians screaming, all of it punctuated by the irregular tattoo of gunfire. Adding to the din were the exaggerated grunts and whinnies of horses driven by fear and the madness of men. Dan watched Steinbrecher beat his way past riders jamming the path up ahead, when Sam drew up beside him.

★ ★ ★

In the chaos Jake fell behind the others. A lone warrior careened out of the dust on his right, coming straight for him. *Sacré bleu!* The son of a bitch was staring at him. Jake cocked the pistol and fired—smoke but no sound. He missed. The Indian raised his rifle and fired—no sound again. The world had gone silent, and everything was moving at a snail's pace. Jake saw the Indian's weapon clearly: a Henry with brass tacks hammered into its walnut stock. The pony lunged ahead, closing on him. Jake couldn't take his eyes off the man's face with black streaks on each cheek. He fired the pistol again. Another miss while the Indian levered the next round into the chamber. Jake thumbed the Colt's hammer back again, just as Scar veered right, straight toward the Indian pony, dumbfounding the warrior and startling Jake into almost losing his pistol. He quickly pulled himself upright as Scar veered back to the left. His right foot came out of the stirrup, and he lost his balance just as Scar brushed past the first tree in a stand of young cottonwoods. The Indian vanished, the pony's momentum carrying him to the right as Jake pitched to the ground. Unhurt, he picked himself up, pistol still in hand, and watched Scar's ass end disappear into the brush. *Jésus-christ!* Remarkably, he could hear again. There were gunshots ahead and to the right, men yelling and cursing, hoofs pounding, and bullets whizzing overhead and smacking into trees. He looked back, hoping to see another trooper, but there were none, so he looked ahead and decided to make a run for it. Suddenly Scar burst through the willows, racing toward him, slowing as he got near. Grabbing hold, Jake half-leaped and half-yanked himself up and into the saddle.

"You come back for me," he said, leaning forward to stroke the horse's neck. "Thanks, but how come you do that?"

Chapter 21: The Race to the River

HAVING CAUGHT UP TO Jubal, Dan looked over at Sam. He sensed that fear had touched the lad for a moment, triggered by the imploring eyes of a downed M Troop Bay reduced to a quivering, bleating half ton of helplessness.

"Reno's heading for the bluffs," Dan said. It was a guess, but he was trying to divert Sam's attention and dampen his qualms. "We can hold 'em off all day up there."

"Iffen we git thar afore … giddown!" Jubal yelled as he yanked the reins back and fired at a young brave who appeared suddenly above the brush and fired at Sam, who shot back but missed, as did Jubal. The brave disappeared. Sam spurred Blaster into a fast trot, leaving Jubal behind as Prince lunged off the path into a tangled patch of roses and mulberry bushes.

"Damn it, horse!" Jubal cried, pulling the animal around. "Git yer ass back on the trail. We gotter catch up!"

Seconds later a bullet smashed into Prince's mouth, sending him crashing to the ground. Jubal sprung out of the saddle as the horse rolled onto one side, his massive chest heaving, the bulging eyes staring fearfully, maybe ready to glaze up. Jubal looked around for help, but suddenly Prince kicked out, thrashed his legs around, and lurched to his feet. Muddleheaded, he stood, swaying only a little, seemingly sound except for the crimson bubbles swelling out of his nostrils with each exhalation.

"Thank you, horse," Jubal said, swinging up into the saddle. "I surely 'preciate you gittin' up like thet." He spurred Prince forward, reloading his pistol as they went.

★ ★ ★

Elvin Crane realized he was trembling, scared to the bone. Why not? Bullets were flying by so close he could reach out and touch them, for Christ's sake. Indians were everywhere, firing from the woods, even charging into the column ahead, which wasn't moving anywhere near fast enough. He had Jack Cobb on his left, which was good, because by then most of the shots were coming from that direction. Funny, it felt like he was getting away with something, a lucky break maybe he didn't deserve, but that was nonsense. It was every man for himself. He hunched down in the saddle and reined his horse ever closer to Cobb, the way a cub stays close beside the wounded she-bear.

★ ★ ★

Troopers reined up as everything ahead got in a tangle. The column abruptly broke into a trot, and Dan saw that Reno was racing directly to the river. Goddamn it, he was right! They were running for the bluffs. He would have been happier if the Major had gotten things organized first, but at least they had an objective now.

Men from all three companies were in the mix together. Where was Jake? Looking around, Jim spotted him far back, coming out of a patch of willows, looking every which way for hostiles. The column slowed, a good thing because Storm had to shy away from a man running on foot ahead of him. Jim had his Colt in hand when a young brave on a red roan broke out of a strand of cottonwoods. He looked barely fifteen and was carrying a six-foot lance. He went straight for Charley, singing his high-pitched wail, coming on so fast that he had the lance ready to hurl before Jim could yell a warning, but Charley was fast, turning in the saddle and shooting him high in the chest. The boy fell back and slid from the pony as it veered off into the bulrushes. The din around them softened for a minute. Looking back again, Jim saw Jake move off into another patch of willows. Damn it, he was heading too far left to reach the ford.

The men reached a small clearing where a G Troop sorrel went down with a busted right foreleg. The trooper's bunkie muscled his mount around and gave the man a lift up behind, but his horse reared, then bolted ahead, spilling the rescued rider off his rump. The man got up fast and was surprised to find a riderless mount standing quietly beside him, grazing on a patch of brown grass like it was just another June afternoon. The trooper swung himself up and went after his friend, whose horse was still giving him a hard time. Nobody had time to kill the horse with the busted leg.

Six men from M Troop charged into the clearing, a sergeant in the rear. They looked relieved to see Jim and the others. Then a cluster of warriors in the trees behind and to the right let fly a volley of shots. Each soldier spurred his horse while scrunching down in the saddle, but one pulled up, turned, and returned fire. *Thwak-wack!* Two rounds struck him in the neck. Dead, he started falling to the side, but his right boot stuck in the stirrup, keeping him in the saddle, slumped over to the left at an inhuman slant with blood cascading over the down-turned face.

In the next open space a horse with an empty saddle galloped across and brushed against another, upsetting the rider, who had to grab hold of his horse's mane. The first animal raced off in a frenzy, forcing a charging warrior to veer off from his attack on a dismounted trooper, who was running for a horse another man held for him.

Jack Cobb appeared from somewhere. Two shots from a Winchester rang out from the trees nearby on the left. Both Jim and Dan whirled and fired. They couldn't see the shooter, but Jim thought they might have discouraged him. Coming up behind, Jubal sent another pistol round into the woods. All their efforts were futile. Two more braves joined the first one and fired off another volley. The troopers spurred their horses, but Jack Cobb's reared up suddenly and turned to the right before straightening out. No wonder the animal jumped; one of the Indian's shots had creased his back just behind the croup. Another volley from the trees sent several more rounds whizzing by. Cobb slumped and grabbed the pommel with both hands, the fiber gone from his spine, his shoulders hunched as he tried to hang on. Jim urged Storm ahead and grabbed for Jack's bridle but couldn't quite reach it. Damn! Blood on Jack's shirt below the ribs, him leaning into that side, pawing at it like he'd been burnt with a hot iron. He raised his left hand but looked to be in a trance, his face chalky, mouth bubbling red. He said something Jim couldn't make out as his horse sprang ahead, then swerved left into the trees, Jack hanging on as it raced out of sight underneath the shady cottonwoods and into the brush beyond, heading downstream. Unable to help, Jim slowed and Dan came up on his right. Elvin was on Dan's other side, tight up against him. His face was gray, like a day-old corpse.

Jim looked at him and said, "Scary, ain't it?"

In a flash Elvin's face turned red with fury. "Wha'd you say that for? An' where's Bull, huh? You seen him?"

* * *

Finally the brush opened up, giving Dan a chance to look ahead. The squad was pretty much together, although stymied for the moment by the tangle of riders ahead. Bull came through the willows, talked with Jim for a second, and then swung to the left and went forward. Charley was beside Jubal when three cavalrymen crashed through the brush and blocked Dan's view. Jubal's horse was blowing pink and favoring his nigh foreleg. In came Elvin, Sam, and Jim—no sign of Ernst or Jake. *Christ Almighty!*

Chapter 22: Escape to the Bluffs

Bent low in the saddle, Bull and Charley turned toward the river just as three men broke away from Reno's ford and moved downstream. Two warriors on the far bank opened up on them. The two men responded with a volley of pistol shots, and the Indians backed off. Three other braves appeared a little farther downstream, but Sam, Jubal, and Dan drove them back with their carbines. Sam hit one of their ponies but it didn't go down. Then Jake appeared unexpectedly from behind a patch of willows.

"What happened?" Jim asked.

"Fell off my horse, but he come back."

"You see Ernst?" Jim asked.

"He ain't here?"

"No. Okay, let's go!"

About sixty yards downstream, the new ford looked inviting, a sloping bank on the near side. Crossing, Bull rode into a hole on the far side, requiring a Herculean effort by his horse to get out. Bull explored a bit before waving Charley over, pointing to a spot some six yards farther down where the climb out looked easier. Unslinging his carbine, he looked for any warriors making a move toward him and the others.

As Charley started across, a trooper's body floated down on the east side and snagged on the branch of a dead tree. Face down, there was no telling whose corpse it was. Upstream the fight at the ford raged on; any bullets that came downstream were spent.

Charley dismounted with his carbine as Bull started toward

the bluffs. Next in line, Elvin hesitated, prompting Jubal to get after him.

"Gitty up, boy!" he shouted. As Elvin looked back at him, the horse heeded Jubal's command, leaping into the water and nearly unseating the dolt. Jubal wasted no time in following him. Prince was still blowing pink bubbles.

Sam was next. Blaster plunged into the water, his momentum carrying him into midstream, front hooves thrashing as they searched for the bottom, propelling him forward. In that instant a warrior jumped his pony straight out of the willows into the water, close enough to blind Sam with the splash of it. Wiping his eyes, he saw the pony standing still in the water a scant six feet away. In the next magically drawn-out instant, it was as if Sam was staring through a telescope, registering only the sun's glint off the Henry's brass receiver, the barrel coming up to find his chest and the young brave's eye behind its sights just as the pony's skull exploded in a burst of bone and brain matter. As the animal rolled to the side, the Henry fired, the bullet howling as it missed Sam's head by a good foot. What stuck in his brain was the fiery hatred in the Indian's eye as he slipped into the muddied water.

Blaster kept churning and went up the far bank with convulsive leaps and then off at the gallop toward Bull, merging into the line of men hurrying across the hundred-yard bench to the hill. The column was climbing a very steep hogback. From thirty yards off it looked even steeper. To the left a narrow ravine was less daunting, but no one was moving toward it. The hogback made for slow going, making them tempting targets for Indian sharpshooters above the ford. Another twinge of fear! *What?* He'd read that fear vanished once the action started, but this was the third damn time. Blaster turned toward the hogback downstream that looked easier. Sam yanked him back in line.

Unexpectedly he recalled hearing Charley shoot. Fear grabbed his solar plexus! He couldn't breathe! *Lord, what if Charley had missed?*

Blaster was laboring so Sam dismounted and trudged upward,

his boots sinking into the powdery soil. It was like climbing in new-blown snow, but this was a sunbaked day in Montana Territory. His mind's eye seized again on the savage hatred in the Indian's glare. He shook his head to let loose of it, then desperately tried to picture the pony's skull exploding in a pink-and-gray spray of flinders, blood, and specks of brain, but there again was the man's withering hatred. *Why must it play over and over and over?*

Dan had to hand it to Jake. He had plenty of sand and he soldiered well. There he was, looking uncertain, but he trusted his mount and didn't hesitate, just laid his face against Scar's neck, grabbed the pommel with his free hand, and put the spurs to him. The horse leaped forward into the water, took in a gulp or two before gathering himself, and lunged again and again until he reached the far bank, where he churned for a second and catapulted himself up and out of the river, then slowed.

"Scar, you keep going!" Jake hollered, spurring hard. He looked up at the towering bluff. "*Sacramère,* that's a fuckin' cliff!" he shouted, and then suddenly angled toward the less-demanding hogback to his left.

"Jake Picard!" Jim yelled. "There's Sioux up there! Follow Streeter!"

Dan was about to cross when Charley hollered to hold up. He resumed firing at a troublesome Indian in the bulrushes upstream. Dan steadied Teddy, massaging his poll, waiting. Blood tinted the brighter patches of water in the speckled light beneath the cottonwoods, catching his eye. Then Charley waved and Teddy leaped, with Jim and Storm right behind. On the far side Charley had already mounted and the three of them headed for the bluffs, catching up to the thin column, while upstream men still fought their way across the river.

Reaching the base of the hill, they waited briefly for those ahead to get a little higher.

"Good shot," Dan said to Charley. "The one with Sam."

"Yeah," he replied, still scanning the brush for snipers.

Most of the troopers led their horses up the steep grade,

sometimes dropping back a bit to prod them ahead, using pistol barrels as goads. Near the top, a Bay took a round just behind the shoulder. His foreleg gave way and he tumbled down, over and over while the trooper stood helpless, watching through the dust as his mount fell freely the last thirty feet, forcing men below to scramble out of the way. It hit the ground with a resounding whomp.

The horse's fall made the climb look more dangerous, but no one slowed. The earth gave way under each footstep; sometimes solid purchase was six, eight inches down. Teddy strained mightily, huffing and groaning with each lunge upward as the baking sun doubled the weight of everything.

A third of the way up they paused to catch their breath. Sweat streamed into Dan's eyes. He wondered about Ernst, then gave a yank on Teddy's reins and started up again. It was getting even steeper. He slipped a bit and never did get straightened up, finishing the climb bent over, almost on hands and knees. There he lurched to the side and sank to the ground, in desperate need of air, cool fresh air. There was none in the unrelenting heat.

Jim staggered up and dropped beside Dan, puffing.

"Sumbitch, what a climb," he said, pulling out his watch. "Near ten after four."

"That all?" Dan said, struggling for air. Only an hour since they had started the charge down the valley—seemed more like three. He pushed himself up on one elbow. Down below men were still racing for the bluffs.

From where they were it was easy to spy out the warriors waiting near the top of the hogback Jake had started for. Fortunately, Reno had done something right for a change; he'd spotted those Indians and led most of his troopers to the right. Dr. DeWolf, the surgeon, and his orderly had paid for not following his lead. Their corpses lay out in the open. The hostiles must have grabbed up their horses.

* * *

It was almost quiet. Charley guessed that most of the Sioux had gone downstream. He could hear gunfire from there, some three miles distant. Springfields, but a lot more from their own pieces, including a Sharps buffalo rifle, from the sound of it.

★ ★ ★

Old Prince was used up. Bleeding steadily now, he staggered off to the left and looked back at Jubal, perplexed. An immense shudder ran through him and his forelegs gave way; he went down in front, the shudder fading. Jubal started toward him, unholstering his Colt when Prince let go and crumpled onto his side. His last breath left a blood bubble that burst as Jubal came close and said, "Sorry, horse, yew was a good one."

★ ★ ★

Elvin let his mount go free, but Jim told him to take the reins again.

"But he ain't goin' nowhere," Elvin whined.

"Shut up an' git hold of him," Jim said. Elvin was pissed aplenty, with a hard-ass look on his face, but he didn't push it. Jim guessed that for once his pea brain worked.

Meanwhile, Jubal was already jawing about the climb. "Tarnation," he said, putting the cork back in his canteen. "Thet was 'bout straight up."

"No, it wasn't," Sam said, mopping his head with a bandana. "No more than a sixty-degree slope to it."

"What're yew?" Jubal asked. "A 'spert on hills of a sudden? Maybe it wa'n't straight up, but 'twas jist shy of it."

"No," Sam said. "I'm no expert, but I've worked on a few roofs. It's sixty degrees at the most."

"Sometimes yew come 'cross bodaciously sure of things."

"I just know about slopes," Sam said.

At that moment Dan thought the boy could be insufferable. Here he was talking about sixty degrees, and it wasn't more than forty. *Christ Almighty!* Some men had ridden up the damn hill. He looked at Jim, who shrugged and kept his mouth shut—a smart move. A steeper angle gave men more to be proud of, and they would need all the bluster to be found pretty soon. Bluster mixed with being furious, they would need a lot of that, and plenty more cartridges. The pack train had better find them and soon.

⋆ ⋆ ⋆

Looking up, Jim watched the thin column winding its way up the broad slope to the ridge, a hundred feet above, a trek of maybe seven hundred yards. High ground was good ground. He only hoped it fell off on the other side. They would need all the help the terrain could give, what with the men they had lost below.

"Okay, boys, move out," he said, standing up.

"I'll catch up, if it's all the same with yew," Jubal said. "I seen a little Bay in thet ravine over there."

"Go ahead," Jim said as they started moving again.

Chapter 23: Left Behind

ERNST HURRIED UP THE path after Sergeant Steinbrecher, his knee still aching. He was a scant two meters from the timber's edge when he tripped over a root and sprawled forward through a mess of half-dead bullberry bushes, the wiry branches and twigs whipping at his eyes. Struggling out of their clutches, he squinted at the open bottomland before him. The sun burned through the dust, halfway through its afternoon descent.

Two troopers galloped past from right to left, then two more, followed by another, all five keeping close to the timber. His eyes still blurry, Ernst made out the shapes of their pursuers in the dust. More than fifty had poured out of the village.

He wiped his eyes. Thirty meters to his right oblique, a lone cavalryman stood behind his dead horse. He was an older man with a swooping mustache, grizzled, short, and wiry, taking aim and firing his Springfield. Farther out, eight mounted Sioux milled around, yelling their mind-searing screams and shooting arrows at the old trooper. Two carried rifles. Ernst stood transfixed—the scene reminded him of a painting he'd seen somewhere. Trying to help the man, he reached around for his carbine before remembering he'd left it broken on the path. Fumbling nervously, he unholstered his Colt; a diversion might give the man time to run for the trees.

Events moved relentlessly toward the inevitable. Ernst raised his pistol skyward. It went off, startling him. An arrow hit the cavalryman in his left thigh, and he jerked and twisted halfway around as he sagged to one knee behind the horse's carcass. Ernst's

Colt went off again. The cavalryman reloaded his carbine and fired it but evidently hit nothing, as two warriors commenced a powerful charge, one on a buckskin and the other on a roan. Ernst fired into the air again, this time deliberately. The cavalryman fired his pistol twice at the two charging ponies—no damage. He aimed the Colt carefully and fired again. The buckskin slowed but still came on. The old trooper paused and stared at his Colt. The second rider pulled up and slid off the roan, an old Spencer in hand. Watching him, Ernst fired again into the sky, then once more. The trooper glanced toward him and turned back to fire again. This time the buckskin's forelegs crumpled. Its rider leaped to the ground, running toward the man, coup stick thrust forward. The old soldier raised the Colt and aimed at him, but the other brave fired his rifle. *Crack!* The shot hit the old trooper squarely in the chest. As he fell backward, the first warrior touched him with the stick and then was on him, his chilling song crowding out every other sound.

Ernst's mind struggled to crawl from under the weight of what had happened. A charging pony and a vigorous old trooper were gone, instantly transported to deathly still. War was killing. His grandfather told it. Other men died today, but he hadn't seen them go down. Maybe what shook him was that he couldn't help because he wasn't *ein Krieger.* Or was it seeing a man refuse to give in to the certainty of death, fighting to the last, the futility of his efforts failing to diminish the splendor of his courage?

Sadness swept over Ernst like the fingers of a gentle wave spilling over a child's sand castle. Holding the long-barreled revolver by his side, he literally swayed, then caught his balance, replaying the scene in his mind: the cavalryman standing, firing; the painted warriors riding, leaping, screaming; the horses running, swerving, crashing down; the dust swirling up. Man and pony so magnificently alive, then instantly dead. In an unseeing trance, he stood on the timber's edge, his mind's eye held captive by those stark images of finality playing again and again, his sorrow a burden.

Suddenly it hit him. The Indians were out to kill him too. He scrambled back out of the light and found a path leading upstream and away from the flats.

"Gott sei Dank," he mumbled. They were out to kill him, yet dying was unthinkable. Ducking into the timber, he ran as fast as he could. But despite his concentration on staying alive, the image of the old trooper firing away remained vivid, demanding a quick look-see every quarter minute.

★ ★ ★

Following the twisting, barely discernible path, he found the runaway sorrel lying on his side, his front hooves feebly raking the dirt. His rear quarters quivered, the spine severed at midback by a .58-caliber musket ball. Bewilderment lay behind his bulging corneas, while his heart pumped blood from an ugly neck wound into the darkening earth. The breaths were heaving, desperate, irregular, but Ernst knew the animal would live another hour. Disregarding caution, he killed the horse with a shot to the head, glad to find good use for his Colt. Unexpectedly remembering Jake's admonitions, he smiled and reloaded it.

The ford was several hundred meters away. He tried going around the Indians, but there were too many of them, so he crawled into a thicket to catch his breath. Two Indian riders passed three meters away. He headed downstream, staying low, pausing frequently to scan the brush. Although he was farther away, the noise from the ford had grown more clamorous.

Minutes later he spotted four mounted braves near the river's edge. One held the reins of a G Troop sorrel, blood smearing its thigh. The warriors rode their ponies across the river and rested, talking. Hoping they would go upstream, Ernst was scurrying from tree to tree, getting closer, when he tripped and fell into a deep trough, landing silently on the spongy ground. He peered over the lip of the ditch. A fifth Indian had met the others. Talking excitedly, he pointed downstream. Ernst strained, as if he could will them to move away so he could cross—they didn't.

Hearing a moan, Ernst turned and there was Jack Cobb behind a clump of willows. He was lying on his side in the heavy grass, arms wrapped around his shot-through chest. His breathing came in convulsive gasps, greedily sucking in air, but it whistled through the blood-soaked shirt. Crawling over, he took his knife and cut away the shirt, revealing a bloody puncture. Beside it a three-inch gash along his ribs oozed more blood. Jack stared into his eyes, garbling through the wheezing and gurgling. He frantically pawed at his pocket.

"In there is something, *ja*?" Ernst whispered. He worked his fingers in and pulled out a small leather bag with a rawhide drawstring. It held eighteen dollars and twenty-six cents, plus two twenty-dollar gold pieces and a small piece of paper. Ernst read it aloud.

"John M. Culhane. Born May 17, 1853. 274 Maple Street, Dover, Delaware. Father, Terrence J. Culhane. Mother, Eleanor Flaherty Culhane."

Jack nodded. With his left hand he pointed to his chest, nodding as vigorously as he could; the result was feeble.

"To this place I send a letter? To John M. Culhane?" Ernst asked. Jack shook his head, pointed to the paper and then back to himself. "What you say I don't know ... oh!" Ernst exclaimed. "John M. Culhane is you! Terrence *Ihr Vater,* your father? And Eleanor *Ihre Mutter? Ja.* Jack Cobb is the army name, *ja?*"

"Uh huh," Jack said, and then he gestured again and pointed to the paper in Ernst's hand. "The letter for your father and mother. Sam Streeter, he writes the English. *Und* this money I send also, *ja?*"

Jack shook his head again, trying to speak. Ernst bent, putting his ear closer.

"Elvin," Jack whispered.

"Elvin to write?"

Jack shook his head again, desperate. "Money for ..." He struggled for enough air. "Elvin," he gasped.

"*Ja*," Ernst said, finally comprehending. "This money I give to Elvin."

Whispering his thanks, Jack's smile sagged with the weariness of one who had caught sight of the end. His eyes clouded momentarily but refocused as he tried to say more and couldn't. He gestured feebly, trying to point to Ernst and then to the woods.

"I go?" Ernst asked. Jack nodded. "*Ja*, after I rest." Jack shook his head and gestured with determination.

"No, *mein Freund*. The rest I need," Ernst whispered, smiling. "I am played out. *Und* Indians there. For them I wait to go." He wet Jack's bandana from his canteen and moistened the dying trooper's mouth.

⋆ ⋆ ⋆

For Jack, life's choices had been few. At fourteen his father forced him to work in his harness shop rather than continue in school, where he'd shown with the best of them. He slaved until running off to sea at seventeen, where he spent three wretched years, sometimes suffering cruelties so humiliating he never talked of them. Half-broken, he returned to work leather, but the old man was too much, so he enlisted. Now he'd been thrown into this unholy ditch where he would die, but this time, *Goddamn it*, he would choose to do it while still conscious and on his own terms. So he let go, even while considering the slimmest of possibilities that Ernst could get him to the sawbones, who would plug the gaping hole in his chest so he could see his mother once more. How silly such notions were. Here he was dying for sure yet thinking of home, which he had left in anger three years before. It was preposterous, even funny. The laugh rose in his throat only to catch on a clot, triggering a coughing convulsion. Searing pain ripped his chest for ten seconds but ended as abruptly as it began.

He lay still, a rag doll in square-toed boots, muscles gone doughy, sensing the moistness of the earth through the back of his hand, dirt made of silt mixed with decomposing leaves, its dampness percolating up from below in June of a year marked by Montana snows as late as three weeks before. The moist coolness was as refreshing as the river's water he'd craved to slake the burning thirst now gone. They'd marched at night through alkaline dust to reach this soundless glade with shade as cool as the Delaware woods he'd left in bitter haste, set on casting his own lot at sea where corrosive shame cost him name and liberty in exchange for serving five full years or less, if death came first. It was too soon, Goddamn it! He had four years to serve as Private Jack Cobb, Seventh Regiment, United States Cavalry. The sky above darkened. What time was it? No matter—death was present. He smelled it, by God, its bitter taste on his tongue. The brightness beyond Ernst's face sank back into itself, losing its depth, the fading outline of an oversized boy whose name had slid into another place now too far away to touch.

* * *

Ernst pocketed the tiny leather bag, stuffing it down for fear it might work itself out on its own. He watched Jack's eyes change focus, looking beyond here and now, catching sight of those gone before.

There he sat in peace on the edge of battle, watching Jack take leave as his own mother had years ago. He grasped tightly the image of her face, then slipped into a fantasy of him beyond the brush and trees and far horizons to where creation does its work with no constraints of time and space; all the while the pastels swirled to embrace them both in that ditch—how long he couldn't tell, but just enough for Jack to catch hold in that other place. Regaining the present, Ernst closed the lids of the young trooper's sightless eyes, wiped his tears, and rose to leave. In the silence he sensed the warriors had left. Keeping to the brush, he headed for the river.

Halfway there it struck him—he'd forgotten to pray. With surprising grace he knelt and prayed for Jack's soul in the manner he'd been taught as a child, and then he cautiously made his way another forty meters into a thick cluster of willows. Looking up he saw troopers and horses disappear over the crest. He wished desperately to join them immediately, but his determination to live held him there. Laying down, he curled around a bush in a hollow. Faint sounds of volleys persisted from downstream. Jack had been so young. Everything had been ahead of him: tinted skies to marvel at, flowers to smell, women to love, little children to toss into the air and catch, songbirds to hear, fires to warm him, a family. This death was a senseless waste; a blasphemy brought on by man's love of war—an enduring and ugly love. Angry, Ernst thrust a hand into his pocket, reassuring himself that the paper with its precious names was still there.

The sound of four shots not far upstream. Minutes later Ernst set out, determined to reach the ford where the battalion had crossed. The faraway sounds of battle from downstream persisted. Coming out of a box elder grove, he sensed the ford was nearby. He dashed across a small clearing and into a thick grove, where he was astounded to hear his name.

"Ist das jung Albrecht?"

"Ja. Ich bin Albrecht," Ernst replied, his eyes adjusting to the shade. "Oh, it is you, *Herr Feldwebel Weihe.* Sergeant White."

"Ja, me and a dozen more, waiting for the Redskins to go," the M Troop sergeant replied. There was blood on his sleeve.

"You are hurt," Ernst said.

"Es ist nur eine Fleischwunde. Those two they hurt more. Over there is the scout Herendeen. He will lead us."

Gott sei Dank! If anyone could get them up the hill it was George Herendeen.

Chapter 24: Forting Up

THE GROUND MAJOR RENO chose was the south end of a four-mile-long curving ridge running parallel to the river. The field measured some 450 yards long and 220 yards across at its widest, a bit more than fifteen acres. Sparse grass, dry as last year's buffalo bones, with pockets of low sagebrush here and there. The final one hundred yards on the south end narrowed while rising about six feet, and then it fell off sharply toward Ash Creek. On the west the ground fell away gradually to the edge of the bluffs the men had climbed. The north end was wider and slightly higher than the south. It would take two companies to defend it. Farther north the ground sloped a little down a ways before rising for five hundred yards to a fairly high ridge. Later that spot would be called Sharpshooters' Ridge. A hollow in the center of the hilltop was deep enough to give both the animals and the wounded a bit of cover. Dr. Porter had set up a hospital and was already at work there. A shallow swale ran west to east through the hollow, then crossed the eastern perimeter and fanned out on the plain beyond. Although dry, it still had a lot of green in it from the spring rains.

On the east side the ground sloped steadily down from both the north and the south ends to a swale, where it was a good twenty feet lower. That area would be the hardest to defend. In front of it the ground barely fell off, leaving no height advantage. About 250 yards out there were two gullies where warriors could hide. A lengthy hill was another two hundred yards out. Disciplined firing would stop a charge on that side, but could the companies work together? Were the rookies trained well enough? On the skirmish line below, some of them had stood a better chance of hitting a chickadee than an Indian.

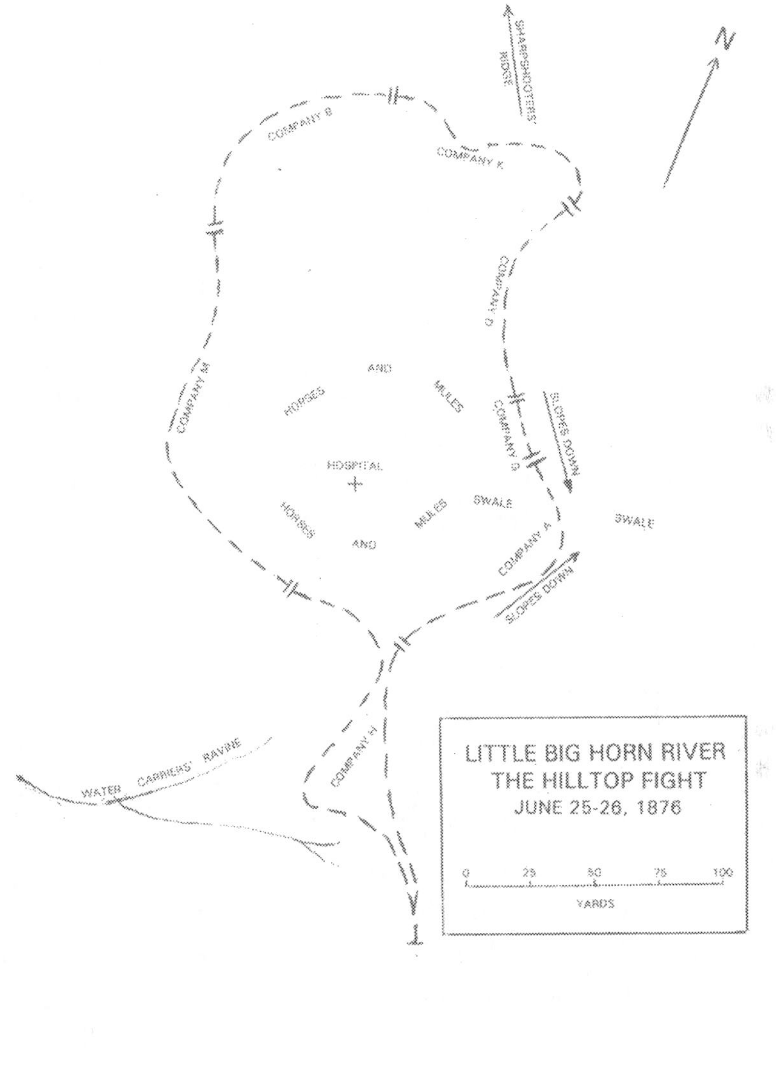

★ ★ ★

Jim returned to his men with some numbers from a quick NCO meeting. There were five officers and about one hundred able-bodied men on the hilltop. Captain Benteen ought to have some hundred and forty more. When B Troop came up with the pack train, they would have over three hundred, counting scouts and teamsters. They would need to throw up breastworks on the east side, but that would be enough to hold the Indians off until the water ran out—a disturbing thought. At the moment G Troop was down to twelve men, clustered near the wounded. M Troop was on the west side and A Troop was on the east. Hopefully Reno was working on a plan of defense. However, it sounded like the sumbitch was more concerned about Lieutenant Hodgson lying dead down below.

At four thirty Benteen arrived, for which Dan was most thankful. He assumed the hostiles were concentrating on Custer's battalion, because they could hear heavy firing from downstream. However, there was no sign that Reno wanted to move in that direction—no orders whatsoever. Instead, the Major took ten men down to the river to find Hodgson's body, and the Crow scouts left for home. *Mother of God!*

⋆ ⋆ ⋆

Jubal came up, leading the smallish Bay he'd seen in the ravine. He was greeted by a challenging holler.

"Hey, where you think yer takin' that there horse?" a skinny rookie from M Troop yelled at him. He didn't look more than seventeen but was showing teeth just the same.

"Who wants to know?" Jubal threw back, stiffening.

"*I* do, damn it," the boy snarled, his voice none too steady.

"Easy, mister. I found him down the hill a ways an' was takin' him over to the picket line," Jubal answered.

"He's an M Troop mount," the young trooper growled. His voice cracked but was no less insistent. "B'longs to my bunkie."

"I sure didn't know thet. Where's he at?"

"Ain't here yet, but it's *his* horse, damn it, not yours."

"I'd guess yer right," Jubal answered.

Jubal figured the boy's bunkie had been left down below, maybe for dead. Wrought up about it, the young rookie needed time to gather himself. At the same time, he needed a horse for himself. "What's yer name, mister?" he asked.

"Carney," the boy-man said. "Art Carney."

"Okay, and I'm Jubal Tinker from A Troop," Jubal said. "Tell you what, Art. I got myself kinder partial to this here Bay, so 'less yew wanna do it yer own self, I'll git him settled with the others. Then if yer bunkie, I mean *when* yer bunkie gits here, you send him on over to me. I'll have his horse brushed out smooth as silk. Won't be no fuss, I g'arntee." He started again toward the picket line, talking softly to the horse. The young trooper flopped onto the ground, grumbling but pacified.

★ ★ ★

Major Reno returned at 4:50 p.m. By then the heavy firing from Custer's fight had faded out. Benteen sent Lieutenant Hare back to the pack train to hurry up the mules with the ammunition. Then Captain Weir, acting on his own, took D Troop and headed north along the ridge to join Custer. Several mules carrying ammunition and two shovels arrived at 5:19 p.m. Benteen seemed to take charge of things when Reno sent Varnum down with a detail to bury Hodgson. Benteen took H and K Troops and followed Weir. Minutes later Company B and the pack train arrived. Half the Ree scouts mounted up to join Benteen; the rest left for Powder River with their captured ponies. This left Companies A, B, G, M, the wounded, and the pack train on the hilltop. By then it had been over thirty minutes since they'd heard firing from downstream, so they assumed Custer had broken off his attack.

With no breeze, the sun bore fiercely through the haze. The lower it sank the hotter it got, as if it was moving closer. It wouldn't set until nearly eight, two and a half hours away. That was plenty of time to cook men, horses, and mules clear through. Most of the canteens in A Troop were bone dry.

Amidst the heat and waiting, a tow-headed ghost suddenly appeared in the hospital area.

"Look at that," Jim said, smiling. "It's Albrecht!"

Sure enough, the German lad had just finished helping a wounded man to the hospital.

"It sure is. That oughtta perk up ole Gus," Charley said, thinking Ernst would see Steinbrecher lying not twenty feet from him, but he didn't. Instead, he turned toward the squad and spotted Jake and Sam. The next couple of minutes were downright comical. Ernst started toward his two friends in a fast walk with a little hitch in it, trying to keep from breaking into a dead run. Errnst's boyish face changed from uncertainty to relief to joy and then to a studied nonchalance as he finally struggled to mask his emotions. On the other side, Jake tried his damnedest to remain unmoved, if not sour-faced, but the best he could manage was to straighten out half of the silly-assed grin on his face, leaving his mouth lopsided. Sam let out a whoop before working hard to contain himself. Unthinkingly, he studied Ernst for signs of injury, not unlike checking out one's little brother after his first schoolyard fight.

Even Charley was grinning. Who wouldn't be happy? Relief and joy were obvious in the three rookies' movements, while the others tried to maintain an air of indifference, remembering they were soldiers in battle, a circumstance in which finding life while expecting death was the best moment in the game. Only the most hard-bitten of men wouldn't feel good seeing Ernst's boyish face flushed with the joy of reunion. Sam kept shaking his head in smiling wonder while trying to remain stoic, and Jake reached out to touch his young friend, unable to hold himself back.

Jim, Charley, and Dan weren't the only ones enjoying what they saw; half the hilltop was relieved to see a trooper return to the ranks, especially good-natured Ernst who nobody could really dislike. Maybe he couldn't handle a carbine, but he was a good, decent, and cheerful young man. On top of that, his innocent face appearing out of Death's shadow below signaled that not everyone they'd left behind was dead. In fact, they soon learned that Herendeen had led not only Ernst but twelve other men up after the hostiles moved downstream.

Jim said, "Life has a way of going on, no matter what." That summed it up for all of them.

There was no time to savor the moment because Captain Moylan called his sergeants over. The remaining companies were moving north, following Captain Benteen. A Troop would shepherd the wounded. Those who could move on their own would walk beside the horses and support the ones who rode. Able-bodied troopers would carry the rest of the wounded on horse blankets. For the next half hour the men did their best to get all the wounded moving, a nearly impossible undertaking. The best description of what happened came later from Jubal Tinker.

"After gittin' catawampously chawed up down in the valley, we set atop thet sun-broiled hill lickin' our wounds. Thar wa'n't nothin' to do, the officers too busy jawin' to give orders, yew know. Then Cap'n Moylan says we're marchin' north, our troop haulin' the wounded. We set to it right quick, fergittin' our troubles like they was yes'day's breakfast; got the walkers leanin' on each other an' propped the riders in the saddle best we could. Them boys hardly peeped, bein' happy they wa'n't left behind, which some was down below. Mebbe I shouldn't of mentioned thet, but I did. Fact is, leavin' men behind wa'n't exactly new in the Fighting Seventh. Yew might of heard 'bout Washita in '68. 'Course, down by the river Major Reno had good reason this time. He was in a hurry, yew know.

"Them what couldn't walk or ride, we used our blankets to carry. Worked in teams of four, but the idea di'n't stand up no more'n a fart in the wind. You jist couldn't git a holt. Blankets tore right outta yer fingers, no matter what. So we tried six men, and thet worked some, but yew couldn't go more'n twenty paces 'fore yer fingers would be slippin' an' yew'd hafta set the poor bastard down, or else he'd drop. I recall Jim Lawton d'rectin' us to put the carry on ole Steinbrecher—yew remember him, the hard-ass German who beat down his recruit last winter? Put him in the hospital?

Well, we grab aholt, an' Jim Lawton, he tells Bull Judd to lend a hand, but he shies off mumblin' 'bout havin' other duties. Bullshit! He jist di'n't wanna be close to Steinbrecher fer fear the sergeant would tell him what to do with his squad, which Moylan had give to Bull. Bull's the kind what piles on the bluster when he ain't sure how to go 'bout somethin' new. Fact is, he might be a good 'nuff sergeant 'cept he di'n't have Steinbrecher's ole German ways nor Jim's sensibilities. He come outta Colorado an' done reconsituated hisself into a non-cussin' teetot'ler with too many axes to grind, includin' a humungous hate fer folks of color gin'rally.

"Well, we put our backs into it but it wa'n't to be done, so Moylan, he gits Cap'n McDougall to lend us a platoon from B Troop, which made things tol'able. We still wa'n't sure how fur we'd git, but it di'n't matter none 'cause ole Charley Smrka points off to the east an' thar goes the scouts headin' south at the gallop, the same ones who'd left forty minutes earlier tryin' to hook up with Custer, an' behind 'em comes a passel of Sioux, which give us pause. Then things changed agin, real sudden-like. Me an' five others was short-steppin' with Steinbrecher, sweat pourin' down our shirt necks. Under thet sun 'twas hotter'n a whore's quim on payday. Anyways, we look up an' here's H Troop racin' straight back at us, Reno and Benteen in the van, comin' hell fer leather past us an' back to where we started from. Dan Murphy, he turns red as a rooster's top-knot an' starts cussin' up a streak, puttin' the Goddamn on Major Reno fer sure. He wa'n't the only one Reno pissed off, but Dan had a real conniption over it. Fer me, I figgered the Major would hafta pony up sometime. Jist when is the Lord's bizness, not mine.

"Anyways, Cap'n Moylan hollers out 'to the rear' so we 'bout-face jist as M Troop comes by hollerin' thet the Sioux was on their heels. At thet we picked up the pace fer sure an' had them wounded all nice and comfy back in horsepistol holler right quick. 'Bout played out we was, but them officers got us busy formin' up the line 'round the hilltop. Put A Troop back on the east side agin. Fact is, our squad had the troop's left flank on the lowest piece of ground.

White men owned thet day, the bottom of a dry wash which run onto the prairie whar the Sioux was gittin' ready to cum at us. A Troop's line run up to the knob on the south. D'rectly behind us was whar Doc Porter had the wounded in a holler up the wash. Had a tent fly fer shade. The animals was in thet bowl too, some of 'em close enough they was apt to step on our hind legs when we stretched out to stay low, which wa'n't a bad idea most of the time.

"Cap'n Benteen seemed to be in charge, what with his givin' out orders and all. He set M Troop facing west, with B Troop on their right, lookin' toward the river. H Troop was on the south end, whar the ground was more exposed, being raised up. On the east side, we was on the south end of it. What was left of G Troop was on our left, an' then after thet D Troop stretched on up to the north-most knob. Comp'ny K come back last. Fours come first with the horses, then the rest of 'em. In good order, they was, lettin' fire an' fallin' back, lettin' fire an' fallin' back, the way yer s'posed to. Thet kept the hostiles a ways behind 'em. Lieutenant Godfrey give them boys some good ossiferin'. At the last they made a run an' fell into line 'tween D an' B.

'Fore long we seen the hostiles clusterin' out thar to the east. Maybe five hunerd stood on the hillside fur enough off so they was like ants, whilst some of 'em was closer, in the draws. I recollect Sam Streeter sayin' it was twenny to seven. An hour till sundown, an' still hot as the devil's own cook stove."

Chapter 25: Holding the Ground

★ ★ ★

THE HILL JUBAL TALKED about was a rise seven hundred yards to the east. Jim had taken the left flank himself to make sure the company held contact with G Troop. He put Charley and Dan on his right and Sam at the lowest point, figuring he could pick off any warriors working their way up the swale. Jake was on Sam's right. He was tough, wouldn't get rattled, and unlikely to get buck fever. Next was Elvin Crane, with Jubal on his right to steady him if things got hairy. Jim told Jake to start bringing their saddles down to the line. They would give some cover if they kept their bellies on the ground. Bull Judd was up the line on the right, having taken over Gus Steinbrecher's squad. Ernst remained with the wounded, more valuable there than on the line.

Elvin was watching the Indians on the hill when Ernst came up from behind and touched his shoulder. He jumped.

"Goddamn it! What d'you want?" he asked, craning his neck around.

"Jack Cobb died."

"Huh? How do you know?" Elvin asked.

"I was with him. Here, for you," Ernst said, handing the little leather pouch to him. He'd already removed the paper with the names and addresses. "Jack says it is for you: eighteen dollars, twenty-six cents, and *das Gold,* two pieces."

Elvin loosened the drawstring and dug into the bag. Cobb had said something about it. Freedom money, he called it. After counting it out he pulled the drawstring tight and slipped the pouch into his hip pocket.

"Okay. What happened to him?"

"Dead by the river."

"Yeah, I knew that already," Elvin lied, almost snarling. "What're you waitin' for, Kraut? We got work to do here, so g'wan back to yer post for Chrissakes."

He turned to gaze blankly over his carbine's sights. A dozen braves were putting on a show four hundred yards in front, racing their ponies in and out of a long gully. He reached into his pocket, fingering the leather pouch. *Goddamn it! Why'd they have to shoot Jack Cobb of all people? Why not Picard?* Heavy-hearted and terribly alone, he tried to rally. *Yeah, why not Picard? Why not Murphy or Streeter? They think they know everything. Why not them sonuvabitches?*

Returning to the hospital, Ernst bumped into Jake dragging two saddles down to the line. Jake was bent over, trying to make himself a smaller target for the spattering of bullets and arrows whistling through the air. Ernst just stood there, paying no attention to the danger. Apparently Ernst's unconcern irritated Bull, because he hollered over.

"Hey, Picard! Tell Albrecht to git down!"

"Huh?" Jake said, pointing to himself. "You hollerin' at me?"

"Yeah you, Private! Tell the Kraut to git down. He's drawin' fire." Bull failed to notice Jim coming down the line.

"Goddamn, you tell him that," Jake hollered back.

"I'm the corporal, you blamed half-breed! So you tell him!" Bull yelled. "An' clean up yer language, Private! You hear me?"

"I hear you good, but I don't tell him jack shit!"

"That's insubordination, soldier!"

"So what, you son of a bitch." Jake smiled.

"Let go of it, you two," Jim cut in. "The boy ain't drawin' fire. Injuns are too far out."

"Mebbe, but what you gonna do 'bout Picard, huh?"

"Not a Goddamn thing!" Jim snapped, his patience used up.

He turned to Jake. "Go ahead, Jake. Git them saddles down to the line."

Bull was furious. "Picard may be yer man, Jim, but he was disrespectful of me. I'm takin' this to the captain when things quiet down."

"Then you are stupid," Jim growled. He started down the line, half-crouching. Slowing, he looked back at Bull. "If you want to rile Moylan up, go ahead. Just remember, he don't take kindly to corporals pissin' on wildcats."

⋆ ⋆ ⋆

Then a mule named Old Barnum with two boxes of cartridges on his back careened past Jim to browse on the few green sprigs beyond. Losing 2,000 rounds to the hostiles would be disastrous, so Sergeant Hanley mounted up, raced out and turned him back amidst a storm of lead. Relieved he'd held onto his hair, he told a packer to offload the boxes before the contrary bastard got it into his noggin to stroll down to the river for a snootful of fresh water.

⋆ ⋆ ⋆

For the first time in his life, Sam couldn't hit what he saw. He thought it might be the light. The whey-thin clouds softened the shadows, while dancing bits of smoke and dust intensified the haze, making him squint when he tried to aim. It took seconds before his eyes adjusted to give him a clear look at the smudge of a warrior who, like as not, had pulled his head back down by then.

He reached around and dragged a cross-buck packsaddle closer, then swung it up onto two cracker boxes. From this perch he was able to draw down on a warrior who was busy trying to hit a man up the line. *Judas Priest!* How could he miss at two hundred yards? The man was in plain sight, his head above the brow of a little rise. After the first shot he'd checked his sights again and then deliberately aimed low. No dust. *Judas!* Sergeant Lawton called him a sharpshooter, said something about counting on him to "kill the sumbitches." What the hell was wrong?

He slid a fresh cartridge in and closed the breech. Squinting in anticipation, Sam thumbed the hammer back, raised the gun up eight inches, and sighted in on the brave.

"Still there," he murmured, letting the front sight fall below the notch. He squeezed off the round, absorbed the recoil, and lowered himself in smooth succession. Again his eye caught no sign of dust as he lowered himself behind the saddle. Then Sam realized that all the while he was shooting, his mind was picturing the warrior at the river glaring at him with such hatred.

"Goddamn it!" he swore. Jake was staring at him from the right. "What're you lookin' at?" Sam growled.

"A good shooter gone bad."

"Think you could do better?"

"Not me, but what're you doin' wrong?" Jake asked.

"I'm shootin' high ev'ry time. Never did that before."

"Take another shot," Jake advised.

"What for?" Sam asked.

"Maybe I see what you do wrong."

"Like what?" Sam said, still flustered.

"How the hell I know that? You want some help? Shoot again."

"Just tell me your hunch."

"No."

"Why not?"

"Jésus Christ!" Jake exclaimed, shaking his head in wonder. "You're more stupid than a pig!"

"Pigs aren't stupid."

"Then how come they eat slops an' we eat bacon? Go ahead, take that other shot."

Sam didn't reply, sensing he'd lost the argument. He got set for the next shot. Unexpectedly, fear sliced through his gut and vanished instantly. He sighed, took a deep breath, rose up, aimed, fired, and then dropped down again. Jake lay on his side, staring reflectively at him. It made Sam uncomfortable.

"So what'd you see?" he asked.

"You flinch."

"What do you mean?" Sam squawked. "*You're* the flincher!"

"Uh huh, but my flinch ain't like yours," Jake replied.

"Huh?"

"My flinch. Me, I flinch back 'cause I don't like that kick. You flinch different. You think you start your head down after the shot, but you start before. Your head, it rolls right, elbow drops, left hand goes up, barrel goes up. You think if you stay up, that Injun shoot you in the head maybe."

"You're sure?"

"Yeah. You think you one sittin' duck up there. Me too," Jake offered in reply.

"I'm not that scared," Sam said, as much to himself as to Jake.

"Maybe, maybe not," Jake replied, then smiled. "You di'n't see it, but I did. You jerk down when you squeeze that trigger."

"Here they come!" Jim yelled, startling both of them. Sam fired his carbine. Jake rose up behind the boxes to aim while Sam hurried his reloading. Three mounted warriors were galloping out of a deep gully, coming straight at them. Troopers along the line were firing. Jake yanked the trigger on his carbine, but he hadn't set himself and the barrel flew up just as Sam's carbine went off. The lead pony went down in a heap, his rider sliding off and sprinting to the rear in one fluid motion, while the other two ponies wheeled around and raced back to the gully, where they disappeared.

"You got that pony for sure," Jake said. "An' you di'n't flinch."

"How come?"

"No time to think," Jake said, chuckling.

Sam resettled himself behind the saddle, keeping one eye on the gully where the riders came from. Jake was right. He'd fired without thinking, but he should have reloaded quickly and killed the unhorsed warrior.

"How d'you think the squad's doin'?" Jim asked Dan.

"Well, you were right about them attacking up the swale."

"But what about the squad?"

"They got to it quick when you hollered."

"Yeah, they drove the sumbitches off. And Sam showed us somethin'. Must of been a heart shot, pony goin' down like that."

"Must have been. There's one good thing, Jim: the Indians have to cross a lot of open ground. Gives us time for a couple shots."

"Or maybe three," Jim said. "But droppin' that pony must of give 'em pause."

"Perhaps. But they'll still try getting in closer in the grass," Dan said. "And one or two young bucks might try counting coup—at dusk, most likely."

Dan saw counting coup as risking one's neck just for bragging rights, nothing more, but young warriors believed it was worth the risk. Here a brave could crawl up inside fifty yards in the high grass without being seen, and then make a dash for the line. And his friends could give good covering fire with their Henrys and Winchesters.

He mentioned his concerns to Jim, who sent him up the slope to the north to ask Mike Martin, D Troop's first sergeant, to keep his eyes peeled for anyone slithering up the swale. He sent Jubal the other way with the same message for Henry Fehler. (Moylan had named Fehler to replace The First, who'd been wounded.) As it turned out, only two braves got closer than a hundred yards, one before sunset and one afterward.

When Dan got back, Jim said, "We're gonna need higher breastworks. Heavier, too, case they come at us hard. Maybe we can drag some dead animals down. After dark, I mean. Charley thinks the sumbitches will come at sunup."

"How come?" Dan turned and asked Charley, who'd been keeping quiet.

"The sun," he said. "They'd be comin' straight out of it."

* * *

Charley figured most of the Indians were several miles north of them, fending off General Custer. Funny thing, though—the sound of gunfire from that direction had faded out completely. The General had probably moved farther north. On the hilltop the cavalry was no threat to the village, and once they forted up, the Indians weren't about to throw their lives away needlessly, so a full-bore charge was unlikely. But in another day the troopers would have to find a way to get water, no matter what.

The Indians in the east kept up a steady stream of rounds coming at them, but they didn't have all the advantages. First, the line being so low, it wouldn't be back-lit if the men rose up to shoot. Second, there were no hollows inside of 150 yards for cover, so groups of warriors couldn't get very close. Most of their rounds still came in high. Nobody in the company had been hit—not yet. The most punishing fire came from the north. Indians pushing K Troop's retreat had settled in close enough to do some damage to the troopers' horses, however. Six or seven had been hit. Three had to be destroyed.

Judging by the sound, the Indians were using a variety of firearms. The characteristic cracks of Winchesters were easy to pick out. Occasionally one could hear the sound of an old muzzleloader. But more and more, they heard the familiar bark of Springfield carbines.

"Hey, Charley!" Jim called over. "Where'd they get them Springfields?"

"Dead troopers," Charley answered. Nothing ever rattled him.

"Sumbitches kicked our ass down there," Jim muttered. Glancing down the line, his eye settled on Elvin, who was squirming this way and that, unable to hold the same position more than twenty seconds.

"Crane!" he called out. The man failed to turn his head. "Elvin Crane, you on an ant hill?"

"Huh?" Elvin looked over, slow to realize Jim was talking to him. "No, I'm okay."

"Fidgety are you?"

"No, I ain't! Jest gettin' settled right, that's all."

"Uh huh."

Actually, the dolt was doing well enough. He wasn't frantic, like one rookie in Steinbrecher's squad, up the line. Twenty minutes before the man had started firing as fast as he could. Bull came up behind him and thumped him hard on the back of the head. It didn't knock him out, but he stopped making like a Gatling.

Chapter 26: Sounds in the Night

ABSOLUTELY DARK, IT WAS eerily quiet, just the sound of men scraping out rifle pits and keeping their voices down, as if that made it safer. Suddenly a single warrior's voice pierced the darkness. How far out was he? Dan couldn't see him. Besides, the unintelligible words demanded his attention, coming through loud and clear. He could only imagine what they meant. Each sentence started off quiet, then got louder, before trailing off into a mumble that sometimes sputtered along for longer than expected. Half the words came from somewhere down in his throat; many ended inside his nose. Each sentence had a definite beginning and end, like the man was concentrating on one thought at a time.

The warrior went on for three full minutes, a long time under the circumstances. It was as if he was telling a story—first this happened, then that, and then something else. He was agitated in telling one part of it. Then he was silent for a time, enough to make men wonder if he'd finished. Everyone on the line became more alert. Dan fingered his Colt. Maybe the warrior was creeping up, getting ready for a crazy charge, firing his Winchester as he came. Instead, he launched into what sounded like a long, drawn-out prayer lasting another half minute, followed by a string of oaths hurled, like he was cursing, calling the men every name in the book.

Mother of God! Dan had to admire the man, just as he had the painted brave standing up in the daylight. Both wove bits of time into majestic tapestries of sound. On a day of near calamity with its heat, sweat, and dust, its whipped-back branches, clawing bushes, lathered horses, and riverside mud, replete with thirst, blood, and shattered bones, searing pain and quick or drawn-out death, in these two Lakota voices there was life—pure unadulterated life. Strident, purposeful, graceful, life transcending dark and light, wounds and thirst, friend and foe. Life matching form with action. Irresistible life rebuking the murderous intentions of the day.

The two braves created crystalline palaces of time, not simply because of their courage or manner, but because of the whole of it: their words, their audacity, their indomitable humanness. Dan knew right then that in later years, when worn down by the burdens of civility, he would replenish himself with incredibly clear recollections of these two extraordinary human beings.

The tirade left some men up the line grumbling. Elvin Crane went on and on, huffing and puffing about it. Sam was indignant.

"Who in hell does he think he is, sneaking up in the dark and hollering at us?" Sam asked. "An insolent son of a bitch, that's what he is."

Jubal said, "Mebbe, but I gotter respect him."

"Why?" Sam asked.

"'Cause he spoke his piece. Don't know 'bout yew, but I wa'n't about to stand up an' tell him what I was thinkin'."

"By my faith, I'm with you, Jubal," Dan said, nursing his pipe, shielding it from the enemy.

"So, Charley, wha'd he say?" Jim murmured.

"Not sure," Charley replied, moving closer to Jim, Dan, and Jubal, like he didn't want the others to pick up on what he thought. "Couldn't get but half of it."

The sound of distant hoof beats rolled across the terrain. The men cocked their heads, trying to make out how many animals were involved and whether or not they were shod.

"Ponies," Charley said.

"Mebbe a dozen, movin' north," Jubal added, and then got back to the Indian. "I niver heard a Injun thet long-winded afore. Did he say somethin' other'n we was maggots in a dung heap?"

"He said somethin' like that," Charley answered. "But first he talked 'bout Lakota warriors killin' plenty soldiers today. He said that four times."

"Was that all?" Jim asked.

"Well, there was a long prayer before he said our goose was about cooked."

"Yes, but was there more before the prayer?" Dan asked.

"Hard to catch. He was talkin' fast, *ota* this, *ota* that."

"*Ota* means a lot, don't it?" Jim asked.

"Yeah, lots of soldiers, lots of horses, lots of rifles. Said they rubbed out *ota Wasicus,* but I couldn't tell where," Charley said.

"Prob'ly the boys we lost by the river," Jim said.

"Yeah. I thought that too. Only ..."

"Only what?" Jubal said.

"Only he said rubbed out in English, which I ain't heard from no Indian before. I'm not sure of what come after. He used a word which could mean a hundred or hundreds. Humaza said it once, talkin' about a herd of buffalo."

With that, Charley stopped talking. Jim assumed he didn't want to put words to the worst of possibilities. But of one thing Jim was certain: that Indian speaking in the dark was intent on killing a cavalryman on the morrow.

Later Charley, Jake, and Dan sat a few yards back of the line, each of them within their own thoughts, Charley with his chaw and Dan finishing his pipe. Jim had gone up the line to meet with Fehler. Jubal and Sam were asleep.

"Them guys with Corporal Ray, their heads gotta be muddled," Jake said. He was talking about Bancroft, McClurg, Harris, Gilbert, and old Andrew Conner.

"What do you mean?" Dan asked.

"They volunteered an' that don't make sense to me," Jake said. "If the sergeant ordered me to go, okay, I ain't no *pissou,* so I'd go. But I ain't gonna volunteer to go sit out there in the dark, no damn way. You could fall asleep and wake up stuck through with arrows or even worse. *Jésus-christ!* In the dark the *maudits bâtards* could snatch you up before you knew they was on you."

"Nah, they wouldn't drag you off," Charley said quietly. "Just slit your throat and leave you sitting there still asleep. Only not snorin' no more." He and Dan smiled in the dark.

★ ★ ★

Rubbing the dust out of his eyes, Sam looked up through the rotted-out timbers. Last thing he recalled was falling into an ancient cellar hole in the woods above Williamsburg. Had he killed someone? General Custer stood above, resplendent in an infantryman's dress blouse, white flannel drawers, and beaded Indian moccasins. He was shouting, the fire in his eyes so bright it almost burned. In the distance two coyotes howled back and forth, but strain as he might, he couldn't hear The General.

"What?" he called. Then he called again, loudly. "What?" The sound of it woke him up.

"Whadaya mean 'what'?" Jake asked.

"Huh?"

"You say, 'What? What?' That a dream?"

"Ayuh. Guess I dropped off. Uh, how long—"

"Just five, ten minutes. Don't worry, nothin' goin' on."

"That's good," Sam said, relieved. "Guess I better check the horses."

"I'll do that. Gotta stretch my legs."

"Okay. See how Ernst's doing while you're up there."

★ ★ ★

Jake returned ten minutes later to say he'd seen Major Reno chasing three troopers away from the supplies. They were probably looking for tins of peaches for the juice. He hadn't seen Ernst, so Dan and Charley headed up to the hospital. Jake went along. They found Ernst talking German with Sergeant White. White was a good man. Despite the nasty wound to his elbow, he was helping Ernst care for the men with more serious wounds. White was also tough. Court-martialed out for threatening a trooper, he came back in a year later.

"How's Gus Steinbrecher?" Charley asked him.

"Strong but it's hurt bad, his leg," White said

"Hope he don't lose it," Charley said. "He's gotta soldier, that Gus."

"Gus? *Er ist in Krieger!*"

"That's for damn sure," Charley said. "Anyway, we're gonna take a look up by M Troop."

They hunkered down behind two Company M men deepening their rifle pit. They could hear the faint splashes of ponies in the river down below. Suddenly a bugle sounded from quite a ways off to the north.

Surprised, Jake asked, "What call was that?"

"Maybe from Custer's bunch," one of the diggers said. He was a young rookie. "Probably lost their bugler an' they got a man blowin' it best he can so they don't git shot comin' in."

"Not likely," Charley muttered.

"Well, some in K Troop seen troopers comin' this way."

"They seen 'em?" Jake asked.

"That's what I heard," the man said. "'Course, they coulda 'magined it."

"A man's eyes will play tricks this night," Charley said. He looked off to the right, down the slope, and then further right toward the ridges to the north. The strange bugle call cut through the night again. All down the line men stirred, wondering if it was Custer. An officer near Reno's command shouted an order, then another. Other voices called, and then there was a flurry of activity around Reno's command. A minute later a bugler from there sounded stable call, followed by a set volley of shots in rapid succession.

"Tryin' to call 'em in," the trooper said. The first bugle failed to answer.

"What you think?" Jake asked Charley.

"A brave foolin' with our heads."

The breeze shifted, bringing more sounds from down below. Drums beat steadily behind the strange singing with its high-pitched tremolos. Mournful wails sounded, sometimes a single voice melded with another, then joined by a third. An occasional gunshot broke through the eerie cacophony from the village, where bonfires lit up the lodges around them.

"Thet singing's weird," said the older trooper. "Plain unnatural. Them's scalp songs. Gits me recollectin' Chancellorsville, how Jackson's boys come chargin' outta the brush hollerin' thet infernal yell they had. Skeery, like it wa'n't human."

"That ain't scalp songs," Jake said, thinking of when he and his brother stayed with their mother's people.

The younger trooper turned his head. "They sure in hell are," he said.

"Maybe not," Charley said. "Maybe some young braves whoopin' it up, but ..."

"But what?"

"But I ain't sure what they're doin'," Charley said. "You boys have a good night." He turned and started to move toward H Troop. Twenty paces down the line he stopped, listening again.

"I first heard songs like that after Washita. You remember, Dan? Don't know what it is, but it's touched me ever since," he said.

"Whaddaya mean?" Jake asked.

"You know what I'm sayin'. It's like you can't not listen."

"Uh huh, that way they go on."

"Yeah. Humaza says some songs got no words, just sounds, animal sounds—even sounds from other places, like their spirit world. You understand that stuff?"

"No," Jake said. "But the songs, they're uh, good."

"Good?"

"Uh huh. I heard 'em before, a long time ago, up north. I like 'em, even the wailin'."

"Yeah, the women wail like that," Charley replied, his eyes not straying from the village. "They lose somebody, I guess they carry on real hard."

They stood there a couple more minutes before the breeze let up and the sounds faded.

"Gotta get back now," Charley said.

"How come?" Jake asked.

"Catch some shut-eye. Be light 'fore long."

"Shut-eye? Goddamn, I forgot that."

— Chapter 27: Second Day on the Hilltop —

* * *

JUNE 26, 1876

In the dream Sam swore to God he'd get home, even though the howling wind piled the drifts higher than ever across the vast meadow, making it nigh well impossible to get across. Fifteen below but keep moving! There! That knoll ahead, the back side of the sugar bush. He'd be drinking water at home in twenty minutes. Was that thunder? Not in January. He tripped and sprawled into the snow. Don't rest, you need water! He tried to push himself up, but someone held him down.

"What are you doing?" he muttered, trying to breathe with his face in the dirt. Dirt? "Damn it, I'll kill you," he said, rolling over. He reached for his knife, but a hand clamped on his wrist. The son of a bitch stared at him with no face.

"You stay down!" Jake said, crouched beside him. "They shootin' again."

"Okay," Sam mumbled, the dream sliding away as he dug in the pocket for his watch. "Almost three." It was barely light enough to see.

"Yeah. They start right after reveille."

"Reveille? I didn't hear it."

"You sleep damn good. Three, four bugles blow same time. Woke them Sioux up, I think."

★ ★ ★

The progression of dawning moves faster than what one would expect. Ernst finished changing Sergeant White's bandages just as the first colors of dawn appeared—pale blue beyond light gray stretches of cirrus drifting over from the west. Down lower, bits and pieces of cumulus hurried toward the southeast, still clinging to the gloom of night. Without warning a brilliant orange appeared, spreading skyward so rapidly he could track its rise as it tinted the high cirrus, leaving the scudding wool packs below an ominous gray, but within a minute the entire eastern sky melded into a fiery orange interspersed with patches of robin's egg–blue. Closer to the horizon, the orange moved more deliberately, sliding over the gray. Once the brilliance reached its height, the process reversed itself. Straight overhead, the orange disappeared in an instant. In five minutes all that remained was a band of pale yellow-orange above the far-off mountains in the southeast, as the sun's giant crown showed above the earth's edge, quickly taking over the show, diluting the surrounding blue as the high cirrus thinned out and the remaining wisps of gray slipped off to the south and out of the picture while the entire sun sat on the horizon. The sun's awesome power warmed Ernst's face as it started baking the land and everything on it.

★ ★ ★

Captain Benteen had ordered every bugler on the hill to blow reveille, supposedly to make sure the Indians knew they were still there and in force. They knew, all right, and opened fire immediately. It was steady too, much of it coming from Sharpshooters' Ridge to the north. Only scattered shots came from the east; in the dim light signs of the Indians out there were blurry wisps of smoke, leaving nothing to shoot at.

"You two got plenty cartridges?" Jim asked, moving behind the line with an ammunition-stuffed haversack.

"Yes," Sam said, yawning. "We filled our belts last night."

"Git some sleep?"

"Enough," Jake said. "Them Injuns come hard today?"

"Maybe. Keep a sharp eye out. They charge, shoot the ponies like yesterday," Jim said.

"Corporal Roy and the others still out there on picket?" Sam asked.

"No, they came in at reveille," Jim replied, moving on to the right.

"Going to be another scorcher," Sam said, shaking his nearly empty canteen. "How much water do you have?"

"Two, three swallows maybe," Jake said. "Them horses, how long they go with no water?"

"Lord knows. I've never seen them stretched out for water. Not a full day, anyway."

"That's first time you don't know 'bout horses."

"Really? Well, if the Indians decide to shoot 'em we won't find out today."

"Indians shoot us and take the horses," Jake said.

By then it was light enough to make out more than a hundred hostiles on the long hill, with fifty more riding back and forth and still out of range. The crawlers in the grass were shooting regularly. It was hot already, and the water situation was worrisome. Thirst is a physical thing. It will gnaw and scratch at the gut and the brain and neither training nor grit can stop the craziness once it starts.

★ ★ ★

Ernst moved from one wounded man to the next. *Der Feldwebel* wasn't alone in maintaining a stoic front. Even those in excruciating pain bit down on it. And despite their growing thirst, few complained loud enough to bother the others.

The Indians' steady fire tore new holes in the hospital's tent-fly. Another mule went down without a sound.

"Albrecht!" Steinbrecher hollered. "Come here!"

"Ja!" He stumbled as he hurried to the sergeant's side. "What do you need, *Herr Feldwebel?"*

"Need? You call me Sergeant. This is *Amerika. Und* be careful—you think the Indian he can't kill you? Keep the cabbage head down!"

"But, Sergeant—"

"No! You stay alive! The wounded need you!"

As if to emphasize the point, a round from Sharpshooter's Ridge whistled by Ernst's head, followed by a sustained fusillade from the east. A mule brayed piteously, his left foreleg shattered. Someone hustled over to shoot him behind the ear.

"Is there water left?" Steinbrecher asked when the volley let up.

"Very little, I think."

"Listen to me. A detail will go later to the river. You do not volunteer, *ja?"*

"Ja, Herr Sergeant."

* * *

Dan watched young braves racing their ponies back and forth, barely in range, trying to get troopers to waste ammunition. Closer in, warriors crawled closer and popped up and down in the tall grass, doing their best to draw fire. He watched one hummock in particular, about a hundred yards out where the ground on the left sloped down into the swale, making a distinct crest. The grass out there remained high. Beside him Charley was getting ready, wiping cartridges with a rag, then setting them on a cracker box in front of him. It was a quarter past five.

"Okay," Charley said, setting his eye behind the sights.

Dan focused on the hummock. A half minute later a rifle barrel slowly came up. Then the warrior popped up.

"Now!" Dan said. Charley fired, knocking the Indian back and down.

"Think you hit him?" It was Jim, back from Moylan's NCO meeting.

"Not sure," Charley said. "So wha'd you find out?"

"H Troop's catching it hard from the north, and there's heavy fire comin' up on the west side. Moylan was surprised they didn't come at us out of the sun."

"What about water?" Dan asked.

"Benteen says we're gonna find a way. Seems like he's runnin' the show, not Reno."

"Good," Charley said.

"Uh huh. Gonna be a long day," Jim said.

"Already has been," Dan said, his eye still on the hummock. "Four of them bunched up out there, we think."

Jim settled into his spot beside Charley. Ten minutes later three warriors rose up suddenly from the hummock and started pumping rounds into the line. Half the shots were high, and the others weren't concentrated on any particular spot. The men returned fire but didn't register a hit. For the next hour the Indians let loose about every ten minutes, with the line answering them. Finally one warrior appeared to fall.

"We might of got one," Jim said.

Several minutes later a rider raced toward the line, expertly zigzagging toward the hummock, while Indian fire erupted all across the front, giving him cover. When he pulled up, two braves quickly lifted a third onto the pony, turned instantly, and dashed back to safety.

"Holy Geehosaphat!" Tinker yelled from up the line, but the last part of it was drowned out by another fusillade.

Jim pulled out his watch. It was past seven thirty.

"How's yer water holdin' out?" he asked Dan.

"Mine's nearly gone. Yours?"

"Gettin' low. You got water, Charley?"

"Enough. We'll make it."

"Until when?"

"Till they leave," Charley said quietly.

"Leave?"

"Yeah, they gotta leave soon," Charley said, still watching the slope out front. "Their ponies gonna need grass. An' Gibbon's comin'."

"What about Custer?" Jim asked.

"Don't know 'bout him."

* * *

Sam was frustrated. The Sioux let loose whenever they chose, forcing him and Jake to hug the ground behind the cracker boxes and stinking dead animals. But he kept trying, getting in a few shots, missing every one. Finally a pair of feathers emerged above the grass 140 yards out. A minute later the warrior wearing them rose up quickly to snap off a shot.

"You see that?" Jake asked. "That guy stuck them feathers in a calv'ry hat. And he's using a Springfield carbine."

"Don't worry," Sam said. "We'll let him take one more shot, and I'll get ready while he reloads. When he comes up again I'll nail the son of a bitch."

For the next two minutes they watched as the two feathers moved just enough to let them know the brave had reloaded and was biding his time. Then he popped up and shot again; this time the round creased the top of one of the boxes as it buzzed past.

"Okay, *gros boque*. Next time we get you."

For the next two minutes Sam held his sights on the spot. When the feathers appeared, he lined up on them as they rose, hesitated, and then rose some more. *Blam!* Sam fired then reached for Jake's carbine.

"You got him!" Jake cheered. "That hat go right back down."

"You sure?" Sam asked, peering through the thinning smoke while aiming again.

"Yeah. Oh, oh, them feathers coming up again. Git ready."

This time Sam took his time in squeezing off the shot, and then he crouched down.

"Shit!" Jake cursed.

The hat with the two feathers was waving back and forth above the grass, held aloft by the barrel of the Indian's Springfield.

"He fool us for sure," Jake said, smiling.

"Son of a bitch," Sam grumbled. "They're a lot smarter than I thought." Disgusted, he slumped down and reached for a fresh cartridge.

"You're learning," Dan said from behind him.

* * *

The butcher's bill always finds a way to grow. Six men on the line were killed outright that morning. More than thirty new wounded showed up at the hospital. Some were able to return to the line, but a number remained and one died hours later. The Indians' fire never let up for long. There were no more deaths in Company A, but Jacob Deihle caught a round in the face, and George King was hurt bad enough to raise doubts as to whether he'd survive.

Company H's problem stemmed from the fact that its ground fell off steeply on the south and west, making it easy for the hostiles to creep up close. By nine o'clock in the morning warriors on the west side were crawling up the ravines and getting too close to the company. Troopers had to stretch out on their bellies along the rim to keep them at bay, but this left their backsides fully exposed to the hostiles on Sharpshooters' Ridge. True, it was inaccurate and much of it spent, but it did cause a batch of wounds. And it was unsettling. It was no surprise that some men pulled foot for the hollow where the wounded and the animals were.

In A Troop Cornelius Cowley went berserk from thirst. They bound him with rope and took him to the hospital. Figuring that others might break before long, Jim sent Dan up to headquarters to ask if they wanted volunteers for a water detail.

Chapter 28: The Water Detail

Returning down the slope Dan ran into two men dragging a fresh corpse back from the line. One side of the head was covered with blood.

"What happened?" Dan asked Andrew Conner, him from the Auld Sod. He sat leaning against an aparejo behind a double course of boxes.

"Ah Daniel, there was Frank Mann, the packer. God rest his soul. Couldn't stay out of the fight," Andrew said, his blue eyes reflecting sadness. "'Twas a while 'fore anyone knew he was hit, us being all busy on the line. Last I saw he was linin' up his piece while the rest of us, we was duckin' an' shootin', ye know, till fin'lly things petered out. That's when we saw he wasn't movin'. Took one in the brain, he did. Wasn't like nobody cared," he added. "Just too damn busy, and he niver made a sound. Death'll do that. Sneak up on ye, do its job an' move on, nobody the wiser."

"Sure there's certainty in that, Andrew," Dan said, turning inward to visualize death not in human form but as a purposeful, enveloping, cloud-like being, a monstrous son of a bitch deserving nothing but a man's spite. "It only wants the next man on the list. Who that is doesn't matter."

"Nor what he's been," Andrew said.

"Volunteering for the picket last night was stout, Andrew."

"Sure it wasn't much," he said. "We come in 'fore the savages got goin'. Roy's a good man, he is."

"Right along with all of you. Well, I've got to get back."

"Good to see you, Daniel."

"Good to see you, Andrew. Mind yourself, now."

⋆ ⋆ ⋆

Around nine o'clock Captain Benteen walked over and told Reno he needed reinforcements to drive back the Indians crawling up the ravine. While he was gone, an Indian shot an H Troop man dead and then got close enough to touch him with his coup stick before another trooper shot him. After considerable argument, Reno agreed to reinforce the captain's company with M Troop. Benteen readied both companies and at nine fifteen they charged down the ravine, killing two braves immediately and sending the rest scurrying down the hill in disarray. Corporal George Lell was gut shot and dragged to the hospital. He knew he was a goner and said as much. Those nearby said he asked to be held up so he could get a last look at his friends. He smiled when he saw them and was dead soon after.

Satisfied that his line was secure, Benteen turned his attention to the north. A number of Sioux had gotten within a hundred yards of the perimeter up there. They looked about ready to charge. This time he had no trouble convincing Reno they had to drive the Indians back.

Jim first learned of the plan from John Hammon, a corporal in G Troop.

"We're goin' up by K Troop," he said. "Benteen's planning to drive the sons of bitches back."

"Glad somebody's finally takin' charge," Jim said. "Good luck up there."

With G Troop off the line, Jim decided to take Dan and move up the line to the left. From there they could see if warriors were forming to charge from the east. As G Troop pulled off the line, a man named Moore went down hard, shot through both kidneys. Later Ernst said the pain soon swallowed him up, and he begged for something to dampen the pain of it. He was dead in fifty minutes.

The men from G Troop returned a half hour later. Hammon said the charge went well. Once they hooked up with Troops B, D, and K, Benteen got them all hollering and firing as they started forward at the run. The Indians fired a volley or two, then broke and ran.

"We was out eighty yards when we was called back," Hammon said.

"You lose anybody 'sides Moore?" Dan asked.

"No," Hammon said. "Funny thing, at the start of it a man in D Troop froze up an' wouldn't leave his hole. He was still there when we come back, but shortly he was hit an' killed, right there. They said he had a premonition beforehand, which was how come he got streaked."

"Seems strange to me," Jim said. "So what're the Sioux up to now?"

"Whadaya mean?"

"Well, the sumbitches ain't shootin' much. Not over here anyways," Jim observed.

"Prob'ly bringin' fresh braves up from the village," Hammon said. "They change off 'bout every hour."

"No more, they don't," Charley said, pointing to the slope thick with Indians earlier. Less than a third of their number remained.

"Chrissake!" Hammon exclaimed. "Where'd they go?"

"Pullin' out."

"Maybe," Jim said. "I'll go ask up on top."

"See what's goin' on down below too," Charley said.

After that no rounds came in from the east, and they heard only an occasional shot from Sharpshooters' Ridge. It seemed like Charley was right about the Indians leaving.

At eleven o'clock Captain Benteen called for volunteers to make a dash down to the river for water. Although casualties were expected, nineteen men volunteered, including Sam, but he was told to help provide cover from above, firing into the brush along the far side of the river. The first group to go down brought up enough water to quench the thirst of the wounded. Among them only one man was hit. He was Mike Madden, K Troop's saddler. The ball shattered his leg below the knee, but they got him back up to the hospital.

Jubal Tinker was in the third group. It was risky, which bothered him, but he insisted on going.

"The wounded had got a swaller or two by then," he told the others later. "Fact was, I was desp'rit to git a snootful of water my own self. An' maybe a swaller or two fer the rest of yew boys."

The detail took three six-quart camp kettles as well as all the canteens they could carry. They scurried a hundred yards down from H Troop's line to the head of an open ravine leading to the bench along the riverbank. The ravine was safe, but from its mouth they had to dash a dangerous twenty yards to the riverbank. The marksmen at the top of the ravine gave them good cover, but a few warriors still made it hot once they reached the water.

The job was as challenging as it was dangerous, exhausting as it was satisfying, and exhilarating throughout. At least that's how Jubal told it.

"Yew know I ain't one to volunteer none. I leave thet to those with more of whatever they got but I ain't. What it is, I don't know, 'cept I ain't niver had none of it in me; jist seen it in boys like Stanislaus Roy an' them last night.

"But today the thirst *drove* me to it. I wa'n't far from bustin' apart like Cowley, bein' half off the track already. It skeered me, so I put my name in fer it. When the first boys git back they was grinnin' wide, havin' doused their noggins in the river. After that I wa'n't thinkin' of nothin' 'cept dippin' my own head in the cold water down thar.

"Fer a second the skeer of it got a holt on me, but it let go quick when we started off 'cross thet hunerd-yard stretch to the ravine. We prob'ly didn't git shot at once, but my ears sure thought so, pickin' up the sound of lead whistlin' past my head, but it coulda been I was runnin' so fast it made fer a whistle in my ears. An' I slid into thet ravine like Jonah down the whale's gullet.

"We catched our wind then flew down that gully like a flock of barn swallows. They was sage an' dead brush an' flat-leafed cactus along it, but we didn't care. I got scratches on ev'ry inch of skin showin' an' some thet don't. This one boy thet went on the first detail, he showed us the way, so when we git to the bottom he showed us an' from there we go one at a time. Scrambled twenny yards to the riverbank where a bluff kind of juts out to keep Injuns downstream from drawin' a bead on yew. We had us three kettles, so the idea was to take one down, fill 'er up an' git back to the ravine. We'd start fillin' the canteens from thet, yew see, an' the next man, he'd take another kettle an' git back with it.

"I'm set to go last, so I watched the others duck their heads under whilst fillin' the kettle up. Yew can bet yer thirteen dollars ever month I was thirstier than a drunk on Sunday morning. So when I git to the water I'm duckin' the kettle an' my head at the same time, while tryin' to hold my own canteen under with the other hand. In thet three seconds an arrow plows through the water two inches to the side, so I pull my head out quick an' there's this young buck straight across reachin' fer another arrow, so I shot him quick with my pistol. Hit him in the arm, I think, the left one. Then I dip my head fer another quick swaller. Thet's how thirst'll rob yew of whatever sense yew had to begin. Anyhow, the buck, he'd sunk back against the willers, so I start hightailin' it back, spillin' half the kettle on the way but lucky fer me thar was enough left to finish off the canteens we had, so wa'n't no call to risk my sorry hide agin.

"By then I'm rarin' to git back up thet ravine jist to see the look on yer faces when yew git yer first swallers, 'cept after jist a rod or two all the sap run outta me, an' my belly's real heavy what with the water sloshin' in it. An' Judas, I got this pain in the side thet's killin' me. Still, I kep' up with the others till we git near to the top. Then my feet didn't wanna move at all. Not a Goddamn inch, they didn't. Fact was, I was streaked. Yew know why? 'Cause I niver volunteered before. An' with my thirst slaked, my thinker's workin' agin, an' it's sayin' what in tarnation am I doin'? Volunteerin's tempting death, sure as shit stinks. Froze me up, my thinker did, till my feet said the hell with it an' got me goin' agin.

"Best thing was none of us got hit 'cept the man what showed the way. Got shot in the hand, but it's s'posed to heal up okay."

"How come you didn't *kill* that brave with the bow and arrow?" Elvin asked. "I sure would've."

"I cain't 'splain it, Elvin," Jubal said. "I still see him, over and over, standin' thar, fumblin' with another arrow. I could of killed him easy but I didn't. Thet's all thar is to it."

After Tinker's group, several more parties brought water up, so pretty soon every man on the hilltop had enough to get him through the day. The animals could have used a bit more, however.

By one o'clock the men were about sure Charley had it right. There'd been no gunfire from the east for some time, and only a few Indians were watching from the hill to the east. They gathered in one spot and tried to relax.

"Either they're done or tryin' some kind of trick," Jim said.

"We'd find out iffen one of yew stood up," Jubal said.

"Why don't you?" Elvin asked.

"Don't git all in a pucker," Jubal cautioned gently. "I was jist funnin'."

Twelve Indians began riding parallel to the line four hundred yards in front. Joined almost immediately by another dozen, they raced back and forth, over and over, a furlong in either direction. It seemed they were either trying to draw fire or getting their ponies worked up for a charge. However, neither turned out to be the case.

"Ain't that a guidon?" Charley asked, pointing to the swallow-tailed pennant the lead rider carried.

"Uh huh. Sam, can you make it out?" Jim asked.

"Seventh Cavalry," Sam said, straining to see. "Can't tell which troop."

"Could be G or M lost theirs down below an' the sumbitches picked it up," Jim said.

Wherever it came from, a company's pennant in the hands of Indians was troubling. It certainly left them uneasy. Two minutes later the horsemen rode off and there were no Indians at all out there, although they heard an occasional shot from the north. Shortly, Elvin started scrambling up the slope toward Bull Judd. Jim didn't bother to stop him.

Up the line men ventured that the siege might be over, although nobody was counting on it. Sure enough, a new flurry of firing suddenly broke out. Some twenty braves had snuck back and were popping up and down, firing into the line.

"Geehosaphat!" Jubal swore. "I thought them buzzards gave up. Any fool kin see we got 'em whipped."

"Just some young ones gettin' their last licks in," Charley said, watching the Indians ride off.

Chapter 29: Fight's End

★ ★ ★

GUNFIRE STOPPED ALTOGETHER AT about three o'clock, leaving a silence that was almost unsettling. Company D reported that the last group of warriors to the north had started toward the village, careful to stay out of range all the way. An hour later Captain Moylan ordered A Troop to stand down. Jim detailed Jake and Sam to remain on the line in case any coup-hunters tried sneaking up the swale. The rest of the squad went up to where the horses were tied, happy to get away from the line. They also wanted to see about getting all their canteens filled. No telling if and when the Sioux would start in again.

★ ★ ★

Jake sat with his back against a packsaddle, only partially watching the field in front. Sam lay beside him, arms behind his head, idly following the wisps of clouds overhead.

"How come Jim Lawton say the both of us stay here?" Jake wondered.

"In case coup hunters try comin' up the swale again. We could hold 'em off till the squad gets back down here." Sam sat up and surveyed the field beyond the barricade.

"Hell, you do that easy without me."

"You're absolutely right," Sam agreed, chuckling. "But I enjoy your company. Besides, I can use you to load for me."

"Sure. You the boss, me the help."

"Ayuh. You're hired to fork hay, shovel horseshit, and keep me in cartridges."

"Yeah, simple as that."

Jake began inspecting his carbine. He shook out a rag carefully before starting to wipe out the breech. When he finished he laid the piece on one of the hardtack boxes and went to work on his cartridges, nearly putting a shine on each one before replacing it in the belt.

"We gotta trade these belts for canvas ones," he said. "That leather corrodes the cartridges so they stick in the chamber."

"Verdigriss," Sam muttered, mispronouncing the word.

"What?"

"Verdigriss. That green stuff the copper gets from the leather. That's what jams them." Sam sounded frustrated, angry.

"I know that, but you don't say verdigriss. It's verdigree. French," Jake said. "But how come you gone sour? Oughtta be glad you still breathin'." He paused, hoping what he'd said would sink in, but Sam didn't react. He shrugged, giving up. "You think them Sioux quit?"

"Yes."

"How come you pissed off then?" Jake couldn't let it go.

"Nothing except I'm, uh, well it wasn't like I thought it would be."

"Whadaya mean?"

"No big charges against us. No hand-to-hand. And I should have gotten a couple of them," Sam said. "I'm supposed to be the best shot in the squad, and I didn't hit anything."

"Huh? You killed that Goddamn pony. He come full bore an' you drop him dead like that."

"I know, but the sergeant was counting on me for more than that," Sam said.

"Oh, you not that big hero, huh?"

"No, it's just that I thought I'd hit at least one brave. At first I was flinching, damn it. Then I couldn't get the range. And the one I thought I had was a lot smarter than me."

"Was your first time in a fight," Jake said. "An' what about down by that river—we get through, huh?"

"Just barely, thanks to Charley," Sam mumbled, picturing the warrior's eyes full of hate. "Never hit a thing there, either."

"Goddamn, we're alive!"

"Uh huh."

"You're a stupid sonuvabitch, you know that?"

"Huh?"

"You stopped them bastards comin' straight at us, an' they don't come no more. We're okay. That's what counts."

"Judas Priest, Jake. You still don' get it, do you?" Sam asked.

"What d'you mean?"

"Droppin' that pony was nothing, just a snapshot, a reflex."

"So what?"

"So what? Listen to me, Goddamn it!" Sam said. "We came four hundred miles to kill Indians, and I didn't hit a one of them."

"Maybe they come back, give you another try."

"But what if they don't? What if they scatter and we don't get another shot at them?"

"That bother you? *Câlice!* You are stupid!"

"It's not stupid to want to do my part," Sam muttered, almost sullen now. "I'm only saying I didn't do what I thought I could."

"You think stupid ideas, they're more important than life? *Tête croche.* You hard to live with like that. That's the Goddamn truth."

Gazing at the sky, Sam remained silent. Jake watched him closely, silently shaking his head. Looking for glory, Sam could think himself out of appreciating life, even now, when they could have been dead. *Sacramère!* His bunkie was a fool, simple as that.

⋆ ⋆ ⋆

At the picket line, Jubal made sure the little Bay was doing okay. (Had he only found the horse yesterday?) Then he went on to the

M Troop line and found Carney standing in his shallow rifle pit. He looked like he hadn't slept in a month.

"Hey there, Art," Jubal said, trying to be extra friendly. "Am I disrememb'rin' or did you move since yestiday?"

"They switched us with B Troop's what they did. We was in the charge down the ravine."

"Really? From what I heard, you throwed them varmints straight off the hill."

The scrawny rookie nodded. "I guess so. They ain't been no bother since."

"Thet's good. Say, I jist checked out yer bunkie's little Bay. Not a scratch on him."

"Thanks. It'll ease Ole John's mind when he gits back up here. He's had Knuckles more'n seven years."

"He been in thet long?" Jubal asked.

"Since sixty-eight," Carney said.

"An old-timer. He must of gone to ground down below."

"That's what I figure. Anyway, I'll tell him to look fer you when he comes up." Worn out, the boy looked away, his eyes drawn to the trees below.

"You jist tell him to ask fer Tinker, Jubal Tinker, A Troop. Meantime, I'll tend ole Knuckles."

Jubal walked away, trying to get the young trooper's face out of his mind, an underage boy hanging desperately onto the chance that his bunkie was alive—awful long odds. Still, the hope of it had kept him going so far. He spotted Dan and Charley and ambled over to them.

The three of them rested on the west edge of the hilltop, Charley kneeling beside Dan and Jubal stretched out next to him, on his side. It was peaceful, and they were quiet for a long time, each with his own thoughts as they gazed at the river down below. His feet in a B Troop rifle pit, Dan got his pipe going. He was more comfortable than he'd been in two days. Jubal spoke first, telling how the boyish trooper couldn't admit to the possibility that his bunkie had gone down, not for all the stump liquor in Hardin County, Kentucky, which Jubal reminded them was his place of enlistment, as if he hadn't mentioned that fact a hundred times before.

Not even the first pipe of the day tempered Dan's foul mood. Staring at the valley below, he looked down the long ravine to where the stream crossed a grassy clearing, the richness of its green creating an idyllic oasis amidst the arid, sage-dotted expanse of hillside, triggering thirty-year-old images from County Kerry: two lovely, old cottages emptied of families half-starved before their eviction. *To hell with all things Irish,* he thought.

Sam and Jake walked up and hunkered down next to them.

"Welcome to the sunny side of the hill, lads. No more Indians to the east?" Dan asked, trying his best to fend off the gloom.

"None we could see," Sam replied. "Captain says they've left."

"We crossed down there?" Jake asked, pointing to the spot of green.

Charley answered, "Fifty yards upstream."

Dan focused on the tiny spot of green. Wasn't that where they had crossed? The clearing's far bank was trampled. What of the near bank? If it was broken down, Charley was mistaken. If not, it was only where the ponies went to drink. He strained to see it clearly, unconsciously stretching his neck forward before realizing he didn't give a damn whether the ford was there or in County Donegal. Fact was, it was a labor to hang on to the here and now, to resist the murky quicksand of a centuries-old rage against the devil's own Brits and, yes, against the impotence of his own kind as well.

"How far to that place?" Jake's query sounded from afar.

"Half mile, maybe more," Jubal answered. "What d'yew say, Charley?"

"Some less'n that."

Locked within himself, Dan struggled against his brainless wrath, pulling himself back into the present only to compare Custer's jingoistic blustering to the overblown myths he'd learned years before.

"Sam!" Charley spoke sharply, pointing toward the river. "Yer the eagle eye. Whadaya make of them hostiles down there?"

A half dozen riders had entered the clearing, a brave on a pale buckskin in front.

"The one with the buckskin's runnin' the show," Sam answered. "Now they're all lookin' up this way."

"Yeah," Charley muttered.

Jubal said, "They're watchin' us fer sure."

"Captain, he watch them back," Jake said, pointing to where Moylan and several of the other officers stood, using binoculars. "Them glasses, how much he see, you think?"

"Prob'ly no more'n Eagle Eye Sam here," Jubal said.

The six Indians dismounted and sat in a circle.

"They're passing the pipe around," Sam said. "Funny thing, they're talking but using sign also."

"Prob'ly a couple are Cheyenne," Charley said.

"And the leader's hair is loose, kind of brownish."

Dan struggled in silence as his fury toward matters Irish surged once more to dangerous proportions. *Goddamn them all,* he cursed in silence. *Goddamn the purveyors of Irish courage and beguiling Irish charm. Goddamn the tellers of tales and the singers of the Kathleen we'd love to take home again. Damn Garryowen. Damn Custer and his braggadocio, his cavalier disregard for precious lives. The Seventh crush the Sioux? Not yesterday, they didn't. And not today, not with their chiefs palavering in plain view, unconcerned with our mighty presence.*

Chapter 30: The Exodus

"WHAT THEY UP TO you think?" Jake asked.

"Plannin' tomorra's doins, prob'ly," Jubal guessed.

"Yes, but Christ Almighty! Look at where they're doing it," Dan said, the venom startling everyone but Charley. "Having a parley right under our noses, they are. Even passing the pipe around, Goddamn it! They're taunting us!" Finding a conveyance in speech, the rage tore through him from soul to tongue. "Christ Almighty, for the past two days they've outnumbered, outfought, and outwitted us! Now they're ignoring us, deliberately, like we're not worth their time, never mind their precious ammunition."

"Why'd yew say outwitted?" Jubal asked.

"Because it's the God's honest truth, that's why! They've had us in a noose, right? And yesterday, how smart was Custer, sending three understrength companies to charge a village that big in the middle of a summer afternoon? We didn't get a glimpse of it! And today, who's got who bottled up?"

"But—"

"Another thing!" Dan cut Jubal off. "If Custer's such a great general, like you think he is, why didn't he know there were so many Sioux beforehand? The scouts knew. Charley picked that up just by talking with them. Did Custer listen? No! All he worried about was they'd scatter and cost him his chance to be cock o' the walk. Now, Goddamn it, we can't find him nor him us. The Fighting Seventh a crack outfit? Jesus, Mary, and Joseph, Jubal, think again." Out of steam, he clamped down on his pipe and stared down the hill, letting his thoughts run their course before they settled. The others were quiet, silenced by the outburst. Jubal occupied himself opening and shutting his clasp knife.

Charley's voice cut gently through the silence. "We weren't outfought."

The truth of it dampened Dan's rage. "You're right, Charley. We gave as good as we got."

"Thet's c'rect," Jubal said.

"What you think them Sioux do tomorrow?" Jake asked Dan.

"I've no idea, lad." Thoroughly drained, he had no interest in the matter.

Charley said, "Sam, that buckskin got white patches on him?"

"Hard to tell, he's so light, but I think so. Why?"

"Just wondered," Charley replied.

Dan knew what he was thinking. After the fight in '73 some men claimed they'd seen Crazy Horse on a buckskin with white patches. Humaza told Charley last month that he still rode a pony like that. Down below, the man in question pointed up at the bluffs, toward the village, and then southwest toward the Bighorn Mountains. Moving unhurriedly, the party mounted up and rode single file into the timber, the leader following the five others. At the clearing's edge he reined the buckskin around for one last look up at the men on the hilltop before disappearing into the trees.

"You think that's him?" Dan asked Charley quietly.

"Prob'ly, but it don't make no difference," Charley said. "The village is leavin'."

"What do you mean?" Sam asked.

"Like I said, they gotta 'cause there ain't no grass," Charley said.

* * *

Jim walked up to join them. It was six forty, almost four hours since the Indians' last volleys. No signs of them leaving yet, but smoke was curling up from behind the timber, plumes of white and gray swirling together. Perplexed, they watched as the smoldering cloud grew.

"What d'yew s'pose they're up to now?" Jubal asked.

"I don't know," Dan said. The others were mute, caught in their own thoughts again. Several minutes passed.

"*Jésus-christ*!" Jake said, pointing farther downstream. Sickly browns and yellows joined the mix as the creeping fire spread into rotting clumps of rush and sedge along the stream. "Real thick, that smoke, color of shit."

"Too yellow for shit," Sam said, absently. Once again, his mind was stuck on his brush with death in the river.

"*Chicken* shit."

"Okay, chicken shit."

The grimy cloud thickened and rose above the trees, a greasy blanket with a trillion flakes of ash, quickly turning the sun into a darkening scarlet presence. In turn, its rays lent a reddish cast to the swirling smoke. Translucent blood smears streaked the spreading blur. Sam found it ominous.

"What makes that smoke red like blood?" Jake wondered.

"Ask Ernst, for God's sake," Sam growled. "He's the painter."

"How come you're pissed off now?"

"Nothin'. I just don't know that much about colors," Sam said, softening his tone.

Without wind, the smoke contained itself in one long stretch from yesterday's skirmish line to more than a mile down river. Upstream the air was clear all the way to the distant mountains, barely discernible on the southern horizon.

Bull and Elvin joined the group, along with three others. Bull asked what the heathens were up to. No one answered for a minute because they were straining to see through the smoke screen, all except Dan. He didn't give a damn.

"Pony herd's movin'," Charley said, pointing. West of the village a dozen riders were pushing the herd off the bench and toward the smoke.

"That means they're leavin' for sure?" Jake asked.

"Could be," Charley said.

"Could be a trick too," Elvin said. "Ain't that right, Bull?"

"Wouldn't surprise me," Bull muttered.

"No, Charley's right," Jake said. "They gotta move out. No grass left."

"What d'you know 'bout it?" Elvin asked.

A smile crossed Jake's face. "Enough to put my money on Charley," he said.

Sam wasn't surprised to see Jake happy. After all, he was alive, which was his main concern. Never mind that the Indians would go back to their murderous ways, more convinced than ever they could act with impunity. Jake had never grasped what this war was about. He didn't hardly care why they were out there. Probably none of the others cared either, although they'd all fought well and hard, even Elvin. An image of the dolt lying dead sped past his mind's eye. *Forget about it,* Sam told himself.

He sighted down the carbine's barrel at the clearing, the rear sight set to the seven-hundred-yard mark. It would take a few rounds to zero in on the spot. No point to it, of course. Sergeant Lawton would explode if he pulled the trigger. He'd sure like to be ready, though, in case more braves showed themselves and taunted them. A man could put up with ridicule for just so long, least of all from an uncivilized enemy. He squinted, picking out a dark-brown smudge in the water caught on a snag next to the opposite shore. Maybe it was the pony Charley shot out from under that warrior bent on killing him. The carbine's front sight dipped a bit as a flash of remembered fear gripped his gut before his mind's eye took over, confronted by the warrior's glare of unadulterated hate. He wrenched himself back to the now but couldn't hold it, as he remembered racing from the skirmish line to the timber, convinced he'd be stone-cold dead any second. *Stop! That was then, this is now!* Raising the sight he squinted down the barrel as two braves rode into the clearing.

★ ★ ★

Welling up in the distance, the smoke thickened, rising higher by the minute. The light itself became strange, untrustworthy, as the laden sky dimmed shadow lines, blurring distance and elevation.

"Lookee thar!" Jubal cried out as the first Indians emerged from behind the smoke. "Where they goin'?"

Jim looked up from his watch. Five past seven. Across the river, thirty-odd people and three dozen horses were heading up the valley. Dogs and children followed alongside, tiny at that distance, yet he could see the kids jumping and skipping, falling back and dashing ahead the way they do, all herky-jerky against the steady walk of the ponies, maybe half of which pulled travois carrying hides, robes, bundles of food, and necessities. A few carried people unable to walk on their own.

It was a full minute before another cluster followed, time enough for some of them to guess wrongly that only a single band had broken away from the village. Gradually, the second bunch ate up the distance separating it from the first. After that it was a steady stream, then a river. A river of hundreds, then thousands of people and animals. A river as wide as the Ohio.

Awestruck, the troopers could only stand there. No one spoke.

★ ★ ★

"Ernst should see this," Jake finally said, starting toward the hospital. He was back shortly. Ernst said he would come when he finished dressing a man's wound.

By the time Ernst arrived the exodus stretched a mile and a half south, its foremost elements so distant that they couldn't tell one cluster from another in the dust-blurred mass inching its way up the valley, an enormous procession with thousands of hoofs and moccasins echoing off the bluffs, blending into a soft, low-pitched rumble that filled the air. On the hilltop the silence was at last interrupted by a ragged "three cheers" from M Troop up the line. Were they signaling a victory? Only if survival constituted victory.

A shot rang out, jerking heads around to the left, and then a second shot sounded. Twin puffs of smoke drifted skyward in the stillness.

"What was that?" Ernst demanded, wiping his eyes to stare down the hill, straining to see if anybody was hit. No one fell.

"Jist M Troop payin' its respects," Jubal replied.

"That was not respect!" Ernst shot back. He was livid. They'd never seen him angry before, not like this.

"Jubal was just jokin'," Sam offered kindly.

"With you I'm not angry, Jubal," Ernst said, his face flushed with emotion. He was literally shaking. "It is the fools that shot guns at those people. Why would they do that?"

"Why not?" Elvin challenged. "We come out here to kill the sonuvabitches, didn't we?"

"Children?" Ernst spit out.

"Shit. Men, women, brats, ponies, dogs. They're all filthy Injuns."

"He's right," Bull said. "We come to rub 'em out, Albrecht. Ev'ry last one. An' next time we will." He glanced past the red-faced Ernst at the others standing there stone-faced. "Is that clear, Private?"

Tight-lipped, Ernst glared back until Bull broke off his stare and looked away.

"Who was it did the shootin'?" Jubal asked.

"Ryan and Captain French," Jim said. "French carries a Long Tom. Prob'ly thought he oughtta hit somethin', that big a target. An' Ryan's got his own Sharps telescope. They hit anybody?"

"I saw nobody fall," Ernst said.

"I'm goin' over to see what Ryan's got to say," Bull announced. "Maybe he did git one of 'em. And, Albrecht, you stop takin' the heathens' side."

The last of the Indians were still emerging from beyond the timber when the smoke finally thinned out. The lodges were gone.

That's when the speculating began. The move was a gigantic trick, the opening ruse in a massive ambush. Or they were moving the village but the warriors would be back in the morning to finish them off. Or maybe they were actually heading back to where they came from. Rumors about Custer abounded too. He was forted up five miles to the north, waiting for Gibbons. Or he had circled all the way around the village and was situated several miles to the west. Or maybe to the east. In any case he would join them in the morning for sure.

And then a small group of horsemen appeared from downstream to move through the abandoned village at a fast walk. It was the rear guard that had been positioned downstream to cover the village's departure. Each man rode straight-backed, proud, his rifle carried erect. Not one glanced up at the bluff, as if no outfit they'd soundly whipped deserved recognition. Some troopers cursed them, vowing to kick their arse the next time, Goddamn it, and there sure in hell would be a next time. But most stood in silence for another half hour until only a faint dust cloud remained, disappearing up the valley of the Little Bighorn.

Chapter 31: Burying the Dead

ERNST GOT HARDLY ANY sleep that night, what with tending the wounded. The most serious case was Mike Madden. The wound he suffered on the water detail turned out to be a double compound fracture. Dr. Porter had no choice but to amputate the lower leg. Before he started, the doctor gave his patient a stiff shot of liquor as an anesthetic and went to cutting. Madden suffered the procedure in silence. After it was over, the doctor gave him another good-sized drink, whereupon Mike smiled and asked him to take off the other leg.

About nine o'clock they spotted a dust cloud three or four miles downstream, moving toward them. As they riders came closer, it didn't look to be Indians, nor was it Custer—no company of gray horses. Maybe the best bet was General Crook's column.

After a while a single horseman started up the bluffs. It was Muggins Taylor, a White scout, with word the column was Colonel Gibbon's. General Terry and his staff were with him. Lieutenant Bradley of the Seventh Infantry then arrived with awful news. They had found the bodies of Custer and his five companies on the hill above the north end of the village. The whole battalion? Two hundred cavalrymen? The very notion of it defied common sense. Indians never set up ambushes big enough to swallow up five companies, not in open country. Besides, that many troopers could hold off two thousand Indians for two days if they forted up. Reno's battalion did. Still, Bradley had no reason to prevaricate, not on such a matter.

General Terry soon arrived with his staff and met with Major Reno and his officers. Some twenty minutes later Terry ordered Captain Benteen to lead H Troop over to inspect Custer's field. The remaining companies began burying their dead on the hilltop and moving the fifty wounded men down close to Colonel Gibbon's camp on the river bottom. They also set about the loathsome but necessary task of killing the seriously wounded horses and mules and dragging all the dead animals to a gully located downwind.

That evening Tom Garvey from H Troop came by and told the squad what they'd found on Custer's field: small clusters of corpses were spread over a stretch of ground almost a mile wide. He said that Benteen thought the battalion must've split up before it all began. Companies were widely separated, with I and L Troops along the ridge, the others on the side hill. It didn't look like any company had forted up. It looked like they'd been surprised by a force large enough to break their ranks before they could defend themselves. Just plain overwhelmed, they were. Bodies lay in twos and threes or alone. Most of them were stripped of uniforms and boots. Many were desecrated—scalped, mutilated—but not all of them.

"What about General Custer?" Sam asked.

"He must of lost his feekin' reason," Tom said. "Splittin' the battalion like he did."

"No, I meant what happened to him," Sam asked.

"Oh, you mean his corpse? He wasn't cut up or nothin'," Tom answered. "Shot in the head and the chest. One leg had a gash in it."

"Was he scalped?"

"No," Tom replied, reaching for the tobacco pouch Charley was offering. "But here's what brought me up short about General Custer. You boys know how he always stood out like he was God's special creation, sitting tall in the saddle on a fine thoroughbred, with them golden locks of his catching the sun. Well, lemme tell you somethin'. Over there he was just another corpse on a field of death. Downright common, he was."

When Tom left, Jubal looked like he'd been mule-kicked in the stomach. "The Gin'ral, he done bungled the job," he said.

"Sure and he did that," Dan agreed. The truth was that the same arrogance that brought Custer to humiliate Jubal in the Black Hills had cost the lives of two hundred good men.

To the east a lone wolf answered the distant howls of a pack to the north.

"What them wolves howlin' 'bout?" Jake asked.

"Hard to tell," Charley said. "Maybe 'cause their bellies are full."

"Oh," Jake said, realizing what Charley meant. "I still don't see why Custer didn't fort up."

"He split up the battalion before seeing what he was up against," Dan said.

"But how come the comp'nies didn't fort up? They must of seen 'em comin'," Jake said.

"We don't know the ground over thar," Jubal said. "The Sioux could of come 'round the back side an' tore into 'em before they know'd what hit 'em."

"If Custer did see them, he didn't react fast enough," Dan said.

"How come?" Jake asked.

"Probably he thought they'd run when they saw him. Then they were at him before he realized he was wrong. Five maybe six hundred of them."

"Or more," Charley added.

"But the gen'ral must of known they would come at him," Jake said. "Sam, he read that Custer said them Sioux fought good."

"What he wrote don't mean nothin'," Jubal said. "Gen'ral Custer, he niver thought he could be beat. Not by nobody."

"Such men don't see trouble until it's too late," Dan offered.

"You think he knew he'd blundered?" Jake asked.

"It ain't likely," Charley said. "He wasn't one to admit bein' wrong."

"No, he wa'n't," Jubal said.

The next morning, June 28, Jubal went over to M Troop to talk with young Art Carney. The boy was down in the dumps but trying to tough it out.

"I checked on Knuckles this mornin'," Jubal said. "He's doin' pretty good, now thet he's got plenty of water and all."

"Thanks."

"How're yew makin' out?"

"Okay, I guess," the boy replied. "Only thing is, I don't know what happened to my bunkie. Sergeant Ryan told me ain't no more men comin' up from down there."

"I'd guess he's c'rect 'bout thet," Jubal said.

"For a while I figured my ole bunkie's was hurt an' got into the hospital down there, but we ain't heard nothin' like that," the rookie said, choking up a little. "Do you think we would have?"

"I would of thought so," Jubal said.

"Uh huh," the boy said. He gulped hard and went on. "Tell me somethin', Jubal. You must have heard that General Terry ordered us to go over an' bury all of Custer's men, all two hundred of them."

"I did."

"Well, how come we gotta do that? I mean, we been fightin' for our lives up here and we're close to bein' played out. Shouldn't Colonel Gibbon's men do it?"

"No."

"How come?"

"'Cause Seventh Calv'ry takes care of its own."

"Oh. I guess you're right."

★ ★ ★

When they reached the sun-broiled field it was far worse than Jim had pictured it. Corpses were scattered all over, from Darby Finley's remains near the river on up to the cluster of dead officers and men just below the northeast ridge. That was a spread of three quarters of a mile. Most of their uniforms had been stripped. Some were desecrated, but more were untouched. All were bloated after two days in the sun. A lot of them were unrecognizable. And the smell—one couldn't get away from it. Company A found about twenty rotting corpses from E Troop in a deep gully not far from where Darby lay.

"What do you think happened?" Dan asked Jim, staring into the gully.

"Someone found Lieutenant Smith up the hill. I'd guess that when he went down, these boys run down here an' tried to fort up."

They set to work with bandannas over their noses, but after a while the cloths only held the smell tighter. Some staggered away and puked up their breakfasts. Between the hardpan and no shovels, all they could do was carve shallow graves and cover them with whatever chunks of dirt they found. That wouldn't discourage the coyotes, but it was all they could do. Before long a lot of men were plain desperate to finish and escape the stench of death.

Halfway through the job Dan stumbled onto the rotting corpse of Paddy O'Malley. The strength swooshed out of his legs, leaving him near the point of falling. His mind was blank for a bit, and then he cursed the banshee, the Goddamn Gaelic specter that didn't exist—never did, never would. Seeing the color drain from his face, Sam started toward him, but Charley gave him a glare, his steely eyes speaking more clearly than words or action, warning him to stay the hell away from Dan for as long as it took.

Dan's sourness rushed back with a vengeance, racing beyond the old struggles with Irish ways and impatience with regimental claptrap. He silently railed at generals, politicians, reporters, and writers by the bushel, excoriating every ignoramus that trumpeted the glories of war. Pictures of torn-up corpses flooded his mind. He saw artillery horses, infantrymen, warriors, camp dogs, drummer boys, children, women with child, ponies, Sioux, Cheyenne, Whites, Blacks, Secesh, and Yankees, wearing blue, gray, butternut, beaded leather, or calico, scattered on a bloody cornfield, in drifting snow and inside lodges at the Washita, heaped at the foot of Marye's

Heights, in windrows at Gettysburg, in sage and cactus at his feet. All of them lives thrown away, wasted by the greed of distant men with great ambitions—spent for political advantage, military ambition, personal power, and financial gain.

And here were two hundred more, struck down in a bloodbath brought on when one man's arrogance overcame the necessity of sensible reconnaissance.

He shrugged off the gloom for a moment, insisting that his own survival was a blessing. But he couldn't accept that, not truly, not ever. One thing was certain: the long-standing anguish of the day would stay with him forever.

When the grim work was finished, they staggered down to the river where they tried but failed to wash away all traces of the stinking job and then proceeded upstream to bury the men killed in the valley fight on Sunday, another gruesome chore. And after that they climbed the bluffs once more, gathered their gear, saddled up, and moved the bivouac down to the lower part of the abandoned village. A scattering of damaged and misplaced Indian trappings lay here and there, suggesting that the exodus was more hurried than it looked from the hilltop. They finished setting up camp late in the afternoon, the tents arranged in some semblance of order, the remaining horses and mules on a picket line.

Chapter 32: Sam and Jake at Odds

SITTING ON THE BANK of the river, Jake absently studied a child's corncob doll he'd found in the weeds. A little girl must have lost it. He imagined a tired mother walking with the crowd, pulling along her weeping four-year-old daughter by the hand while promising to make her another. The image tumbled his mind into the formless past, not so much a memory as a boyish state of being, a warm emotion, and with it an uncertain yearning. Irritated, he grabbed hold to the safety of the present. He felt good, almost buoyant. *Mon Dieu*, he exclaimed to himself, and why shouldn't he? He glanced northeast, toward the Godforsaken hillside. He was alive, damn it! And unhurt. He'd learned some things too, from Charley, who showed him that no trooper had been tortured alive, not even the two boys from M Troop they'd found later, the ones whose runaway mounts carried them straight into the village. (What Charley said made sense. If the cavalry was attacking your village, what would you do to anyone charging straight toward your family's teepee? Take time to catch him so you could torture him? No, you'd shoot the sonuvabitch dead and reload.)

He'd been in deathly struggles before and had always savored coming out of them alive, proud of his skills and guile. This one was different. All he'd done was keep his head down. That, and he'd become a fair horseman in the six months before. But there was a lot of plain luck in it. Experienced men like Steinbrecher and The First got hit. *Jésus-Christ!* Every dead guy in A Troop was a better soldier than him. Like Dalious and Rollins, they'd been in since

'72. And what about the poor guys with Custer? Some of them were soldierin' during the War, like Charley and Dan. No sir, he was lucky. In addition, Scar was one damn fine horse. Of course, he owed Sam for part of it, him being the one who'd taught him how to ride. And he owed Charley as well for showing him how to soldier. But mainly, being in one piece was the luck of the draw, and that left him feeling really happy—and kind of proud too. Not like proud of what he brought to the table, but a proud that he couldn't really explain.

Sitting next to him, Sam appeared lost in thought, twirling the Colt's cylinder over and over, glowering at nothing in particular. Next thing he knew, Jake was giving him a hard time.

"How come you look bad like that?" Jake asked. "Buryin' them guys today?"

"No." Sam hardly looked up. "But it was bad. I nearly puked when I stepped away to get some air."

"Me too. But we're done with that, so how come?"

"It's just remembering how I couldn't hit a damn thing."

"That still got you pissed off, huh?"

"Yes. I know I ought to be thinking more about the boys that went down, out of respect, but uh ..."

"What?" Jake was incredulous. He stood up, still clutching the tiny girl's doll. "Them guys, they're gone. You're here. Be glad for that!"

"I am."

"Bullshit!"

"No, really, I'm happy. It's just that I kept missing—"

"Jésus-christ! You don't kill nobody so you piss in your boot. *Stupide."*

"You just don't get it," Sam said, getting to his feet.

"Get what?"

"How I'm supposed to be the sharpshooter, and I plain fucked up. No excuse, I just—"

"Hey!" Jake interrupted, trying to brighten him up. "I hear

right? Sam Streeter say fuck? *Jésus-christ,* you one damn tough guy!" He laughed.

"Well, no use denying it. I didn't do my job" Sam said, still serious.

"Bullshit! You drop that pony—one shot!"

"Just a reflex shot," he said morosely.

"*Câlice!* That's more bullshit!" Jake cursed, standing up and starting back toward the bivouac.

"It isn't bullshit to me!" Sam said angrily. "We're here to defeat the enemy, and I—"

"Bullshit!" Jake said, turning back. "They don't tell us to defeat nobody. They say kill them Indians: men, women, old men, kids too."

"Stop it! We're soldiers ordered to drive them back to the agencies, and if they put up a fight, we've got to respond."

"Ain't like that, Sam," Jake said quietly. "We start the fights. Here, at the Washita, Sand Creek."

"You're wrong," Sam said, starting to heat up. "That was a rogue outfit at Sand Creek. And the Seventh is—"

"More bullshit!" Jake interrupted. "They got the same orders we got. Nothin' 'bout drivin' no Indians any damn place. Reno, he say shoot ev'rybody that moves. Women an' kids an' old folks here like Sand Creek."

Unfazed, Sam said, "Seventh Cavalry's an honorable regiment."

"Honorable? *Câlice!* What you mean by that honorable shit? Huh? Custer, he wanted to charge at sun up, ride through like the Washita. Kill them braves sleepin', kill women with babies, toothless old men takin' their mornin' piss." Jake raged. "Goddamn it, Sam, wake up! Here! Take a trophy from this honorable fight!" He tossed the doll toward Sam, who fumbled it.

"What is it?" Sam asked, frowning as he picked it out of the dust.

"The prize for you drivin' them savages back to the agencies. Look at it! A little girl had that doll. The orders say if she move, blow her head off. Maybe that happen! But then her father an' the rest of them they scare Reno shitless an' chase us up the damn hill. Then they rub out Custer so we don't kill no more women an' kids."

"That wasn't the way it was going to be," Sam said weakly.

"No? What was it gonna be? Shoot that girl's father, then dance with her mother?"

"That isn't what soldiering's about," Sam said, his voice rising.

"Marde! Soldierin's 'bout followin' orders," Jake shot back. "They say kill that guy, I do it, but I don't swell up over it." And with that he stomped off toward the latrine.

⋆ ⋆ ⋆

Late that evening Charley and Dan were gnawing on their crackers when Jake dropped down beside them.

"That Sam, he one pain in the ass," he said. "How do I get a diff'rent bunkie?"

"Tell Jim Lawton," Dan answered. "But his mind's on other things."

"Like what?"

Charley smiled. "Like gettin' Elvin Crane into Bull's squad."

"Guess I wait then. Thing is, Sam's not a bad guy. But with the army he *le gnochon.*"

"Huh?"

"Got brains but he don't think right. Read too many books, I think. Says the army is the honorable profession. No honor in killlin' women."

"No, there isn't," Dan said.

"Worse," Jake went on, the words coming faster. Fumbling, he pulled the makings out of his pocket, careful not to lose any of it. "Big thing for him is he gotta be the best Goddamn trooper in the outfit. Can't trust him like that."

"Why not?" Dan asked.

"He's gotta be the hero, even a dead one," he said, pulling in a lungful of smoke.

"Like that's all he cares about?" Charley asked.

"Yeah, that's it," Jake said. "If he ain't the best soldier, he ain't nothin'. He thinkin' 'bout shootin' good all the time. Nothin' left to watch my back when we catch them Sioux."

"Don't worry about that," Dan said. "Terry's in no hurry to catch them."

"So how can I get a new partner?"

"You tried workin' it out with him?" Charley asked.

"*Marde*! He don't hear me," Jake muttered, taking another drag.

Charley said, "It ain't my business, but in the fight, did he ever hang you out?"

"No."

"Could be it's just his talk that's got you pissed. Besides, he thinks you're great. Why I can't figure," Charley said, smiling, but Jake didn't catch the humor.

"Sam's basically a good trooper," Dan added.

"Yeah, I gotta say that," Jake agreed. "But he's a pain in the ass, sayin' that killin' women and kids is okay."

Charley said, "You know 'bout killin', so—"

"What's that mean?" Jake cut Charley off, flaring up.

"You already know about it," Charley said flatly. "You know a man kills 'cause the other guy's gonna kill him or 'cause he hates real hard like Bull, or maybe he's just a cold sonuvabitch. Sam don't hate, and he ain't cold."

"No, Sam's got a cold streak in him," Jake said.

"What do you mean?" Dan asked.

"It's like, I don't know. Sometimes it's like he's a killer. After I had it out with Elvin, he said he'd kill him one day. It sounded like he would."

"Maybe, but I don't sense a cold streak," Dan said.

"Then how come he talks 'bout killin' Indian women an' kids?"

"'Cause he read it," Charley said. "Indians ain't people for a lot of writers. Some gen'rals too."

"Okay, but you think Sam gonna learn diff'rent?" Jake asked.

"Someone will learn him."

"Who? An Indian like Humaza?"

"Nah. Humaza ain't got time for Whites."

"'Cept you, Charley," Jake said, smiling. He pinched the butt between thumb and forefinger, took a last long drag, let it drop, and kicked dirt over it. "Okay, I put up with *le gnochon* for now, but when you think he gonna change?"

"In time," Charley said.

"How long that mean?"

Charley shrugged and said, "In time."

Chapter 33: The Butcher's Bill

★ ★ ★

JUNE 29, 1876

The next morning Dan and Charley talked about casualties. Charley had heard that 210 died with Custer, including his nephew and the reporter. Reno lost forty or so between the initial charge and reaching the hilltop, and then another thirteen before it was over. Including scouts and civilians, it came to 263 dead out of 645, more than 40 percent dead.

"How many wounded?" Dan wondered.

"Not sure," Charley said. "Ernst said more'n fifty."

"Jesus! That's half the column. How many do you think the hostiles lost?"

"No way of knowing. They only left eight in them ceremonial lodges."

"They must have done something special."

Charley pulled some tobacco out of his pouch, his fingers working it into a wad. "I guess so. But thinkin' 'bout it, I doubt we hit more'n three up on top," he said.

"You mean on the east side," Dan said.

"Yeah, and the north. And H Troop got that one with the coup stick."

"That's three, and maybe two more. That's not many. We must have killed some down below."

"I heard we got two maybe three at the skirmish line," Charley said. "And maybe four or five in the timber."

"I heard two or three went down by the main ford," Dan said. "Didn't you get that one going for Sam?"

"No, just the pony. The brave slid off and went downstream a ways. I seen him crawl out with his Henry but couldn't get a shot off 'fore he was gone."

"No telling how many Custer's men took with them," Dan said.

"Nope," Charley said, stuffing his cheek with the wad. "Word is, it didn't take long, so there must of been twelve, fifteen hundred warriors. No time to get off many shots. Probably got fifteen, twenty. Less than fifty, I'd guess."

"Poor Sam," Charley said. "Didn't have no chance to be a hero, gettin' turned down for the water detail."

"Yes, poor Sam," Dan said, half-smiling. "Besides the water detail, the only stand-outs I know were Roy and his party."

"And Hanley from C Troop, catchin' up that mule with the ammo."

"Jesus, yes. How could I forget about Hanley? Talk about poor shooting, they must have fired a hundred rounds at him. And what was Hanley thinking, risking his hair like that?"

"From what I heard, he was so pissed off at the mule that he didn't give a damn. After that it was pure luck and bad shootin'."

"Actually, he was lucky to be with the pack train. Otherwise, he'd be buried with the rest of C Troop."

"Huh. I hadn't thought of that," Charley said. "Anyway, I shouldn't of said 'poor Sam.' It was a good fight for him. He learned Indians ain't stupid, for one thing. And he got the chance to deal with bein' scared. Next time it won't throw him."

"I guess not," Dan said. "Actually, he soldiers well, and being part of the army's what counts for him. Like Jubal, don't you think?"

"Not exactly," Charley answered. "Jubal's like a lot of us. Cavalry gives us a set of rules to live by."

"Yes, and it gives a man a chance to learn some things well," Dan added. "Like how to take care of a horse, and—"

"How to drink rotgut whiskey," Charley said and laughed. "But Sam didn't need no set of rules. He had a good trade, was sober, never in trouble, a good and decent man."

"You're right. Even so, the army's giving him something."

"The chance to be a hero," Charley growled, shifting his chaw to the other side. "He's still starry-eyed, you know. Mopin' 'cause he didn't kill nobody."

"That's a good way to put it, moping." Dan got his pipe going.

"The fight didn't change that hero stuff in him, not a bit." Catching Dan's eye, Charley gave him that icy glare of his. "He was lucky this time, but the next—"

"Yes, I know. We better do something about it," Dan said.

"Not we, Goddamn it, you! What you gotta do is—"

"I know, for Chrissakes! I've got to do exactly what you told me at the Powder. You said I had a way with words, so I should use them to change the flag-waving pictures in his head. Tell him about Antietam, you said. Tell him about the windrows of dead, the blown-off arms, the close-up grape shot, and the canister, the screams, the running for your lives. Tell him how his darling Dad went down, how Franny went down. Make him see it, you said, make him feel it."

"Well, that ain't it exactly," Charley said, a shit-eating grin on his face. "But you sure got the gist of it."

Chapter 34: A Summer of Misery

★ ★ ★

THAT EVENING THEY STARTED for the Bighorn, where the steamboat *Far West* was supposed to be ready to take aboard their wounded. However, the column hadn't gone four miles when General Terry called a halt because carrying the wounded on improvised litters was slowing the march too much. The next morning Lieutenant Doane of the Second Cavalry had his men put together mule-litters and travois. Finished by evening, the new litters worked beautifully, so Terry decided to get going immediately. Before long it started to rain, making for a miserable night's march. It was half past two the next morning when they reached the Bighorn. There the wounded were loaded on the *Far West.* Ernst stayed on the steamer with the wounded as it started downriver to Fort Lincoln.

Together with Colonel Gibbon's column, Seventh Cavalry marched down the Bighorn to Fort Pease on the Yellowstone's north bank. The squad was far from cheerful. Jubal was downright touchy, not like himself at all. Elvin Crane spent even more time pandering to Bull, who'd made sergeant and taken over Steinbrecher's squad permanently. Sam was plain down at the mouth. Jake spent most of his free time in one card game or another. Neither Jim nor Charley spoke more than was necessary.

July fourth was the nation's hundredth birthday, a warm, sunny day that found Dan deep in a hog-trough of gloom. Nevertheless, it gave him reason to drink, so he found and shared a pint of rotgut with Charley, but gloom drowned the celebration and he only managed to get half-drunk. The next morning found him even more sullen, with a splitting headache on top of it. *What better time to confront Sam?*

He should have known better. Irritation had begun clawing at his gut when he first saw Sam sitting alone with his coffee, gazing at nothing, lost inside his own head. But he went ahead anyway.

"You still want to hear about Antietam?" he asked.

"When? This afternoon?" Sam asked, brightening up immediately.

"Yes, this afternoon, but tell me something," Dan started in, suddenly pissed off. Sam was all wide-eyed again for Christ's sake. "We've just been through a terrible fight, lost near half the regiment, and buried two hundred and fifty corpses under a blazing sun. Why in God's name are you so feekin' eager to hear how twenty-five hundred men went down in one bloody day? Jesus Christ, lad, why?"

"Because my father died there!" he fairly bristled. "I've got a right to know how it happened, and you were there."

"That's right, and what did I see? No flag-waving heroes for sure." With that a jolting pain split Dan's skull, while pictures of Franny's bloodied remains flashed through his mind. He turned away.

"What's the matter?" Sam asked.

"No, not today, I can't," Dan growled. "I cannot tell it today." He'd bitten off more than he could chew. Maybe he'd get it done after they got back to Fort Lincoln.

* * *

Sam stomped off. What business did Dan have turning snarly like that, practically questioning a man's honor, a man who sacrificed his life for the country? Judas H. Priest! Oddly, he found himself thinking back to Simpson's sheep farm in Middlefield, of all places—colder than a witch's tit in January, sitting on a wind-swept ridge halfway to Albany. The county stuck him there when he was ten. He had to wrestle sheep at shearing time, ticks crawling all over him. Mr. Simpson blew up when he caught him petting the dog. "That's a *workin'* dog!" he'd hollered. "Leave it be!" The man had grabbed the ox whip and come at both of them. The dog scrambled under the barn, so Sam had to take it for both of them. He hoped someone had put that crazy old man down, the narrow-eyed son of a bitch.

★ ★ ★

On July seventh a party of Crows rode in with word that back on June seventeenth Crazy Horse had soundly whipped General Crook's column of twelve hundred men, fifty officers, and over two hundred Crow and Shoshone allied warriors. It took a while for the news to sink in. Not only had the Sioux and Cheyenne renegades soundly whipped the Seventh, but a week earlier they'd driven a force twice its size hightailing it back to Wyoming. General Sheridan remained determined to punish them and ordered Crook and Terry to combine their forces into an expedition to find and destroy them.

At Fort Pease Seventh Cavalry reorganized itself into seven companies. Late in the month they joined Gibbon's column, marched down the Yellowstone's north bank, and set up camp opposite the mouth of Rosebud Creek. Someone dubbed the temporary bivouac Fort Beans (to go with Fort Rice and Fort Pease.) The renegades were thought to be in the Bighorn Mountains, so Terry planned to hook up with Crook on the Rosebud and move on them as soon as possible. On the second of August the *Josephine* came upriver, carrying badly needed provisions, remounts, recruits, and some artillery. The column spent the next four days ferrying everything across the Yellowstone, preparing to march up the creek.

★ ★ ★

The first evening of the march Jake asked, "Hey Charley, where them Sioux now, you think?"

"All over. Some bands gone back to the agencies, some gone north to Canada."

"So how come we gonna chase 'em south into them mountains?"

"Following orders."

"It doesn't make sense to go where they aren't," Sam offered.

"It's the army way," Jubal said.

"Still doesn't make sense," Sam insisted.

"Makes sense to Sheridan," Dan said, breaking out of his shell. He'd been especially churlish ever since getting wind of Sheridan's plans.

"Huh?"

"Sheridan's got to restore his feeking pride!" Dan said, angry enough to cause the others to look up. "Look, first he sends Crook out into the snow, all for naught. Then he gets Custer from under Grant's foot and orders him and Crook and Gibbon to box the hostiles up like they were a foot-sore Secesh outfit. What happened left him lower than a snake's pecker. So now he can't let go of it till we kill a few stray Indians. Then he'll ballyhoo it to the newspapers and we'll go home."

"Who knows? We might find another big village," Sam said.

"Sure, and come winter, bullfrogs will grow whiskers."

"How long you think we'll be out?" Jake asked.

"How in the name of Christ would I know?" Dan snapped. Weary of the whole damn thing, he got up and headed for his tent.

* * *

The next two weeks made for nothing but misery for everyone. It was a march from hell, thirty miles south, fifty miles northeast, twenty miles east, and thirty-five miles north again. The men were thoroughly soaked and chilled by rain, baked by the sun, short on rations, and without forage in a country fire-blackened by the Indians, using up the horses while the officers argued about the meaning of pony tracks some three weeks old. Out of supplies, Crook headed back to Wyoming, and on August eighteenth, Terry's column reached the Powder River depot, played out, living on hard bread and waiting for supplies. Scurvy, dysentery, and rheumatism swept through the ranks. Those well enough grumbled and bickered. More than a few deserted.

⋆ ⋆ ⋆

A few nights later Charley called Dan on his churlishness.

"Dan, you been a pain in the ass since we buried them boys by the river, and it's gettin' worse," he said.

"I know that," Dan growled.

"So do somethin' 'bout it! Deal with whatever's eatin' you up."

"I keep thinking how many lives the generals throw away," Dan said.

"Bullshit. You know that's what they're paid to do, and it's never got to you like this."

"So what else could it be?" Dan asked.

"Christ, how should I know?" With that Charley rolled over and was snoring inside of three minutes.

Dan finally drifted off only to be forced awake by the revulsive sight of Paddy O'Malley's corpse, the flies busy at the work of procreation amidst the cadaveric poisons. He usually pushed the image aside, but this night was different. Why that picture? The answer emerged in an unending string of thoughts. The banshee had called Paddy for Christ's sakes! Then the tinny sounds of "Garryowen" filled his ears, followed by a string of recollections peculiarly Irish: Uncle Dev's rants about Clontarf in '43, Great Blasket through the mist, his first sight of Boston in '48 (he was almost seven), Franny's premonition that one of them would die, "Garryowen" again, Father Duffy, the rheumy-eyed lecher, the cottage near Kilmurry, Uncle Kevin's wake—all ancient history, nonsensical, and the stuff of being Irish.

Truth be, Dan's memories of things Irish carried the double-edged sword of conflicting truths. On one side was the righteous truth that tyranny was wrong—to drive starving innocents off their land was the Devil's work. It was equally true that charging into tyrants' guns made for naught but grieving mothers and fatherless babes. Of course, Irish humbug would muddle the brain, blinding it from the second.

As a wee lad in County Kerry he had learned of the faeries and their magical powers. It was fascinating stuff for a boy caught within the dreariness of poverty. Like a thirsty sponge he absorbed it all, right along with the fancies of the Church that in the end strengthened the bonds of misery. In America he grew to trust in what was real and see through the magical trappings of self-serving priests. Shunning the hollow promises of superstition, his brain separated the real from fantasy. Logic and reason forced him to dismiss Franny's half-spoken premonition and O'Malley's banshee tale, but Paddy's brogue sat locked inside his brain: "Did ye hear her mournful keenin', Daniel?" *Not on your life, me darling Paddy,* he had thought, although he wouldn't insult a friend by scoffing at his words. He'd gone on that day, thinking he'd erased Paddy's words just as he'd forgotten as best he could the slip-away little ones he'd briefly seen when he was five.

Still, if he was a rational man, why the fleeting "maybe" when he saw poor, dead Paddy, his eyes flat-staring at the sun. Did a corner of his brain still hold on to those idiocies, indifferent to the power of reason?

"Damn it!" he cursed. "Truth be, I half-believed the old hag *did* call him that black night. Nothing but hocus-pocus, that part of my brain, infected by the taradiddles of childhood."

Fact was, Dan hated that hodgepodge of absurdities. Looking to get rid of them, he chose to talk it out with Charley. And if Charley couldn't help, at least he'd say so with neither reluctance nor hesitation.

The conversation the next night was shorter than Dan expected. After explaining his dilemma, he said, "Christ Almighty, Charley, that old hairball of hocus-pocus holds fast in my brain, fairly mocking my love of reason. I've got to get rid of it!"

"You can't," Charley said.

"Why not?"

"It's a part of you. Always has been."

Taken aback, Dan sat silently, stupidly thinking a man of so little learning shouldn't be so cock-sure about another man's nature.

"But reason's the only way to make sense out of this life," he said.

"Horseshit!" Charley shot back, eyes narrowing. "There's more to life than what makes sense. You think there's logic in who lives, who dies?"

"Maybe not, but—"

"Ain't no maybes about it!" He was furious. "That's why gamblers got hunches an' professors got philosophies. All hogwash, sure, but it helps 'em through it. Real Catholics go to confession. Jews, I don't know 'bout them, but I'm sure they got something. Indians call on the spirits. Your faerie stuff is the same thing. It's all to help us fill the holes in life. 'Course John Daniel Murphy's gotta be diff'rent—ev'rything's gotta be reasoned out."

"It'd be a help," Dan said, trying to lighten things up.

"Horseshit again!" Charley growled.

"What do you mean?" he asked, eager for him to go on. When Charley got that intense, it paid to hear him out.

"Look, you're a man of reason. I listen to you reasonin' ev'ry Goddamn day. But the faerie stuff is a part of you too. Piss on it and you're pissin' on yourself."

Speechless, Dan reached in a pocket for his dudeen only to fumble it onto the ground. "Where's that leave me?" he asked, recovering the pipe.

"Here with the rest of us, usin' our brains as best we can. What's left over we leave to God or faeries or spirits or whatever else we got."

"And all the hocus-pocus in my brain?"

"Let it sit," Charley said, looking at the stars above, then locking eyes with his partner. "Live with both sides of yourself, Dan. The rest of us gotta. Why shouldn't you?"

★ ★ ★

On the first of September Major Reno led the regiment north from the Yellowstone on a fruitless, two-hundred-mile search for hostiles as far as Wolf Point and Fort Buford before heading down the Missouri. They reached Fort Lincoln on Tuesday, September 26, their clothes in tatters and their equipment in sad repair. Both men and horses were played out ... and bone thin.

Chapter 35: At Fort Lincoln

THEY'D HEARD RUMORS ABOUT Sheridan's plans for three weeks, but nothing about what he had in mind for Seventh Cavalry. Now they got the details. Dan had fallen far short of the mark when he said all Sheridan wanted was to regain his pride. No, sir—he wanted vengeance. He wanted vengeance for Crook's defeat; vengeance for killing Custer and 265 good men; and vengeance for destroying his grand plans to force the renegades back to the agencies once and for all. Now he was going to get it—every bit of it and more. He'd emasculate the Sioux and make them completely dependent on the government for enough food to avoid starvation. Proud men could no longer provide for their families.

Terry and Crook were to construct permanent bases in Powder River country to maintain the war against all Indians outside of the reservations. He convinced Sherman and President Grant to replace civilian agents with officers backed by garrisons of regimental strength. Nine companies were placed at Standing Rock and nine at Cheyenne River. Red Cloud Agency got a mix of cavalry, infantry, and artillery—eighteen companies in all.

The Treaty of 1868 was trashed. The Indians lost their vast hunting grounds in Montana, Wyoming, and Nebraska Territories. The Great Sioux Reservation was cut by at least a quarter. The government took the sacred Black Hills and forced the Sioux to allow Whites to cross their reservation freely in order to get to them.

Sheridan aimed to dominate the Sioux; their lives would never be the same. Any renegades returning to the agencies would be arrested and treated as prisoners of war. Sales of arms and ammunition to Indians were outlawed. The cavalry would invade the agencies and seize every rifle, pistol, and cartridge it found—by force, if necessary. Worse yet, cavalrymen would take away all of their ponies.

For now Seventh Cavalry needed rest and food—three squares a day of it. Its equipment needed repair and replacement. Five hundred recruits had arrived to fill the ranks. They needed training. Company A picked up two new officers, forty-two men, and forty-three remounts, swelling the troop to one hundred men and eighty horses. The squad picked up four rookies: Rooney, Kessler, Connelly, and Holland. Fortunately, none of them were starry-eyed "Custer's Avengers," and they looked like they would work out okay. And Elvin Crane gained his transfer to Bull's squad, which greatly pleased the others.

Returning to the post settled Jake down, while Sam was quiet, even somber, still wrestling with not having killed an Indian. Ernst was happy, assigned to the hospital. (Jim suspected his fondness for Ernst came from him being the only gentle human in this scratch-and-claw country.) Dan was no longer surly, but Jubal was the big surprise. He remained downright contrary, complaining about everything.

"Jubal, you're not one to piss and moan all day and half the night," Dan said. "Been going on since the fight, it has."

"I jist got the sorries, is all," he answered.

"What about?"

"Well, yew'd prob'ly understand," he said, looking like he wasn't all that convinced. "Thing is, Dan, I keep seein' thet young brave, the one by the river."

"With the bow and arrow?" Dan asked, as Charley joined them.

"Uh huh. It's like he's still sittin' thar in my mind, his arm bleedin' hard," he said, nodding to Charley. "I keep wishin' I'd of gone over an' tied it off."

"But you couldn't."

"No, 'cause I had to git back right quick," he said, looking away, disquieted. "But thet wa'n't it. See, I tole y'all he was a young buck, but shoot, he was no more'n twelve. Sap-green, yew know, an' leavin' him bleedin' like thet ..."

"The ugly part of soldiering, a time like that," Dan said, knowing it wouldn't help a bit. "He keeps haunting you?"

"His face does," Jubal said, looking inward. "How long you think it'll go on?"

"I don't know."

"Charley?"

"No tellin'."

★ ★ ★

Dan was free after morning stables on Sunday, the first of October. The day promising to be warm, he settled under a shade tree with a book from the post library. Mark Twain, it was, a book of stories that started with the tale about the jumping frog. He was into the fourth story where Twain lists the ingredients of killikinick when Sam walked up, all bubbly with excitement.

"You got a minute?" he asked, knowing full well Dan didn't; he'd waited for the book since last March.

"What is it?" Dan asked pleasantly, being a kind and forgiving man.

"The July *Galaxy* came in."

"So?"

"There's a new article by General Custer!"

"Back from the dead, is he?"

"'Course not," he said. "No, it's about the Yellowstone fight in '73. I read through it fast 'cause I wanted to tell you about it. I'll read it carefully later on."

"That's good of you, lad, but right now—"

"Wow! What a fight that was," he said, interrupting Dan and rushing on, unable to contain his excitement. "Custer was really a brave man, Dan, riding four hundred yards ahead of the party like that."

"Oh, he was brave, all right," Dan said, his irritation growing. "But four hundred yards?"

"Maybe I got it wrong, racing through it like I did. Anyway, he sure outthought Crazy Horse. Tells me that if he'd been leading us the last three months, we would have caught Sitting Bull for sure."

"What?" Dan put the book aside, his blood starting to boil.

"Well, we wouldn't have been bogged down by the infantry. And all those wagons really held us—"

"What the hell is wrong with you?" Dan exploded, jumping to his feet. "You read a few pages about a fight three years ago and you're back to being a schoolboy again, hero-worshipping a dead man for Christ's sakes. That's right, your feekin' hero is dead! Just threw away two hundred lives, he did. Why? 'Cause he thought he could get away with splitting up an undermanned regiment, split it up not once but twice."

"But—"

"But nothing, Sam. But nothing," Dan said, holding up his hand to keep him quiet. Far past exasperation, he took a deep breath, wondering what to do with the lad. Then he realized he knew exactly what to do. "It's time, Goddamn it, time to hear about Antietam and how your darling Dad was killed."

"Really? When?" Sam asked, his eyes lighting up.

"This evening, north end of the stables." Dan gestured him away as he sat down. A storyteller of Mark Twain's caliber never deserved to be interrupted, certainly not by a lad idolizing a general brought down by his own arrogance.

Later when Dan told Charley his plans, Charley said he would go along and bring Jake and Ernst. Sam's friends being there would help the story stick in the lad's mind. Sure and it was a very good idea.

★ ★ ★

After supper the two men walked down to the little grove of cottonwoods.

"We start with a map," Dan said, scraping a patch of dirt clean and level.

"I was there a year ago," Sam said. "Walked all over the battlefield: the Dunker Church, the farms, Hagerstown Pike, Burnside's bridge, Bloody—"

"The ground wasn't the same in '62."

"It couldn't have changed much," Sam said, all wide-eyed. "I've read some stuff with maps too, which showed how the two sides maneuvered and all."

"A regular professor, you are." Dan took a deep breath. "Look, I won't belabor you with what happened unless you're going to open your ears and hear me. Do you understand?"

"Yes."

"Okay, but first admit you know not a damn thing about how your Dad was killed."

"How d'you know that?" Sam asked, the color draining from his face.

"Because I watched you go starry-eyed talking about it, which says you've got made-up pictures running through your head. Jesus, a month's pay says you see your heroic father carrying the Fifteenth's colors out front in the line of battle, looking back and waving his stalwart companions forward as they charge into the very heart of the blazing maelstrom."

Turning red, Sam gulped and looked toward the river.

"Am I right?"

"Not exactly," Sam said, attempting a smile. "I thought about him carrying the colors, but—"

"That's what I mean, lad. You have it wrong. Color sergeants carried the flags. So now I ask you: do you want to know what happened to your Dad or no? If you want to go on with those heroic pictures in your mind, just say so and I'll stop."

It took a moment for him to respond. "I better hear what really happened," he said without looking up.

"Don't give me 'better.' Choose."

Sam looked up, his eyes unfocused, looking inside. Then his gaze shifted quickly and he was staring into Dan's eyes with an intensity that set Dan back for a moment. Something wild in that stare, there was.

"I want to know."

"So you'll let go of the nonsense you've read and try to hear it?"

"Ayuh."

"Good. Here comes Charley and your two friends." They were quite a ways off, taking their own sweet time.

"Judas, why are they coming?"

"They should hear it too." Dan smiled. "Besides, expert historian that I am, I require an audience larger than one."

"I still don't see ..." His words trailed off. He shrugged and turned to welcome the others.

Dan began sharpening the end of a stick while reminding himself to tell it through Sam's father's eyes. That should be easy enough. His own Twentieth Massachusetts was in the Second Brigade, almost directly behind the father's Fifteenth. Old images began to come: the quiet time before sunrise; the coffee's bitterness; the fetid smells of the catch-as-catch-can bivouac of men far better suited for Hampshire farms or Boston tenements than a Maryland creek-bottom blanketed in dripping mist; the stand-arounds, coffee in hand, pushing down the impatience of men waiting to throw their lives like dice upon the hay fields, corn stalks, and woodlots that lay to the west. Whatever war was to the philosophers, it was nothing but a miserable gamble for the man caught inside the iron trap of luck.

His thoughts leaped to the wilderness, twenty months later. Pat Foley rising to a crouch, moving forward through the shattered trees, Dan stride for stride to his left and just behind. The ball hit Pat's face with a thunk and spun him around, stone dead but still standing, leaning against him for half a second. *Thunk!* The second ball was meant for him, but it hit Pat in the back. Alive, he was, yanking his arm out from under the fresh corpse. Dan always pictured him the day they met in Readville. Freckled with orange-red hair, he laughed in a full-blown way, sometimes braying like a mule when he gasped for air. He came from Fitchburg, or was it Fiskdale? They partnered up after Antietam. Never knew why—just glanced at each other and that was that. Soldiered well together, they did. Dan never would forget him, yet never missed him.

The silence was broken by a meadowlark's flute-like song, then silence again. The waste, the Goddamn waste of it infuriated Dan. Could Sam comprehend that? Could any man grasp the waste unless he'd been there to see the color-drained faces, flies busy on dry mouths, and unseeing eyes before noon? Maybe one like Charley, born old enough to marvel at seeing life's persistence in a fly creating maggots. *Make him feel it,* Dan urged himself, thinking that he'd welcome a bit of the Creature, just a taste to smooth the edge of his snarliness.

The four men were fast approaching. Christ Almighty, the jauntiness was back in Sam's step, once again the schoolboy. Eager to learn, he was.

"I saw Bloody Lane when I was there," Sam said immediately.

Dan didn't reply, catching a flash of bright yellow, the songbird disappearing beyond the trees.

"Meagher's Irish Brigade took it, didn't they?"

"Men dying took it!" Dan snapped. "And it was called the Sunken Road that day," he added, trying to calm himself.

Offended, Sam shot back, "I know that!"

"Easy, lad, you're like a cat thrown in the drink—all whiskers an' wet fur. Calm down and listen."

"Okay, I will," Sam said, no less irritated.

"And I'll hold you to it," Dan said.

Motioning the other three to come close, Dan asked Sam to fill them in on events prior to September 17, 1862. He did a good job of it, explaining that the Union had suffered a succession of defeats before Lee crossed the Potomac into Maryland and McClellan moved to stop him, first at South Mountain, then at Antietam Creek near Sharpsburg. The young bastard did an impressive job.

Dan spoke to Jake and Ernst. “I’m tellin’ this mainly for Sam’s benefit, you know. I’m sure he’s told you his father was killed there. Now he needs to know what went on. You boys ought to hear it too.”

Chapter 36: Antietam

"HERE'S THE GROUND," DAN began, drawing with the pointed stick. "North's this way. Here's Antietam Creek running south to the Potomac, Hagerstown Turnpike out of Sharpsburg, and Smoketown Road here. They come together here at the Dunker Church here. Three woodlots, North, East, and West—hardwoods. Slow rolling farmland, but it generally sloped up from the creek going west. Fairly flat after the East Woods, except there's a rise just past the West Woods, giving the Confederates a clear field of fire from here, on Hauser's Ridge and here, on the hill beyond the Nicodemus farm. You see that?"

"I think so," Sam said.

"Picture it," Dan said. "You got it? Now, First Corps was bivouacked by these woods on the north. At dawn they started marchin' south an'—"

"Where's the cornfield?" Sam asked.

"What?" Dan was nettled by the interruption, but Sam was right. "It's here. The Sunken Road slants across here. It's a deep trench, actually, seven or eight feet. Now remember, the ground slopes up from the creek going west, then mostly flat after the East Woods."

"Distance?" Charley asked. "And the guns."

"Thanks, Charley, I forgot. From Smoketown Road here to the West Woods there is some four hundred yards, maybe a bit more. As for guns, the Confederates knew their business. Horse artillery up on Hauser's Ridge plus more on this rise behind the Nicodemus place. Regular artillery down this way, both south and east of the Sunken Road. I say regular, but those boys ran their guns from place to place so quick you would think they were moving slingshots."

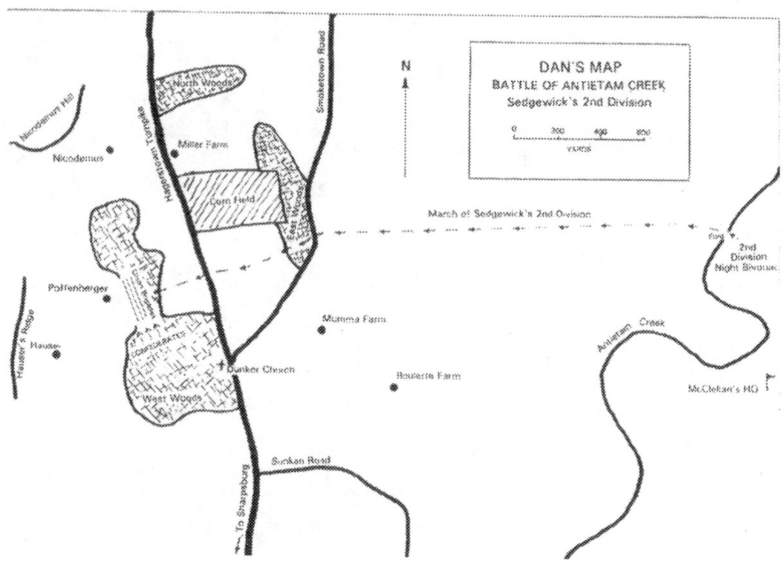

"What about our guns?" Sam asked.

"Early on, mostly close by the woodlot on the north. More batteries east of Smoketown Road," Dan replied, pointing to the map.

He took a minute, gazing at the map, and then it was time to get on with it. He locked eyes with Sam.

"Okay, let's follow your father's footsteps, best we can. What was his name?"

"Huh?" Sam was startled. "Oh, it's Jonah."

"Private Jonah Streeter of the Fifteenth Regiment Massachusetts Volunteer Infantry, Gorman's First Brigade, Sedgwick's Second Division, General Sumner's Second Corps. Right?"

"Yes, but how'd you know all that?"

"I did some studying myself. Now I can only guess what went through your Dad's mind, but maybe we can get the feel of it. How tall was he?"

"He was tall, ah, close to six foot, I'd say. Why do you need to know that?"

"To get a sense of his stride and what he could see. All right, it's Wednesday. We'd pushed the Rebs off of South Mountain three days before, sending 'em back toward Virginia. Felt good to drive them back for a change. The Fifteenth had to be happy, because they'd been hurt bad at Ball's Bluff and beaten up at Fair Oaks in May."

"Were you at Fair Oaks?" Sam asked.

"Yes. At Ball's Bluff too." Dan took a breath, remembering. "On Monday your father marched the eight miles from South Mountain to Antietam Creek. Tuesday morning a hard fog hung in the hollows, but it cleared off early. We knew by noon there'd be no fighting that day. Talk was that Lee was about to retreat straight across the Potomac. We relaxed more and more as the day went on, jawing some, passing rumors along. Then Lee holed up in Sharpsburg—so much for a retreat. Rebel guns and ours lobbing shot and shell over, feeling each other out. Nothing came close to your father's outfit. Weather was pleasant enough. Maryland countryside is real green."

"Not like here," Sam said.

"No, not like here," Dan said. "Not in any way."

"There's a stir late in the afternoon. First Corps's pulling out and crossing a bridge half mile to the north. Hearing that, your Jonah would know it meant something is on for the next day. Rumor is the Fifteenth would cross the creek first thing in the morning. Still, during the day he relaxed some, thinking there might not be a fight. You understand?"

"I guess so."

"Then he hears what sounds like First Corps is in a fight. It's near dusk though, and the noise fades out. Word comes down: no fires. Now that's plain disgruntling. They say we must keep the Rebs from seeing where we are, but they've been watching us all day from the high ground to the west. You can't move First Corps' seven thousand men without giving them a hint of McClellan's plans, not after they got into a skirmish up there. About then it starts to drizzle and then rain. Jonah was miserable, chewing on ground coffee and hardtack.

"Things get quiet, finally. Just the ordinary sounds of camp. You know, someone's always moving around, your bunkie shifting a hip off a hard spot, a voice here and there. Some men will nod off and sleep right on through. Most won't. Then just after eleven word spreads that Twelfth Corps will move across the creek to join with First Corps, so the next day's sure to bring on a fight. In the distance the sputter of muskets opens up again, then it's quiet. Between all the distractions, your Dad had a fitful night. He was dozing, waking, half-dreaming, sometimes startled, generally a mite nervous. He probably got up to piss once."

Dan paused, listening to the meadowlark before recalling Franny's voice calling him in the dark. A dream woke him up, he'd said, but he'd had no wish to tell it. A premonition? Nonsense! Five thousand men had premonitions that night, and most of them lived through the next day, bloody though it was.

"'Twas real dark, with the rain and the overcast. Still, it's surprising how much light there was. Maybe it was all those tents lined up. I remember looking at the clouds to the east. Might have been my imagination, but it looked like they were brightened up by the sporadic rifle fire.

"Nothing is calm, you know. But again, there is nothing to worry about. Kind of like how they'd been eating. They weren't starving, but Jonah wondered how many days he could go without getting something substantial.

"He's mostly awake when reveille sounds. Glad the night is over, yet dreading the day, he crawls out in the dark. Rain has stopped but everything's wet. Heavy dew, thick mist hanging in the hollows, chilly.

"Picture it, Sam. There's your darling Dad, one of fifteen thousand men, battle ready yet sitting still. Around your Dad were the fifty men of Company C, sitting, standing, hunkering, stretching, scratching, grumbling, farting, pissing, rolling blankets, stowing gear, nervous but not nervous too. Hungry yet knowing they'd be eating mush again. And coffee—thank God for coffee. Your Dad probably changed into the extra socks he'd washed and dried over the fire yesterday. Knew enough to take care of his feet.

"Sun's not up, but it's light enough to see six hundred men all doing the same as him. Beyond are more regiments, then some more, thirty-seven of them. Over by some trees the artillery's tending their horses, limbering up. Then the sergeants come by, giving men the once-over, telling this man that, that man this, hurrying one squad up, sending another to fill their canteens. From somewhere come the generals: Sumner, Sedgwick, and Gorman, maybe Howard and Dana too. And the regimental colonels. There's a bunch of wide-eyed lieutenants acting like they're more than the messenger boys they are. Brigadiers on high-stepping prancers follow Sumner off somewhere important, each general his own monkey show. You can picture that, for sure. By now Jonah's finished both his ablutions and his cracker mush and stands around, knowing he's in for another wait but hoping he's not, still not sure if the Fifteenth will fight today. They'd been in reserve at South Mountain. Maybe the same today, maybe not. All he knows is he has to wait, so he stands or hunkers, no place dry enough to sit. Sun's still not up. He begins to worry they'll stay there all day. Or maybe he was hoping they would. That's what I did."

Taking a rest from remembering, Dan realized his legs were aching from hunkering down, so he stood up and took a few steps before coming back to the makeshift map. The others shifted around some too, except for Charley. He just sat on a stump, quiet-like, his eye on a sky that had turned a soft orange. Dan settled with one knee on the ground, pointed stick in hand.

"Okay, back to Jonah. Time did one of those fast slides ahead, if you know what I mean, slipping past five. Men talking, doing their best to keep the rumors flying around, except they keep one ear cocked toward the west, their minds plotting out who's moving which way and with how much. Guns—five, ten, maybe more—seem to be coming from behind a woodlot up the hill. *Blam-blam blam.* He feels the percussion of it. Small arms fire mixed in sounding like popping corn: *tut-tut-pop, tut-pop-pop-tut.* Skirmishers. Doesn't get louder, just more of it, murderous volleys of it. It stops and then starts again.

"Jonah's compelled to look to the east because the sun is gliding up fast from behind the mountain, lighting up the clouds." Dan pointed with the stick. "Just then the Rebel artillery up here by the Dunker Church gets to thundering—*ba-bam bam bam!* Our guns answer, a nonstop roar from the east, louder and louder. After the first volley it's scattered, then more rapid. Twenty-pound Parrotts banging away, six batteries of them, firing faster and faster as they get into it. Twenty shells the first minute, then more and more. He stops counting. The sound is a kind of sharp clang which splits the air, bangs on your eardrums, like pails of water flung against the side of your head. Doesn't really hurt, but it staggers you, and it won't let up. Shells stream over, searching out the Confederate guns. Twenty-four cannons, laddie, all at once! The noise? The worst thunderstorm you ever went through is like a colt running on grass by comparison. Your Dad, he'd heard it before, back at Malvern Hill. Only this time the roar is straight from hell. Strange, though. The longer it goes on, the less he hears it."

"What d'you mean?" Sam asked.

"You get used to it, like working in a foundry. The noise slides back to where you don't notice it. Of course, if it stops you're going to look up. Right?"

"Ayuh."

"About then word comes down: the company will form up and march west, up the slope toward the fighting. Nothing happens, of course. Funny thing about moments like those. By my faith, you're out of harm's way but almost itch to get the waiting over with no matter what. Still, you stand and wait some more, ready to go, but no orders come down. Jonah starts worrying again about his socks, of all things. Maybe he should have saved the good ones. Probably he chews on a twig or maybe a cracker to quiet the stomach twinges.

"General Bull Sumner, he's more eager than anybody to get his Second Corps moving. But McClellan won't even meet with him. Instead, he has his staff tell Sumner the smoke and noise up on the hill is Confederate rear-guard action. Lee is pulling out, they say. Fact is, McClellan was dead wrong. Couldn't see a damned thing as far back as he was. He could hear, though, like the rest of us. Sure, it quieted for a bit, but it picked up again. What happened was that Hooker's First Corps came out of the North Woods, here, and drove south down both sides of the pike, here and there. Confederate guns up on Nicodemus Hill tore them up something awful before Rebel infantry drove them back out of the East Woods and the cornfield and they had to pull back. Shortly, Mansfield's Twelfth Corps tried pretty much the same thing and got no farther."

The meadowlark had gone silent.

Chapter 37: The West Woods

"OKAY, THE FIFTEENTH MASSACHUSETTS is here in Gorman's Brigade," Dan said, jabbing at the map. "Steppin' off straight toward the Hagerstown Pike five hundred yards distant. Jonah sights on the rail fence beside it, gauging the distance as they go. A man will pick out one thing to focus on while he moves toward it.

"The line picks up the step. The beat takes hold. A soldier trips and falls, scrambles back in line, back in step. Got to keep up. First Sergeant shouts. Nobody hears. Jonah stares straight ahead, straight at that fence four hundred yards distant. Three rails or four? Land falls off, then rises. Four rails, definitely. That's all he sees, all he wants to see. Woods quite a ways past it. Jonah glances that way but keeps his eyes fixed on the four-rail fence. Short steps around a wounded Reb lying there, eyes full of scared. Ten yards farther, mind goes back, recalls the Reb's eyes, dark brown, kind of sad. Quickly he thinks ahead, to the fence. Rail fence, no, they're poles not rails—heavy, solid poles, five, six feet high. Got to climb over it. Judas Priest! Fence on both sides of the pike. Two hundred, one fifty, a hundred yards. Soldiers lying by the fence. More blue than brown. One hanging *on* the fence. Why'd they leave him there? Smoke and dust. 'Where'd my air go?' Step, step, keep the step, step. Tongue's dried out, pats his canteen, got water. 'Who's praying? It's me, Goddamn it!' Fifty yards, thirty, twenty. Too soon! Five rails not four, and poles not rails. *Bam! Ba-blam!* Rebel six pounders. *Blam!* Damn! He twists an ankle and falls.

"A blur to his right, the man flies backward, taking the man behind him, gone. *Ba-bam!* Twelve pounder?" Dan pointed. "Guns from here on Hauser's Ridge blasting away, lobbing shells over the green, shady trees, solid shot barely over his head and into the brigade behind. He trips and falls. On one knee he twists his neck, looking right then left. Two, three men go down. *Ba-bam! Bam!* Solid shot straight into them. He jumps up and darts for the fence, grabs hold, up and over and drop. Across the road and over again. Sergeant shouting, 'Double quick!' Glued right there, he is, until his feet take over and he's running across two hundred yards of clover for the woodlot. Shells! Goddamn lampposts flying overhead! The cold knife of fear cuts deep into his gut, but it's gone in an instant while a scorching force like a skinner's bull whip drives him and he's racing for those trees. Someone's yelling loud. It's him; it's the whole company, a growing roar and then the line is out from under the shells. No! One explodes overhead! He goes down, tripped by a fresh-cleaned Springfield on the ground. Who dropped it? *Not one of us*, he stupidly thinks as he falls, turning to the side, keeping his own rifle up. Goddamn it! Downcast eyes light on a single shamrock reaching up like 'twas just another sunny day. Four seconds frozen into forever. Get up! Catch up! Watch the ground. 'To Hell with it!' he says, angling forward, rifle swinging in time with his double-quick. Four yards behind the line, legs pumping, lungs screaming, he catches up, a line of blue more ragged than before. Just fifty yards to go, now forty. It's so quiet all he hears is his feet hitting the ground, the soft clover almost springy. Thirty yards, twenty. Man beside him catches his eye for an instant; smiling, he smiles back—in this together. Sun on his back, and then it's dark, they're inside the woods. The line slows, others catch up, eyes strain to see. It's too dark in here, too quiet. A deep breath and then a shudder; shakes it off, looks ahead. Oak and hickory, maples. Ground broken with ledges, holes, outcroppings.

"Confederate guns four, five hundred yards to the front. First Sergeant hollering; the rank straightens some. Jonah looks right, then left. Where's the Thirty-Fourth New York? Only three regiments in the line. Dana's brigade's thirty, maybe only twenty yards back.

New York's Fifty-Ninth directly behind Jonah's regiment. Me, I was in the Twentieth Massachusetts, one outfit to the Fifty-Ninth's right. Union men stretched through those woods like strands of blue trading beads coming undone. The shadow-blotched ground is spongy, spotted with men from First Corps—dead, wounded, dying. Rebels, too. Pockets of them ahead in the trees, loading and firing. Murderous fire. Jonah looks left. Still no Thirty-Fourth New York. My God, they're supposed to be on his flank! More and more musketry beyond where they're supposed to be, and artillery going at it now. Maybe the Thirty-Fourth ran into trouble. He puts it aside, focuses on what's in front. A man's eyes keep darting ahead, you see, looking for the next thing to shoot at, or step around or over.

"Time slows down, his company keeps moving over the broken ground. Still catching his breath from the run. No push to get out of there. Halfway through more guns join the thunder to the south, Rebs hollering that yell of theirs over there, a steady crackle of musketry, fierce. The Thirty-Fourth New York catching that fire? Jonah stumbles over a Rebel corpse, sidesteps another, spots two wounded on his left, regains his step. Trees thinning out some. It gets lighter up ahead—a smoky haze, flicks of orange fire in it. Only forty yards more, thirty, twenty. Someone in the rank behind grabs a Confederate battle flag from a wounded man. A holler goes up off to the right, the line swelling ahead, men at the quickstep. Leave this shade? Into the heat? Into the fire? How come? Look! Old Bull Sumner spurring his horse out front, First Minnesota following like they're hitched to his traces. Fifteenth picks it up too, but by the time it gets to Jonah, it's only a hurry-up pace. Gets his breath again. Fifteen yards, ten, five, and out. A wagon road at woods' edge. The light is blinding! *Blam!* Six pounders on Hauser's Ridge sighting down on them, letting loose from what? Three hundred yards? No more than four. Infantry too, rifles poking out of barns and sheds, even the haystacks, only sixty, eighty yards to the front. *Zing!* Rounds fly over their heads mostly, but the bastards keep at it, getting the range. Sergeant shouts. Jonah fires, loads. *Thunk!* A man grabs his arm, sags, goes down. Behind, the two other brigades coming up close, still in the trees. Your Dad's out front in the open, firing, loading, firing.

"Ramming home a load, it's like something's not right. At first it's just a feeling, but then he hears the sound of it, off to the left and a bit behind. Guns for sure, but now it's one hell of a lot of muskets too, for God's sake. Now he's sure of it. The flank's been turned! A storm of Rebels coming at them through the trees from the south! It can't be, yet the Fifteenth's line is turning left and then they're dropping back into the trees again. Two minutes more and the air's too full of lead to breathe. Another man is hit, then two more. There's no stopping it!"

Spent, Dan sat lock-jawed, caught between his last thought and the next as the old pictures tumbled through his mind, chaining him to that bloody day. Motionless except for his fingers making fists, he stared not at Sam but through him. His hand relaxed, then repeated it all. Suddenly he stood and began pacing back and forth, his arms flying out and retreating in jerks, a hebephrenic obbligato to the steady beat of his steps until he broke off, sat down, and leaned forward, chin in hand.

"What's wrong?" Sam asked.

Dan held his breath, further reddening his face.

"What's the matter?" Sam asked again.

"What's the matter? What do you think's the matter?" Dan said, throwing his hands up, eyes following. "You studied the battle. Lee, he sent McLaw's division and another brigade north at the quickstep, another three thousand men. The Thirty-Fourth New York had fallen behind, moved toward the Dunker church, here," Dan said, pointing. "Together with a Pennsylvania outfit, they were holdin' off two Confederate brigades when a third one hit them on their flank. Swept them clear across the turnpike. Then the Rebels ran north, putting themselves in the rear of our three brigades stalled in the woodlot. You see? Three Union brigades, one close behind the other, facing west! Jonah's out front loading an' firing at Rebel infantry not eighty paces distant, with guns on the ridge pouring shot and shell straight into them. Now lead is zinging in from the left and the Goddamn rear! What's going on? A man cries out he's hit, a horse screams, the storm of musket fire on the left rises into a fury. The flank, the Goddamned flank! There's a fresh Confederate company charging into it. A company? Hell no, it's a whole brigade, a Secesh mob, screeching straight out of the bowels of hell. Rolling us up! Solid shot, canister and musketry in front, musketry from behind, and now a bloody cyclone from the left. We tried to swing around, but there was rank on top of rank, no room to maneuver. God help us, it was too damn late. A thousand rounds flying from three directions all at once and canister smashing into trees and men alike!"

Dan's mind flashed to the Creature. Christ Almighty! He'd give his left ball for a drink, but he pulled himself together.

"Smoke's so thick Jonah can't tell east from west—five thousand men caught inside the jaws of hell. Howard's Second Brigade's the first to go, his left flank crumbling, four Pennsylvania regiments running north for their lives. Jonah tries to hold on, him and the others firing at anything gray in the smoke. Trapped ten, twelve minutes by then. Each man fighting a battle in his head: stay or run? Here and there a soldier drops his musket and pulls foot. More often a man goes down, bleeding bad, leg broken, or stone dead. Your Dad spots Sumner on his horse again, hollering something fierce, but the din's too loud to make it out. Did someone yell we're going to move north? Or is it just him thinking he ought to go?

"It's too damn loud to think. Furies coming at them from the west, south, and east, tossing them back, body parts on the ground, a head here, an arm there , bloody guts splat on the living. Picture that, Sam! Picture your father. Go ahead, *picture* him. He's not waving anybody on, just doing the job of loading and firing while a solid shot plows through the man on his right, cutting a leg clean off the one behind, and two Minie balls thunking into the third man to his left. *Thu-thunk!* Wiping his eyes, he can't see for the smoke. Soldier dashes by before him. He spots a man in gray, raises his rifle, man's gone. Musket fire behind, awfully close. Another man hit, pitches forward. Still another down the line, same thing, hit in the back. Rebs can't be that close."

Dan went limp again, nearly played out. A shudder rolled through him. Framed in his mind's eye was dear Franny's face, his smile as sweet as ever. The shudder diminished, and he caught his breath and hurried on, his voice softer.

"There he is, Jonah Streeter in the smoke, everything helter-skelter, more strangers near him than men he knows. Cannons blasting from the ridge, musket rounds buzzing past from every direction. Loading and firing, deaf to all except a voice down the line hollering. He can't make it out. And now it's bright, the sun's streaming through the hickory. Nearly ten in the morning.

"Picture it, Sam, *picture* it!" Dan said, his voice a Goddamned roar in his ears. Sam flinched, pulling back as the words ran together. "Inside of this hell your Dad's alone, loading and firing, biting and tearing cartridges, ramming them home, aiming, firing, over and over. He doesn't think, doesn't hear, doesn't even see except for what he's doing. And then, remember that fire from the rear? It's a Goddamn storm! He wants to turn around, damn it, wants to know who's killing them. And he wants to run, Goddamn it, but he won't.

"Your darling Dad," Dan croaked, a sob melding with the words, "he rams home another load, straightens up to aim, and *thunk!* A chunk of iron smashes through his breastbone, blasts through his heart, and shatters his spine on the way out."

"What hit him?" Sam asked, chalk-faced.

Dan locked eyes with him. "Who knows? Solid shot, canister, grape, Minie ball, Confederate, Union—makes no difference. It killed him dead."

Sam's eyes lost their focus as he slid inside himself, clenching one fist then the other, over and over. Rage swept over him but vanished just as quickly. Dan drove the stick into the dirt, prying up a hunk of the tromped-down clay that he took in his hand and kneaded, like a farmer testing its readiness for the plow. Strange, he was anything but a farmer, yet he liked the feel and smell of dirt. He rolled it into a ball and slung it into the meadowlark's tree.

He looked at the others—Jake keeping one eye on Sam while rolling *une zigoune;* Ernst looking solemn, his mind probably recalling his *Großvater*; and Charley working on a new chaw.

Chapter 38: At Standing Rock

OCTOBER 27, 1876

Three weeks later Major Reno led Companies A, C, D, and G down the Missouri's west bank to Standing Rock to gather up all firearms and ponies from Sitting Bull's Hunkpapas. The supply cantonment there was garrisoned by a detachment from the Seventeenth Infantry. The cavalrymen would drive the ponies back to Fort Lincoln when they finished. Then they would move to Fort Rice for the winter.

Dan was wrought up again. What in the name of Christ was Sheridan thinking? Punish the whole tribe for the renegades' victories? Actually, Sheridan aimed to humiliate the tribe by stripping proud men of the tools they needed to provide for their families. What does that do to a man? Even at Appomattox, after the Union had lost 350,000 dead, Grant allowed the Confederates to keep their horses and mules so they could feed their families. In the event the cavalry got the job done, they left behind a dazed people, dependent on handouts from the government to survive the winter. Of course, some of the Indians took to the boonies and hid out. Halfway through the week Captain Moylan called a sergeants' meeting. He ordered the first sergeant to take a party to check out a band that was thought to be fifteen miles to the northwest. There was possibly another band some twelve miles west. Moylan told

Jim to lead his squad plus four of Bull's and find them. Both scouts were strictly for reconnaissance.

After the sergeant's meeting, Bull Judd walked down the slope to where Elvin Crane was sitting in the sun outside the stables. The usual swagger in his walk was absent, although his flat face still had the look of somebody entrusted with an important mission.

"How'd yer meeting go?" Elvin asked.

"Okay. Bunch of heathens are by a creek west of us. We gotta find 'em."

"You think they'll put up a fight?"

"I sure hope so. Thing is, Moylan's sendin' out two recon parties. Lawton's leadin' one of 'em. His squad plus four of us," Bull said.

"Which four?" Elvin asked.

"Me, you, an' two rookies, Finzer an' Runny LaCrosse."

"They're good, 'specially LaCrosse. If we find some bucks hidin' their ponies, we could learn 'em."

"That's right," Bull said, pleasantly surprised. Pretty good thinking for a dimwit. "Don't say nothin' 'bout that, 'specially to Smrka and Picard."

"Don't worry. I don't talk to no half-breeds."

Starting for the barracks, Bull thought about Custer for the umpteenth time. The newspapers said he rode into a treacherous Sioux ambush—hogwash. Indians aren't that smart. The General plain outthought himself, that's what happened. Split the regiment up, then found three times more heathens than expected. He paid the price, and that was the end of it. If the whole regiment had charged the village, the slaughter would have made Sand Creek look like child's play. Bull's mind jumped back to '64: racing through the swirl of it, Cheyenne running everywhere in the pandemonium, carbines barking, bullets whizzing, horses snorting, the screams of women and brats, an old chief staggering backward, his chest filled with lead, one of them weird death songs cutting through the hullabaloo, the feel of silky black braids in his hand as he sliced the bloody scalp from her devilish skull, the sound of it tearing from the bone, a ripping, gristly sound.

"If they fight, you think we'll get some scalps?" Elvin asked, cutting through his reverie.

"Dang blast it, Crane. Can't you see I'm thinkin'?"

No shame at Little Bighorn—and he'd made sergeant! It excited him, knowing that now he'd lead men in killing the heathens as the Lord had intended. After all, that was his calling.

⋆ ⋆ ⋆

They were in the saddle before sunrise. The first sergeant walked over to make sure they knew the job was strictly reconnaissance.

"First of all, go out twelve miles or so, and if you don't see nothin', head on back. And I don't wanna hear 'bout no fight 'less they come at you firin'."

That was good news as far as Dan was concerned. The Little Bighorn was all the fighting he needed for that year. Having the rising sun behind them was a good thing too. There was ice in the little brook by the bivouac, and his backside could use the warming of it.

Jim had Dan and Sam take the point ahead of the squad by a good five hundred yards. While they trotted out, Sam started talking about how they'd disarmed the Indians at the agency. Dan was a little surprised by his thoughts on the matter.

"Taking those people's rifles was bad enough," he said. "But taking their ponies was really tough. I almost choked up over it."

"You did?"

"Yes. Especially the kids. You remember that boy wearing an eagle feather? He was about ten and wasn't about to let go of his pony. Father made him do it. Judas Priest! The hate in that boy's eyes looking at me. Even the ponies were mad; you could see it. I don't understand why we took their ponies."

"Just following orders, right or wrong."

Nine miles out they rode up a gentle slope and could see all the way to the western horizon. Dan scoped it out with the glasses. The ground ahead was marked by six or seven coulees running mostly toward the northwest. A half mile to the south was a shallow canyon, its rim lined by a scattering of pines. Three miles ahead a solitary flat-topped knoll rose some three hundred feet above the plain with a cluster of pines on top. A barely visible thread of smoke was rising from a meander of trees five miles west of it. Figuring it to be the Indians' camp, Dan sent Sam back to tell Jim. When Bull heard what they had seen, he wanted to take his men into the canyon and round up any ponies he found. Jim disagreed. The First hadn't mentioned rousting ponies.

"He didn't hafta. We're here to dismount Injuns," Bull said. "I say we split up."

"No, Bull, we ain't out here to fight. You stumble on them people, there'll be trouble."

"So what? They don't scare me. I say we pitch into that camp of theirs."

"No, Goddamn it! The orders are we go out twelve miles an' turn back. That there knoll's as far as we go," Jim said.

"Who said twelve miles is the limit?"

"The First. Now let's head for that knoll."

"Uh uh. I'm gonna oblique left, then head west afore I swing back toward the knoll," Bull said. "I'll meet you on the west side of it. That way we don't miss nothin' 'tween here an' there."

"I'm sayin' diff'rent," Jim said.

"Say what you want, but I'm obliquin' left," Bull growled, his toe tracing a line in the dirt. "You wanna push it, The First can settle it later."

Apparently Jake saw something comical in the way Bull got all puffed up, because he couldn't resist smiling.

"What are you grinnin' at, Private?" Bull asked him. Before Jake could answer Bull motioned to Elvin and his two rookies, mounted, and started off to the southwest. Jim stared after them for a minute, his mind seemingly frozen.

"God*damn* that sumbitch!" he sputtered. Then he turned to Sam. "You take Charley an' git atop that knoll right quick an' keep a look out. Anything happens, get back to us an' we'll come at the gallop."

Sam and Charley caught up to Dan and then they pushed their mounts hard, reaching the top of the knoll twenty minutes later. What they saw spelled trouble. To the west twenty mounted Sioux were in a wide coulee moving toward a pie-pan-shaped depression, ninety yards across. It was situated immediately below, at the southwest edge of the knoll.

"Judas Priest!" Sam exclaimed. "Look at them!"

"No paint, anyway," Charley said absently, gazing toward the meandering line of trees. "See that dust the other side of the trees? The village is movin' out. Them braves are comin' out to meet us, give 'em time to get away."

"How'd they know we were comin'?"

"It don't matter. Now where the hell is Bull?"

"Back there," Sam said, pointing.

"Oh shit!" Dan said.

Below, two young Indian riders emerged from a gully, moving west. One was leading a tall sorrel. Starting into a wider coulee, they failed to see Bull a few hundred yards behind them, coming at the trot. Elvin and the two rookies were pressing hard to catch up to him.

When Bull burst into the second coulee a minute later, the Indian boys whipped their ponies into a gallop, but the four troopers gained on them steadily. Bull hollered at his men and dashed ahead. Directly under the south side of the knoll, the coulee narrowed and deepened before emptying into the pie-pan depression toward which the twenty-three braves were heading.

"Damn!" Charley muttered, turning to Sam. "Get back to Jim fast as you can. Tell him to get up here at the gallop, straight to the top of this knoll. Tell him Bull's got trouble."

— Chapter 39: Bull Judd's Comeuppance —

★ ★ ★

CHARLEY WORKED A FRESH chaw into his cheek. Below, Bull was ahead of his men by twenty yards. Coming fast from the left, he was still a hundred yards behind the Indians but gaining. One boy had the sorrel on a lead rope, a handsome, powerfully built stallion. He was cantering smoothly, making it look easy while the boys were getting everything they could out of their played-out ponies. Bull closed to fifty yards. The boys reached the shallow pie-pan just as the twenty braves entered it from the west. When the leader saw Bull he shouted back to the others, causing them to move to the sides of the coulee's mouth. Blinded by the boys' dust, Bull didn't realize he was racing into an ambush. Charging flat-out, Bull pulled his Colt.

"Goddamn it!" Charley muttered.

The Indians in the depression were waiting. Thirty yards behind the boys, Bull raised the Colt and fired. *Pop!* A Chinese firecracker at that distance. *Pop!* A second round, then a third. Damn fool! In the hollow the braves began making themselves visible. Immediately one of the boys let out a high-pitched whoop, prompting Bull to fire again and slow up. Elvin and the other two were catching up to him. Bull shouted back to them and sped up as the boys galloped into the hollow and pulled up twenty yards from the line of braves who were holding their rifles at the ready. Instantly, Bull threw up his gun hand to signal a halt. Unfortunately his pistol went off again. At the same time LaCrosse's horse veered right and crashed into Finzer, sending LaCrosse flying over his mount's neck into the grass.

Dan almost smiled, watching LaCrosse struggle to his feet, then reach back down for his floppy-brimmed hat. Red-faced, the chubby rookie winced as he grabbed the shoulder he'd landed on. Finzer nudged his horse up and took hold of LaCrosse's reins.

"Dismount!" Bull called out, then instantly thought better of it and reversed himself. "Mount! Mount!" he yelled. He glared at the Hunkpapa leader, a tall man holding a Winchester, its stock decorated with brass studs. The man glared back, a flicker of amusement on his face. He hadn't moved nor had the others.

Bull looked down the line of warriors and waved his Colt, then shouted, "Give up them ponies an' yer firearms!"

Immediately, every brave except the leader raised his rifle. "Oh my God!" Finzer blurted out. Not a single Springfield had been unslung.

"Put them rifles down!" Bull commanded, more pugnacious than before. He waved his pistol threateningly. A string of clicks cut through the morning air as the warriors cocked their weapons.

"Hau!" Charley yelled down to the leader, easing Augie out of the shadows. *"Hau!"* He went on in a mix of English and what Dan hoped was good enough Lakota, saying that Bull and his men weren't worth troubling with. Any man could see that the sergeant (here he struggled for the right words) was a *wasicu waslolyesni,* a stupid White man trying to scare twenty Lakota warriors with his last bullet. The chief sergeant was a man of honor, a *wicasa wokinihan.* He was coming with more soldiers. Soon! He was leading the soldiers on a lookaround. His orders said do not take ponies and weapons. He would lead the *wasicu waslolyesn* and all the other troopers back to the agency. But if the warriors fired at the soldiers, the chief sergeant would bring many soldiers to hunt the warriors down and put them in the agency jail.

The Indian leader answered in a clear voice, combining English with sign, demanding that the soldiers with Charley step out where they could be seen. Dan moved quickly into the sun. Now the leader mixed Lakota and English, going on to say he was glad the chief sergeant was *wicasa waste,* but he asked why *wasicu waslolyesni* was chasing young boys.

Suddenly Bull broke through, hollering up to Charley.

"Hey, Charley, that there's a G Troop sorrel. Tell this blasted heathen—"

"Shut up!" Charley yelled down sharply.

"He don't give it up, we're gonna kill ev'ry last one of 'em!"

"Goddamn it, Bull, shut up!" Charley hollered. He thought that if Bull wouldn't listen, maybe his men would. Sure enough, Elvin began to whine, begging Bull to let Charley palaver with the chief.

"You shuttin' up?" Charley hollered again.

"Yeah," Bull said.

"Then holster your Colt!" Charley yelled. Sullen, Bull obeyed. "An' secure the flap!"

"Jim's about three minutes away," Dan said quietly.

Charley turned back to the Indian leader, saying that maybe the beautiful stallion caught the sergeant's eye. He kept at it, stalling, saying the animal was worth ten or maybe twenty ordinary ponies and the sight of him running like a *tahcha tanka luzahan,* a big, swift deer, would cause some men to lose their reason. Lacking the words, Charley tried to put this last into sign but had no trust in whether he was getting the point across. Changing tack, he told the Indian that Bull was *waslolyesni,* stupid. The beauty of the sorrel made Bull *witko tko ke* (crazy). He hesitated as if he wasn't sure how to frame it, but then the Lakota words tumbled out anyway. It must have gotten through, because it brought a laugh from the leader and several others.

"Charley!" Bull hollered up, unable to contain himself further. "That sorrel's US property!"

"No!" the Sioux responded angrily, raising his Winchester. Obviously, he understood English, because he called back to one of the boys who led the handsome animal forward and paraded him before Bull. There was no "US" on its shoulder, no regimental brand on its rump.

The jangle of accouterments sounded and Jim arrived, his horse all lathered up. Lowering his voice, Charley told him what was happening and suggested the squad go up to the edge of the trees, where they could be seen but not counted exactly. Jim told Dan to disperse the men accordingly.

"*Hau!* The chief sergeant is here!" Charley shouted down to the Indian as Jim nudged his mount into the open. "He talks to *wasicu waslolyesni*."

"Bull!" Jim shouted. "Do exactly what I say, you dumb sumbitch. First off, raise yer right hand up an' look peaceable. Right! Now ease yer mount around an' start walkin' back up the coulee. You others, follow him. Go easy, damn it! Walk yer mounts back to the east end of the knoll and wait. We'll meet you there in a bit."

The wrangle ended easy enough. The leader simply raised a hand to Charley and said, *"Lila pilamaya, wicasa waste!"*

"Pilamaya! Wakan Tanka nici un!" Charley answered.

Once Bull was a hundred yards back, all but two Indians turned and headed west. Charley figured those two stayed to make sure the squad moved east, while the others caught up with their families moving further into the boonies.

Jim told Charley and Dan to remain there for a while to watch the Indians leave, and then he led the squad off the knoll. Suddenly a kestrel swooped up from the plain below, paused in midair for an instant, and settled onto the branch of a scraggly pine only six feet from Charley. Folding its slate-colored wings, it glared unblinkingly at him, as if possessing great authority, the impression enhanced by its distinctive face with its vertical stripes of black.

"What kind of bird is that?" Dan asked.

Charley was silent. Dan watched slack-jawed as man and bird remained rigidly erect, eyes locked, oblivious even to Augie nervously tossing his head against the tightly held reins. Then, as suddenly as he'd arrived, the bird took to the air and disappeared through the trees.

"What was that?" Dan asked, relieved the eerie encounter was over.

"Sparrow Hawk," Charley answered absently.

"Yes, but you looked like he spoke to you."

"Yeah, he told ...," Charley started to answer, still absorbed in what had gone on. "I mean, he didn't make no noise, but he told me plain as day."

"What was it?"

"Told me savin' Bull's hide wasn't my doin'."

"What saved him, then?"

"Somethin' else, I guess."

Chapter 40: A Peaceful Summer

April 1877–September 1877

While Company A spent the brutal winter of 1876–1877 at Fort Rice, Colonel Nelson Miles's Mounted Fifth Infantry hounded any Indians refusing to come into the agencies. He went after villages from the Canadian border to upper Rosebud Creek for six months. He scattered Sitting Bull's camp in December and killed the Minneconjou leader Lame Deer in the spring. Sitting Bull and his Hunkpapa band finally settled in Canada, and Crazy Horse returned to the Red Cloud Agency in May with nine hundred Oglalas and Cheyenne. With that, the war against the Sioux and Cheyenne was pretty much over.

However, in June more Indian troubles boiled up in Idaho. Out there the Nez Perce had gotten along with Whites for decades, even after their country was opened to gold miners in 1861. They avoided hostilities despite the aggravations caused by thousands of Whites on their land. In '68 many of them agreed to live on a reservation, but those in the Wallowa Valley quietly remained on their ancestral land. Finally, under unremitting pressure from the government, the nonreservation people gave in. In early June they were complying with General Howard's orders to move to the reservation when some hotheaded braves killed at least a dozen settlers. Howard immediately sent out two companies of First Cavalry to corral all seven or eight hundred Indians. In White Bird Canyon the column of a hundred troopers was ambushed by seventy warriors. Thirty-four men were killed. Howard then mounted a force of four hundred men and drove the Nez Perce from the field at Clearwater River in July. Led by Chief Joseph, the Indians fled east through the mountains to Montana Territory, then south until they reached the Big Hole River, where they were attacked by General Gibbon's command on August 9. Despite losing more than sixty people, the Indians escaped with their pony herd and kept moving toward the upper reaches of the Yellowstone. General Howard worried they would reach Canada and join Sitting Bull.

Company A left Fort Rice in April of '77, long before the trouble began in Idaho. Seventh Cavalry then spent several months patrolling north of the Yellowstone before bivouacking at Colonel Miles's Tongue River Cantonment in August. To Charley's surprise, his friend Humaza was there, scouting for the Mounted Fifth Infantry.

★ ★ ★

Two evenings after they arrived Charley went over to the scouts' village.

"*Hau, kola,*" Humaza said, smiling.

"*Hau,*" Charley said, unprepared for how good he felt. "So you're back to scoutin'."

"*Han*, for soldiers on ponies. Greasy Grass, you not hurt?"

"No, we all come out okay. How'd last year go for you?"

"Okay. At Greasy Grass with Crow Dog."

"You were there?" The idea of his friend being on the other side hadn't occurred to Charley. "Did you fight us by the river or when we was on the hill?"

"*Hiya,*" Humaza said, shaking his head. "Sicaŋju with Crazy Horse. Fought Custer. Pony go down."

"Your pony?"

"*Han*. Took C Troop horse," Humaza said. "Next day by river,

Tinker get water." He locked eyes with Charley, just a hint of a smile on his face.

"Goddamn!" Charley said. "You seen Jubal?"

Humaza nodded. "Now you an' me talk of Greasy Grass no more."

"Yeah. Some men would get riled up knowin' you was there. But one other thing: Jubal says he shot a young brave in the arm by the river. Do you know if that brave lived?"

"*Han.* Tell him that brave is good."

"I will," Charley said. "How're things at your *tiospaye*?"

"Bad. Soldiers grab up ponies. Me an' Chetanzi hide out. Cold winter. People hungry."

⋆ ⋆ ⋆

The mail finally caught up with them at the cantonment. Sam got three magazines, several *Bismarck Tribunes*, and a book—enough to keep him happy for weeks. Ernst's father wrote him from Germany, which left him all smiles, and Jake had a letter from his brother. René was moving to San Francisco and wanted Jake to join him. His sister had a baby, making him an uncle, and Marguerite had married a big-time lawyer. The best news was that Boss O'Reilly was dead. Apparently, O'Reilly had a habit of beating women and one lady decided enough was enough. She went to cut off *ses balloches,* but O'Reilly twisted to the side and she missed, severing his femoral artery instead. This led Jake to ask Charley and Dan how to get out of the cavalry. He couldn't stand to spend three more years there while thinking of San Francisco, where it rarely got hot and never got cold. They told him they'd have to think about it.

⋆ ⋆ ⋆

For the next few days Charley spent most of his free time with Humaza, who introduced him to Nagin, an *iyeska* from his *tiospaye.*

"*Iyesk*a tells what spirits say," Humaza explained.

In the evening the three men smoked while Nagin told stories. Each one was filled with humor about humans' basic foolishness, like how a swellheaded man carved an extra-long and ornate pipe stem befitting a man of his importance. He proudly showed it to friends, but when it came time to smoke, his arms were too short to light it.

Between thoughts Nagin would pause, a half smile on his face, appreciating a story as it unfolded. His onyx eyes were powerfully friendly, almost mesmerizing, putting Charley at ease, except for an illogical, gnawing idea that the old man knew he had killed his father thirteen years before.

Nagin was curious about what it was like in the mines. Charley spoke of the shadowy darkness, the black dust filling the foul air and the damp cold, which got inside your bones.

"After the mine, the cold in Dakota ain't bad. My horse, he groans 'bout it more'n me," Charley said, going on easily. "You know, I never rode no horse till I joined the cav'lry an' now, uh—" He stopped abruptly, realizing he was prattling on like an old lady.

"Now?" Nagin prompted, smiling.

"I was gonna say, out here you ain't got no choice 'bout horses. You depend on 'em. I trust Augie. I even like him."

Nagin nodded, still smiling. He said something to Humaza. Charley made out the words *sunkawakan* and *wicasa waste* (horse and good man) but couldn't decipher the rest of it.

⋆ ⋆ ⋆

It was mostly curiosity that compelled Charley to accept the scouts' invitation to a sweat lodge with six other men. What happened there defied description: a stream of sounds, images, and sensations swirling around and through him, always changing, only the heat and the darkness staying the same inside the round-topped oven, the dominating power of the super-heated rocks barely suggested by the wavering glow of red in the dark. Lakota songs, the verses cascading down the scale. Nagin praying without end, lung-scalding steam, coughing, hacking, the door pulled open, cool air, light, water, laughter, then dark and hot again, the rocks pulsing waves of heat through skin and muscle to cook his bones. Tiny green sparks flitted about in clusters, leaping through the dark to dance around his head. Nagin's raspy voice singing on and on, the others praying in turn while Charley suffered an abyss of aloneness, a ridiculous yearning for a house. His own turn to pray but silently refusing to acknowledge a God he'd never known, and then a shower of green sparks spun about him, a few touching his arm.

A voice cut through the suffocating heat: "Accept your crime!" Who spoke? Now a frenzy of sparks circling his head, dancing on his nose, crackling like flaming twigs of pine, then sliding away and were gone. Someone poured water on the rocks creating heavy, choking steam. *Mitakuye oyas'in!* Door opens, cool air comes in. They all smoke the pipe. Door closes. Fourth round. What happened to the third?

Nagin says, "Charley! They say you want a house. Not army house."

Afterward the *iyeska* spoke at length with Humaza, then turned to Charley.

"Listen good. Charley *wicasa waste,*" he said. "They say you a man in between. White not *wasicu.* Not army here," he said, hand on heart. "You stand alone."

Nagin knew! As close as Charley was to Dan, he was still alone. In the sweat lodge the aloneness was clear, a blanket wrapped tight around whatever he was. In a real home he would shed the blanket—now that was a crazy thought. And the voice he heard? What was the crime? His father would have killed him. He looked up to find Humaza and Nagin watching him gently.

"Man in Between alone," Nagin said, chuckling.

Charley twisted nervously, digging in his pocket for tobacco. *Old man thinks he knows everything,* he thought.

The next evening they sweat again. Charley was surprised to

find himself praying for a home with a parlor stove. And the eerie voice repeated, "Accept your crime."

Afterward, Nagin said to him, "They say you choose to kill."

"No choice to it. He was gonna kill me."

"You choose to be there," Nagin said.

"I lived there," Charley shot back.

"Man choose his house," Nagin said. "We sweat next time."

"What next time?"

"At Spotted Tail Agency."

"Huh?"

"We sweat there someday. *Wakan Tanka nici un,*" the *iyeska* said, leaving for his teepee.

Charley told Humaza he found the *iyeska's* words frustrating.

"Spirits make you angry," Humaza said. "Nagin only tell you they say you stay there so he beat you."

"Goddamn it! I worked there so I lived there!" Charley growled. "Anyway, I don't see how I'm gonna see Nagin again."

"They tell him that."

— Chapter 41: Nothing Stays the Same —

★ ★ ★

ON SEPTEMBER 2 THE squad returned from escorting a supply train to the Powder. That evening Charley told the others he wouldn't reenlist in October.

"But soldiering's all we know," Dan said, suddenly pissed off.

"Uh huh, but ten years is enough," Charley said, reaching for his oilstone.

"What got you thinking that?" Jim asked.

"It started a year ago. When we disarmed the Sioux, I guess. But the past couple months I got to thinkin' hard on it."

"Why?" Dan asked.

"Partly it's what we're doin' out here."

"Christ Almighty!" Dan exclaimed. "You're into politics!"

"No, not that. It's how we fight. This old man named Hawk Holds On said things 'bout the Little Bighorn," Charley said, putting an edge on his knife.

"What did he say?" Sam asked.

Sam's question made Charley fidgety, but he went on. His story wanted out. "He was talkin' 'bout us on the hill with Reno. Said we fought with honor up there, but most times there's no honor in how we wage war."

By this time Jubal had arrived, and Charley seemed to get a second wind. Dan lit his pipe, marveling at how his partner's words tumbled out like a free-running brook, telling how the old man talked about each year having its own story, its own reason. This was the year for staying put.

"What was last year for, slaughtering troopers?" Elvin Crane asked from the shadows, his voice a surprise.

"No," Charley said quietly. "It was the year for coming together."

The Sioux remembered the previous year as the biggest gathering ever of people from every Lakota nation and the Cheyenne too. It was one village so big that the army had to fight the Indian way, soldiers against warriors, where any man could have honor if he took hold of it—any man, Indian or White. Afterward, most of the bands went to the agencies like the government wanted, but there the army stole their ponies and rifles. There was no honor in that. Some bands found wintering places protected from the wind and snow, but Crook and Miles burned their lodges and robes, stole their food and ponies, and killed the helpless ones. No honor in attacking winter villages. The White man's way of war was a scourge, like smallpox. It killed more women, children, and old people than warriors. It had started at Blue Waters twenty years ago when General Harney attacked a peaceful Sicaŋju village. Helpless ones were slaughtered and their bodies mutilated. Soldiers took women for themselves. The army promised to return the women when Spotted Tail surrendered, but it didn't. Since then every Sicaŋju has carried the Blue Water in his heart.

Charley continued like a seasoned storyteller. Now the *Wasicu* were everywhere. Buffalo were scarce and renegades starved. When Crazy Horse brought his starving people in, the army arrested him and murdered him. Now there was no choice; the Sioux were done fighting. It was a year for quiet.

"But I thought the scouts here trusted Colonel Miles," Sam remarked.

"When I asked about Miles, the old man snorted," Charley said. "They work for him, but he's like Custer: destroys winter villages like at Washita." Finished, he fumbled in his pocket for tobacco.

"Whad'you mean there ain't no honor in war?" Elvin asked.

Charley answered with quiet patience. "He said honor in war is soldiers against warriors, not killin' the helpless ones."

"Them helpless ones are killers same as the bucks," Elvin said.

Jake said. "You're nothing but *un poltron* that likes killin' women."

"What's a *poltron?*" Sam asked.

"Un branieux, a coward."

"Yer callin' me a coward?" Elvin said, his face turning crimson.

"Until you show me diff'rent," Jake said.

"That's enough!" Dan cut in. "So, Charley, all I heard was the Sioux are done fightin', yet they worry the army will try and get even for Custer."

"That's right," Bull said. "Someday we'll get even."

"Maybe, maybe not," Dan said. "One thing's for sure, though. The Sioux will suffer for generations."

Dan and Charley stayed while the others began to drift off.

Jim spoke to the two of them. "The bad blood between Jake an' Elvin's gettin' worse."

"Yes, I fear the day will come when one of them must die," Dan said.

"Yeah, so we just gotta see how it plays out," Jim said. "But there's somethin' else. I don't mean no disrespect, Charley, but I don't wanna know too much 'bout the people we gotta fight." He paused, watching Charley tuck more tobacco into his cheek. "I don't wanna be thinkin' while in the heat of it. Give me some of that, will you?" he asked. It took him a couple of minutes to get his own chaw going. "Fact is, I like the cavalry, but I don't take to the killin'. Not like Bull—he lathers up just talkin' 'bout it."

"True," Dan agreed. "He's one of those that—"

"Wants to kill," Charley said. "Most of us choose who to shoot in a fight. Like at Washita it got frantic real quick. Some men was chargin' this way an' that, shootin' wildly. Those of us been in The War stayed pretty calm. I'd say we chose our shots."

"Whadaya mean?" Jim asked.

"Me, I kept an eye out fer anybody pointin' a gun at me or Dan. I seen a couple, and I shot 'em."

Dan said, "We didn't fire much till some braves holed up an' we had to root them out. Fact is, most men can't kill the helpless unless things get crazy."

"Hadn't thought about it like that," Jim said.

When they were alone later on, Dan asked Charley about what he had said.

"It's not like you, going on like that. Told it well, you did. What got you going?"

For a moment Charley sat there, thinking, and then he said, "I guess it just needed to be told."

* * *

On the tenth of September Humaza sent a Cheyenne boy to ask Charley to come over. When he got there they smoked the pipe in silence, and then Humaza gave him the news.

"Yesterday man come from *Mahpiya Luta* (Red Cloud Agency)," Humaza said, his voice soft yet powerful. His eyes never left Charley's face, searching out his *kola's* reactions even as he delivered news that marked their separate fates. "Soldiers and Indian police take Crazy Horse to Camp Robinson jail. Soldier stab Crazy Horse. Kill him."

"Goddamn," Charley whispered, picturing the man he watched from the bluffs above the Little Bighorn. He shuddered, sensing a cold and fearsome rage rising in his chest. Cleaning the pipe, his *kola's* face remained the same but for a terrible pain deep within his eyes.

Humaza rose, motioning for the boy to bring his horse. He put the pipe bag in the parfleche and stood motionless, gazing silently into the distance, while Charley searched his face as if to memorize every detail.

"Our paths cross again, *kola*," Humaza said, mounting the horse.

"I hope so," Charley replied. And what Charley said next surprised him. "God be with you, good friend."

— Chapter 42: Chasing the Nez Perce —

★ ★ ★

SEPTEMBER 16, 1877–SEPTEMBER 28, 1877

On September 12 Colonel Miles ordered six companies of Seventh Cavalry to leave Tongue River and intercept the Nez Perce. His column clashed with the Indians at Canyon Creek, but the Nez Perce fended off the cavalry and headed north again.

Worried they would join Sitting Bull in Canada, the army ordered Miles to march 250 miles northwest and cut the Indians off near the Bear Paw Mountains. He put together a column of six cavalry companies: three each from the Seventh and Second Cavalry, ninety mounted men from Fifth Infantry, forty unmounted infantrymen, a Hotchkiss gun and crew, thirty Indian scouts, and a pack train. All in all it was more than four hundred men. The Nez Perce had a five-day head start, so time was of the essence. The column was ferried across the Yellowstone the night of September 15 and on the march by ten o'clock the next morning.

★ ★ ★

To Bull Judd this meant a chance to make up for his mortification at Standing Rock. But first he had to make sure his squad was clear about how to fight the Nez Perce. He got a surprise when he spoke to Elvin about the recruits.

"Yer gonna have to tell 'em hard," Elvin said.

"Whadaya mean?"

"Last night they weren't sure 'bout who to shoot. They might of been listenin' to Smrka."

"Uh huh. He's an Injun lover fer sure."

"Him an' Picard."

"Yeah, that breed oughtta be dead."

"I'm gonna do it, Sergeant," Elvin said.

"For sure?"

"First chance I get."

Bull was surprised. Until now he hadn't thought the dimwit would go after Picard, but now? Well, he was stupid enough to try it, for sure.

* * *

On September 27 the men were treated to a sight unlikely to be seen again. During a long noon halt on the north bank of the Missouri, about sixty buffalo slowly came their way to feed on the good grass close by the mules and horses. Cavalrymen stood entranced by the tranquility of it, buffalo and mules and horses grazing together, the prairie's past melded with its future—a welcome island of peace.

That evening the squad got a sincere blaze going, taking the edge off the evening chill. Jim said the rookies had been talking with the boys in Bull's squad about what happened at Washita.

With that Dan's stomach began to churn and he walked away, immersed in his own thoughts. Would they never end, those searing memories bursting from the cave where he put them?

When he returned, the rookies were going at it with Jim. They had questions about the upcoming fight, especially fighting in a village. Jim said they'd be paired up with one of the veterans and should follow their lead.

"Okay, but who we s'posed to shoot?" Rooney asked.

"Anyone holding a weapon," Jim said.

"Sergeant Judd's boys said, 'Shoot anything that moves,'" Connelly said. "We asked 'em if that meant women and kids too."

"An' Crane said we damn well should," Holland said. "Runny

LaCrosse, he told us General Sheridan wants every Indian dead, includin' the little ones 'cause nits make lice."

Jim glanced at Dan, then came back hard. "Forget Sheridan!" he said. "He don't run A Troop, Captain Moylan does. You see anybody holdin' a weapon, shoot him. If not, don't."

"But what about Washita?" Rooney asked.

"Orders said shoot the warriors an' take the rest prisoner," Charley said, glowering. "But it got wild an' more helpless got shot than warriors."

"They killed women and children? Why?" Ernst asked.

"Some men like doin' it," Charley said, glancing at his partner.

Dan waited a moment, putting a lid on his ire, and when he spoke, the words came slowly. "Yes, murderers in soldiers' clothes, there are some of those. Some others do the same, fools unhinged by murky commands and the wildness of the fight."

"They are murderers also?" Ernst asked.

"God only knows. To judge a man who's been made crazy is His chore, not mine. But you and me, as sane as we are at this moment, we surely know that killing women and kids is not a part of soldiering."

"What do you mean by murky orders?" Holland asked.

"Orders coming down that aren't clear, like, 'Shoot what you have to.' At Washita, Captain Moylan was clear, like Charley said. And he'll be clear when we fight the Nez Perce. That's his way. There are others who order the opposite—commanders like that lunatic Chivington at Sand Creek, who told his men to shoot every Indian they saw. He's the one who said 'nits make lice,' not General Sheridan. What's important here is that Captain Moylan runs A Troop, and we take our orders from him and The First, and from Jim."

"No two ways about it," Jim said as Bull and Elvin walked up.

"Now I cannot say our war against Indians is wrong—not and draw my pay as a soldier, I cannot," Dan said, eyeing Bull. "Fact is, war is part of human nature, I fear, and innocent folks perish in war. Prisoners starve and die of the bloody flux. Civilians are caught in crossfires. But deliberately killing innocents is murder. Period."

"Good to hear yew philosophizing again," Jubal cut in. "Been too long since you give us some educated preachification."

Good old Jubal, always there when a man needed to catch his breath. Smiling at him, Dan started in again.

"Lastly, there's the matter of pride and shame. Killing the helpless shames us as men. It destroys our pride in self and in the regiment. And by all that's holy, it corrupts our souls forever."

"That's hogwash, an' ye know it," Bull said. "Fightin's killin', and who ye kill don't matter none, long as it's Injuns."

"Christ Almighty, Bull. You just don't get it."

"He cain't, Dan'l," Jubal offered. "It jist ain't in him."

⋆ ⋆ ⋆

Late the next evening Bill Finzer went to Jake with news of Elvin's intentions.

"It ain't my business," Finzer said, "but I heard Crane tell LaCrosse somethin' 'bout fixin' you good 'cause you're gonna desert. Said Sergeant Judd knew he was going to do it. Sounded like he meant shootin' you."

"He prob'ly did. Thanks, and I owe you big."

Later Jake found Elvin by the horses. Staying quiet, he came up behind and grabbed his arm with his left hand, holding his knife in his right.

"What d'you want?" Elvin asked. He started to turn but felt the knife's point in his ribs.

"Get movin'," Jake growled, propelling Elvin down the company street. "You an' me, we talk to Bull."

"Whadaya want, Picard?" Bull squawked.

"He's got a—ow!" Elvin whined.

"Shut up!" Jake barked, shoving him so violently that he stumbled and fell at Bull's feet.

"He pulled a knife on—"

"Quiet!" Bull commanded. "What're you up to now, Picard?"

"I tell you if this sonuvabitch come close to me, I cut him bad!" Jake said, his eyes on fire.

"That's a threat, Picard! I'm reportin' ye to Captain Moylan."

"You do that, but keep this piece of shit away or I stick him good." With that Jake turned and there were Jim and Sam not ten paces away, coming up the street.

"What's goin' on?" Jim asked.

"Crane says he gonna fix me," Jake growled. "I tell Bull I'll cut the sonuvabitch. He say he goin' to the captain about it."

"Okay, I'll handle it," Jim said. Steaming, he started in on Bull straight off, telling him to "keep the dimwit away from my men" or there would be hell to pay. Bull replied that he was reporting Picard. Jim told him that would only piss Moylan off.

* * *

After Jim left, Bull turned on Elvin for not standin' up to Jake.

Although mortified, Elvin managed to say, "Yer right, Sergeant. I shoulda fought the runty breed, only he surprised me with that knife. It was real sharp."

"So what are ye gonna do about it?" Bull asked.

"First chance, I'm gonna shoot the bastard," Elvin said.

"Think you can do it?"

"Just watch me."

"Well, if you kill a half-breed, ye gotta make sure he's dead or he'll cut yer heart out."

"Not with a bullet in his brain, he won't."

* * *

After dark Jake told Charley and Dan that he was worried about Sam.

"He's a good guy, only sometimes I think he's gonna kill Elvin for sure."

"Really?" Dan said.

"He can see himself doin' it, he says."

"Sam's got a good imagination," Dan said. "He wouldn't kill a man, not in cold blood. What do you think, Charley?"

Gazing up at the stars like he often did, Charley was thinking it through, while Dan wondered for the hundredth time how he kept the juice from his chaw from running down his throat with his head cocked back like that. Of course, there was always the possibility that he didn't.

Finally Charley spoke. "Sam might surprise you."

Chapter 43: The Chill of Dawn

★ ★ ★

SEPTEMBER 30, 1877

Insisting it was the cold that woke him, Dan surveyed the heavens where a sky so clear it teemed with stars proclaimed there'd be ice on the streams that day. A bit of the dream crept back and he tried to push it aside, but his mind's eye got a glimpse. The evil in her eyes—'twas a fading image, thank God. Wasn't the banshee like Medusa, who killed her brother and her children? No, that was Medea. The wonderful Greeks. A grand assemblage of deities they had, enough to satisfy every fancy and fear. He hadn't seen the hag—damn it, he hadn't—nor had he heard her keen. A sense of dread washed over him, leaving behind the clinging film of sorrow.

"Good morning." It was Sam, sitting in the dark on a cracker box not ten feet away.

"Sure and the top o' the marnin' to you, lad," Dan answered, laying on the brogue to mask the ancient gloom. "If it's idle chatter you're seeking, drag your fine perch over here."

"I didn't want to wake Charley up."

"Not to worry, lad, Charley wakes his own self, and then only for reveille or the first whisper of trouble. What woke you? You hear something?"

"No, I woke to stop dreaming about a snowstorm back home. Not surprising. The dew is close to frost."

"Yes, there's the coming of winter in the air," Dan said, fumbling for his dudeen. "And the whisper of death," he mumbled.

"What?" the boy asked.

"Ah nothing, just a soldier's worthless premonition."

Probing diligently, Dan finally located the pipe deep within the coat's inside pocket. Sam handed him his tobacco. He took his own sweet time filling the bowl, set a match to it, and started puffing like a smithy's bellows. In an instant he was coughing, a speck of tobacco lodged in his windpipe.

"You okay?"

"Aye, lad, and thank you," Dan answered, still hacking as he set about firing up the pipe again carefully.

"Your enlistment's up in October," Sam said. "You're staying in, aren't you?"

"Can't say. That's a long ways off, lad."

"What do you mean? October's the day after tomorrow."

"True, but time is more than days. The twists and turns 'tween now and then could make a month of it," Dan said, pausing to frame what he wanted to say. "Suppose something happened which changed everything. What I'm sayin' is, I'm waiting on something."

"Like what?" Sam asked.

"Sure and I know not the answer, lad," he said truthfully. "But what about you? You still set on a lifetime of soldiering?"

"No. For one thing, I've done a lot of thinking about my notion of glory in battle. At Antietam, what happened to my father, the way you told it, there was no glory in any of it. Actually, it was a lot like Ernst's grandfather's story."

"That's true."

"And none at the Little Bighorn either. What Jubal did in getting water took a lot of guts, but he didn't seem to think it was glorious."

"Far from it," Dan said.

"And the sergeant who brought that mule back in."

"Hanley."

"If there was any glory in that day, it goes to men like him. But like you've said all along, it's not like the pictures they draw for *Harper's*. Not at all," Sam said.

"Anything else change your mind about soldiering?"

"Well, like I told you at the time, disarming the Sioux kind of soured me," he said. "And then there was Bull charging through the dust straight into those braves. Lucky for him Charley was there."

"Sounds like you've thought it through pretty well," Dan said, starting to get up.

"Ayuh," Sam replied, looking up at Dan like there was more. "Couple other things too. For one, folks will always be looking to get land for themselves, so I suppose we'll have to corral the Indians until the country's all White. But what Charley was saying about fighting war honorably got to me. I don't think I want to be part of it anymore.

"And one other thing," he went on, a smile breaking out. "Before the Little Bighorn, I thought fear wouldn't bother me 'cause I was on the right side. But running for the timber, I thought I was a goner. Judas! I've never been so scared. And crossing the river, fear sliced through my gut like a red-hot knife when I saw that rifle pointed at me. Christ! If Charley hadn't shot that pony, I'd be dead," he said, then looked up at the sky. "My hero dreams ended in the middle of that river. Tell me, does a soldier ever get past being scared?"

"I don't know, but I'll tell you what made it easier for me," Dan said. "After Fredericksburg I realized the chances of making it through The War were next to nil. So I began thinking I was dead already. Sounds strange maybe, but it made it easier. Out here there's much less chance of being hit, so fear is a warning—tells you to move aside before you look for the man aiming at you. Do that and maybe you'll live."

"Unless you're with Custer's battalion," Sam said softly.

"Yes, that's true," Dan muttered, remembering Paddy O'Malley.

Gazing upward, Dan thought there was nothing as beautiful and humbling as the plethora of stars over Montana. Then he heard himself say, "Every once in a while I find myself praying for the souls of the boys who died beside me—unusual for an old skeptic. And now I actually wish to live a while longer, which also surprises me, it being the night before a fight."

"You think they'll stand?" Sam asked.

"Yes."

"Why?"

"Just a feeling, but it's one I trust."

They went back to watching the stars. Before long a lone comet streaked across the blackness of it. *Exhilarating in its way,* Dan thought.

"Are you certain it wasn't something you heard that woke you?" he asked Sam.

"I can't be sure, no," Sam said. "All I know is that I was in a snowstorm back home in Williamsburg. Winters there were hard too."

"Yes. Hardness is in the north."

"What's that?"

"Warmed over cabbage, lad. An aphorism for every occasion, the Irish have."

"What's this one?"

"By my faith, lad, it's not worth a tinker's dam." Dan sighed, vaguely aware of the purpose behind his eagerness to keep the talk going. Might his mind take them to a better place? "In every land hardness is in the north of it, softness in the south, industry in the east, and fire and inspiration in the west."

"You're right. The Irish have a proverb for everything," Sam said.

"Most peoples do, whatever their God. Tell me lad, what God is yours? Which church?"

"I guess that would be Congregational."

"Aye, and there you spoke of God and read of Him in scripture. But did you believe in that God? I mean, sitting in your church could you feel His presence?"

"Not that I remember," Sam answered.

"I'm not surprised. Your Pilgrim's church shuns the mystery of God, while my Catholic church makes much of it, with robes and bells and incense and all the rest. The problem is that religion will clutter up a man's mind with an accumulation of nonsense," Dan said.

"Like what?"

"Like the twiddledeedee a boy swallows whole."

"Twiddledeedee?"

"Superstitions and the like. Dangerous in a fight. Takes your mind off the matter at hand—watching out for your partner, staying whole, that kind of thing."

"I guess you're right," Sam said. "What time is it, anyway?"

Dan fumbled for his watch and lit a match. "One thirty," he said, dropping the match. "Well, tomorrow being here already, we can stare it down if we choose. But who can glimpse the day after, being over the horizon as it is?"

"No one, I guess," Sam said, shrugging.

"Ah, but that's what I love about the army. It's predictable, telling a man what's coming."

"You'll reenlist?" Sam asked. "I certainly hope so."

"Why, so you can hear three more years of Irish blatherskite?"

"Why not? It's refreshing to me—preeminently rapturous!"

"Sweet Jesus, how did you come upon such elocutionary refinement?"

"Where else but from you, with your prodigious vocabulary. It nearly wore out my dictionary," Sam said, smiling. "But it's your Irish—what did you call it, blatherskittles?"

'Blatherskite's the word, laddie."

"Blatherskite then. That's what charms a man, all the Irish twattle."

"Not all of it charms, it doesn't. Do you know of the banshee?" Dan heard himself ask. Slipping out like that, it should have surprised him, but it didn't, not really.

"A banshee?" Sam repeated. "Isn't that an Irish panther? His growl's a high-pitched scream or something?"

"No, she's neither a he nor a painter, nor does she growl or scream. She keens, lad, she keens," Dan said. "The sound is, well, if you hear it, you'll know it is her—simple as that. But enough of fairies. This is the day we catch the Nez Perce, if we catch them at all."

His hand fell on his pipe, lying near his hip in the grass. He relit it for the last time, taking his time about it, putting thoughts of the hag aside as best he could. It was the cold that woke him, or maybe it was coyotes. They'd woken him before, although not for some years.

Cold again, Dan pulled his coat's collar up, his mind returning to the morning before the Little Bighorn fight. Was it fate meeting O'Malley, or had he deliberately sought him out? And if so, why did he choose Dan? There were plenty of Irish in his own troop. No matter, it being long past. And this morning, it must have been a coyote—or maybe a Nez Perce signaling his friends in the dark.

"Look," Sam said, glancing toward headquarters. "They're getting up."

"They are indeed, so I'd best be off for me morning piss."

— Chapter 44: A Cold Morning's March —

SAM PULLED UP HIS cape, but the cold was already inside. Dan, the old skeptic who believed in God—couldn't help it, probably, being raised Catholic and Irish, with all its blatherskite. And the banshee, who was she? Another Irish mystery. The business about God bothered Sam. Troopers never talked about God except for Bible-thumpers like Bull, and only dimwits would listen to him. Still, Sam would like to believe in God the way Dan did. The fact that he couldn't believe left him uneasy, separate. He remembered sitting next to Mrs. Thompson on the hard pew, wearing the hardly used trousers and brogans she'd found for him. It felt good, like he almost belonged with the worshipers. What about Aunt Ida? Now there was a Bible-thumper, for sure.

He'd sat down to settle his account that last evening with her. She'd looked at his figures and agreed she owed him eighteen dollars and twelve cents. They talked some about the weather. Then he heard himself ask her what happened to his father's farm. She said it was sold it to a Mr. Sumner; the proceeds were invested for his sister's future. (The "investments" included eighty acres of bottomland next to the Ohio farm, a prize Holstein bull, plus room, board, and tuition at Harvard for her two sons.) Lifting her chin, she stared down her nose at him, and then the venom of self-righteousness spilled over to puncture his memories of a caring father.

"Jonah was a wicked man if ever there was one!" she hissed. "Running off was just the last of it!"

"He didn't run off! He volunteered!" Sam insisted, suddenly furious, although it came out in a red-cheeked whisper.

"Of course he did," she said. "And I had to clean up behind him, the shiftless reprobate. Years before he sweet-talked my sister when she was but a child and had his way with her. Why, the lies he—" She put her hand to her mouth, as if the rush of indignation muddled her sensibilities. "I'm sorry, Sam, may the Lord forgive my wrath, but charity does not come easy to me, not after what he did to Sarah and ran off."

"But he volun—"

"Don't interrupt your elders! He skedaddled, like the fox in the coop come sunrise. Plenty like him in the army, sidestepping honest labor. Yes, I sold the farm to Sumner. How else was I supposed to raise Sarah's child?"

Sam sat frozen, her words challenging the major truth of his life, that his father was a good and brave man.

"No, my Pa was a hero. He died fighting," he mumbled without passion. It was all he could muster.

"Jonah Streeter a hero? A pity, you thinking that. He was a wicked slugabed who would dazzle young girls and then deflower them. A dreamer and a runner—ran from work, shirked responsibility. He probably died running!" She dabbed at the spittle on her lip, caught her breath, and returned to her rant. "He was a sniggardly coward! A coward and a wicked fool. Yes, he was wicked all right. Only good to come from him was dear Maddie. She's a fine and virtuous girl, bound to marry a man of prominence, perhaps one of George's friends or Franklin's. You know George has been appointed ..."

Sam heard little of what she said as she prattled on about the Lord's reward for her own righteousness. Within Sam's mind the echoes of her contempt for his father gradually faded away.

"Friends from Harvard who're drawn to good Christian girls like Madeline. Just last week George was saying ..."

Sam recalled the old farm, the grown-over west pasture. Unintended, his words burst into consciousness and found voice.

"What about me?" he asked.

"What?" Ida responded, startled.

"Why'd you leave me with the county?"

"Because you were not my responsibility! I had my hands full with my own flesh and blood, our own two boys and Madeline!" she said, glaring at him, her eyes burning. "That fool Jonah, he filled your head with nonsense, just like he did Sarah's. Tell me, young man, where'd you come from? What'd he tell you about that?"

"He said I came from God," Sam answered.

"That's exactly what I mean! Jonah was a designing prevaricator, sliding around the truth whenever possible. What did he say about your mother?"

"He said Ma loved me more than anything."

"You mean Sarah. Perhaps she did in her way, but she wasn't your mother."

"What do you mean, she wasn't my mother? Why'd you say that?"

"Lord have mercy!" Ida gestured as if to shoo a troublesome fly. "Truly, you didn't think Sarah was your mother?"

"Of course!"

"Well, 'the counsels of the wicked are deceit,'" she said, citing scripture. "That was one of Jonah's evil lies, but it's time you got the truth, just as God intended. Sarah was not your mother!"

He knew that what she had to say was important, but it seemed distant, muffled in a cloud of fear and disbelief.

"God only knows who gave birth to you, never mind the profligate man whose blood you carry. But know this, young man: in her trade you were an unwanted hindrance. Gave you up to an old hag. Jonah picked you up in Northampton and made up one of his lies to hide that you were a bastard," she declared. Sam looked away, not wanting to listen. "Then he brought you home to cheer up Sarah, who'd been melancholic since losing a stillborn some months before. Poor girl, she was only sixteen, but Jonah ... well, no need to say more."

She pretended a sigh and went on and on. Nothing short of a

tirade, it was but an unintelligible mumble in Sam's ears. Numb, he headed for the door when she finished.

"Where's your manners, young man? I said good night!" she called after him.

Sam stumbled to his room, his mind slowed by a dense, protective mist, behind which lay what is all too common in cast-off children: an undeserved shame and the certainty of lifelong aloneness.

He went to work in Columbus four days later for an outfit needing a man to put a fresh six-horse hitch to harness. It was a good job with considerable challenge to it. But he slept fitfully as fragments of the tirade he'd shut out peppered his thoughts, phrases such as "prating fool" and "wicked prevaricator." The most piercing was "probably Jonah died running!" Unable to sleep, he paced the floor, muttering imprecations half-aloud to drown out her vicious sanctimony. She was the liar, a flint-hearted, waspish Bible-thumper who maligned the innocent to hide her sins of greed and avarice.

God Almighty, his pa fought and died in the War, while she stayed home and got fat off it. Pa a runner? Judas Priest, she was the runner. Sold Pa's farm, took the money, and ran to Ohio. Goddamn the old woman.

In time these rejoinders won out, shutting off her vituperation. Still, he was restless and would have returned to Williamsburg if the idea didn't bring with it a new yet vaguely familiar sense of embarrassment. One thing was for sure: he'd get the hell out of Ohio. A week later he was on a train heading for Jefferson Barracks in St. Louis, a recruit in the United States Cavalry.

⋆ ⋆ ⋆

At two thirty the column started out across rolling grassland, broken only by the occasional shallow coulee. By five it was light enough to make out the Second Cavalry companies ahead.

★ ★ ★

Ernst was half-napping when they halted a little after six o'clock. He shook himself alert to discover Thor stretching out the reins to browse on the frost-covered grass. But a minute later they were off, filing past K Troop. He nodded off again and again until they picked up the trail of the Nez Perce and stopped. It was close to eight o'clock.

The cold morning air barely stirred. Harbingers of the killing storms of winter, a blanket of silvery-gray cirrus, swept eastward. Bereft of its leaves, a lone cottonwood stood beside the stream, a black, skeletal presence against the grayness of the day. Up and down the line men grumbled, cursed, kibitzed, and joked, the sounds melding into a low-pitched murmur, one easy to ignore in listening for the sounds of other life. The meadowlarks, robins, and sparrows were gone. Even the squawking jays had left for warmer ground. Winter was coming—also a battle. There would be wounded—also the dead.

A wolf's howl broke the silence, hanging in the stillness for a moment. To Ernst it was a mournful lament, registering a sorrow soon to come.

"That ain't right," Charley mumbled. "Wolves don't generally howl after sunup. Not like that with no answer."

"Maybe an Indian?" Dan asked.

"Prob'ly," Charley growled.

On the march again, one of the Sioux scouts drifted back and rode beside Charley for a minute. Already stripped and painted, he rode a fine piebald pony that danced excitedly from side to side, reluctant to slow his pace to match that of the column.

"He says the village is seven miles ahead," Charley said, turning to Dan. Then he looked back at the scout, who had more to say before he rode off, angling across the wide pony trail toward Second Cavalry's left flank up ahead.

"Says the ground ahead keeps on risin' for five miles, then falls off gradually," Charley said. "The village is in a hollow by Snake Creek."

Dan heard him, but barely, his mind still cluttered with the banshee nonsense. Shaking himself alert, he checked his watch: 9:40 a.m. Fate was running against them, he feared.

Chapter 45: Charging the Village

★ ★ ★

THE COLUMN WENT TO the trot with the Indian Scouts and Second Cavalry in the lead, followed by the Seventh in a column of fours. Jim's squad rode second in A Troop. Jubal, Ernst, Sam, and Jake made up the first rank, then Rooney, Kessler, Connelly and Holland, with Charley, Dan, and Jim in the rear. Bull Judd's squad rode behind them.

Dan saw the ground rising gradually ahead, just as the scout told Charley it would. No point in trying to see the village until they reached the crest. Supposedly over six hundred people were there, 130 or more warriors, better than a thousand ponies. But the column was big enough to keep them from getting to Canada, unless they were on the run already. Up ahead it looked like the ground was furrowed with wide and deep coulees running into the hollow. Gray clouds had settled in, blocking the sun entirely. The stiff northwest breeze chilled his cheeks, but Teddy loved it, his neck straight out, sticking his nose into the cold.

It was almost ten o'clock, not exactly the best time to attack a hostile village.

"Christ Almighty!" he called over to Jim. "How come we don't hit them at dawn anymore?"

"Not my business," Jim answered. "Right now I gotta worry 'bout them," he said, nodding at the four rookies.

Jim had brought all four recruits up to standard or better. Fact was, the whole squad was ready, especially without Elvin to foul the waters. Of course, actually pitching into a village was going to be new for everybody but him and Charley. That led his mind back again. Goddamn the Washita. That was then, this was now: September 30, 1877, 10:03 a.m. on a Sunday morning. *God forgive us,* he asked, remembering this was the Lord's Day. Again.

Moylan should have ordered their coats off. Too cumbersome to fight in. Made it hard to get at the cartridge belts. Dan looked ahead, inspecting like he still wore the stripes. Christ Almighty! Holland had on wool mittens.

Jim was on it. "Holland!" he shouted ahead, gesturing. "Pull them mittens off!"

There was a strangeness in the air. Nothing you could see, hear, or smell, but by all that was holy, it was there. It made Dan almost lightheaded. Overly warm, he wanted out of his overcoat, but he shivered. A streak of cold lay just behind his lungs, like a foot-long, icy worm lying snug up against his spine.

The old banshee still lurked in the crevices of his brain. Uncle Kevin's wake came to mind. Back in Ireland, it was. Dad was telling Franny and him about the gray man, a half-sized faerie who'd drive his cart up to a dying man and collect his soul before it flew away in the breeze. Went by the name of Ankou in the time of the ancients. Hogwash, his darling Dad said, but he half-believed it himself. Sure and Dan did too, as a lad. Now here he was, an old soldier bearing down on the enemy, stuck with it still, with death coming for him thanks to the old hag's keening. *Goddamn her!*

Then it was his darling Dad he saw, snatching the runaway Morgan's bridle before one shake of the horse's frantic head cast him onto the stones and under the buggy's wheels, snapping his neck, dead in an instant. No banshee there, just his Dad's compassion for a drunken swell coming round on him—another of God's cruel jokes.

To hell with it, he said to himself, digging for his watch: ten fifteen. They went to a gallop a minute later with Teddy happily surging into a three-beat gait. Passing the crest of the rise, the terrain ahead stretched out for miles, falling off gradually to give a look beyond the column. There was no sign of the village but a blur of something stirring to the northeast. Buffalo? Maybe, but what were those riders a half mile ahead? He reached down to stroke Teddy's neck. The blur became a pony herd barely moving. And the riders? Four Nez Perce sitting their ponies, watching the cavalry galloping ever closer.

The column slowed to a walk, gathering itself a mile and a half from the hollow where the village sat. Second Cavalry's three companies swung out to the left, the Indian Scouts milling around ahead of them. Excited, one or two of them dashed forward and back, and then all thirty obliqued left at the gallop, heading for the pony herd with Second Cavalry close behind.

Jim kept an eye on the Second Cavalry battalion. Looked like they were going to pitch into the village from the west. The Seventh would hit it directly from the south. Smoke rising from maybe two miles ahead. It had to be the village, hidden in the hollow, waiting. The squad was ready. No two ways about it.

The battalion was a mile and a half from the village when ordered into line of battle: Company K on the right flank, D Troop the center, and A Troop the left. In the changeup Jim mixed the rookies in with the others. He rode on the left, and then came Kessler, Sam, Jubal, Ernst, Holland, Charley, Connelly, Jake, and Rooney, with Dan on the right. As they went to the trot, First Sergeant McDermott raced up from behind to join Captain Moylan in front. Colonel Miles and his aides broke away from K Troop and drifted back toward the mounted men of Fifth Infantry. A trooper galloped over to Moylan with orders from Captain Hale. Minutes later the bugle sounded and they went to the gallop. Teddy leaped ahead, nearly yanking the reins out of Dan's hand, startling him into pulling back for a second. *Christ Almighty, Daniel, pay attention!* He'd fallen back a good ten paces, but Teddy caught them up in seconds.

The ground ahead stretched out flat for miles, but they couldn't see where it fell off into the hollow. Down the line every man was pushing his horse hard to match the pace set by the officers. Pistols were at the ready. With about half a mile to go, they were running parallel to a fair-sized coulee maybe four hundred yards to the right. A minute later things started happening really fast. Another coulee appeared on the left, gradually deepening and turning to the northeast. Company K diverged to the right, heading for the first coulee, which had turned sharply toward the northwest. Then they disappeared down into it. Companies A and D kept on between the two coulees, like into a funnel. And the village was still out of sight.

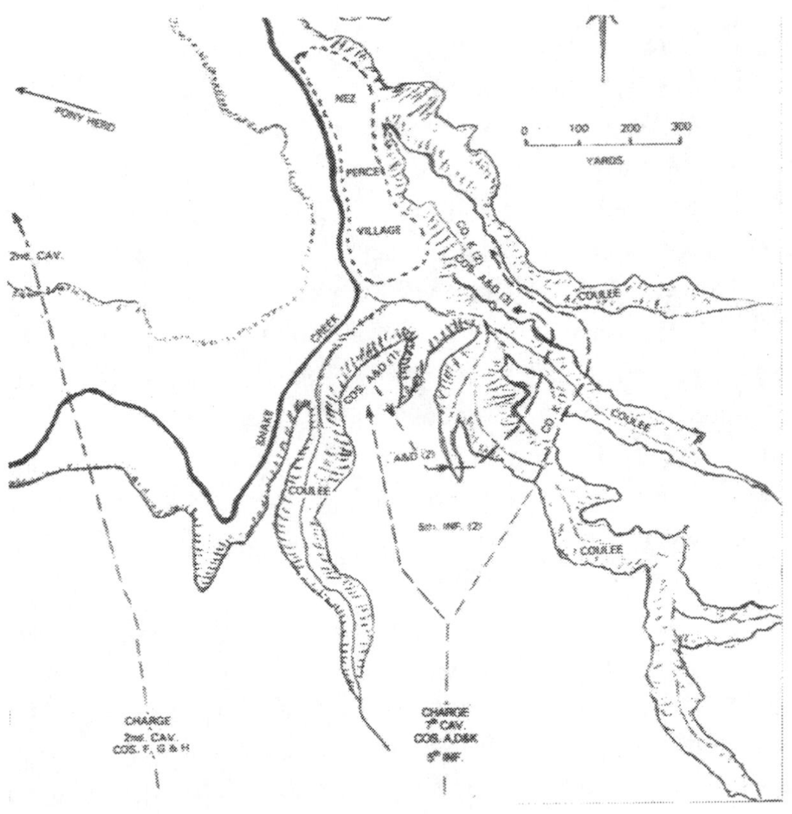

With five hundred yards to go, they galloped into a slight depression running across their path, then out of it, and pressed on, keeping the line with D Troop. Two ponies far ahead ran away and disappeared. *Into the hollow?* Dan guessed. Still no tops of lodge poles in sight; the hollow had to be forty feet deep. At three hundred yards they crossed another depression, the east end of it becoming a swale.

To Dan's right Elvin had his head pressed against his horse's neck. Next man over was Bull, hollering at his squad, "Keep the line, boys! Let's kill us some Injuns!"

Dan shot a quick look in Second Cavalry's direction just as its 150 troopers followed the Indian scouts straight into the pony herd and were lost in a swirling melee of men and horses. *Goddamn it!* He'd thought they were going to pitch into the village! K Troop was still in that big coulee off to the right. Captain Hale was going to attack from the east rather than bunch three companies up between the two coulees. Ahead, the first puff of smoke from a rifle, a warrior shooting from the hollow's edge. There was another yellowish puff, then a rapid succession of rounds whining overhead.

Two hundred yards to go and the bugles blew the charge. Teddy leaped ahead with the rest of the line, every man spurring his horse into an all-out run. More smoke ahead, a wall of it. Bullets filled the air, *zing-zinging.* Dan was sure the gray man would grab him up. Elvin drifted over behind him, then settled between Rooney and him.

Chest to pommel, Elvin spurred his horse mercilessly. *Bull said we'd surprise them. Bullshit! How'd Dan Murphy get on his right? Sonuvabitch must have dropped back and come up behind.* Crumph! He sensed himself leaving the saddle, soaring through the air as his mount went down in a heap, spilling him into the dirt on his face. His carbine banged against his spine as he came up spitting dust and grass, Colt still in hand, bullets whining by. He ducked involuntarily and turned in a running start for the rear, his face bloodied up where it was scraped. Ten steps and his boot found a hole. This time he stayed put on the ground, watching two, then three downed horses struggling to get back on their feet. Dragging a leg, an unhorsed trooper was crawling toward him when a round thunked into the side of his head three paces away. It was Stilson of D Troop. *Stilson or Simpson? Better stay down.* He checked his Colt.

★ ★ ★

Sam sensed rather than saw the trooper's horse go down on his left, quickly lost behind as they charged full out toward the sunken village. They went seventy yards, into a slight depression, twenty yards, and then came out of it, the ground starting to rise. A round buzzed past his ear. Forty more yards and the Nez Perce let loose a terrific volley. Another mount went down to his left. A round went by close, strangely sputtering.

Warriors peered over the rim of the slope, levering their Winchesters and Henrys, firing nonstop. *Brzzow!* A round ricocheted off Blaster's poll. He stumbled, quickly regained stride, and kept going. Blood speckled Sam's coat. Suddenly he could see the tops of lodges, forty feet below and a hundred, two hundred yards away. Christ Almighty! The bank was too steep! On the right a horse went down in a heap. They were pouring it in. Blaster slowed, dancing a bit to the side.

★ ★ ★

"Fours left about!" came the call. Dan's Teddy turned instantly, and Dan and Rooney wheeled around Jake, while eighty-five others struggled to do it by the book although every instinct dictated they just get the hell out of there. In fact, some did just that, but no matter how ragged, the company got it done and raced back to the last depression, where the Indians' fire went over their heads. Coming out of it Dan saw a gray horse go down in a heap, throwing his rider hard into the grass. It was Captain Godfrey, staggering as he got up. His trumpeter came racing back to get between him and the enemy, and Godfrey started back afoot.

Galloping for the rear Jake spotted Elvin on all fours, forty feet ahead and to the right.

"Marde!" he muttered, turning Scar toward him and pulling his left boot out of the stirrup. Finzer came out of the dust from the other side, spurring his horse to shield Jake from the warriors. Scar barely stopped as Elvin stuck his foot in the stirrup, grabbed Jake's arm, and clambered up behind him as the horse leaped forward to catch up with the others.

★ ★ ★

Suddenly, Teddy reared and twisted right to avoid a man crawling painfully toward his downed horse thrashing helplessly a few yards away. "Christ Almighty!" Dan muttered as he swung to the ground, the momentum carrying him forward a few steps before he could scramble back to the man who had a scalp wound and couldn't see for the blood in his eyes. Dan gave him a leg up onto Teddy then ran ahead, reins in hand, his mind jumbled, hating the Goddamn coat for being so heavy. He thought he'd die any second. *Sweet Jesus, why not get it over with?* A trooper with an ugly hole in his brow stared sightlessly up at his mount, standing patiently over him. Dan snatched the animal's reins, jammed his boot into the stirrup, and swung up. They set off at a fast walk with him still leading Teddy. Looking back to see if the wounded man had good purchase, he sensed his back tightening up, itching for the bullet meant for him and no one else. Damn the old hag!

"I got a holt!" shouted the man with the bloody face.

That's good, Dan thought, *because after I'm gone Teddy can get you to the rear on his own.* He pushed the borrowed mount into a fast trot as they started into another shallow depression.

They came up out of the trough and over a slight rise before reaching the mounted Fifth Infantry boys waiting in reserve three hundred yards back. Dan turned the wounded trooper over to Major Tilton, the surgeon, and then brought the Bay to the picket line. Teddy was favoring his right leg, a trickle of blood working its way down from a gash on his shoulder. Dan thought it didn't look too serious but brought him over to the farrier to be sure.

First Sergeant McDermott had gone down close to the bluff. Three others in A Troop were wounded. Captain Godfrey was able to catch a riderless mount and get back. His trumpeter took a round for his trouble; the surgeon said he was a goner. No one in the squad had a scratch. They all just sat there, hollow-eyed, watching

K Troop's fight some four hundred yards away. Dismounted, they were desperately beating off the Indians, who had them practically surrounded. A minute later Captain Moylan ordered A Troop to dismount and get over there at the double time.

Chapter 46: A Perilous Run

Colonel Miles's command was fragmented. Two of Second Cavalry companies were half a mile north, trying to corral hundreds of ponies. The third company was even farther north, chasing 150 Nez Perce making a run for Canada. The Seventh's K Troop was 450 yards to the northeast on the bluff overlooking the village. They were supposed to be attacking the village from the east and southeast, but at the moment they were stalled, being practically surrounded by warriors. A and D Troops were regrouping near the mounted Fifth Infantry, three hundred yards back from the bluffs. Many of the warriors who'd stopped their charge were moving east, using the coulees for cover to get close to K Troop. Seeing this, Colonel Miles directed Fifth Infantry to move north to the bluffs where A and D Troops had been stopped. He ordered those two companies to move northeast on foot at the double time and reinforce K Troop. Captain Moylan stayed in the saddle to lead Company A.

It was eleven fifteen. Dan shook out of his coat despite the cold. It was too cumbersome for a run past Nez Perce riflemen. The others followed suit. Charley and Kessler took the horses.

Jim quickly surveyed the ground they'd have to cross. Fifty yards to the first coulee, a narrow one and not so deep. Down into it, catch their breath, and then sprint across and up the far side and cross a forty-yard stretch, then down into the next coulee, which was a bit more than a hundred yards wide. Twenty yards wide? Twenty-five? It would be worrisome getting across it, with

Indian rifle fire from the high ground north of K Troop. There were sharpshooters southeast of K's line, as well. Sam could keep those braves occupied while the rest of the squad crossed the second gully and clambered up its far bank. Then they'd have to run like hell across a hundred yards of level ground and down into the third coulee, that one eighty yards wide. Down in there they'd be exposed again to fire coming from both the north and the south. From the village too. One hell of a lot of enemy fire until they climbed out of it and reached K Troop.

Captain Godfrey's D Troop was going first. In A Troop Jim's squad was third and Bull's last. K Troop had fallen back from the bluff and was taking fire not only from sharpshooters in rifle pits on the north but from warriors that had scaled the bluffs from the village and were firing from close range in the company's front. A few braves were concentrating on K Troop's fours, trying to drive them to cover so they could grab up the horses.

"Sam, you see them warriors over there?" Jim asked, pointing to the east. "After we cross that first coulee, you settle on the rim of the next one an' keep 'em duckin' till Bull's squad reaches the far bank."

"Okay," Sam said. "And then what?"

"If it's clear, catch up best you can. If it ain't, git back to Charley," Jim said, turning to the others. "Rooney, you an' me will lead out with Sam. Holland an' Connelly, you go next, then Jubal, Jake, and Ernst. Dan, you follow an' make sure nobody's left."

With that Jim took a deep breath and sprinted for the first gully. The others followed, staying low.

* * *

Dan started about ten yards behind Ernst. The first gully was shallow and only thirty yards wide. Although he never broke stride, it seemed like the men ahead of him were running faster. Jim, Rooney, and Sam were already scrambling up the far slope. He was halfway across when Jubal and Ernst were climbing out of it. When he finally got out he tried to catch his breath, but a round whizzed by his ear, sending him into an all-out dash, pushing him to stay ahead of the devil's own. He caught only a flash of Jim and Rooney as they disappeared down into the next gully. Holland and Connelly were right behind, looking like they were joined at the hip, making for a good target. He'd tell them about it later. On second thought, that was Jim's business not his. Besides, in his faerie-infested mind there was no way in hell he would make it that far.

He glanced to his right and there was Sam setting up behind a meager collection of rocks. Three warriors were on the far side of the next coulee trying to hit the men running across that gully. Sam would put a stop to that, what with his eagle eye.

He careened headlong down into the second coulee, half-running and half-sliding on the slippery grass until his heel caught on something and he tumbled downward, narrowly missing Ernst bent over a sergeant. It was Jim Alberts from D Troop, dead less than a minute.

"He's gone! Dead!" Dan hollered, taking the Colt out of the lifeless hand. "C'mon!" he yelled, pushing himself up. Two braves were set up near the coulee's mouth, their fire whizzing by terribly close. Still bent over poor Alberts, big Ernst was a tempting target, so Dan gave him a shove and dashed after him. With the whining lead coming from the left, he knew one of those shooters would get him. On the other hand, it would be like death to let him go on for a while and then nail him with an errant round at dusk.

* * *

Running across the first coulee, Sam's mind was busy remembering the turmoil at the top of the bluffs. Horses were going every which way, trying to get out of there. Colonel Miles was ordering Moylan to get over to Company K as quickly as possible. Then Sam was up the slope and running for the far rim, his mind gone blank while his eyes searched for where to set up. And there it was: a pile of rocks not two feet high. Next thing his body settled itself behind them, his eyes scanning the other side of the coulee, spotting two, no, three of them on one knee 150 yards off, aiming lever-action rifles into the coulee. While laying six cartridges out on his bandana, for some reason Sam pictured Katrinka, her last litter lined up on her belly, and then he recalled how the deer crumpled when he killed him from two hundred yards with Caleb's Spencer 50-56. His thinker shut off as he pulled the hammer back while his eyes chose the sniper on the right and brought the front sight up just a tad over the notch. Finger squeezed off the round. Hand took over. Hammer back, breech bolt up, snatch a cartridge, insert, bolt down, eyes move sights left, squeeze off the round. Survey them again while his fingers reloaded. One was down and two were looking his way as they scrambled back and hugged the ground, looking for a safer perch.

Pzzzzing! A bullet ricocheted off the rocks. Eyes right. A fourth sniper in a hole. Sam got off a quick shot and ducked to reload. *Pzzzzing!* Another shot hit the rocks. Sam popped up and *zzzzing!* A round tore through his coat sleeve. Flat on the ground, he pulled out his pistol and used it to raise his hat barely over the edge of the rocks. *Zzzzzing!* Quickly he rose up and fired, knocking the Indian down. Reloading, his eyes went to the other two. Too hastily, he snapped off a shot. Looked like he hit one of them. Both went scrambling for cover. He reloaded. *Zzzzing!* Another shooter appeared to the left the others. Sam hit him in the head with his second shot. Reloading, he looked down into the coulee. Dan and Ernst were thirty to thirty-five yards from its far side. Elvin was close behind them, the son of a bitch. The rest of Bull's men were up ahead.

He made sure his Colt was loaded, and then dropped a couple 45-55s into a pocket in case he had to reload his carbine on the run. Racing down the hill, he lost his footing and tumbled ass over tea kettle, ending up half-dazed at the bottom, thinking it was plain luck he hadn't shot himself with the Colt. He started up but his mind was elsewhere. Judas Priest! He'd just killed a man, maybe two—the thought of it hit him unexpectedly. There was Sergeant

Alberts's body, and Ernst and Dan were reaching the crest of the opposite slope. Elvin was limping along behind them. Sam loped along, looking for Nez Perce shooters, until a round practically screeched as it zipped past his head, sending him into an all-out run.

★ ★ ★

Dan and Ernst had only thirty yards to go in the second coulee when they stopped by a man on all fours with blood running down the side of his face. A glancing round had knocked him down, leaving a two-inch gash above his right ear. He was shaking his head, trying to regain some sense of clarity. They hunkered down beside him as Bull's squad ran by, drawing considerable fire from the left. They were so close together it was a miracle they hadn't been hit. Elvin was trailing way behind, hobbling along on a bum leg.

It seemed like Ernst was taking entirely too much time checking the man's wound. It was only a bloody scrape. He pressed the man's folded bandana against it, told him to hold it there, pulled him upright, and tried to get him running.

"My Springfield," the trooper muttered, hesitating.

"Here!" Dan said, tossing the piece to him. "Go!"

Still foggy, the trooper stumbled ahead, trying to shake the fog out of his head, then he broke into a run. *A lucky man,* Dan thought, turning to see if Sam was following.

— Chapter 47: Unexpected Casualties —

★ ★ ★

COMING UP OUT OF that second coulee, Dan took a quick look over at K Troop some two hundred yards to the north, beyond the third coulee. Heavy smoke hung over them. A scattering of troopers were coming up behind them out of the third gully. Probably the first of D Troop and maybe some of A Troop too. About a hundred-yard run ahead over level ground, but God only knew how long it would take while sticking with Ernst. There was a man down thirty yards ahead, and Ernst was making a beeline for him. Nothing Dan could do but follow.

The man was lying on his side. He'd been hit in the left arm and was bleeding slowly but steadily. Ernst folded the man's bandana, pressed it against the wound, and told him, "Hold this *fest* to the wound *und* run!"

Dan looked around for snipers. Up and running again, he swiveled his head as he ran, half-expecting a brave to rise up from a hole and kill him. Without thinking, he glanced over his shoulder, looking for the little gray man. No sign of him, but Sam was there, coming out of the second coulee.

★ ★ ★

Elvin's ankle hurt like hell. He had passed Murphy and Albrecht, bent over some poor sonuvabitch on the ground. The stupid Kraut was tending a dying man. He looked to the side—no troopers on the right, none to the left. Nothing for the Redskins to shoot at but him. *How come Moylan had us afoot when he was up ahead on his horse? Goddamn officers!*

Up ahead Bull and the squad grew smaller, then disappeared down into the next coulee. The pain forced Elvin to his knees, but a shot whistled by his ear and he leaped up and started running hobbledehoy, like a fyce dog with a cut foot. The hell with the pain—if he slowed down they'd shoot him dead. Sixty yards more to the third gully. Maybe some cover down in there.

★ ★ ★

Dan and Ernst reached the third coulee quickly enough. Right off, Ernst spotted a wounded man and plunged down the slope. Dan hunkered down to survey what lay ahead. This gully was maybe a hundred yards across with a shallow ditch running the length of it. He got his first clear look at the village, three or four hundred yards to the left. A cluster of braves near it were getting clear shots at the troopers ahead. And one of the snipers who'd exchanged shots with Sam had moved northeast to enfilade the coulee from the right. A Godforsaken gauntlet, that's what it was.

He saw Jim on the far side, just starting up the slope behind Rooney. Jubal and the other two rookies were close behind, but Jake was only halfway across the coulee, down on one knee near a shallow ditch. He was looking back, like he was waiting for him and Ernst, only he was too smart for that. Something was wrong. Bull and his boys were about to pass him, except for Elvin, who was far back, hobbling along as best he could.

Dan hurried down to Ernst. The wounded man lay on his side, knees pulled up, the ground already soaked in his blood. The bullet had torn all the way through the belly, leaving a fist-size hole in his back. There was no way to staunch the flow of blood. Ernst cradled his head, knowing there was no sense staying but unable to let him die alone. That's when they froze, transfixed by what was unfolding.

⋆ ⋆ ⋆

Jake had taken a bullet high up in his left calf. He thought it was a spent round, but still, his knee hurt like hell and he could barely move. He looked back and saw Ernst and Dan. Suddenly the air was filled with lead as Bull went by with his squad, running straight out as they crossed the ditch. *Zzzzing! Whizz! Zzzzzzz.* Some guy was zeroing in on him from the left. *Thunk!* A half-spent ball smashed into his holster, the force of it staggering him enough so he fell to the ground, cradling his carbine. His mind went blank as he searched. *Whizz!* There he spied the brave by the smoke, aiming again with a brass Henry. No paint. Shifting the carbine, he found the sonuvabitch just above the sights. *Bring it up, not too far. Don't shoot high. Zzzzz* chunk—a round dug into the ground on his right. Taking his time, he squeezed his finger as slowly as he could, while his mind sped up, remembering the skirmish line last year. *Marguerite! Whizzzzz!* Another round overhead. *Bam!* The carbine went off by itself. *Marde!* The Indian was moving back, clutching his shoulder. Surprised, he heard himself mumble, "I got the sonuvabitch!" as he rose up and tried to move, but an invisible shovel whacked him in the leg, knocking him sideways and into the ditch like a quail hit by buckshot. *Zizing-zing!* Three more shots flew by where his head had been. He was halfway up again when a round glanced off the back of his skull. The brownish grass went dim, then black nothingness.

⋆ ⋆ ⋆

Ernst and Dan were watching as Jake struggled to rise, his back to them. Then they saw Elvin raise his carbine and fire. Jake's head jerked forward and he slumped.

"Christ Almighty!" Dan yelled.

Elvin started hobbling toward Jake, shifting the carbine to his left hand and drawing his Colt.

Ernst shouted "*Nein!* Elvin, No!"

His hollering seemed to trigger a deadly sequence as rapid as a sketch artist's pencil. Elvin stopped fifteen paces from Jake, thumbed the pistol's hammer back, and took dead aim. He fired. He must have missed because Jake didn't jerk; he just continued to slide down.

Elvin started forward just as Sam came running into view on the right. Elvin got right close to Jake and thumbed the Colt's hammer back again. Sam stopped, and in one smooth motion he raised his carbine and fired, dropping Elvin like a sack of onions. Then he dashed ahead, covering the forty yards in no time flat. Coming close to Elvin, he slowed to a stiff-legged walk while sliding his Colt out of its holster, then pushed Elvin's body over with his foot. The front of his coat already soaked through with blood, he must have been dead or close to it. Sam cocked the pistol and fired a single shot into the coward's forehead. Then he went down on one knee beside Jake.

Dan and Ernst raced over, their eyes glued to Jake's body, hoping for signs of life. His chest rose and fell as Ernst knelt to examine the wounds.

"Is he breathing?" Sam asked, sounding dazed.

"*Ja*," Ernst answered. "Get down!"

Dan got down but realized that, although the Nez Perce were still firing, none of their shots were coming close.

"What do you want me to do?" Sam asked, lowering himself.

"You and Dan go!" Ernst commanded.

"No!" Sam said. "We're not leaving you and Jake behind!"

Dan checked Jake's leg wound. It showed gristly white bone where the bullet had grazed the knee, and there was no pulse to the oozing blood. That was good.

"*Ja, ja*," Ernst muttered, cradling Jake's head, the back of which was sticky with blood. Rolling him part way over, he probed for softness. *Gut!* The ball had torn the skin away but didn't break bone. Jake moaned.

"*Sie sind gut*, Jake. You are good," he said, turning to Dan. "Give me your bandana." He used it fashion a compress for the scalp wound, then unslung his carbine. Rising, he effortlessly tossed Jake over his shoulder and started running.

Most of the fire was coming from the left now. Apparently this registered with Sam because he caught up with Ernst and stayed on his left. Still, no rounds came near.

Dan looked ahead. Jim and the others were on the slope, Bull's men too. Moylan was spurring his big Black over the crest, the sight of him a surprise. He hadn't seen the captain since they started out. How long ago was that? Five minutes? An hour?

* * *

Jim stumbled halfway up the slope. Forty yards back he'd run into a vicious crossfire. Three men ahead went down, but looking back, his men were okay. Then a round hit him just above the hip, shoving him somewhat to the side before he recovered his steady. It must have glanced off the cartridge belt. Hurt some, but no blood to be seen. Ignoring the dull pain, he'd pushed himself to go all out and almost caught up with Rooney at the base of the slope, but he was slowing considerably. He paused for a second and looked back. Jubal and the two rookies were catching up. Was that Ernst by the ditch? And Dan? He wiped his eyes, unable to make it out so good. He started up the damn slope again, slowly. Damn! Not enough air. No matter. *Just keep climbing, you dumb sumbitch!*

* * *

The slope was much steeper than Dan thought, but Ernst kept moving fast. He was ten yards below Finzer when he saw him grab his leg and fall beside Jim. Ernst lumbered up and hunkered down, handing Jake off to Sam and telling him to go ahead. The sound of gunfire from K Troop was intense, and there was plenty of lead in the air overhead. Some of it was close.

Finzer's left trouser leg showed blood, so Ernst slit the kersey with his knife. The bullet had passed clean through the calf muscle; blood flowed slowly. As Ernst fashioned a bandage out of the man's bandana, a shot sent Rooney tumbling back down. Wounded in the right hip, he almost landed on top of Dan. In the midst of all that, Ernst noticed the blood on Jim's side.

"You are hurt, Sergeant," he said.

"Just a crease," Jim said. "Dan, you and Ernst get these two up. I gotta get them others moving." He pointed to the knot of men above.

"No," Dan said. "Finzer can make it himself. I'll take Rooney and get after them while Ernst takes a look at you."

"I told you it's just a crease. You two go on an' get up there," Jim said, smiling through the pain. "And don't give me no shit, Private. I'm the Goddamned sergeant."

Rooney couldn't do much more than crawl, so Ernst dragged him up. Finzer did fairly well without Dan's support, although their boots kept slipping on the sunbaked grass. When Dan stopped to catch his breath, he found himself downright belligerent about death's plan.

"What's taking you so long, old reaper?" he taunted. As if in answer a flurry of shots came close, some digging into the ground close by, others whizzing barely overhead. "To hell with it," he mumbled, starting up again.

Jubal was amongst the cluster of men near the top. Two dead troopers were on the left, Percival and O'Leary. LaCrosse was to the right of the dead men, scrunched down on his side, paralyzed with his knees up, his hands grabbing them. Two men from D Troop crouched beside him. Devine was just below, sitting bent over on one hip, holding the other. He was telling Jubal that he was grazed in the shoulder as well.

"Don't fret none," Jubal told him. "We'll git yew up thar." Turning to the men from D Troop, he said "Yew boys git a move on, Goldurnit!" He jabbed at them with a carbine lying close by. "Stay here an' yer goners fer sure."

"You okay?" Dan asked him.

"Oh yeah. I jist stopped to git ole Runny goin'." He turned to LaCrosse. "Cain't stay here, Runny!" he yelled. "Git a move on!"

LaCrosse stared blankly at him, pointing feebly at Percival. The corpse was hunched over strangely on its knees, feet uphill, nose buried in the grass below, his left temple no more than brain matter in a gaping hole.

"Niver mind him, git on yer feet!" Jubal yelled as Jim struggled up and crouched beside LaCrosse.

"Where's Sergeant Judd?" Jim asked.

"He left," Runny said mechanically.

"Where'd he go?"

"Up the hill, I guess."

"C'mon, Runny! Git up!" Jubal demanded. That's when he saw the blood stain under Jim's cartridge belt. "Damn it, Jim, you been hit," he exclaimed, pointing.

"Huh?" Jim glanced down at his blouse. "Just a graze. Ricocheted off my belt."

"Ain't no graze, Jim," Jubal said, moving toward him. "Here, lemme take a look."

"Ain't no time! You git up on top!" Jim hollered over the din. "You too, Dan. I'll be right behind, soon as I get LaCrosse goin', or shoot the sumbitch, one. Now get a move on, Goddamn it!"

"Okay, but you git up there, hear?" Jubal said, taking hold of Devine. They started up again, hurried by a new spate of bullets thunking into the ground and zipping past their heads.

"And you boys keep low!" Jim threw after them. He turned to LaCrosse. his bile rising at the sight of the plump sumbitch as he clawed his way over to where his face was only a foot away. "Git up!" he barked. "If you don't, I'll beat the shit outta you!" Not a twitch from the trembling sumbitch. "Git the hell up!" Jim shouted, pulling LaCrosse's Colt out of its holster. He cocked it, jammed its muzzle against Runny's wet nostril, twisting and flicking it to scare him into moving, but the man was beyond scaring, no two ways about it. He eased the hammer down and grabbed him by the collar, yanked him up and slapped him across the face hard. He did it again and again until the hurt of it finally broke through and he responded reflexively, rising as he tried to fight Jim off. With that Jim sat back, cocked the pistol, and fired twice, barely missing Runny's crotch. That sent the sumbitch on his way. He was running straight out when he disappeared over the crest.

As Jim started to rise an insistent wave of weariness swept over him, leaving him perplexed, leaning with one arm just barely holding him up. He wondered what was going on. He willed his arms to push him up, his legs to start moving, but nothing worked, not even his eyes. The world began to fade, his mind humming along at a gentle pace, musing. Getting darker. *How long they been at it? Hours? Cold. Snow tonight maybe—maybe not.* Silence. His ears must have shut down. Fact is, it was better like this. *Was the fight over?* Tired, he laid down. He didn't want to; it just happened.

Spring of '76, tracking the two deserters. Eagle-eye Streeter puking. Hogan's corpse in the dust, the lifeless eyes staring out at nothing. Those dead eyes, he saw them but couldn't look at them, not really. The side of his face rested on the sparse brown-gray carpet. Not much of a cushion, but warm. Felt good. Blades of grass a few inches away. Buffalo grass. Scant feed. *Rich green pasture back home, by the cattle barn.* The First went down in the charge. Now he was used up too. No two ways about it. Looking inward, he strained to shut his eyes before ...

Chapter 48: The End of It

WHEN JUBAL AND DAN returned from bringing the wounded over to the hospital, A Troop was moving to join the skirmish line on the west side of the bluff. They were under heavy fire. Some of the warriors had wormed their way to within a hundred yards of them, but there was too much smoke hanging in the cold air to get off a decent shot.

Several men lay dead in front of the line. Lieutenant Biddle was among them. Occasionally it seemed like one would twitch when hit in the arm or leg. Captain Moylan was hit in the right thigh and headed for the hospital, and Captain Hale went down minutes later, shot dead through the neck. The only officer left was Lieutenant Eckerson. More than a few troopers, Dan included, thought he wasn't worth much.

When Dan saw Fifth Infantry moving up to the bluffs south of the village, he figured that would take some of the pressure off the skirmish line. Sure enough, half the warriors facing them scrambled down to the village. The firing soon became sporadic and the company shifted into a slight depression a few yards back. That gave Charley a chance to scurry over the edge of the slope to check on Jim. He was back quickly. Jim was dead.

Dan turned away, biting down on the pain of it, but it persisted. Losing friends in battle was part of soldiering, but Jim was special, a damn fine sergeant. Like today, setting Sam up to cover them. And he was that most rare of men: sweet, kind, and so comfortably honest with himself. Dan thought back to the time he'd playfully scolded Jim for lording it over young Streeter. He told him he was even more frightening than Gus Steinbrecher himself. "I hope so," Jim had said.

He smiled at the memory and thought, *May the devil hear not of your death till you're safe inside heaven.* Turning to the others, he said, "A good sergeant, he was, and a good man as well." There was only the slightest quaver in his voice.

The look on Jubal's face was one of pure misery. "He must of bled out gittin' LaCrosse goin'. I shouldn't of listened to him."

"Where was he hit?" Sam asked.

"In the side. They was a stain on his blouse."

Charley said, "He bled out inside. Wouldn't of made it even if he got up here. Like Dan said, he was a good man. Leave it at that."

Nobody spoke, each man caught in his own thoughts. Finally Jubal asked the time.

"Eleven, a little after," Sam said.

"So how long we been at it?"

"Went to the charge just after ten," Dan answered. *Had it only been an hour?*

Although surrounded by over three hundred soldiers, the eighty-odd warriors weren't about to give up. Miles ordered the Hotchkiss gun into action, but from the bluffs its muzzle couldn't be depressed enough to hit the lodges. Worse yet, the accuracy of the Nez Perce snipers sent the gun crew scurrying for cover.

Later Charley asked, "How many did we lose?"

"All three troops, I heard maybe thirty, maybe more," Sam said.

"Thet many?" Jubal asked.

"Yes," Dan said. "And the Indians know what they're doing. They killed Captain Hale, Lieutenant Biddle, all three firsts, and four other sergeants. Wounded Moylan, Godfrey, and two more sergeants. I doubt the colonel wants another charge, not with the Seventh, anyway."

He was wrong.

★ ★ ★

Miles had a two-pronged attack in mind. He sent Fifth Infantry's Company G over to join Seventh's three companies, with their Lieutenant Romeyn taking command. Army sharpshooters on the bluffs would concentrate their fire on the southernmost tepees, while nineteen infantrymen charged into the village. Simultaneously, Romeyn was to lead the charge to regain the bluffs on the west side.

It went off at two o'clock and was a complete disaster. The Nez Perce were hidden in rifle pits and under the crests the gullies. Others were hidden inside the village. On the bluff Lieutenant Romeyn rose up, waved his hat, and the men started off with a holler. Immediately the Indians let fly a fusillade that stopped the charge cold. Romeyn was shot through the right lung and Kessler was killed instantly. Down below the infantrymen charged straight into the village but were greeted by volleys from warriors in pits and tepees. Eight men were hit (two mortally), and they were forced to retreat, leaving some of their wounded behind.

Except for occasional exchanges between snipers, that was the end of the fighting that day. The cold and snow made for a long and grim night, and they woke up on Sunday to five inches of snow. Dan wasn't surprised when Captain Moylan sent word that he was acting sergeant, replacing Jim.

A truce was arranged while Miles tried to negotiate a surrender with Chief Joseph. During the truce both sides recovered their dead. After Charley and Sam brought Jim up, the squad paid their last respects before the body was taken over to the mass grave the infantrymen had dug next to the hospital. When the negotiations with Chief Joseph failed, Colonel Miles tried to coerce the other Nez Perce chiefs to surrender by holding Joseph hostage, a reprehensible act. His trickery failed, however, because during the truce the Indians caught a Second Cavalry lieutenant moseying around their positions. They held him until the next morning when Miles agreed to return Joseph.

Seventh Cavalry lost heavily, with a casualty rate of 46 percent. Twenty men were dead and thirty-three wounded. More than half the men in K Troop were killed or wounded. Company A suffered five killed and nine wounded out of thirty-six. Of the wounded, Private Savage was in the worst shape. Shot in both thighs, he was in for a long stay in the post hospital, if he could make it back there alive.

The ball that struck Jake's leg plowed a wicked furrow that Major Tilton sewed up. Tilton predicted a permanently stiff knee, which pleased Jake. A bad knee would earn him a surgeon's certificate. One thing for sure, that knee wouldn't bend again until he had his discharge in hand.

With the promise of more miserable weather, Charley and Dan appropriated several gum blankets the dead wouldn't be using and rigged up a larger shelter. Word was the Nez Perce might try to slip through the lines. Charley was slated to stand watch at two in the morning.

Unable to sleep, Dan started talking. "The Irish in me took hold two nights ago," he told Charley. Freezing rain tapped a steady beat on the canvas. "The banshee woke me, keening she was, so why didn't death take me?"

"You sure it was her?"

"Might have been a coyote, or an Indian making like one."

"So it wasn't her."

"I thought it was. All day I did."

"You're alive, so it couldn't of been her!" Sometimes Dan pissed him off. "Or maybe she changed her mind. Keened for Jim, instead."

"But Jim, he uh … I shouldn't laugh but that can't be right, Jim not being Irish."

"Which he's tellin' her right now," Charley said. "He's sayin', 'Are you blind? I ain't fat-cheeked and ugly like that sumbitch Murphy. No two ways about it.'" They lost themselves in the mirth of it, picturing Jim railing at the spectral crone.

When the chuckles ran out they sat without words in the dark.

A blast of wind shook the makeshift tent. It had worked its way around to the north, bringing more snow than rain.

"Going to miss the way he soldiered," Dan said.

"I'll miss the man, not the soldierin'"

"A man's soldiering doesn't matter?"

"Not no more," Charley said.

"What does matter?" Dan asked, suddenly aggravated.

"The next corner and whatever's around it."

"But—" he started, but Charley held up his hand.

"Soldierin's a meanderin' river, Dan," he said, thinking before he went on. "Most of the bends are signaled ahead of time by a call—reveille, stables, mess call, tattoo, charge, retreat—so you know what's comin'. Outside soldierin' there's corners where you gotta react or choose: the job is gone, your uncle's dead, Jameson or Bushmills, which girl to go after. You see? When you come home from The War, you got to hatin' them corners and the Goddamned surprises. So you joined the cavalry, where the corners are few and the meanders are easy."

And with that Charley rolled over and was snoring softly three minutes later. Dan stayed awake while his mind buzzed with memories, and then he stood Charley's watch, growing increasingly despondent. *Mary, Mother of God,* he thought, *Jim's gone, Charley's leaving. But however long the road, there comes a turning. Sure and there's an Irish saying for every occasion, but too often they helped not a bit.*

* * *

Charley had no more than opened his eyes in the morning when it hit him. Ever since the sweats he'd been pestered by what Nagin said—"You choose to be there"—which he denied. In fact, he'd done okay on his own, so he could have left earlier. He didn't have to kill the old man. It was time to accept it.

★ ★ ★

All Dan wanted was some decent coffee. What he got was no closer to decent than what they'd had on the march, but he couldn't complain, not after getting word that Teddy was still on his feet and looking better. Sweet Jesus, what a relief! Old Teddy, with more heart than most, was not ready to give up the ghost, not ready at all.

Sam showed up. You could see he wanted coffee, the way he looked at the steam of it.

"Want some?" Charley asked, holding out his cup.

"No, thanks," Sam said. *A Massachusetts boy through and through,* Dan thought. Good manners trumps truth every time.

"You look like you could use it," Charley said, holding out the cup. "I've had one already."

"Okay, thanks. Dan, I have to tell you something, you being the sergeant now," Sam began.

"Okay, if you must."

He took a swallow of coffee and launched straight into telling how he killed Elvin. The way he told it wasn't like him. Instead of pausing to think while talking, he ticked it off one step at a time, as if by rote, an unvarnished, emotionless succession of events: running, pulling up when he saw Elvin fire, Jake falling, raising his own carbine, the shot knocking Elvin down, checking the Colt while approaching the fallen son of a bitch, thumbing the hammer back as he raised it slowly, aiming, and then blasting him straight into hell. It was like finishing off a Whitetail, only just above the eyes instead of behind the ear because he wanted him to see it coming just in case he was still alive, but dead or alive, it made no difference.

Dan was intrigued. That Sam shot Elvin wasn't surprising—*Christ Almighty, he had no choice.* It was putting that extra round into the Elvin's head. That, and the mechanical way he did it and told it. Sam Streeter a cold-blooded killer?

Dan sipped some coffee, and then asked, "And why would you bring it to me?"

"'Cause I don't know what to do with it," Sam said softly. "Tell me, what are the regs on killing a man like I did?"

"You'd have to ask the captain. However, hearing the question would disturb him enormously what with his wound."

"But it's important to set things straight," Sam said. He slumped as if exhausted at the end of a foot race. He looked up at Dan, then over at Charley, who locked eyes with him.

"Been set straight already," Charley said.

"What do you mean?"

"Elvin Crane was killed in action while fighting the Nez Perce. That's it."

"But I murdered him."

"No, you stopped the murder of your partner."

"But I'm not sure about—"

"About what? Guilt?" Dan snarled.

"No, I'm not sorry I killed him. It's doing it without a thought, then or since. That makes me a cold-blooded killer."

"No!" Charley said. "It makes you a man who kills when need be."

"And now you know that you can kill with neither passion nor remorse," Dan added. "Maybe it surprises you, but it's true."

"But I'm not like that," Sam insisted.

"You are. It's a part of you," Charley said.

"How come I never saw it coming?"

"War brings out things in a man he don't know about."

"So what do I do with it, with knowing I can kill like that?"

"Live with it," Dan said, smiling at Charley. "We must live with whatever we find within." He lifted a boot and tapped his pipe on the heel, spilling the ashes to the ground. "Look, Sam, it's just one part of you. There's also a kindness in you. Fact is, it's the kindness that needs the harness. It makes a man vulnerable, so you must use your head with it. Mind yourself when it comes out. Now if you'll excuse me, I must go and see a wounded friend."

"Who?"

Charley answered him. "His horse."

★ ★ ★

Sam mulled over what Charley had said: "It makes you a man who kills when need be. It's a part of you."

The fact was, Sam couldn't disagree—not and be honest about it. Katrinka. There she was again, and now he knew why. He raised her, took care of her, sat up with her through her litters. Then, when the time came, he'd killed her for the meat. He'd helped Mr. Thompson carve her up, clean the guts, and stuff them with sausage meat. They made scrapple from the rest—without a second thought about any of it.

Truthfully, he could kill if he had a reason for it. He'd been that way from the start. It should trouble him, he supposed. In the event he might act like it did, but it didn't, not really.

Chapter 49: Promises

THE STANDOFF CONTINUED UNTIL General Howard and his column arrived the evening of October 4. He brought with him two elderly Nez Perce men and an interpreter, Arthur Chapman, who was a friend of Chief Joseph. The three of them palavered with the Indians the next morning. Before noon the two sides agreed on surrender terms. General Howard and Colonel Miles promised that the Nez Perce survivors would be brought down to the Tongue River Cantonment for the winter and then transported to the Lapwai Reservation in western Idaho, some seventy miles from Joseph's home in Oregon's Wallowa Valley. Chief Joseph and the other elders agreed. The formal surrender would take place on the morrow.

Late the next day, Charley, Jubal, and Sam came back from watching the surrender. Charley said Howard and Miles arrived first. They stood waiting long enough to understand that Joseph kept to his schedule not theirs.

"Gin'ral Howard, he looked a mite hang-dog, kind of slumped with his one arm left from preservin' the Union," Jubal said. "Colonel Miles, he tried to look right smart. His back was set straight an' his jaw stuck out like it does, but yew cain't git wool an' leather to look trim when they're four days wet. We seen he was rankled, thinkin' Joseph's one bodacious, uppity Injun, makin' him wait like thet, an' yew jist knew he was schemin' as to how he'd fix him later.

"They stood there long enough to worry thet Joseph changed his mind. Looked as if the colonel was 'bout to tell the guard to do somethin', when the chief, he come out 'tween the lodges on this fine black hoss with one of them Mesican saddles. Nigh on forty years old, he was all spruced up, with a clean shirt and a gray woolen shawl over his shoulders. Looked like they was some bullet holes in it. Had his hair fixed up too; didn't he, Charley?"

"Yeah. A topknot like the Crows tie with otter fur and two long braids. Marks on his forehead and wrist like he'd been grazed in the fight."

"Real slick, he was," Jubal said. "And 'bout big as Ernst. Anyways, he had a Winchester carbine an' he followed the crick with five of his men walkin' 'longside. Dan'l, yew should of seen the way he rode. It grieved me, him lookin' real sad. Yew could feel it. At the same time, he was holdin' his head high. Lemme tell you, they wa'n't a body there but had to watch the man. Yew know what I'm sayin'?"

"I think so."

"He was solemn," Sam cut in. "With dignity."

Accounts of the event in later years mentioned that Chief Joseph delivered a heart-stirring speech of surrender, including the unforgettable line, "From where the sun now stands I will fight no more forever." While those few words accurately reflected Joseph's intentions, he had voiced them earlier in the day, perhaps during the negotiations. From what Jubal said, Dan could picture the event.

Chief Joseph remained silent, his face awash in sorrow. He thrust his rifle out toward General Howard, as if with that sudden move he let go of hope for his people. A tragic moment, it was cheapened when Howard didn't reach for the rifle but gestured to Miles instead, indicating that the chief must surrender to him.

"Nobody said nothin'," Jubal said, "but yew could see what was goin' on. When Gin'ral Howard points to Miles, the chief looks down at him an' shrugs, like he'll go 'long with it, but it jist ain't right givin' in to a lyin' scoundrel. But when he turns he don't give the colonel the piece right off. First he glares at him fer a bit, like he was sayin', 'Yew kin fool the gin'ral, but yew cain't fool me, 'cause we both know yer a split-tongued, fancy-ass, storytellin' polecat.'"

"That's it exactly," Sam said, smiling at Jubal's way of putting it.

"Right," Jubal said. "Sam, yew tell the rest of it."

"Okay. The chief moved off to the side and his warriors came up and laid down their arms," Sam said. "It seemed like every Nez Perce around came out—women, kids, sick, lame, really old ones, even some that looked to be blind. I imagine they were glad it was over, but you couldn't tell from their faces."

"They were tired," Charley said.

* * *

A half hour later Charley stood on the edge of the bluffs overlooking the coulee where the Nez Perce shelters were located. Starting a new chaw, he thought that surrendering was painful enough, but it had to be awful for those warriors to stomach the idea of their families being prisoners. Bull walked up and stood beside him. Down below, five braves were bending an older man's ear. Apparently he agreed with their argument because when they started toward their dugouts they were walking tall.

"They're talkin' escape," Bull said.

"Maybe."

"They try it an' we'll shoot 'em dead."

Charley remained silent, remembering Humaza in his village.

Down below a six-year-old boy walked next to three other kids, an elderly woman, and an old man. The old woman stopped at one of the shelters and held the flap so the old man could enter. Then she turned to say something to the children, adding a final few words for the six-year-old. The boy hunkered down while the others played. He was keeping an eye out for someone. Behind him a woman came up and stopped, gazing at his small form squatting beside the path. She called out, softly. Surprised, he looked around, then jumped up and ran, slowing to a walk before he got to her.

Charley smiled. The kid was delighted to see his mother, but it wasn't that important, not for a big boy of six.

"Dang blast it!" Bull exclaimed. "We should of rode straight through them heathens, you know."

"We'd of all gone down."

"Not if Second Cavalry come in from the west. Between them an' us, we would of rubbed 'em out," Bull said. "As it is, one day them kids will slice up a settler's wife. Then we'll hafta hunt 'em down all over again."

"Bull, you're nothin' but a snake." What pissed Charley off was the sonuvabitch interrupting his enjoyment of the little boy, as tough an Indian as any full-fledged warrior.

⋆ ⋆ ⋆

The troop finished burying their dead in the common grave on Saturday. The next day the whole army and Nez Perce column headed out, carrying the wounded in wagons and on travois. The prisoners included eighty-seven men, 184 women, and 147 children. Many of them rode ponies from the captured herd. Thunderstorms hit their camp that night and they remained there the next day, Monday, October 8, because it rained cats and dogs all day. It took them another five days to cover the ninety-odd miles to the Missouri River. There the three Seventh Cavalry Troops joined the rest of the regiment and went into camp on its north bank, while the infantry and the Nez Perce were ferried across.

On the evening of October 14 the squad was sitting around the fire, talking quietly. Dan had just asked how Jake was getting along when Ernst came into the circle with Jake slung over his shoulder, splinted leg sticking out straight to the side. Sam produced the first bottle. When it got around to Dan the second time, he held it high, signaling a forthcoming speech.

"Fear not, lads," he said. "There'll be no lengthy oration, just one toast to those no longer with us. As for our rookie compatriots, too bad you didn't get to know Bull Judd's predecessor, Sergeant

Gustav Steinbrecher, who knew the cavalry in a time and place where men were well trained and well led. He told of old-time cavalry fights and the glory his Prussian regiment garnered. Such glory is not for the Seventh, partly because of the kind of war we've been waging. But if we've seen no regimental glory, we have seen valor. And by my faith every one of you fought with valor. You've soldiered well, for which you can be proud, and I am proud to have served with you. With that said, let's get on with our drinking, for which I thank Sam who brought the Creature to us this night, demonstrating that he's learned far more soldiering than I dared hope two years ago."

★ ★ ★

On October 15 the wounded boarded the *Silver City* for transport to Fort Lincoln. Due for discharge, Charley and Jubal went with them.

★ ★ ★

Apparently the Nez Perce's flight had embarrassed both Sheridan and Sherman because they quickly nullified the promises made to Chief Joseph by Howard and Miles. Their superiors decided the Nez Perce should be punished as an example to other Indians and never be allowed to go home. In November the Nez Perce were shipped to Fort Leavenworth and corralled in tents on an abandoned racetrack. The following July they were sent to a malaria-ridden reservation in Indian Territory. It wasn't until 1885 that the remaining 268 people finally were allowed to return to the Northwest. One hundred and eighteen went to the Lapwai Reservation in western Idaho. Chief Joseph and the other 150 settled on the Colville Reservation in Washington, some two hundred miles north of his home in Oregon's Wallawa Valley.

★ ★ ★

After a month of heavy drinking in 1880, Sergeant Henry Judd got himself into a violent brawl in a saloon and was discharged per general court-martial order for "attempted murder with his service revolver." Bull reenlisted in the Seventh six months later and made sergeant again the following year.

Upon his discharge, Jubal Tinker went to Wisconsin, where he worked on the family farm of his old bunkie, Bobby Thorsen. He enjoyed being one of the family but found that things weren't the same between him and Bobby, who was about to be married. Jubal reenlisted on April 10, 1878, and was assigned to Dan's squad in Company A.

After his discharge Charley made his way south to the Spotted Tail Agency, where he found Humaza and his *tiospaye*. Charley spent the winter there, helping out by bringing in fresh meat for the village. He quickly became fluent in their language and his many conversations with Nagin helped firm up his resolve to find his own way in life. Realizing the Lakota way was not his, in the spring he gave his Winchester and 382 rounds of .44-40 ammunition to Humaza and headed west to San Francisco. In 1880 he married Angelina Germano, a twenty-year-old seamstress. A year later, she gave birth to their son, James Daniel Smrka. Two other boys followed in short order.

Jake was discharged with a surgeon's certificate of disability on November 20, 1877. He returned to Chicago, and then joined René in San Francisco in January. Two years later they opened a first-class restaurant modeled after Chapin and Gore's in Chicago. In 1881 he ran into Charley and hired him as a bartender. A year later he bought a building on Hyde Street and made Charley a partner to run the saloon on its ground floor. Jake took the apartments upstairs to serve as his business offices and living quarters.

Ernst was discharged as a private of excellent character by regimental order in September 1878. A freelance illustrator and painter, he eventually gained national recognition for his paintings of Western landscapes and American Indian life. He also settled in San Francisco, where he married and started a family. In the autumn of 1890 he spent three months on the Pine Ridge and Rosebud Reservations, compiling illustrations for a series of articles about the state of American Indians.

Sam Streeter was promoted to Sergeant in October 1878. Discharged in 1880, he found work at an Omaha newspaper. In 1882 he went to work for the *New York Times.* Two years later he married Katherine Willoughby, the daughter of a prominent New York financier. He entered the family business but grew increasingly restless in the world of finance and returned to the *New York Times* in 1888.

After visiting various Dakota agencies in 1889, Sam wrote a series of articles that questioned General Crook's claim that three-fourths of the Sioux had "touched the pen" to the agreement taking nine million acres away from the tribe. Later that year he looked into the causes of the Johnstown flood that claimed more than 2,200 lives. His report was one of several that blamed the flood on the failure of a dam constructed to create a lake for a millionaires' sporting club. It was acclaimed by social critics but sparked the ire of prominent men of wealth, including his father-in-law. In December of 1890 he traveled to South Dakota to report on what was known as the Sioux Ghost Dance.

Dan remained with Company A. After turning forty on September 16, 1880, he went absent without leave for three weeks, costing him a month's pay. He lost his stripes too, but Captain Moylan returned them just before Christmas. A month later Dan married Sheila Sullivan, a young widow with two girls, ages four and six. In October she bore them a son, Francis Carl Murphy.

Company A relocated to Fort Meade, Dakota Territory, in 1879. Later it was garrisoned at Fort Riley, Kansas. During the fall of 1890 eight companies from the Seventh were sent to Pine Ridge. On the morning of December 29 they were at Wounded Knee Creek, escorting Big Foot's peaceful band of 360 people to the agency. While disarming the Indians someone fired a gun. After an initial flurry of shots, during which both troopers and warriors were struck down, the cavalry turned its Hotchkiss guns on the people, and the cavalry hunted down those who fled. Official estimates were between two hundred and 250 Indians dead. Fewer than a hundred were men of fighting age, and less than half of those had firearms. The remaining dead were women, children, and the very old. The army's official casualty list included Captain Wallace, twenty-five troopers, and one enlisted Indian scout killed in action. Thirty-six men were wounded, of which at least five eventually died of their wounds.

In government documents the event is known variously as an incident, an affair, an encounter, an engagement, a fight, and a battle. In American history it is known as the Wounded Knee Massacre, a slaughter of innocents that marked the end of the Indian Wars for the Seventh Cavalry.

Epilogue: A Letter From Dan

★ ★ ★

Pine Ridge Agency, S.D.

December 31, 1890

Dear Charley,

I haven't written in a long time. Sorry. First thing's first. Our beautiful girls are fourteen and sixteen. Our darling son, Francis Carl Murphy, is nine. He's brighter than a firefly on a cloudy night, and he's good looking. Takes after his mother, he does.

I saw Ernst Albrecht in November. He said you and Jake owned a saloon that is doing a bang-up business. That sounds like a good deal for you, Jake being a trustworthy man. I should come out there and get a taste of what you're serving the swells.

By now you know they killed Sitting Bull two weeks ago. It reminded me of how Crazy Horse was done in. You surely will know about Wounded Knee too. There were enough reporters around here to write it a thousand times over. No matter what they wrote, it was just plain bad. Seventh Cavalry killed women and kids like never before. There's no good count. My guess is more than 250. Men like Bull Judd went wild, killing every soul they could. You and I know the higher ups will never tell the truth of it.

Colonel Forsyth tried to do right. Big Foot was sick, so he put him in a tent with a stove at night. He separated the women and kids from the braves before disarming them. Then the troopers searched the teepees. Some of them got rowdy and it agitated the warriors. Someone fired a round and all hell broke loose. Dismounted, B and K Troops were crammed between the braves and the village. It was close quarters, so some men were hit by cavalry fire. Then the Hotchkiss guns on the hill opened up on the village, and the six other companies joined in the killing.

Sam Streeter's been here since the middle of December as a newspaper reporter. When the four Hotchkiss guns on the hill opened up on the village, he helped some women and kids scramble into the ravine. The artillerymen wheeled one Hotchkiss down from the hill to enfilade the ravine, killing and wounding more innocents. Shrapnel hit Sam in the belly. He's in the hospital having a tough go of it, but this morning he perked up a bit. He asked me to send his regards to you and Jake and Ernst.

January 1, 1891

I had to stop writing yesterday because Sam's condition worsened. He's got a fever and gets terribly fitful. I hope he can hang on long enough to get better, but the surgeon isn't optimistic.

The day after the massacre the colonel had us chasing the Sioux north of the agency. He didn't put flankers out. The Indians let us "catch" them, and so we were half-swallowed up. Unsure of himself, Forsyth dismounted us and sent back word three times that he'd run into one thousand warriors. Jubal says the colonel has his own way of counting Indians: "A handful's fifty an' two handful's two hunerd. Any more's a thousand." Bull made like a hero and rode off alone, chasing two braves over the next hill. We figured he was done for when he didn't come back.

Two hours later four companies of the Ninth Cavalry came to our rescue. They deployed into the hills dismounted. The Sioux slid away and went back to their village three or four miles away. Later we determined there were less than fifty of them, some without rifles.

Bull returned red-faced, escorted by men from the Ninth. You recall that's a colored outfit. Jubal asked where they found poor Bull. "They went to grinning real wide-like," he said. "Said they durn near missed him, cause he'd lost his horse and was under a pile of tumbleweeds in a ditch. Couldn't tell who he was hiding from, the Sioux or the Ninth. I said prob'ly both." There's humor in that, but the laughter went out of me with the massacre. By my faith, Bull deserves a good whipping, being the mean son of a bitch he is.

General Miles suspended Forsyth and there's an investigation. But in week or so they'll declare a great victory and give out a bunch of medals to the officers and fools like Bull. Sure, and that's the army way.

North of the agency I caught a spent ball in my arse. Moylan thinks it's worth a surgeon's certificate. He's getting out next year himself, which will give him thirty-five years in.

I've lost the heart for soldiering. Fact is, we're just arm-twisters called out to put down any little threat to business as usual. Killing starving Indians because they dance is worse than the Pinkertons shooting up the Molly Maguires, but you knew that long ago. Anyway, I'm getting out. Maybe I'll travel to California and try the good life.

JANUARY 2, 1891

Humaza came in late last night from the bad lands to spy out the situation. He talked with Jubal and me. Times have been hard. After a terrible drought, the government cut the size of the reservations and the beef rations too. Looks like he's weathering it okay personally. He asked me to say "How" to you and say he's still "Man in Between's *kola*." It must be true, for him to still be friendly with us after what's happened.

Sam Streeter died yesterday after supper, God rest his soul. Another good man's life cut short by the sons of bitches who like the killing. Do you remember when he came to Fort Lincoln wanting to be a top-notch trooper in the worst way? By my faith, he succeeded. He soldiered as well as any man, and died protecting the helpless from butchers in uniform.

I plan to get the certificate in the spring. A snowbird at heart, I won't leave the cavalry until it's warm.

Mind yourself, old friend.

Dan

THE END